Bleeding Star Chronicles
Collection 2

Ethan Russell Erway

ISBN-10: 1503137252
ISBN-13: 978-1503137257

DEDICATION

This book is dedicated to all those men and women who have bravely served by defending the freedom we all hold so dear.

Contents

ACKNOWLEDGMENTS

Special thanks go to my wife and family for their love and support. I would also like to thank my readers, who are the best fans on the planet- thanks for your ongoing support.

Book 6

Reckoning

The lush rain forest canopy swished and swayed as Boreas guided the Shiv along, just above the leaves. Jungles such as these reminded him of the pictures he'd seen of Draconia, his peoples' home world, and although the reptilian had never visited the planet himself, he had a great desire to do so. He longed to find a way to free it, and his people from the grips of the Nazerazi Alliance. But how? He knew there had to be a way. He had only to find it, and he would, he promised himself yet again.

Captain Winchester, who was sleeping in the seat beside him, was missing the view, but Boreas would not disturb him. The poor man had been exhausted lately, and with all of the trauma that came with losing one's home and family, it was no wonder. Boreas knew how

Galin felt, how they all felt, because he was in the same boat himself, as the humans might say. Perhaps these new friends would be able to help him find the answers he sought, so that they could defy the Nazerazi together. After all, there was something special about the Katara, some secret thing that their enemies wanted, and Boreas hoped that whatever it was, it might help them break free of the Alliance's grip.

Before long, the Shiv approached an area that was rumored to be a drop-zone for human prisoners, and Boreas activated the scanners. A few small pockets of uninfected people popped up here and there, but the overwhelming majority of humans in the scanners range were victims of the virus. It was perplexing to see so many showing up in the jungle. Given these numbers, there were probably thousands of zombies inhabiting the surrounding jungle, which didn't make any sense when one considered the historical record. Any new prisoners being dropped upon the planet's surface by the United Earth Government should have been immune to the disease, so where were all of these victims coming from? Boreas decided to ask the captain about it after he awakened.

Some interesting structures had also appeared upon the scanners. Abandoned buildings from back when the UEG still had a presence on this world. *Very interesting*, thought Boreas. And then something even more interesting caught his attention in the skies above the structures.

Galin stirred in his seat, then looked up groggily and wiped a bit of drool from his chin.

"Captain, I'm picking up faint traces of the robot's energy signature," Boreas told him, rousing Galin from the remnants of his nap.

"Finally." The man rubbed his eyes, and examined the scanners. "What's that up there? An old military compound?"

"Yes, I believe so." Boreas ran some additional scans. "It appears that the compound has been overrun by what your people refer to as 'zombies', though I believe the term 'ghoul' would fit more appropriately. I'm not picking up any non-infected humans."

"That's strange," Galin responded, tracing the android's path. "I wonder what the T30 found so interesting down there. It looks like he busted his way into this building here," he pointed at the screen, "and then blasted off into space. Hero said he'd transmit a report if he found anything, though. This just doesn't seem to make much sense."

"Agreed," the reptilian told him. "However, I suggest we continue our investigation elsewhere. It would not be advisable to set our ship down anywhere near that compound."

"Oh, I'm with you there. We'd have to fight our way through hoards of those things to get a good look at anything, and getting eaten alive by freaks is not on my to-do list for the day. Let's see if we can trace the robot's route and find out where he came from. Maybe he discovered something that sent him here to search for information."

Boreas adjusted the short-range scanners to better capture the T3038's energy signature. "The trail is faint, but we have a direction. Shall I set course?"

"Yeah," Galin told him. "There's nothing else we can do here, let's get going."

The shiv came about and blasted off over the trees. It hadn't gotten far when the com lit up and beeped with an incoming transmission.

"Looks like the Katara is hailing us. It's about time," Galin said, answering the call. "Hey guys, where've you been hiding? Boreas and I have been trying to reach you. I was starting to get a little worried."

Ulrick's face popped onto the screen in the dash. "Let's just say we've had our hands a bit full since you two left. We had a little run-in with some pirates, and they blocked out our transmissions. I'll tell you all about it when we get to Necron."

Galin glanced at Boreas and cringed, then looked back to Ulrick. "Pirates? Is everyone all right?"

"Everyone's fine. I'd tell you all about it, but it's a long story, and we've got a lot of repairs, a lot more than we did before you left. We were actually able to commandeer the pirate ship. We handed it over to some folks who were being held onboard as slaves. They were picked up by the pirates after being abandoned on Necron. Right now, they're towing us to your location with a tractor beam. They seem pretty intent on getting back to help the others who got left behind. Some of 'em were forced to abandon family and friends down there."

Galin shook his head and tried to keep himself from laughing. Those pirates didn't know who they were dealing with when they took on Ulrick. "I can't leave you alone for five minutes, can I?"

"I just wanted to let you know that we're headed your way, and if you need us you'll be able to get ahold of us from now on- theoretically. Have you two had any luck with the search yet?"

"We've picked up the android's trail. He appears to have broken into an old military complex down here. We're retracing his steps to figure out why. No luck on finding Peter or Joseph yet, though."

Ulrick nodded. "That reminds me, there's somebody here who wants to say hello."

"Okay." Galin waited to see Jace pop onto the screen. The poor kid had really been put through the ringer, but hopefully his time in the regeneration chamber had made him as good as new again. Galin nearly fell out of his chair when the face of Joseph Stormcrow appeared. He couldn't help but laugh, and a smile spread across his face from ear to ear. "Joseph! Where the heck did you come from?"

"It's good to see you, too." Joseph's face was just as

stoic as ever, but Galin knew he was doing it on purpose, as if nothing unusual had happened.

"Did I miss something, or what?" Galin pressed him.

The chief cracked a grin. "Peter and I were stranded on the surface, in the jungle with a few hundred other captives, but we got separated in the confusion." The grin was short-lived; Joseph couldn't hide how much pain the memory caused him. "People were dying all around us. It was...not something I'd care to describe. Anyway, I never saw him after that, but there are a lot of pockets of survivors down there, and we all know how resourceful he is. Hopefully you'll have some good news for us soon."

Galin nodded. "I hope so. But how'd *you* end up back on the Katara?"

"Black-backed Jack would make routine visits to Necron. He liked to round up zombies to use as weapons against his victims, and snag uninfected people to turn into slaves. He even made some of the survivors crew members if he thought they'd be good pirates. He's been doing it for years. I was only on the surface for two days before a party of buccaneers rounded up the group I was with." He suddenly looked angry. "They were a mean bunch of bastards, but they didn't have to work very hard to convince us to go with them; it was a better option than the alternative."

"Wow," Galin said, shaking his head. "I look forward to hearing the whole story."

"I look forward to telling it." Joseph smiled. "It's good to see you. I didn't think I'd ever see *any* of you again."

Galin got a lump in his throat. For a moment he simply smiled back. "Well, that ship isn't going to fix itself. Break time's over, chief. It's good to have you back safe."

The chief smiled and gave him a parting nod before the com clicked off.

Galin looked over at Boreas and let out a long sigh. "Life is really strange sometimes, you know that?"

The Draconian looked back at him with a whimsical grin. "Yes, I agree. Here's something else you might appreciate as being a bit odd. It appears that a Dagger class starship has been docked in a large cave beneath the mountains up ahead."

Galin frowned. "You want to run that past me again?"

—GCW NAVY EARTH STAR-BASE FOURTEEN YEARS BEFORE—

The gym smelled of moisture, equipment cleaner, and human sweat, just like every other gym Galin had ever been in, and the air seemed even stuffier in here than it did on the rest of the station. He knew at once that the environmental controls needed to be adjusted, and if he was in charge, he'd of already put his foot to someone's rear end about it.

The sound of clinking steel could be heard from all directions, as officers and enlisted men alike pumped iron and adjusted the settings on a variety of equipment. He knew the sounds and the smells of this place well, but Galin wasn't here to work out. Scanning the room with a determined furrow of his brows, he soon found the man he was looking for.

Allen Carver sat on a weight bench huffing and puffing, presumably having just finished a set. Galin didn't like the looks of him now any more than he had the first time he'd laid eyes on him. He just had one of those faces, always wearing a stupid, holier than thou smirk that let everyone in the room know he was better than them. He was wearing it now, even as the bandages across his broken nose seemed to stretch to their limits because of it. Lines of sweat dripped from the short black hair on his head, which had been cropped to resemble freshly mowed grass, and landed on the floor around him as he rubbed out his shoulders and neck.

Above him stood a short, muscular man in a soiled wife-beater t-shirt, waiting to spot the next round. His forehead glistened under the dull light of the lamp hanging overhead, and he snorted like a pig as his companion told him something he seemed to find hilarious. All things considered, he looked about as charming as his companion.

Galin bee-lined for the two men, having to side step several lifters to get where he was going.

"Nice face," he said with a sneer as he stared at Allen's nose. "My sister does good work."

"What do *you* want, Winchester?" the man scowled. "You get re-assigned to services? Did you come to bring us some fresh towels?"

"I know you've been harassing Jamie. Maybe you don't like the fact that she ended your relationship by breaking your face, but I've come to put you on notice. Leave my sister alone, or you're going to have to deal with *me*."

Carver laughed. He looked Galin over from head to toe. "You pilots. You really do think you're something special. You think you've got balls because you can fly a starship? I leave chunks of guys like you in the toilet every morning." He lied back on the bench and motioned for his friend to begin spotting him on the next set of presses. Both men glared at him like he was some out of place thing. It was as if he'd just intruded on a quasi-religious ceremony for steroid filled meatheads.

Galin looked back down at Carver in disgust. What a filthy pig. What did Jamie ever see in losers like this? He wasn't handsome, charming, or intelligent; she could do a lot better. "I'm not here to argue with you, *Lieutenant*. Just to give you some friendly advice. Stay away from Jamie."

"Listen to this guy," Carver barked out in a strained

chuckle, pressing up the weights. He quickly pumped out a set of eight. Then he slid the bar onto its bracket and sat back up. "He's coming onto our station and pulling rank, because he thinks his little sister can't take care of herself."

"Leave rank out of this. I'm not delivering an order; I'm giving you a promise. Come near my sister again and you'll have more than a broken nose to deal with. You got me?"

"Oh yeah," the man chuckled, taking a towel and wiping the sweat from his brow. "I got you. I'm shakin' in fear." He rolled his eyes at his friend before looking back to Galin. "Now would you get the hell out of here? I don't enjoy yammerin' with chicks while I'm trying to work out."

His friend snorted another little chuckle.

Galin turned to leave, and just before he got out of earshot, he heard Carver laugh. "Someday, that little slut's going to get exactly what she has coming to her."

Galin clenched his fists. He suddenly had a gleeful vision of smashing the man's teeth in with a dumbbell. *Just let it go,* he told himself. *He's just trying to yank your chain.* As he walked through the station's long, empty corridors back to the docking bay, he tried to steady his breathing and focus on more positive things. Hopefully, Carver would take the warning to heart. There were too many good things happening in life for Galin to have to worry about beating someone up. What was this- high school? The whole thing was just stupid. Soon, he would be heading back to the surface of Earth to pick out a ring for Starla, and knew he needed to be in the right frame of mind. It had to be perfect, all of it. The ring, the way he asked her, everything. Thinking of Starla, he couldn't stop himself from smiling. She was so beautiful, so loving, so special. And soon, he would be the luckiest man on Earth.

If she says yes, he reminded himself.

—NOW—

A rather sizable crowd had gathered on the ground where the Shiv alighted down into the grass. Galin had been able to pick up the entrance to the caves on the scanners, and once the surrounding people got wind of a ship, it hadn't taken long for them to begin showing up.

Boreas glanced at him nervously, and he guessed what the reptilian was thinking. These people looked like they'd been stranded down here for quite a while, and probably wouldn't mind getting their hands on a ship. Hopefully the Shiv wouldn't be over-run, and the two of them clobbered before they could explain that more help was on the way. These people looked friendly enough though, and downright delighted to see them coming. Galin quickly decided that they weren't in any real danger, besides, how were they going to get answers if they didn't get out to talk.

He shrugged at Boreas and instinctively checked to see that his sidearm was there, and then he popped open the hatch. Much to his relief, the outsiders stood at a respectful distance, greeting him with joyous and hopeful smiles.

When they saw Boreas, however, a few of them looked like they were about to bolt.

"Some of these people might think you're a Nazerazi," Galin told his companion. "The rest of them probably think you look like a big scary lizard."

Boreas frowned at him.

"You know," Galin went on. "Because you're a big, scary looking lizard. Anyway, hang back here for a sec while I go and talk to them."

Boreas nodded, and Galin walked out to the man standing at the head of the crowd, who was waiting for him with an outstretched hand. He took it. "I'm Galin Winchester."

The man gave his hand a welcoming squeeze, but his expression changed to something a bit hard to read. "James Locke. It's a pleasure to meet you, Captain. I've heard a lot about you."

Galin raised his eyebrows. "You've heard a lot about *me*?"

"Yes, actually I have. I think we need to talk. Are you up for a bite of lunch?"

"A free lunch. I reckon you *have* heard a lot about

me," Galin told him with a grin.

After introductions were made, and the castaways were convinced that Boreas wasn't going to eat anyone, James led the way into the caves. Dozens of others gathered around to listen, and fruits, nuts, and venison was served while James recounted the events of the last few weeks. Galin could hardly believe what he was hearing. His son had been among the people dropped in the jungle, and had found his way to these very caves. It was too good to be true.

"Where is he now?" Galin demanded, suddenly feeling scared by the look on James' face.

"He was taken." The man sighed uncomfortably. "By a woman dressed all in black…riding a black horse." He winced when he said it, as if he didn't expect Galin to believe him. "That's not all. Your friend Peter was here, too. I'm sorry; he didn't make it. He died trying to protect David. The woman in black killed him just before she rode off with your son."

Galin felt like he was being punched in the stomach as James explained the details of Peter's death. Peter had been a good friend; had always been there to pull him back from the edge. He'd been a brother. And now, he was dead. If only they'd arrived a few days earlier, all of this could have been avoided.

"I'm very sorry for your loss." James put his hand on Galin's shoulder. "We can take you to his gravesite, it's not that far from here."

"I...I appreciate that." Galin's head was spinning. "But first, I need to go find out what happened to my son." He rose to his feet.

"We had a team of volunteers leave yesterday morning to go and look for him, but they haven't returned yet," James said. He looked worried. "I assume you know about the android? We spoke to him, and he said he was going to look for your son too, and would contact your ship when he found him."

"Yes, we know about him. We followed his path back here from that old military compound on the edge of the jungle. It looks like he infiltrated the place before heading back out into space. We didn't pick up any healthy humans when we scanned the compound, though. Just a bunch of zombies."

James looked at the ground, and then back up into Galin's eyes. "I'm sorry to hear that. I was hoping...."

"The android broke into that facility for a reason, I'm not going to believe my son is lost until I have proof." Galin remembered the things he'd seen back on Earth while speaking with Nicodemus. *'A changing of life, and life without life'*, the reptilian monk had told him. Had he been talking about Peter, or was it David? Maybe it was both.

Boreas scratched his claws against the black and red scales of his armor. "Captain, perhaps your son is still out there in the jungle. Our scans picked up dozens of groups of uninfected humans."

Galin nodded. "Let's go take a look." He turned to James. "The Katara's en-route to Necron as we speak. It's coming with another ship, a ship that can take you all out of here."

Upon hearing that, the castaways began to clap and cheer. Galin wished that he could celebrate along with them, but all he felt right now was grief and fear. The cave walls were suddenly growing tighter and tighter around him; he desperately needed fresh air.

Boreas followed him out, and James wasn't far behind them.

"Captain, is there anything we can do to help?" James asked once they'd gotten outside.

"I don't think so. Not right now, anyway. But thanks for offering. Boreas and I are going to run some more scans out over the jungle, just in case we missed something. We'll keep an eye out for that search party you mentioned. If we can do anything to help them, we will."

"Thank you, Captain. And good luck. I hope you find your boy."

Galin nodded appreciatively and headed for the Shiv. If such a thing as luck existed, he should be about due for some that was good.

—GALILEAN SHIPYARDS, JUPITER
FOURTEEN YEARS BEFORE—

Galin sat in a dark corner of the bar, nursing the same beer he'd been holding for the last half hour. He was in a foul mood. Having to sit around and wait for his father always seemed to do that to him. The old man loved to keep people waiting, Galin knew. It was all just a part of the mind games that he played. He looked at his watch and growled out a sigh. Just then, as if his son's exasperation had been his summons, Admiral Winchester arrived. He hovered near the door and scanned the room, arms held behind his back, and he somehow reminded Galin of a vulture perched on a tree branch, watching the crowd below and waiting for something to die. It only took him a few moments to find his son, and soon he was sitting down beside him.

"So tell me more about this Allen Carver boy I've been hearing so little about."

"There's not much to tell," Galin sneered. "He's just like all the others." He downed about half of his remaining beer. "One thing about your daughter, she definitely has a type."

The old man grimaced. "I keep hoping that will change someday. One thing I've learned over the years, however, is that people change when they want to. There's nothing that you or I can do to *make* it happen."

The bartender drifted over. Galin ordered another beer; for some reason, being around his father always gave him the urge to drink.

The admiral ordered vodka on the rocks. "So, you had a talk with this young man," he said rhetorically. "Do you think it did any good?"

"I don't know. He doesn't seem like the kind of guy who takes a hint very easily. But Jamie will let me know if he comes around causing any more trouble."

"If he does, I want you to notify me immediately. If I'm feeling kind, I'll have him transferred to some backwater, deep space outpost so far away that he'll forget what his own mother looks like."

Galin knew that his father would do it. In fact, he was surprised that it hadn't been done already. "So why don't you just go ahead and have the guy transferred? What are you waiting for?"

"I only pull my little strings and call in favors when I have to. That's why so many people owe them to me." He sipped at the vodka. "Besides, maybe having a stalker will finally frighten that girl into behaving herself for a while."

"I thought you just said there wasn't anything we could do to change her."

The admiral gave his drink a few twirls, and took another sip. "We can't. But perhaps facing some of the consequences of her own foolish choices will convince her to start taking more responsibility for them. But, if you think this man could actually be dangerous, I'll be counting on you to keep an eye on her while I'm away. I've been called out to help resolve a mining claims dispute in the Tritanium Seas on Epsilon Eridani Beta. If everything goes well, I'll be back in about two months."

"Two months? You're going to miss Jaimie's graduation ceremony."

"It can't be helped. The President of the UEG asked me personally."

"You don't answer to *him,*" Galin growled. "What's President Earnheart have to say about it?"

"The two governments have been striving to improve relations. That's why President Lindell asked me in the first place. I know for a fact that the man doesn't care for me. This assignment is both an honor and a huge pain in my ass." With that thought, he downed the rest of his vodka, and gave Galin a sour look. "I'll make it up to her when I get back."

"How do you plan on doing that?" Galin asked him. He and his sister had been hearing promises like this all their lives. Most of the time, their father did try to make up for the times he wasn't there, the things that he missed out on; Galin gave him some credit for that. But some of the most important things in life just couldn't be made up for.

His father shrugged, and let out a long, heavy sigh. He looked tired. The man had always been a relentless worker, and now that he was a newly promoted admiral, he seemed to be even more consumed with military life and duty. Suddenly, Galin felt a little bit guilty for asking him to come. The trip had been out of his way, he knew, but Galin had some very important information to share, and he'd wanted to do it in person. Looking his father over, though, he wasn't sure now if he wanted to drop the news of his engagement just yet. He was sure to receive a long lecture, and the old man just didn't look like he had it in him. Normally, Galin would have considered this a good opportunity to get off a little easier, but the man looked so very tired, all he could do was pity him. Delivering the news would be easier to do over a view screen, or better yet through a text transmission, but he *had* gone out of his way to come, and he might even be suspecting what Galin had to tell him.

"I'm going to ask Starla to marry me," Galin blurted out. The alcohol was definitely helping.

"Are you really?" his father asked with wide eyes. "Good for you. I love the girl like a daughter already, and I'd say it's about time."

Galin was a bit taken aback. "You aren't going to try to talk me out of it?"

"Why would I do that?"

"Because," Galin insisted. "You try to talk me out of *everything* I do. Everything I've *ever done*."

"Nonsense," the admiral protested. "What I've tried to do is make you think things through. Ensure you've considered all the possibilities before you make a decision. You've always been rash, charging into things while damning the consequences."

Galin frowned at him challengingly. "And you're not afraid that I'm doing that now?"

"Are you joking? Starla is the only decision I've ever watched you deliberate over for so long like this. It's gone on for years, and has been quiet entertaining, to tell you the truth." He gave his son a rare smile before taking a piece of ice out of his glass and chewing it. "Don't worry. You're going to make an excellent husband." He clapped his son's shoulder. "As well as a father."

Galin just sat there, unsure of what to say. The old man was seldom this agreeable, much less complimentary.

"Well, I need to get some rest. My shuttle takes off at five o'clock sharp." He rose to his feet, and reached out to shake his son's hand. "Congratulations. I know she'll say yes. That girl has been head over heels for you from the first day you met." He started to leave, and then turned back with his usual frowning face. "Remember to keep an eye on that sister of yours. I'm afraid the girl is going to drive me to an early grave."

Galin nodded and gave the man a grin, and then he was gone. He took another swig of his beer, and wondered if he was sometimes too hard on the old man. He *could* be a real piece of work, but he had a soft side too, for anyone that was around long enough to see it. His father's words had caught him off guard. *Would* he be a good husband and father? It was something he'd found himself worrying about, although he'd never admitted it to anyone. How had his father known it was something that bothered him? Maybe it was his way of acknowledging his own failures, telling Galin that he wouldn't make the same mistakes.

Maybe he would, and maybe he wouldn't. Perhaps he had his own unique string of failures waiting to be unleashed upon whatever children he and Starla were going to have. Whatever the future held, he would try his best, he promised himself. He would be the best man he could, for Starla, and for their kids.

—NOW—

As the Shiv re-entered the skies above the military compound, Galin suddenly realized that he'd forgotten to ask the people back at the caves about the ship docked in their mountain. Apart from the Katara, he'd never laid eyes on a Dagger class starship before. Even when they were still in service there were only a handful of them, and Galin was intrigued by the fact that one had somehow ended up buried in a cave on Necron. Peter would find it just as fascinating as he did, and for a fraction of a second Galin was excited to discuss it with him, but he quickly remembered that such a discussion would never occur. There would be no more talks with Peter, ever again. The news of his best friend's death had hit him hard, and along with the idea of getting so close to his son, only to lose him all over again- it was all too much to bear.

Boreas let out something like a yawn, and then cocked his head from side to side while examining the scanners. Then he suddenly squinted in disbelief. "Captain, there appears to be a vessel launching from the midst of the facility."

"What? What kind of vessel?" He sat up straight and put it on the view screen, in order to get a better look. "I don't recognize the make." He scanned the ship. "Looks like it's got a lot of firepower, though. I'm detecting eight life forms inside. It's too well shielded for me to pick up anything else."

"It appears that there is more going on here than we first suspected," Boreas said. "I wasn't aware that humans infected with the Solanum virus could perform complex tasks such as operating a starship."

Galin shook his head. "They can't. But, years ago there were rumors about zombies who could think like normal men, living on this planet. It was said that they traveled into space, looking for victims to bring back to Necron. Nobody was safe, not even the pirates. I think they were called *reapers*."

"And do you believe these rumors?"

"I asked my father about it once," Galin told him, tracking the other ship's movement across the scanners. "He used to have men who patrolled this sector, and told me it was all just a legend, that there was never any real proof for it. Looks like there may be some truth to those legends after all."

"Shall I follow the vessel?"

Galin thought about it for a moment. If the things on that ship were reapers, they'd be out looking for victims, and following wouldn't serve any purpose other than to get them caught. For now, they needed to focus on looking for uninfected human life signatures. If David was down there someplace, perhaps he was being held, stored with other people like some kind of cattle. The thought made Galin sick.

"No, take us in over the compound. Let's run those scans. We need to take a real thorough look this time."

Boreas guided the ship into position over the center of the compound, and began to configure the scanners for deep penetration. Whatever was going on down there was being well concealed.

Galin watched as the escaping vessel disappeared off of the short-range scanners, but it was soon replaced by something that nearly made him jump from his seat. "WHOA, where the heck did that come from?"

A massive ship had just de-cloaked right above them. It was so close that Galin might have reached up and touched it, but experience told him that taking evasive maneuvers might be a better idea, and he reacted before Boreas even knew what was happening, steering the Shiv down and out over the edge of the facility's barriers.

"Captain, that vessel is preparing to fi—."

And then all hell broke loose. The ship let loose upon the grounds down below with a flurry of attacks that shook the air around them. Galin guided the Shiv over the canopy of the jungle until they'd reached a safe distance, and turned her around to get a better look at what was happening. Behind the ship's hull, the sun peeked out at them, blaring back and making it hard to see. Still, Galin was certain that he recognized the massive form of the ship before them. He looked down at the scanners to confirm what he already knew was there. It was the Claymore.

"Captain, that is your father's vessel, is it not?" Boreas asked.

Galin was at a loss for words, but he managed to give his companion a somber nod. What was the Admiral doing here? What business could he possibly have on Necron, at this old abandoned compound? Was he somehow aware of Galin's presence?

The two of them watched as the Claymore decimated the base. Although there were a few feeble attempts at returning fire, the pathetic displays of resistance were no match for the destruction that rained down from above.

Just a few minutes later, nothing remained but a charred wasteland of rubble, and patches of fire and smoke rising up from the surrounding jungle.

Galin just sat there, looking at the destruction with a hanging jaw, trying to steady his breath. What if David *had* been down there? If he had, the chance of finding any of his remains, even enough to confirm his death, would be nearly hopeless. With shaking hands, he reached up and began to type into the communications panel.

"Captain, you aren't going to hail them, are you?"

"Don't be ridiculous," Galin growled. "I'm sending my father an encrypted message. It's over a private channel; no one will see it but him."

"Theoretically."

"Theoretically," Galin conceded.

"Whatever evidence we'd hoped to find here is gone now," Boreas said. "A shame we didn't arrive earlier. Shall we try to track the ship that departed a few minutes ago?"

The reptilian seemed so damn cold sometimes. For a moment, Galin felt like tossing him out of the side of the ship. He pushed his irritation aside, and considered their choices. Following the other ship might be a viable option. Had they known the Claymore was coming somehow? Perhaps it had been an escape vessel, taking away someone who could answer as to the whereabouts of his son.

He was about to give the reptilian the go ahead when the Claymore changed course, and headed out as abruptly as she'd arrived. "Looks like they had the same idea," Galin said, nudging his head toward the view screen. A few moments later, his father's ship was gone.

"Hopefully the old man will get back to us soon. In the meantime, we'll head toward the caves. Maybe we can locate…that search party." *Or David,* he thought, though he somehow felt afraid to say it aloud, as if it might jinx them.

"Or someone else who needs our help," Boreas added.

Galin nodded. He felt miserable, powerless to do anything when there was so much that needed to be done. With any luck they'd find the search party Locke had spoken of, and with even more luck they'd have some answers for him. But he was getting sick and tired of having to rely so much on luck.

—OUTSIDE OF SALZBURG, AUSTRIA
NEARLY FOURTEEN YEARS BEFORE—

The cobblestone road was slick, and a bit icy in spots from the previous night's rain, causing Galin to watch his feet as he crept across to the marketplace on the other side. Upon safely reaching his destination, he gazed off at the snow-capped Alps, and took a long, deep breath of air, trying to calm his nerves.

Heading to the door of the bakery, he reached for the door handle and noticed that the closed sign was still up. A pretty young woman in a brown apron winked at him through the glass, flipped over the sign, and unlocked the door, then she pulled it open for him. He was instantly greeted by the smell of fresh baked pastries and brewing coffee, and the warmth of a welcoming fire that danced from the hearth in the middle of the room. The young woman led him to a table by the window, where a stunning view of the mountains awaited, and he sat down.

The hostess, whose long blonde hair was tied behind her head in pig tails, looked him over with a mischievous gleam in her eye. She put her hands on her hips and inconspicuously pushed out her chest, a feature of which she was obviously proud. "Coffee?" she asked him cheerfully.

"Please," he told her, returning a friendly, non-suggestive smile.

She pursed her lips, as if preparing to blow him a kiss, before spinning around gracefully to leave.

Galin sat there alone and gazed into the distance for a few moments, tapping his fingers on the table and focusing on the beauty of the landscape, until she came back to fill his cup.

"Would you like *anything* else?"

"Thank you, no. I'm waiting for some friends."

She gave him another wink before disappearing into the back.

He was alone with his thoughts for about ten long minutes before the little bell hanging above the door rang, and two men walked in. He turned to see them. One was his friend, a man he'd met in his academy days,

Captain John Nolan. The other was a tall, muscular man with straight, blonde hair, who wore a determined frown.

Galin stood. "John, it's been a while." He met his friend in a firm handshake.

"It's good to see you again. I just wish.... Galin, I was so sorry to hear about what happened to Jamie. It's horrible. How are you holding up?"

Galin shrugged. "I'm just keepin' on. There's really nothing else I can do."

John looked at him mournfully, as if wishing he could say something to help. He glanced over at the other man. "This is the guy I told you about, Ulrick Von Liechtenstein. Ulrick, this is Galin Winchester."

The big man gave him a nod, and shook his hand, and then they all sat down together. The hostess returned and brought more coffee.

"You three want something to eat?"

Galin was just about to tell her no when John spoke up. "Three orders of bread rolls and ham. And bring us some jam, if you would, sweetie."

"She turned her head and beamed at him, perhaps deciding that he might be more fun than Galin, and then ran to fetch their order.

"I know you may not be in the mood to eat anything," John explained. "But just in case we're seen, it's better this way."

Galin conceded a nod. He was eager to get right to it.

"So, Ulrick, John tells me that you overheard some things in the gym on the Navy Star Base?"

The big man nodded. "I was stationed there briefly while doing contract work for the UEG, refurbishing some blaster rifles and special weapons maintenance. Anyway, I went to the gym to work out. Three men were lifting weights together, and there wasn't much of anyone else around, just me and another guy or two." He took a swig of coffee. "Anyway, those three were off in the back doing biceps curls, joking and carrying on like morons, the type of thing that pisses off everyone else trying to work out. They didn't know I was listening to them. I head headphones on, but I turn my music down real low, it helps me relax while I'm lifting. I heard one of them say something about...."

He looked at Galin nervously.

"I can take it, just tell me," Galin assured him.

"I heard one of them say something about 'teaching the slut a lesson', and turned my music off. I was only able to catch about half of what they said, but it was enough."

Galin found that his eyes were tearing up. He wiped them, and ran his hands through his hair. "Go on."

"One of them seemed to be bragging to the others about what he'd done. He, uh...he described how he'd tracked the girl down, how she'd fought back...I suppose you know the rest."

Galin felt enraged and heartbroken all at once. He'd

known Carver was responsible, but until now there hadn't been any real proof. Besides, for some reason this was almost like hearing the news all over again for the first time. He couldn't stop the tears. "I'm sorry. I, I didn't mean to do this."

"Don't apologize," Ulrick told him.

John reached over and gave his shoulder a squeeze.

Ulrick continued. "He went on to brag about how he'd never get caught. He used a DNA cleanser, he said, and had even set off an electro magnetic signal scrambler in case there were any surveillance systems in the area. The whole thing made me sick. I wanted to go over there and bash his head in with a dumbbell, but luckily, I thought better of it."

"You didn't report what you'd heard to anyone?" Galin asked him.

Ulrick shook his head. "I was thinking about it, but I have a criminal record myself, and I wanted to get more information before I approached anyone. It would have been my word against his, and I wasn't sure that would be enough. Anyway, a few hours later in the mess hall, I overheard Captain Nolan speaking with a friend. He seemed pretty upset. Said a friend's sister had just been murdered. I got him alone and told him what I'd heard, and he asked me to keep quiet about it until we spoke to you."

"I checked this Carver guy out pretty thoroughly," John said. "He looks like a big, stupid jock, but he went out of his way to cover all the bases. Galin, he planned the whole thing out. He even has a real good alibi, and some friends that can vouch for his presence someplace else. Turns out his father was a police detective down in Alamogordo, which must be where he learned all his tricks."

The hostess returned with their food, and she flirted with John for a minute before heading off again into the back.

After she was gone, they all remained silent for a few long moments.

"I just want you to know," Ulrick told him. "Whatever you decide to do, you can count on me, to talk, or to be silent. The choice is yours."

Galin moved his eyes over to John; the look on his friend's face was enough to say that he felt the same.

"One more thing," Ulrick said, sliding something across the table to him. "I took the liberty of scanning and duplicating the guy's room key. Do with it what you will. As far as I'm concerned, I've never seen the thing."

Galin picked up the small, transparent card, and looked it over thoughtfully before sliding it into his pocket. He nodded gratefully. "Why are you doing this?"

"You're not the only one who's lost somebody," Ulrick told him, adding jam to his roll. "Besides, guys like that...who knows if he's done something like this before? And who's to say he won't do it again?"

Galin looked out at the mountains. They suddenly seemed even bigger than they had just a few minutes before. "I won't forget this," he told the large man seated across from him.

"You don't owe me anything," Ulrick assured him. "Pay for my breakfast, and we'll call it even."

—NOW—

The search party was almost home. They were just about to move across the tree line of the jungle, and then they had only to maneuver their way down the cliffs, where a nice hot bath awaited. There weren't many perks to living in the caves, but the hot springs was one that Angelica always looked forward to.

Her heart nearly stopped as she watched a hole being torn in the canopy of clouds overhead, and a large mass come descending down right over the entrance to their home. It was a pirate ship, she realized; a ship she'd been unlucky enough to encounter once before. Three fourths of her own ship's crew had been massacred, and the rest had narrowly escaped with their lives, and that was only because the United Earth Government's forces had intervened. Black-backed Jack had battled and destroyed the ill-timed police cruiser, giving her own crew a few precious minutes to limp away and get the warp engines back online. She and her friends had been a few of the lucky handful to escape the wrath of the most notorious pirate in the quadrant.

"Hey look at *that*, what a ship!" April said, walking up beside her. The woman was a wonderful and loyal friend, but could sometimes be a remarkable airhead.

"That's the *One Eyed Whore*," Angelica told her. "Its captain is probably the most evil man I've ever had the bad fortune of crossing paths with."

"I've heard of that ship," Roger said from behind them. "It belongs to Black-backed Jack. When I worked on that mining transport out in the badlands, I heard all kinds of stories about him."

"I don't know what you heard, but if it was horrifying then it was most likely accurate. You can't make up stories any worse than the truth about that ship and its captain."

"So what are we going to do?" Carl asked, trying to catch his breath from the hike. "We've got all these blaster rifles now, if we can get down there fast enough, we may be able to help."

Angelica frowned. "I can't speak for the rest of you, but I'm willing to die trying."

The others all looked back at her with a somber determination. Whatever kind of fate awaited their friends down below, they would not be left to face it alone.

Despite being tired from the day's walk, they picked up the pace, each of them knowing that mere seconds could make the difference between life and death for their friends.

Roger adjusted the straps on his backpack. "Why's she coming in so slowly? Don't pirate's generally try to use the element of surprise?"

Angelica had just noticed it as well. The ship was descending at an unusually unhurried speed. She squinted her eyes. It was then that she saw the other vessel, partially hidden by the One-Eyed Whore, coming in beside it. "I think it's towing in that smaller ship with a tractor beam." That didn't make much sense. If the pirates had come to cause trouble, they wouldn't be towing in another ship, and why would they be assisting anyone? They weren't exactly known as good samaritans, either; especially this lot.

"The whole thing seems pretty weird to me," Carl observed. "Let's just get there as quick as we can."

Angela's father, an avid hiker, would have referred to their movement as "hoofing it," she reflected as they descended down the cliffs. She had been feeling particularly sentimental since Peter's death, and had found herself thinking a lot more about her family, and how much she missed them all.

The group made very good time, reaching the bottom of the cliffs just as the pirate ship extracted its landing gear and alighted down. Angelica saw a large group of the castaways gather together around the base of the ship. It looked like they were.... "Celebrating?" she barked. *"Are they celebrating?* What in the WORLD is going on down there?"

"I don't know," April laughed, breaking into a run, "but we must have missed out on some pretty exciting news."

Angelica was running too, and the others as well. Only Sammy lagged behind, as he had a bum knee and couldn't keep up. Angelica felt sorry for him, but not sorry enough to slow down and wait. He wouldn't have wanted her to anyway.

As they drew near, she brushed her hair out of her face and met eyes with James Locke, who urged her on with a wave of his hand.

"How do you like our new ship?" he asked her in something not unlike a giggle.

"Ou, our…*our* ship," she huffed, struggling to catch her breath.

He hugged her, and nodded. "That boat she towed in is the Katara- Galin Winchester's ship. His crew helped some captives who'd been picked up from Necron in a mutiny, and they've come back to retrieve the rest of us. How do you like them apples?"

Angelica wanted to answer him, but she was too busy laughing, partly from the good news, and partly because April had seized her and begun showering her cheeks with excited kisses. *What a weirdo,* she thought, finally managing to push her friend away.

As the crew from each ship descended, the crowd

around them erupted in claps and cheers.

Angelica didn't recognize any of the people descending the steps from the pirate ship, but she did see a few folks from the Katara who she could put a name to, thanks to Peter and David's descriptions. The big blonde man had to be Ulrick, and the Native American was Joseph Stormcrow, but how the heck had he gotten back onto the ship? He must have been captured by Jack's crew right after being dropped. There was also a young, Asian man who waved enthusiastically, and a pretty blonde woman who smiled back timidly as the people clapped for them. She looked for the other woman Peter had mentioned, what was her name? Scarlett? No, it was Starla, she decided, but there was no sign of her.

And then she saw a very strange thing indeed. Trailing behind Ulrick, all shackled and chained, was the largest, ugliest woman that Angelica had ever seen. Was it a woman? It definitely wasn't a man; or *was* it? Not with a figure like that. She had long black hair, a face a smooth as a baby's bottom, and a big potato like nose. She wore men's clothes, which did not seem designed for, or capable of containing her large, hairy bosom. One thing was for sure, she was a pirate. The hateful, murderous look on her broad face made that clear.

James looked at Angelica whimsically, knowing what she must be thinking. "That? That is the infamous Black-backed Jack."

—GCW NAVY EARTH STAR-BASE NEARLY FOURTEEN YEARS BEFORE—

A thousand thoughts trickled through Galin's mind as the shuttle rocketed toward the Navy Star-Base. What would he say to the man? Would he say anything at all, or just sneak up from behind and open his worthless throat for him? He'd never killed a man before, not like this; not in cold blood. Sure, he'd seen his share of battles, shot enemy pilots down and sent them to meet their maker, but never anything like this. Even enemy soldiers were due a certain amount of respect. They were honorable opponents, fighting for their lives and the prosperity of their peoples. Even if they were misguided, they were men- warriors. Allen Carver was not. He was a contemptible animal. No, even the lowliest of animals was more worthy of life than Carver. And not even the worst of animals deserved what he had coming.

There was no doubt that Carver deserved to suffer, deserved to die a thousand deaths for what he'd done to Jamie, and then rot in the bowels of hell so that he could mull it all over. Of that much, Galin was sure. But for all that, something inside was gnawing at him. Something inside was telling him that what he was doing was wrong.

Why?

It wasn't because he was afraid of being caught. That wasn't his intention, but if it happened, it happened. He was willing to go to prison if it meant getting vengeance for his sister.

Perhaps it was all this sneaking around. Galin was a man who respected the rule of law. He didn't like having to go beyond its bounds, but what else could he do? In this case, the law had failed him completely. It had failed his family, his sister, and it had failed to uphold justice. He had voiced his reasoning for believing Carver was responsible, but the man had come out smelling like a rose all the same. Bringing up Ulrick's testimony would only be an exercise in futility, just thought of as something he'd concocted with the man to try and get something to stick.

No, he told himself again. *This is the only way.*

Galin adjusted his thick spectacles, and wondered again if the grey coloring in his hair was convincing enough. He'd spent half the morning in front of the mirror, working to change his appearance just enough to avoid being recognized. He'd donned the drab, blue jumpsuit of an enlisted maintenance worker, put together a toolbox with the appropriate equipment in it, and tacked on about twenty five years to his appearance. His disguise was simple, convincing, and made him feel utterly ridiculous. It all seemed like some sick, stupid game. Was this the kind of justice that his baby sister deserved?

His communicator vibrated. Galin took it out of his pocket and read the latest in a long series of messages from Starla.

Galin, where are you? Please answer me, please come home and let me help you. I love you. I always have, and I always will.

He slid the thing back into his pocket without responding. He just couldn't bring himself to talk to her, not now.

The shuttle pilot guided her craft into the docking bay and alighted the vessel as delicately as if she were setting a sleeping baby into its crib.

"And here we are folks. Welcome to the Galactic Confederation of Worlds Navy Earth Star Base. I hope you enjoyed your flight. Thanks for traveling with Star Hopper Express, and have a great day."

The three dozen other passengers got up to depart around him, but Galin hesitated, and ended up being the last one off. The docking bay looked crowded today, he thought. And as he made his way into the market area, things got downright crowded. There must be something going on, a graduation ceremony perhaps. Not that it mattered; this was actually a good thing, the more unknown faces around, the better.

Holding his head down and avoiding any eye contact, Galin bee-lined toward Allen Carver's quarters. If he was on his regular schedule, he'd be getting off of duty in about an hour, and return to his room to prepare for the gym. Galin would be waiting for him.

His stomach was tightened and his heart was racing as he made his way to the turbolift. The officers' living quarters were on deck seventeen. If he was lucky, nobody else would be around when he got there.

The communicator in his pocket vibrated once more.

Come on, Starla, he thought. *I don't have time for this right now.* Despite his irritation, he took the thing out of his pocket to have a look. After that, he promised himself he'd shut it off.

He looked at the screen and nearly dropped it. The message was from his father.

Do not deliver your package. The young man has already been transferred.

What did this mean? How could his father know what he was doing? Nobody knew. He had been so careful. The Admiral, however, was an extremely resourceful man. But none of that really mattered now. What did he mean that Carver had been transferred? Had he really been transferred, or had he been.... Galin needed to know. He had to make sure that the job got done. If Carver was gone, he would find out where he'd been sent, and follow him there. No matter how long it took, or where he had to go, Galin would find him. Allen Carver would pay with his life for what he'd done to Jaime.

The turbolift ride was agonizing. It felt as though time had ground to a halt, and the world began to spin all around. The walls were now closing in. Galin needed air. He needed to find some open space. But above all else, he needed to get to Allen Carver's quarters. The lift came to a stop and the doors slid open, and he nearly ran over a young enlisted woman who was waiting to get on.

"Hey, watch where you're going," she grunted as he bumped her out of the way.

"Sorry about that."

He rushed down the hall, trying to look as natural as he could. Luckily, nobody else was around. He examined the number on each door as he went, and before long, the sign for room 1734 was displayed there before him. He glanced over each shoulder before sliding in the key, and much to his relief, the lock clicked and the door swished open. He stepped into the darkness and waited for the door to close, and then he flipped on the light.

The room was a mess, and it smelled like a bachelor pad. The counter was covered with empty beer cans and old pizza boxes, and the floor was littered with clothes. Electronic gadgets and a variety of sports gear was scattered about, and memorabilia for the Juárez Bonecrushers, obviously Carver's favorite football team, covered the walls. Galin noted the absence of any family pictures or books.

Carver had not been transferred, that much was clear. Even if he'd been rushed off quickly, he wouldn't have been allowed to leave his quarters in this kind of disrepair. He was obviously the type of guy who partied hard and cleaned up everything fast whenever he got wind of a room inspection. What a pig.

Galin made his way to the bedroom and stepped through the door, and then his question was answered. There in the corner of the room was Allen Carver, hanging from a rope tied to a punching bag stand. It looked like a suicide. There was even a note on the stand beside the bed.

To Whom it May Concern,

I, Allen T. Carver, can no longer live with myself. I confess to the murder of my estranged girlfriend, Jaime Winchester, and pass my heartfelt apologies on to her family. I am paying the price for what I have done. Please distribute all my belongings to my family.

Short, to the point, and sincere. There wasn't a snowball's chance in Texas that Allen Carver had written a word of it.

Galin was overwhelmed by the things going on inside of him. Hatred, sadness, regret, all welled up to the point that he could barely stand it. But there was something else there, too, he noticed. He also felt relief.

Was it because Carver was dead, or because he hadn't had to do it? He wasn't sure, maybe it was both.

Making his way back out of the apartment, he

hesitated to take a deep breath before opening up the door. Stepping out into the hall, he turned to head back to the lift, and was startled when a voice came up from behind him.

"Hey, who the hell are *you*?"

He instinctively turned to see who it was, and recognized the man as Carver's weightlifting buddy. Without a word, Galin cracked the toolbox over his head, and the man crumpled to the floor like a lumpy, muscular sack of potatoes. Galin turned and bolted for the turbolift. Had the man recognized him? Probably not, it had been months since they'd seen each other, and at the time it had only been for a few minutes. Still, there was a chance. He needed to get off this base as quickly as possible. Luckily, there was another shuttle leaving in fifteen minutes, and he was going to be on it.

—NOW—

As the Shiv shot out over the edge of the rainforest, Galin looked down anxiously to see two ships resting in the grasslands near the bottom of the cliffs. "There she is, poor old girl. I hope those frackin' pirates didn't tear her up too badly."

Boreas' eyes grew large as they approached the pirate ship. It was unlike anything he'd ever seen before. "That really is quite a vessel, isn't it? I don't know how your crew managed to commandeer it, Captain, but I look forward to hearing the tale."

"So do I. And remember Boreas, you're part of the crew now, too. Let's set 'er down right over there where we won't squash anyone."

As they exited the ship, Jace and Hero came to meet them. While Boreas greeted Hero, Galin met Jace in a firm handshake and hugged him with his other arm.

"You're looking a sight better than the last time I saw you," the captain told him.

"I'm feeling a lot better, too," the young man responded in a half laugh. He suddenly looked more serious. "They said you headed out to look for David. Did you find anything?"

"Uh, it's kind of a long story. But no, I didn't find David. I haven't given up hope though."

Hero rushed in and gave him a tight squeeze before gazing up with teary eyes. She looked like she wanted to say something, but couldn't seem to find the words.

"I'm glad to see you're all right," Galin told her, wondering if she actually was.

She gave him a feeble grin, and he returned her squeeze with a tighter one, as he might have to his daughter, then he planted a kiss on her forehead.

"Where are Ulrick and the Chief?"

"Well, the Chief is down in the Katara's engine room, fixated on the repairs. Some of the crew from the One Eyed Lady is helping him out."

"The One Eyed Lady?" Galin chuckled. He supposed that was a nicer name than the One Eyed Whore. "They're going to have to get some more dignified clothing on that figurehead."

"She doesn't look very lady-like at the moment, does she?" Jace agreed.

"And Ulrick?"

"Ulrick is with the uh, prisoners." Jace stuttered, sounding like he didn't want to talk about it.

"Prisoners huh? Well that sounds interesting," Galin said, watching the young man's eyes suspiciously. "All right, let's go take a look."

Jace gave Hero a frown and turned to lead them off toward the caves. Castaways were waving and greeting him enthusiastically as they passed, and Galin filled the two in on how they'd traced the robot's path, and how the Claymore had appeared to destroy the compound.

"We haven't received any messages from the bot," Hero told him sadly. "If he'd found your son, he would have contacted the Katara."

"Maybe he got damaged," Jace suggested. "Or maybe he's still confused about detecting that Nazerazi energy signature from the CPIC they installed."

"Not likely," Hero answered. "He doesn't even know it was the Katara he woke up on. His programming should be fine, and I don't think he'd run into anything here on Necron he couldn't handle."

"I just hope my father responds soon. Maybe he

knows something that could help us find David. I don't know why he hasn't gotten back to me yet."

A small group of castaways ran past them excitedly, and Jace had to dodge out of the way to keep from getting run over.

"Hey, Captain," Hero suddenly said with an excited grin on her face, as if the castaways' excitement had been contagious. "Did you notice the Dagger class ship docked in this mountain?"

"Yeah, we did," Galin told her. "It's kind of hard to miss on the scanners; sticks out like a sore thumb."

"Apparently it belonged to one of Bios' settlers. He was going to try and fix it up or something. The thing was abandoned after the Solanum virus hit. The cave dwellers had hopes of fixing it up, but I guess it's missing some crucial system components. I haven't had a chance to take a look at it yet, but it sure would be nice to bring her back to life. Pretty exciting, huh?"

The young woman was smiling through tears and an exhausted set of eyes. She was hurting, that much was clear, but was also trying to remain positive, despite what she was going through.

Galin put his arm around her as they walked. "It's very exciting, you're right. And I'm sure we'll be able to get the old girl into the stars again. If we can't do it, nobody can."

She answered with a confident nod.

As they approached the outskirts of the crowd, Galin

looked up to see Ulrick, James Locke, and a few other men gathered around the prisoners. He squinted to get a better look at the big one in the middle, who was spitting and cursing at the captors. Galin had seen wanted posters for Black-backed Jack, and now he could barely believe his eyes. He glanced back at his two young crewmembers, and then frowned accusingly when he saw the guilt on their faces.

"Is that him?"

Jace nodded halfheartedly. He could tell the captain was not pleased.

"*Frack* it all, Jace. Start at the beginning and tell me what happened."

As the young man filled him in, his blood began to boil, and he locked his eyes onto the prisoners. These men had threatened his ship, his mission and his crew. They had endangered his family. And now, standing here before him was…what? They'd put Jack in the regeneration chamber and reprogrammed his gender? Was this supposed to be some kind of joke?

When the story was finished, Galin turned his gaze back upon Jace and Hero.

"Is that everything?"

"Pretty much, yeah," Jace answered, "the short version, anyway."

"Captain, I'm sorry," Hero told him. "I, I was just angry. I wasn't thinking."

Galin turned back to Jace. "And you and Ulrick

went along with this, like it's some kind of a damned *game*? Is that what you think all this is?"

Jace shook his head fervently. "No, I don't. None of us do. It's just…it's hard to explain what happened up there." He shrugged nervously. "I don't know why we did it."

"We'll talk about this later," Galin warned them, and then stormed off through the crowd toward the prisoners.

"WELL, HERE HE COMES NOW," Black-backed Jack called out in a surprisingly high-pitched voice.

"You know me?" Galin asked him.

"Oh, yes. You're the captain of that piss-poor little tub you people call a starship. We've all been waiting for *you* to show up. You must be a man of some importance," the pirate guffawed.

Galin looked up at Ulrick with eyes that could have curdled milk, then he exchanged glances with James and the other men standing nearby. "So, what was the plan?" Galin asked them, "To let them go free here on Necron? While we leave with the ships? That way they'd be imprisoned here on the planet, but have a fighting chance?"

James ran his fingers through his long, grey beard, and shifted uncomfortably. "That's what we were leaning toward," he said thoughtfully, "but we wanted to get your input first."

Galin looked back at the pirate, who hadn't stopped

mumbling and cursing since he'd walked up. "And what do you have to say? Anything that might sway our decision?"

"Oh, absolutely. Please let us go, we promise to be good," the pirate sneered as his men laughed heartily. "We won't try to find a way off this bloody planet. We won't track you down like the worthless scum-sucking dogs that you are, and put you down like filthy mutts." He laughed, which caused his unseemly bosom to jiggle, and shifted his eyebrows up and down. "Or will we?"

"They're no threat to us now," James told Galin with a shake of his head. "What are he and four of his men really going to do, once we strand them here and leave?"

"That's right," the pirate agreed. "Listen to your friend. I'm just trying to scare you a bit," he laughed again. But then he stopped laughing, and gave Galin such a cutting look in the eye that his soul could feel it. "I'll tell you what I'm going to do, you frackin' weakling. I'm going to claw my way off this miserable rock of a planet, and have these little *alterations* corrected. And then I'm going to track down every member of your pathetic little crew, and have more fun than any pirate should be allowed to have, by slowly murdering them. And last of all," he looked at Hero, "I'm going to settle the score with that tricksy little fox over there. She thinks she's so clever," he laughed and spat, "doing this to me. It's not anything compared to what I'm going to do to you, girl. You've got a long, long life ahead of you.

You're going to be my special little slave, and I'm going to love you until you beg for—."

Suddenly, the pirate's head exploded within a cloud of red mist.

There were shouts of confusion as several bystanders ran for cover, and a moment later, everyone's eyes came to rest on Galin. They watched with surprise and horror as he calmly squeezed off blaster shots into the chests of the four remaining prisoners.

Then he re-holstered his pistol, and turned to walk away.

James Locke gaped at him in disbelief. "Captain...I, I...."

Galin shrugged. "I believed him." And then he walked back toward the Katara.

Galin was down in the engine room, working with Hero and Chief Joseph on the repairs, when Jace came scooting down the ladder with a fresh pot of coffee. He filled each of their cups, and was about to head back up when the conversation seized his attention.

"So I guess we have no choice," Galin said to the chief as they looked over the CPIC, which had been fried while chasing William Marshal. "This thing's completely junked. I guess we'll have to install the original."

Joseph frowned. "I really wanted to check that thing's programming unit first, just to be safe."

Jace turned toward them. "Why don't you just reinstall the same unit we had in here before?" he asked.

"Because, it was taken when we docked on the Claymore," the chief told him. The Nazerazi took it out for examination.

The young man immediately stooped to lift up the grating, revealing the compartment where he'd been hiding before everyone else was taken off the ship. Jumping down into the crawlspace, he grabbed something wrapped up in a towel, and handed it up to Joseph.

"The Katara's CPIC?" He raised his eyebrows, unwrapping it.

"I decided to yank the thing out and hide it right after you guys left."

"Why?" Galin asked him with a chuckle.

"You two made such a fuss about the information that might be hidden on the original unit, I just figured that it would be a good idea to hide this one, too."

Galin laughed. "Well, I wasn't too worried about that, I'd deleted anything they could have found useful, but I'm sure glad you hid it anyway."

Hero beamed over at Jace and rolled her eyes at him before trying to take a sip of her coffee, but it was still too hot. "I spoke with a mechanic who lives down here in the caves. He said that the ship docked in this mountain is missing a CPIC. It's one of the main reasons they were never able to get the thing going."

"I thought you guys said that a ship could be flown without one if you had enough crew members," Jace said.

"Enough *experienced* crew members," Galin explained. "But these Dagger class ships have all kinds of security lockouts. If they weren't disengaged before the processor was removed, they'd be nearly impossible to get past. I doubt anyone on this rock has that kind of skill."

"Well, looks like we have a spare," Joseph said, tucking the unit under his arm. "If we want to help them get that other Dagger back online, you just need to decide which unit to install in each ship."

"We'd have to install the original in the Katara," Galin told him. "As many concerns as I have about putting it back into this ship, I'd be downright scared to install it in that other one. With the security lockouts, who knows what might happen. At the very least, the CPIC would probably be fried just like this one." He tossed the destroyed Nazerazi processing unit onto a junk heap under the workbench.

"Well, I'm going to head outside and see if Ulrick wants any coffee," Jace told them, and then added with a smirk, glancing at the recovered processor unit- "Let me know if you need anything else."

Hero gave him a little chuckle as they exchanged smiles, then he disappeared up the ladder. It was only a few seconds later when James Locke came clunking down the rungs.

Galin glanced at the man for a moment before resuming his tune-up on the shield generator. "Well, here I am, let's hear it."

James Locke sighed. "Captain, I'm not here to lecture you. In fact, I'm not even sure that I disagree with your decision to execute those men, but the way you went about it…."

"I know," Galin conceded. "It was thoughtless of me. I scared people, and for that, you have my apologies."

"Thank you, I'm glad to hear it." Locke continued to stand there and stare at him, as if something else was on his mind.

Galin looked back at him expectantly.

"Do you think we might speak privately for a moment?"

Galin shook his head. "I don't mean to be rude, but I've got work to do. Whatever you've got to say, you can say in front of them."

James looked hesitant.

"Seriously, just let me have it."

James scratched his head. "Well, to be honest, I'm worried about you, Captain. We don't know each other very well, and I don't mean to be intrusive…. It's just that I've heard a lot about you. David spoke about you so much that I almost feel like I do know you. You're a good man. But, to shoot an unarmed prisoner the way you did…. Well, it was brutal. Barbaric. It just doesn't seem like the actions of a stable man."

Galin laughed a little, despite himself. "I wish I *could* assure you of my stability, Mr. Locke; tell you with a straight face that I'm okay, that I have all my wits about me." He looked over at Hero and the chief, who were pretending to mind their own business. "But if I told you that, I'd be lying. I'm *not* okay. Maybe I've even lost a bit of my sanity these past few months. I don't know."

Locke looked him over with what seemed like genuine concern.

"But, you're wrong about one thing."

"Am I? And what would that be?" the man asked him.

"I didn't shoot any unarmed men today. And although I'm sorry about how I did it, I don't regret my decision, or my actions. That pirate and his men were armed with something more dangerous than any weapon."

Galin kneeled, and turned the screwdriver, which was resting inside the electron dampener, as gently as if he were stroking a kitten. James waited for him to continue.

"Each of those men was armed with hatred. Their leader especially. He carried an insatiable hunger for revenge."

"Yes, but—."

"Monsters like those have a complete disregard for any form of morality. They are men without honor. And

I will not allow my family to be harmed by men without honor. Never again. Not when I can do something about it."

Galin looked over at the members of his crew. Joseph was wearing a knowing grin, and Hero stared at him lovingly, with eyes filled with tears. He turned back to Locke. "And family sometimes extends beyond blood. But I don't have to tell *you* that, do I?"

"No," James said. "You don't." He stood there silently for a few moments. "Very well, Captain. I'll assure my people that you aren't going to flip your lid and kill anyone. Can we expect you and your people for dinner tonight?"

"I never turn down a free meal," Galin assured him. "Besides, we still have a lot of things to talk about."

"That we do. Good luck with your repairs. Please let me know if I can be of any assistance."

They shook hands, and James disappeared up the ladder.

Galin went back to concentrating on his work, and a moment later felt a hand touch him gently on the shoulder. He looked up to see Hero standing over him, wiping the tears from her eyes.

"Thank you," she told him. "Thank you for protecting me. For protecting all of us."

He let out a deep breath. "I'm just sorry I wasn't there bef—."

"No," she said sternly. "What happened wasn't your

fault. Bad things, evil things are going to happen. That's just a part of life. But what you did.... Well, I just want you to know that I understand, and that I'm glad you did it. Not because of what happened to *me*. I mean, not because I wanted revenge, but because Jack and his men wouldn't have stopped. They would have kept destroying people's lives."

Galin smiled at her sadly. He was struggling to find the right words when the chief came over to save him. He clapped his old friend on the shoulder, and smiled warmly. "We know you didn't want to do it, but you were willing to do what needed to be done."

"Thanks," Galin told them.

"But, in Mr. Locke's defense," the chief added with a grin, "a little warning next time *would* be nice." He gave them a wink and went back to his repairs.

Hero stayed right where she was. She looked like she was about to burst into tears.

"Captain, there's something I need to talk to you about," she said nervously. "Some things about my past that I really think you need to know."

"Okay," Galin told her, standing up and taking her hand in order to calm her down.

Just then, Jace came in over the com. "Hey Cap, we just received an encrypted message from the Claymore. You want me to patch it through?"

"YES," Galin sighed, dropping the girl's hand and heading for the nearest screen.

Joseph watched him, trying to read the look on his face. "What is it?" he asked hesitantly.

Galin ran his fingers through his hair. "It's my father, he's coming to talk. Says he'll be here in about forty five minutes." Without another word, he scurried up the ladder out of sight.

—UST SPACE NAVY HEADQUARTERS, AUSTIN, TEXAS
NEARLY FOURTEEN YEARS BEFORE—

Admiral Marvin Savage was his name, and it fit him well. This titan, who sat frowning behind the bench at Galin, was possibly the largest man he had ever seen. His size and demeanor alone were enough to command his respect. His eyes were sharp and piercing, and his ebony skin was not far from the color of pitch. Galin got the feeling that if you lied to him, he might crash his way through the bench, pick you up like a tasty sausage, and finish you off in a few large bites.

To the admiral's right sat Brigadier General Jack Reynolds, whose stoic expression reminded Galin a bit of his father, and to his left, Admiral Thomas Harper, a pinkish man with puffy lips, who looked like he'd just taken a swig of spoiled milk.

"Galin Winchester, you have been accused of committing the murder, and faking the death of

Lieutenant JG Allen Carver. The evidence against you has been presented, and as you know, it is the purpose of this tribunal to reach a verdict and determine your fate," Savage spat. "Is there anything else you'd like us to consider before we deliver our verdict?"

Galin lowered his head for a few moments to collect his thoughts. Could anything he said now affect their opinions on what had happened? He could see from the looks on their faces that their minds were already made up.

"I didn't kill Allen Carver," he told them again. "But it was my intent to. Would I have killed him had he been alive when I'd gotten there? I can't honestly say for sure, but I think I would have." He looked each of them in the eye. "I'm not asking for this court to show me any mercy. My only regret in all of this is that I didn't put that animal down before he murdered my sister. If I could trade my life for hers, I would. But I can't." His eyes darted between the three men glaring back at him. "I hesitated when I should have acted, and for *that* I *am* guilty."

The men just gazed at him with stony expressions. Was there any sympathy there? Any understanding of what he'd done? Perhaps. But facts were facts, and these officers had sworn to uphold the law.

"And you maintain," said General Reynolds, "that you have no idea who might actually have killed Lieutenant Carver?"

"I can't attest to that, Sir. As the evidence clearly proves, Carver had been dead for nearly two hours by the time I arrived."

The three men exchanged knowing glances. Galin suspected that they were just as confident as he was that his father had seen to Carver's death. They had even discussed the message he'd received, which told him that the man had already been transferred. His father had covered his tracks well, even going so far as to ensure that Carver actually received transfer orders earlier in the day. It was why he hadn't been at work. He had been sent to his quarters to pack.

Admiral Savage took in a deep breath and let it out slowly, through pursed lips. "Captain Galin Winchester, the evidence has been reviewed, and it seems very clear that you had nothing to do with the murder of Lieutenant Carver. For that crime, we find you innocent." He paused. "However, by your own admission, you unlawfully entered the man's premises with the intent to commit that offense. You obviously believe that Carver murdered your sister, but he was never so much as charged for that crime. We cannot take your feelings for him into consideration. We find your behavior to be despicable, and unbecoming of an officer of the United States of Texas Space Navy. Our delegate from the United Earth Government concurs." He looked at Admiral Harper, who nodded back in agreement.

Savage continued. "Therefore, it is the decision of this tribunal that effective immediately, you be stripped of your commission and separated from service." He smashed his gavel down as if trying to split the table in half. "We're done here."

Galin felt numb as he exited the room, where Peter was sitting there waiting for him.

"Well? How did it go?"

"Better than it could have. But my military career is over."

Peter sighed. He didn't look at all surprised. "Well, I guess that's that. You want to go get a drink?"

"Yeah, I do. But I'm not going to."

"Music to my ears," Peter told him with a slap on the shoulder before setting off down the hall. "So what's the plan now? You headed back home?"

"No, I don't think so. I'm gonna go traveling for awhile, get away from everything. Can you give this to Starla for me?" he asked, handing over a letter.

Peter frowned as he took it. "Do I look like a fracking delivery boy to you?"

"Yeah," Galin told him, removing the pilot's wings from his jacket. "In a way, you do." He tossed him the wings. "And the next time you see my old man, you can give him those."

"I'll hold on to them for you."

"I just figured he might as well have them. He's the reason they're no longer attached."

"Maybe he *is* responsible," Peter whispered, "but if Carver hadn't already been slagged when you got there, it'd be your *life* those paper-pushers asked for instead of these wings, you think about that?"

Galin just scowled at him.

Peter held his arm to Galin's chest, stopping him in his tracks. "Hold on, you're actually ticked off about this, aren't you? You're mad because you didn't get to kill that piece of garbage yourself?"

Galin didn't say anything; he just pushed past Peter's arm and continued walking.

"Maybe I'd feel the same if I were you, I don't know," his friend said, catching up. Peter had always been perplexed by Galin's strict code of honor. It was like something from days long past, yet its rules weren't exactly clear to anyone but Galin. "I assume you're leaving right away?"

"As soon as I can find a halfway decent ship, I'm out of here."

"And where exactly are you headed? Got any ideas?"

"I've heard they have some very nice beaches on Epsilon Ceti B. Apparently, some intergalactic investors have turned the whole place into a vacation planet. Maybe I'll head there first. After that, who knows. I'll need to figure out what to do with the rest of my life."

"Just be sure to keep in touch," Peter told him, placing his arm over Galin's shoulder. "If you go off the radar again, I promise to give you a beating twice as bad as the last one."

"*That* fight wasn't fair," Galin protested. "I was so drunk I could barely stand up."

"And whose fault was that?" Peter asked with a menacing stare. "You're a fighter pilot, you should know that you always have to be ready for an attack." He took a swing at his friend's stomach, but Galin saw it coming and dodged out of the way, letting out an irritated chuckle. Peter always knew how to cheer him up, or at least he always tried to.

Galin looked up to exchange glances with Admiral Savage and his companions as they passed. Galin was glad that looks couldn't kill. Peter snapped to attention and let the three men go by.

"Fracking paper pushers," Peter whispered when they were too far away to hear.

Yes they were, and Galin would never have to deal with the likes of them again.

Galin was waiting in the grass when he heard the sound of the Admiral's shuttle. At first the noise blended in with the thunder, but a few moments later, it came shooting through the lightning stricken clouds like a rocket, heading right toward him.

As blades of grass shimmered in anticipation, the transport alighted to the ground a few dozen feet away. Two fully armored space marines were the first to descend, taking position at the bottom of the steps. They surveyed the surrounding terrain before one of them motioned to someone above that it was safe to proceed.

Admiral Winchester came trudging down, wearing his trademarked grim frown. He had black circles around his eyes, and appeared even gaunter than he had the last time Galin had seen him.

“I don't have much time,” he said.

“Hello to you too, Dad.”

“I was surprised to receive your transmission. I thought I'd told you to get as far away as you could with that ship of yours. Why didn't you listen?”

“I'm working on it. But first, I need to track down David and Sarah. And Starla.”

“Yes, I suppose you do. But this planet isn't safe. There are things going on here that you and your people know nothing about, things more sinister than a few infected cannibals running through the jungle." He drew in a deep breath and softened his expression. "At any rate, let me make your mission a little easier.” He gazed back up into the ship to give some unseen person a nod. “Bring down the boy.”

A pretty, stern faced female lieutenant proceeded down the steps, holding the hand of a confused child.

“DAVID?” Galin gasped. He ran to his son and caught the boy up in his arms, squeezing tightly. Then he took his head and looked him in the eyes. He was stone faced and lethargic. “What's wrong, son? Are you sick?"

The boy didn't answer; he just stared back, blankly. It was almost as if he didn't recognize the man speaking to him.

"Those monsters did something to him," the admiral spat, his face turning red. "But they won't get away with it. I'm going to find them. I'm going to make them pay."

"Who are you talking about?" Galin asked. "What...what do you think *they* did to him? Who are *they*?"

The Admiral suddenly seemed to snap out of it. He regained his composure and gave his jacket a good straightening. "We'll talk. There are things that must be discussed, and soon, but now is not the time. I need to go after them. I just came to drop off David, and to warn you. You and your friends need to evacuate. General Soth has given the order to re-terraforming this planet, and as soon as the Genesis Torpedo is completed, we'll be back to initiate the launch."

"Re-terraforming? Why? Why would the Nazerazi want this planet reformed?"

"Soth agreed to the process based on *my* recommendation. I want these miserable zombies eliminated once and for all. It was a horrible mistake for me not to have seen to it long ago."

"But, there are a lot of uninfected people on this planet. People who were illegally dumped here by the UEG. What about them?"

"Evacuate as many people as you can, and get that ship of yours out of here, too. If the Nazerazi discover your location, I won't be able to stop them from coming for you." The Admiral turned to leave, and took a few steps up toward the shuttle before turning back around. He gave Galin and David a longing look. "Good luck, son." And then he strode up into the ship. The young lieutenant followed, as did the Space Marines, and a minute later the shuttle lifted off and quickly disappeared through the clouds.

Galin stooped to have another look at his son. The boy looked a terrible mess. He was pale and had dark circles around his eyes as if he'd not had any sleep for days.

"David, you're all right now. You're with me." He waited for the lad to answer, but the boy's eyes fluttered around as if he'd never seen grass, and sky, and clouds before. "Where…where's my mommy?" David stuttered.

Galin felt as though the boy had stabbed him. He couldn't tell David about his mother's death, not now, not like this. "Come on," he said gently, stooping to pick him up again. "There'll be plenty of time for talking later on, but for now you just need to rest." He turned to head back toward the Katara, and saw a disheveled, but beautiful, dark haired woman standing about a dozen feet away. She frowned at them with concerned eyes, and looked as though she was thinking of saying something.

"Can I help you?" Galin asked her, not unkindly.

"Is he all right?"

"I think he just needs to rest."

"I'm Angelica," she said, coming closer. "I was with him when he was taken. When Peter was killed." Her eyes began to well up, and she turned her head to hide the tears.

"You were on that search party too, weren't you? The one that went out to try and get him back?"

She nodded.

"Thank you," he said softly. "I'd like to talk to you about what happened. Would you consider meeting with me later?"

Again she nodded. "Of course. I'd like that, actually."

"Good. I'm going to take him onto the ship, see if I can get him down to rest a bit. I'll catch up with you later."

Angelica brushed the hair from her face. "If you'd like, I can show you where he stayed inside the caves. He was always very comfortable there. It might be quieter than your ship while the repairs are underway."

Galin considered it for a moment. "All right. If you think he'd rest better there, then lead the way."

Angelica gave him a warm smile, and led them off toward the caves. As they walked, Galin saw that she kept gazing down at the boy, concern flashing through her eyes.

"Whatever happened out there, when he was taken, I mean- it wasn't your fault. If Peter couldn't stop that woman, I'm sure there was nothing you could do either. Anyway, we have him back now. Thank God for that."

She nodded. "I know it wasn't my fault, not really, I just wish that we'd believed him. He told us about seeing a woman in black. He'd spotted her several times, hanging off in the distance as if she was watching him. Nobody thought he was making it up, but it was a hard story to swallow. We just figured his mind was playing tricks on him or something. Turns out he was right all along."

Galin squeezed his son's shoulder. "Kids tell stories. Besides, I imagine a nightmare planet like this could have even the greatest skeptics imagining things."

"And Peter, he didn't have to die." At the mention of his name, Angelica's voice broke. "We…we had something. We'd only just met, but there was definitely chemistry between us. It was like we'd known each other forever. I hesitate to use the word love, but…."

"But no other word seems to fit?"

She nodded. "I know he felt it too. We loved each other, and now he's gone."

"The man was the closest thing to a brother that I ever had," Galin told her. "He was always there for me. I owe him my life, several times over. And his final act was to die trying to protect David." He reached over and took her hand. "If I could trade my own life for his, I would."

She smiled, and shook her head. "No, don't say that. Everything happens for a reason. You were meant to live. You have a son to care for, and a daughter to find." She gave his hand a grateful squeeze and looked him deep in the eyes. "I only wish I knew how to turn back time. Fix some of the mistakes I've made, some of the things that I could have done differently. Have you ever felt like that?"

Galin let out something like a chuckle. "I've spent the last half of my life feeling like that."

Galin listened to the crackle of the bonfire, and watched the mixture of light and shadow dance happily across the cave walls behind Ulrick. The man looked like a big, hungry bear as he pawed through yet another piece of fish. Chief Joe, who was also watching him, appeared to be thinking the same thing.

"You know any Native American legends about furless, blonde-headed bears?" Galin asked.

The chief just rolled his eyes, while Boreas looked at him expectantly, as if hoping he might actually have one.

James Locke stepped up in front of the fire and called the people to attention.

"All right, everyone, now that we've all enjoyed a splendid dinner," he gave his belly a rub, "there are some important things that must be discussed. The last few days have been very interesting. Very exciting to say the least, and the time has come for some important decisions to be made. I want to take this opportunity to share some of the things that I, Captain Winchester, and the elders have discussed, and give you all the chance to offer any concerns or feedback that you might have." He pawed through his beard to shake out any remaining crumbs from dinner, as he was want to do, but then realized how silly he must have looked, and put his hands to his sides.

"First of all, we have our *own* starship now." At this point, he was interrupted by a copious amount of whistles, cheers, and applause. "But, as you know," he said, trying to calm the people down, "as you know, having the means of escape will do us no good at all if we have nowhere that we can escape to. Our home world has fallen to the Nazerazi Alliance, and the United Earth Government, which stranded us here, is no more. It is essential that we find a place of our own, somewhere that we can lay down roots, and build new homes and lives.

"It has also been revealed that a month from now, a Genesis Torpedo will be launched upon this planet. Necron has been scheduled for re-terraforming, and when that happens, every living thing residing here will be killed." He tugged his beard and looked down into the fire. "There are still many people scattered throughout the jungle, either in small groups or by themselves. And there may be others who have escaped, living on other continents of this planet. Since we now have the means to search for them and offer assistance, the other elders and I believe it is our duty to do so." There were many muttered words of agreement. Only a few of his listeners looked like they weren't at all thrilled with the idea.

"In order to expedite this process, Captain Winchester and the crew of the Katara have agreed to stay here and help. One of the ways they will do this is to assist with the repairs of the ship that was abandoned in this mountain. If the vessel can be repaired quickly, then search and rescue operations can be expedited, and we'll have more room for evacuees. And now, I'd like to turn things over to Captain Winchester, who I've asked to say a few words."

Galin turned to his crew, and chewed his lip nervously before rising up to stand before the crowd. He'd never been thrilled with the idea of public speaking, and as he looked at the people staring back at him expectantly, their faces illuminated by flames, he felt as if the telling of some old ghost story or folktale might be more appropriate.

"Evening, everyone. I've, uh, never been much for speeches, but James asked me to say a few words, so.... To begin with, I wanted to personally apologize if I scared anyone with the, uh, earlier events today. I know that everyone here has been through a lot of tragedy and heartache lately. We've all seen things that we never thought we would, and some of us have done things that we never thought we'd have to do, either."

He let out a long breath, and looked at the chief, who returned an encouraging nod.

"I've come to a point in my life, where I've realized that…I'm willing to do whatever it takes to keep my loved ones safe. We're not playing some kind of game here, but I know I don't have to tell any of you that."

He clenched his fists, and decided it was time to just let everyone know what he was thinking, and let the chips fall where they may.

"We need to be strong. We need to be unyielding. We need to stick together, and protect one another." He looked around, wondering how badly he was messing this up, and then his eyes fell upon David. The boy looked shell-shocked, but Galin told himself that he just needed time to rest.

"I was lucky enough to get my son back, but my daughter is still out there, somewhere. The woman I love is *still out there*. OUR PEOPLE are still out there, on this world and others. And I don't know about you, but I'm just a little sick and tired of being used as the universe's *fracking* punching bag." He saw a lot of sympathetic, determined faces staring back. Some of them looked angry, some were nodding in agreement, but he couldn't see anyone who appeared to disagree with what he was saying.

"We must all work together to get off this God-forsaken rock, but after that, each of you needs to choose. Will you stay and fight? Or will you try to find a place to rebuild- to start a new life? You must each choose the path that seems right to you. Who knows if one way is more correct than the other? I wish I knew myself. All I can say is, for those of you who still have something to fight for, you're welcome to join me. I'm going to get out there and find the people I love, and if the Nazerazi stand in my way, whoever or whatever they are, they're going to end up just like those pirates I slagged." Was this the right thing to say, he wondered? The people before him looked like they were ready to jump up and fight. They would have, if only some enemy stood before them. *They understand*, Galin realized. *These people are tired of being victims, just like I am*.

Orange flames twinkled in Galin's eyes, and his chest heaved as if he were preparing to breathe fire. "There's going to be some major pay-back coming, and I promise you all that I'm *not* going to stop until I find a rope big enough to hang the Nazerazi Alliance. I'm not going to stop until I find a way, until WE find a way, to take our planet BACK. The reckoning begins *now*."

As Galin sat down, many of the people clapped, some just murmured in agreement, but it was James Locke's face that caught his eye.

"There's one important difference," the man said soberly, "between those pirates you shot and the

Nazerazi, I mean. The Nazerazi can fight back."

Galin put his arm around David's shoulder and ruffled the boy's hair. "Yes," he agreed. "Unfortunately they can."

Book 7

Kill Switch

Galin Winchester had spent so much time on ship repairs over the last few months, he was beginning to wonder if he'd missed his calling. It struck him almost immediately how foolish the thought had been. He didn't know any small starship captains who didn't spend twice the time on maintenance and repairs as they did sitting behind the controls of their ships. Well, maybe that was overstating it a bit, but it sometimes seemed like that much. It was just part of the job.

A few more minor adjustments and the Katara would be raring to go once again. She'd taken quite a licking from her encounter with the T3038 and, then again with the pirates, but as always, she seemed to find a way to keep on ticking.

Galin pulled off his gloves and let them drop to the engine room floor before wiping his brow and reaching for the ladder.

"I'm heading up to the bridge to see how things are coming along. I'll let you know when we're ready to fire the old girl up."

The chief nodded. "I'll be ready when you are. Hey, if you see Hero, send her down here for me, would you? She left her tools all over the environmental controls panel. She's a talented mechanic, but you can always tell where she's been."

"Will do, but why don't you just call her on the com?"

"She's not answering. Jace probably snuck off with her again. Kids these days."

Galin laughed. "Well, who can blame him? She's a gorgeous young lady, and I think our young friend is beginning to fall hopelessly in love."

Joseph nodded. "Do you think she feels the same way, though? I haven't known her quite as long as you, but it seems to me she still has a lot of grieving to do. It hasn't been that long since her husband's death, after all."

"Jace knows that. We've talked about it, and I've warned him to take things slow. She still has a missing boy somewhere out there, too." His face grew sad and serious. "With Sarah gone, my not knowing where she is, or if she's even alive- I can't even imagine trying to develop a romantic relationship. I know Hero feels the same. The...obsession, and the heartache that comes along with having a missing child don't really leave much room for anything else."

Joseph finished tightening the bolt he was working on and stood to his feet. "I can't imagine what either of you are going through. But, at least we'll be back in the air soon. And remember that the rest of us are here for you both. She isn't alone. Neither are you."

"I know that, Chief. And I appreciate it." Galin turned and began to climb up the ladder. Now that he thought about it, he and Hero had a lot in common. They each had a leg caught in the bear trap of a traumatic event, and continuing to try and get out was tearing them both to pieces. It was like being anchored in a storm, yet driven to move forward. It wasn't a matter of choice; neither of them had any choice, not until their children were found, or their fates determined. Galin felt hollow, helpless. It was like being drowned, only squirming and kicking did you no good. You just had to try and stay focused on heading toward the surface, and pray you'd make it to air in time.

And then there was Starla. Her absence haunted him day in and day out. This is what having a ghost limb must feel like, he thought. She was supposed to be there, but she wasn't. Now, only the echo of her form and voice reverberated through his mind. The smell of her hair wafted over him whenever he closed his eyes.

How had he managed to screw everything up so

badly? To push her away further every chance he got? He'd been acting so stupid for so long. If he was ever given the chance to set things right, he would.

Then again, denying reality would do no good. There was a chance he'd never see her alive again, and the guilt of that fact seemed to rush through his veins like a river of tiny, scalding blades. For now, all he could do was keep putting one foot in front of the other, progress toward rescuing Starla and Sarah, and pray that someday he'd be given a chance to make things right with both of them.

The door to the bridge slid open, and Galin was surprised to find Daniel and Matt waiting for him.

"Hey," Daniel said. "We ran into Jace a few minutes ago. He said he didn't think you'd mind if we helped run diagnostics on the Katara."

"You're all finished up with the repairs on the One Eyed Maiden?"

"Knocked the last ones out this morning." Matt pointed out toward the other ship. "We've had a lot of good people helping out. Everybody's seems pretty driven to pick up off from this rock and move on."

"Gee, I wonder why?" Daniel smirked. "This planet seems to emanate nothing but death and nightmares. There's just been too much blood spilled in this place."

"For all of us," Galin agreed. "Anyway, you're always welcome aboard my boat. In fact, since the two of you plan on assisting with the repairs of that Dagger class docked in the mountain, the sooner you start getting familiar with this class, the better."

"Exactly what we were thinking." Daniel pointed and shot his finger like a gun.

Galin checked for new messages on the com. "Where is Jace, anyway?"

"He was heading off for a picnic with Hero," Matt said. "It looked like they were taking off for the apple orchard. That was about fifteen minutes ago."

"Good," Galin said. "They've both been burning the midnight oil. They deserve to get away." He reached over to pick something up from the co-pilots chair. "But I'll tell you one thing- If Jace leaves his communicator behind again, I'm going to staple the thing to his forehead."

Daniel shook his head. "I don't blame you. Just because we have weapons now doesn't mean those zombies aren't still a threat. Still lots of pirates around, too."

"I think there was a pretty big group heading out there to pick apples today," Matt put in. "They should be safe enough. Besides, Jace and Hero are both smart kids, I don't think they'll wander off too far."

"You're right," Galin shrugged, "They'll be okay. But these days...I guess I just don't like to be out of contact with any of my crew. Makes me feel uneasy." He sank down into the pilot's chair and rubbed his head, fantasizing about a nap. "As soon as all the systems get a clean bill of health, we'll install the CPIC. Then we can head out and retrieve the rest of the parts the other dagger needs and complete evacuation efforts. All things considered, we could all be off this rock in another two or three weeks."

Matt took the diagnostics checklist Galin offered him. "And then you're off to look for your daughter? A few weeks must seem like an eternity."

"It does. Every bone in my body is screaming to fly off out of here right now, but I won't abandon the people stranded on this planet. What kind of man would I be? Besides, I found David. I'll find Sarah, too."

"I believe you will," Daniel said with an encouraging nod. "You mentioned a woman the other day as well. Starla, wasn't it?"

Galin nodded.

"Who's she," asked Matt. "Your wife?"

"She will be someday, if I'm lucky." Galin reached out to fire up the control panel. "I'll tell you both all about her sometime, but for now, we have work to do. Let's make this old girl sing."

Hero lunged up to catch the apple that Jace had just launched to her, but it rolled from the tips of her fingers to land with a thud somewhere on the grass behind.

"You're throwing them too high." She giggled.

Jace loved it when she giggled. It made her smile

seem even more beautiful, if that was possible. "No, you need to learn how to jump. You could have easily caught that one."

"Didn't you used to play sports in school?"

"Yeah, what of it?"

"You throw like a retarded monkey, that's what of it." She placed her hands on her hips and sneered playfully.

Jace tried not to stare at the way her black t-shirt hugged her beautiful upper form. When the wind lifted her dirty-blonde hair from her shoulders to reveal her smooth, slender neck a chill ran through his body.

He shook off what he was thinking and picked up another apple. "You're in for it now." He wound up his arm, and let the thing fly.

It streaked through the air like a red snowball, splattering in Hero's hands just a few inches from her stomach, and sending a spray of over-ripened apple mush across the front of her chest and face.

"YOU HORSE'S ASS," she shouted, but immediately began to laugh.

"I'm *so* sorry," Jace called sheepishly, running over to her. "I didn't know. I should have been more careful."

"It's not a big deal. Besides, I can wash off at the river. You wanted to stop by your friend's grave, right?"

"Yeah. I kinda feel like I owe it to him whenever I'm in the area."

Hero reached out and took his hand, giving it a reassuring squeeze. "I'm sorry I never got to meet him.

What was he like?"

They started off toward the ruins of the old homestead. "Peter was the greatest. He and Galin taught me everything I know about flying. He was a great pilot. One of the best."

"Was he married? A girlfriend, maybe?"

Jace shook his head. "He had girlfriends from time to time, but there was never anyone too serious as far as I know. He was one of those guys who makes an awesome friend, but it would have taken a special girl to put up with him and make him settle down."

"From what I hear, he and that Angelica lady hit it off pretty well. That's what she seems to think, anyway."

Jace shrugged. "Could be. I haven't really talked to her that much. She looks like his kind of girl though."

"Is that right? And what do you mean exactly by "his kind of girl?"

"She seems really smart. And she's gorgeous, too. Peter had pretty high standards."

Jace peeked over at her. She had a bit of a funny look on her face. Was it jealousy? God, he hoped it was.

"Yeah, Angelica's probably the best looking woman I've seen on this planet." He allowed that to sink in for a moment before turning to grin at her. "But she still isn't half as beautiful as you." He clasped her hand a little tighter, and was happy to see the smile light up her face. It was sweeter than watching the sunrise.

"I love you, Hero."

What had he just said? He looked at her in terror. Perhaps he hadn't said it; perhaps he'd only thought it. His heart skipped a beat, and the surprise on the young woman's face confirmed what he'd just done.

Her grip loosened, and he let go of her hand.

"I'm sorry. It, it just came out. I...." He looked ahead. They were nearly to the ruins now, and he almost wished he were buried beneath them. How could he have been so insensitive, so stupid? Little more than a month had passed since the death of this girl's husband, and it wasn't fair to lay something like this on her. "I didn't mean to make you feel uncomfortable. I really am sorry."

After a few awkward moments, she reclaimed his hand. He looked up to see that a few tears had escaped down her cheeks, but she wiped them away. Her eyes met his. "When I'm with you, I feel safe. And,...and special. Even with everything else that's happened, I can always count on you to make me happy, if only for a while."

For now, it was enough. He stooped down to retrieve some daisies, and offered them to her. She accepted, and held them up to her nose to smell.

"Not the nicest smelling flower, but they sure are pretty." She gazed up into the sky. "Kind of smells like rain. You think a storm might be coming?"

Jace looked up as well. "Hard to say. There might be, but I think we've still got a little bit of time left."

At Peter's gravesite, a light breeze was blowing, and the sound of trickling water could be heard from the nearby river. The noises seemed to point to the silence of the place. It was as peaceful as sleep, or perhaps even death. Hero and Jace sat down on the grass together.

"This really is a beautiful spot," she said. It was good of those people to bury him here."

Jace nodded. "It is. And you're right, it was very thoughtful." He suddenly felt strange, kind of sick. His hands went up to his head.

"You okay? You don't look so good all of a sudden."

"I'll be fine. I'm just.... I've got a bit of a headache." The world began to spin all around him. He stooped forward and struggled to steady his breath, trying to keep from throwing up.

Then he felt a strong hand upon his shoulder.

"Hey, kid, you okay?" Peter asked him. He knelt down and looked into his friend's face. "This isn't the best place to lay down for a nap. You never know when more of those zombies might show up."

"I was just resting my eyes," Jace told him, instinctively feeling for his sidearm to make sure it was there. "Got a little dizzy all of a sudden. Besides, the people at the caves told us those things almost never come out this far."

Peter gave his blaster rifle a few loving pats. "Not

usually. But they do when they're with *her*. Until we've taken her down, just be sure to keep your head up. Even out here, okay?"

"I will," Jace told him. "I'm heading back to the Katara now. You coming?"

"Not yet. I'm supposed to meet Angelica out here for lunch. Change of atmosphere and what not. But when you see Galin, tell him I'll be back soon."

"Can't you just call him on the com?"

"What?" Peter scoffed with a smile, "you don't expect me to bring my communicator along on a romantic picnic, do you? That's no way to win a lady's heart."

"I guess," Jace chuckled, turning to see Angelica walking up toward them. "Hey, speak of the devil. There she is now."

As Angelica walked toward him, she was gazing back with a really odd look.

"What's wrong with *her*?" he asked, looking back up at Peter.

But Peter wasn't there anymore. It was Hero, and she was looking at him strangely, too.

"Where is he?"

Hero placed her hand upon his forehead. "Where's who? Who do you think you were just talking to?"

"Peter. Where'd he go? He was here a second ago. Hey, Angelica. We were just talking about you."

She looked like she wanted to cry. "What is this? Some kind of sick joke?"

"No," Hero insisted. "He kind of got sick all of a sudden, and then he started talking to himself. He thinks he was talking to Peter, I guess."

"I was. He was just here. He said Angelica was on her way to meet him for a picnic." Jace looked around for his friend, but it was like he'd vanished into thin air. Had he slipped behind the tree? He turned back to Hero. "Come on, why are you two acting so weird? Where'd Peter go?"

"He must have heat stroke or something." Hero tried to make him sit back down, but he wasn't having it. "Jace, Peter's dead, remember? He's buried right beside this tree."

"Right here," Angelica stood next to a spot where the earth had been disturbed, pointing down.

What was she saying? It just didn't make any sense. His head began throbbing again, and everything seemed cloudy. For the first time, he noticed the boy standing next to her.

"David? Is that you? What are you doing on Necron?"

The boy just stared back at him. His cold, emotionless eyes were unmoving.

Suddenly, it all came rushing back into his head with a wave of pain, and he staggered.

"Uh, yeah. Of course Peter's dead. I know that." He looked up at them warily, closed his eyes, and opened them again with a sensation of trying to lift something heavy. "I'm sorry. I…I don't know what happened. It all seemed so real."

"Let's get him back to the caves," Angelica said, turning to Hero and offering her canteen. "Here, give him a drink of this."

Hero took it, and made him take a long drink.

"I'm sorry," Jace repeated. He felt weak and embarrassed.

"Stop apologizing," Hero commanded. "Come on, we need to get back anyway. The Captain will kill us if we aren't there when it's time to fire up the ship. We probably shouldn't have taken off in the first place."

Jace gave her a mischievous grin that said he didn't regret it, and she surrendered a sigh and grinned the sentiment back.

As they walked along, Jace began to feel stronger, and his head soon cleared. Halfway back to the caves he was as good as new.

"So, David, are you excited about getting to fly on the Katara? Your dad told me that you've never really spent much time on it."

The boy just kept his eyes forward, and continued to plod along.

Angelica reached down to take his hand, and smiled at Jace sadly. "David, we've talked about this, remember? It isn't polite to ignore people who've spoken to you."

After a few moments, the boy nodded. Then he

turned to look up at Jace. "Yes. I'm excited. I'm very excited."

But he didn't sound excited. He didn't really sound like anything.

"That kid is really starting to creep me out," Jace whispered, leaning over to Hero. "It's like the lights are on, but nobody's home, ya know?"

"Just give him some time," she whispered back. "He's been through a lot."

Jace met Angelica's eyes, and all he saw was worry.

Hero was right, the boy had been through a lot, but then again, all of them had. That woman who'd taken him had done something to him, and when he looked in Angelica's eyes, he knew she thought so, too. Hero and Galin might not want to believe it, but somehow David just wasn't the same boy anymore.

Hero arrived back in the engineering room to find Chief Joseph and Boreas finishing up some adjustments on the environmental control systems.

"Welcome back, did you have a nice picnic?" Boreas asked.

"Sure. It was nice, but…interesting."

Joseph raised an eyebrow. "Everything all right? You sound a little shaken."

"Yeah," she said with a smile. "Jace just got kind of sick. He gave us quite a scare, but he's feeling better now. I think he just got a little dehydrated."

"Well, I'm glad to hear he's feeling better," Joseph said, looking somewhat unconvinced. "Everything else okay?"

Hero just smiled back and nodded. A moment later she began to cry. "I'm, I'm sorry. I just...I...never mind. It's stupid. I'll be all right."

Joseph took her by the shoulder and gave it a gentle squeeze. "Whatever you're feeling, it's not stupid. Just remember, you're a very strong young woman. I haven't known you long, but that much is easy for me to see."

Boreas nodded in agreement

"Just hang in there," Joseph said, handing her a wrench and pointing to the tool box. "We all know what you're going through. You're not alone. And nobody expects you to act like you aren't hurting."

"Thanks," she said, beginning to cry a little harder. "It's nice to have friends. But I know I'm a mess, and I'm sorry." She picked up some of the other tools she'd left out earlier. "I just feel so confused and lost. Like I'm in a lifeboat out on the ocean, just floating along. Unable to steer. No control. Dying a little bit more each day."

"It's because of your hatchling, isn't it?" Boreas asked.

Hero nodded.

"Yes," the reptilian said. "My people are not so different from yours, I think. The love of a mother for her child is one of the strongest forces in the universe. I still remember the wails of my own mother when I was taken from her. It is my earliest memory, and it still haunts me, even now."

Hero stood gaping expectantly at him, tears rolling down her cheeks.

"But my mother didn't have the capability of searching for me, as you do for your son. And I was reunited with her eventually. I have a strong feeling that you will be reunited with your son, too. And much more quickly than I was with mine, because you are working so hard to find him."

Joseph gave her a warm smile. "You may feel lost, but you've still got your compass."

"What do you mean?"

"Sometimes the simplest tools are the ones that work the best," he said, pointing to her heart. He handed her a flat head screwdriver. "This is just a simple little metal rod with a flattened edge and handle, but without it, we couldn't travel through space in this starship. So tell me, what's your compass saying to you?"

Hero wiped the tears from her eyes. She looked back and forth between the other two, and thought for a moment before answering. "It's telling me that Stephen's still alive, and that I'm going to see him again soon."

Joseph patted her lightly on the back. "Sometimes you just need to have a little faith."

Hero placed the screwdriver back in the toolbox. "Maybe. But I'm not so sure I know how."

"Then the two of us will have faith for you," Boreas answered.

Joseph nodded and gave her a wink. "That is, as long as you promise to stop leaving your tools all over the place. Deal?"

She surrendered a little grin. "Okay, deal." She walked to the other side of the room to retrieve the remainder of her mess, but stopped to take a look at the CPIC, which was resting on the workbench next to its future home in the central processing control panel.

"So, Chief, what do you think is going to happen when we light this thing up? The captain seems a little worried about it. How about you?"

The chief shrugged. "I don't think we have anything to be terribly worried about. Worst-case scenario, the thing locks us out of the ship's control systems, but even if that happens, we'll just use the kill switch you hard-wired in. The software we've installed will prevent the systems from taking any real damage."

"Why would hooking up this processor cause any damage in the first place?" Boreas asked.

"You just never know with these old military ships, especially with a class like the Dagger. These ships were used for espionage. For all we know, installing the original CPIC could automatically trigger a self-destruct sequence, for instance. To protect classified information or what not. Who knows?"

"But even if that happens, you're confident that

adequate measures have been taken to prevent an incident?"

"Well, the technology we're dealing with is thirty years old. Even if the ship's systems were still configured to accept those old military protocols, which they aren't, the new software should overwrite and delete those kind of commands. And even if all that fails us, which it won't, the kill switch will shut 'er right down. If we have to resort to that, we may have to recalibrate of few of the systems, but nothing too significant if we act fast."

"So why does the captain still seem so concerned?" Hero put the last few tools away and closed the drawer. "Every time the subject comes up he acts nervous about the whole thing."

"Yes, he does. He hasn't said as much, but I can tell he's got a bad feeling about plugging that thing back in. Probably due to the fact that we never should have found it in the first place. There's no logical reason for it to have been left on the ship. It's all a bit of a mystery, really."

"One that we may be on the verge of solving, though," Hero added.

"True," Joseph nodded. "But not all mysteries have convenient or satisfying answers."

Boreas, who seemed to be enjoying the conversation immensely, hissed out in laughter. "And what do *you* believe, if anything, will happen when we turn the processing core back on?"

"Nothing," Joseph said with a grin. "Or something. We'll find out soon enough."

"All right, Captain," Jace said, running his fingers across the display screen, "non crew members have left the ship, all personnel are in position, and each station is reporting as ready to go."

Galin took in a measured breath and let it out slowly. "Okay, this is the moment of truth. Chief Joe, get ready to plug in the CPIC. Hero, are you ready with that kill switch you and Boreas put in?"

"Everyone's ready on this end," came the chief's voice back over the com. "Just like we were when you asked fifteen minutes ago."

Galin looked over at Jace and rolled his eyes. "Better safe than sorry kid, always remember to measure twice and cut once."

Jace tried not to grin as he nodded back, but he just couldn't help it.

Galin sneered back at him, then checked the systems on the screen in front of him, yet again. Everything was ready. "All right, Chief. Plug 'er in."

"Copy that. Interfacing in 5...4...3...2...1....

Galin stared at the control screen as the Katara's computer rebooted.

"Everything looks good from here," he said, as the

system popped back online. He watched attentively as each of the ship's systems reported back with a successful self-test. "How about down there on your end?"

"Looks good," came the voice of the chief. "I'd say that the interface is a success. Not seeing any glitches yet, but we'll continue to keep an eye on things."

"Thanks, Chief," Galin said in relief. "Talk to you in a few." He leaned back in his chair, and let out a deep sigh. "Thank God. I'll tell you, kid, I wasn't really sure what to expe.... What the heck's wrong with you?"

Jace just sat there in the chair next to him, staring into the air directly behind Galin's chair. He turned to look, and nearly jumped from his seat to see a young woman standing there behind him.

"Where's Captain Patel?" the girl demanded. "And just who are you people?"

Galin was at a loss for words. It took him a moment to process what he was seeing. The young lady standing before him had a strikingly pretty face. She was Asian, most likely Japanese, he thought, and was in her mid to late teens. She had two long braids in her hair, and wore a vintage black and grey UST military command uniform. "Are you a...a hologram?" Galin asked, reaching out to touch her. The tips of his fingers disappeared through her skin just below the left breast.

"Keep your hands to yourself, pervert," she barked at him, sending a mild electrical shock through his hand, which made him yelp and jerk it back.

"Now, tell me who you are?" Where's the crew of the Katara?"

"We're the crew of the Katara. I'm Galin Winchester. I own this ship now."

She looked incredulous. "That's impossible. You're lying."

The girl closed her eyes as if thinking, and Galin could tell from the sounds coming from the control panel that she was scanning through the ship's computer, searching for information.

"I don't see anything about a change of command. Something fishy is going on here and I don't like it! Computer, initiate Security Protocol 28, Subsection D. I'm taking command of the ship."

"The frack you are!" Galin lunged for the control panel, but it was too late. He was already locked out. He flicked on the com. "Hero, hit the kill switch, NOW!"

"Inter-ship communications have already been disabled," the girl said. "And if you're referring to that hard-lined disruption switch you somehow managed to install in the engineering room, there's no one awake down there to use it. I've flooded the area with thruster engine coolant, enough to make sure all your friends are sleeping like babies by now."

Galin's head was swimming. He couldn't believe what was happening. He hadn't known what to expect, but he'd never expected this. Mutiny, on his own ship, a ship he thought he knew so well. There had to be a way to stop it. He just needed to focus and think.

"Computer," the girl said, "verify the location of each ship in the Bleeding Star Squadron."

"Verifying," came the soft, female voice of the Katara's computer. "UST Rondel- decommissioned-location unknown."

"Decommissioned? What? But how...." The girl closed her eyes for a moment. "2390? This is the year 2390? But that means I've been deactivated for the last 26 years." She looked as if she were about to cry.

"Yeah. You have. The Katara was decommissioned in 2364. That's what I've been trying to tell you. I'm her new captain." He was doing his best not to sound angry.

The girl just stood there, and pursed her lips sadly at him like she still couldn't believe it. Only a moment passed before she got a stern look and eyed him over disapprovingly. "If that's true, I don't know how the Katara could have fallen into the hands of the likes of you, but I'd rather see this ship destroyed than belong to some kind of...some kind of...what are you anyway, some kind of a space pirate?"

That made Galin laugh, which only served to heighten the girl's anger. She pointed her finger at him and was about to speak when the computer interrupted.

"UST Dirk- destroyed in battle. UST Corvo-destroyed in battle."

The girl looked shocked and heartbroken. Her lips began to tremble, and her eyes teared up. This was by far the most emotional hologram Galin had ever come into contact with. She genuinely appeared to be grieving.

"UST Yoroi Toshi- location confirmed- Bleeding Star Initiative Command Center."

"Set a course," the girl said, looking hopeful amidst her tears.

"Hey, wait a minute," Galin demanded, standing. "We're right in the middle of a rescue operation. We can't go anywhere."

"That's not up to you," the girl told him. "I need to find out what's happening."

"At least let me explain." Galin softened his tone, hoping to reason with her. "We're on a planet called—."

"I know where we are."

"Course laid in," the computer reported.

"Take us out."

The ship lifted off, and for a few moments, Galin could see the confused faces of the onlookers outside, then the clouds shooting past, and finally the surface of the planet Necron, getting smaller, far below.

"What's your name?" Jace asked, and the girl looked at him in surprise, as if just noticing he were there.

She looked him over suspiciously for a few moments before deciding to answer. "TAII."

"Tie?" Galin repeated. "As in neck-tie?"

"No, smart-ass," the girl huffed at him. "T.A.I.I. As in, Tactical Artificial Intelligence Interface. But unless you want to call me that, then you can call me TAII."

"I'm Jace. Jace Chang. Nice to meet you."

Galin smiled. What was the kid up to? It was almost as if he were flirting with her. Maybe he was just trying to play the good cop, or in this case- the good prisoner.

"Nice to meet you, too, I guess," TAII told him. "Are you a pirate as well?"

"No. We're not pirates. I wish you'd just let us explain. This ship really does belong to Captain Winchester now."

"We'll just have to see about that," TAII frowned. "Computer, maximum warp."

Hero awoke to the throbs of a pounding headache, and forced her eyes open to see the steel grated floor that had been serving as the mattress for her unexpected nap. Sitting up, she felt her face. It was sore and had the indention of the floor pressed into it. A thin line of drool had escaped to run down her cheek. "What the heck is going on here?" she mumbled to no one in particular. "Hey, are we moving?" She could feel the familiar rumble of the ship's engine as it plowed through space, humming in her bones.

Chief Joseph sat up beside her. "Yes, I think we are."

She looked over to see Boreas sprawled out flat on his

back, his thick tongue hanging out to lie beside him on the floor.

"What happened?" Hero asked.

"Looks like we all took an unscheduled siesta. Can't think of a reason for that, though my head is still pretty clouded."

About that time came the sound of the hatch clanking open overhead. A heavy pair of boots came trudging down, and a few seconds later Ulrick hopped to the floor. "Rise and shine, you sleepyheads. Captain's called a family meeting up in the dining hall."

"Ulrick, what's going on?" Hero asked as Joseph helped her to her feet.

"You'll see. Just come on up."

"What about him?" she said, stooping down to Boreas and trying in vain to rouse him.

Joseph retrieved a medical scanner from the first aid cabinet and ran it over his body. "He'll be all right. Just needs to sleep it off, I guess."

"We'll fill him in later," Ulrick said, beginning to climb back up. "Come get some coffee. Though you may soon be wishing for something stronger."

Hero went up next, and the chief followed her. When they reached the dining hall, Galin and Jace were waiting for them. David was there as well, along with a young Asian woman. *Where the heck could she have come from,* Hero thought.

"Boreas is still sleeping," Joseph announced. "He's

okay, but it doesn't look like he'll be joining us anytime soon."

Galin nodded. "Okay, let's get down to brass tacks then. Everyone, this is TAII, the Katara's old Tactical Artificial Intelligence Interface. She's commandeered the ship, and has decided to take us for a little spin across the sector."

The captain was struggling to sound calm and collected, Hero knew. She could tell that on the inside he was fuming. "So, we woke this thing up when we installed the CPIC?"

Galin snapped his fingers and pointed at her. "Yes we did. Had a funny sort of feeling about that whole thing. Guess I should have listened; Captain's intuition and all that. But, at any rate, now we're in a pickle for sure, aren't we, old girl?"

TAII folded her arms and grimaced back at him. "As long as you all behave yourselves, we won't have any problems. But if you'd prefer to sleep for the rest of the three day journey to the command center, I'd be happy to oblige."

"The command center?" Joseph asked. "What's she talking about?"

"Seems that the old girl here is a bit stuck in the past. Doesn't want to swallow the fact that the Katara hasn't been a UST ship for nearly twenty-six years. So, we're going to pay a visit to the old command center, way out in the badlands, because she thinks there might be another Dagger class ship out there."

"That's not the only reason." The girl was obviously annoyed by Galin's sarcasm. "There are a lot of things at stake here. Things that you wouldn't understand."

"I assume you know we were in the middle of staging a rescue operation," Ulrick growled. "Hundreds of lives are at risk. What's your cold, refracted heart have to say about that?"

TAII narrowed her eyes. "I'm not some kind of monster. I would never interrupt a *legitimate* rescue effort unless it was absolutely necessary. You speak of hundreds of lives being at risk? How about billions? Yeah, you heard me right. So you tell me, whose agenda is more important?"

She'd gotten Galin's attention, though he looked quite doubtful. "Billions of lives? What are you talking about? How's that possible?"

"I've already said too much. The fact of the matter is, I don't owe any of you an explanation for what I'm doing, and even if I did, you don't have the proper clearance to know." She crossed her arms. "But, since your story seems to ring of truth, I haven't jettisoned you all in to space. But I can, and will if you don't behave yourselves. If you're telling me the truth, we'll work everything out when we reach Central Command."

Galin put his face in his hands and slowly shook his head.

"But you have no idea what's going on," Ulrick said,

as calmly as he could muster. "The Nazerazi Empire has conquered Earth. The Space Navy has been destroyed."

"I'm well aware of what's happened. I've spent the last few hours downloading and reviewing historical logs. All the more reason to return to Central Command."

Galin lifted his gaze and waved a hand to stop the conversation. "Look, everyone, we've been over all of this. The little lady won't budge. We're just going to have to play along over the next few days and hope for the best."

Not if I can help it, Hero thought, searching for the same rebellious intentions in the eyes of her companions. Was the captain really going to go along with this? He didn't seem like the sort of man who would take such a thing lying down. Even if that was his plan, though, there had to be some way to kill this girl's program. They simply didn't have time to waste on some meaningless excursion to an old, abandoned military station, as this outpost most likely was. What they needed to do was move along the rescue efforts on Necron so they could get back out there and search for Stephen.

"Again, let me be very clear," TAII said challengingly, "you'd all better behave yourselves, or I'll take measures to see that you can't cause any trouble."

We'll just see about that, Hero responded inside her head.

"Having any luck yet?" Boreas asked as he appeared at the bottom of the engine room ladder.

"No, he's not responding on his own frequency or any others," Hero sighed. "I've tried to hail him on every possible channel, even on subspace. Wherever he is, he doesn't seem to want to chit-chat."

"I hate to suggest the possibility, but perhaps he's incapable of a response. He may be damaged, or even gotten himself destroyed."

Hero smirked. "I don't think so. I mean, that's the easiest idea to believe, but I just can't swallow it. For whatever reason, that bot is choosing to ignore our hails. It made sense when he thought we were a Nazerazi vessel, but he doesn't have that excuse anymore. No, he's purposefully choosing to ignore us. Why?"

"I don't know," Boreas said with a shrug, "but at least it appears he's taking his mission seriously. He did try to rescue David Winchester, and the people in the caves said he seemed quite innocent and friendly upon interaction."

Hero nodded, and gave him a little grin. Boreas' words were true, and that made her feel better. Wherever William Marshal was, he was looking for Stephen and the Winchester girl, like a silent guardian angel who refused to return phone calls.

"Here, I brought you something to eat," the reptilian said, handing over a paper sack. "Ulrick made it for you.

He told me it was called a peanut butter and jello sand bitch."

She covered her mouth, trying not to laugh. "Thanks. My favorite. To tell you the truth though, I'm not really hungry."

"Ulrick was preparing himself a hot-dog. I was unaware that humans are so fond of canine meat. Don't you have a saying, that dog is mans' best friend?"

"We don't eat dogs. I mean, I guess a few humans do, but not many. Hot dogs are made out of pork, usually. And sandwiches…oh, never mind. I don't even want to think about food right now."

"You haven't been eating enough. I know that your heart has been hurting, but you need to stay strong in order to continue the search for your son."

"What's your home world like?" Hero asked, eager to change the subject. "Do you remember it at all?"

"Yes, I remember it, though I was very young when the Empire conquered my people and took me away. The jungle where I was born was very warm and humid. I remember that warmth to this day, and long to return to it." He closed his eyes and tilted back his head, imagining himself there. "I can still see the red light of Draconis, our star, shining through the leaves of the trees. The images are quite vivid, as if burned into my mind by that star, but there are few of them." He looked at her. "I never had a chance to see any other parts of the planet, though I am told it consists mostly of deserts and jungle, and there are many mountains and flowing rivers, and rarely a bit of snow on the highest peaks."

"You said you were re-united with your mother afterwards. What happened?"

"It was a rare chance, really. On one of my first duty assignments, I was stationed as an environmental control systems mechanic aboard a Nazerazi battle cruiser. Some Draconian women were stationed there to prepare food for the members of my people on board, and my mother was one of them. We had the pleasure of being together for almost one year, as you earthlings count time, before I was transferred. I have been able to keep in touch with her since then. At least, I did until I defected and escaped with you."

"That's wonderful. Do you know where she is now?"

"Still stationed on that same battle cruiser the last time I checked, though I don't know the ship's current location. I can only hope that she lives to see the day when our planet regains its independence. Our people have been away long enough, they deserve to return home."

"I hope that, too." She gazed up at him longingly. "Do you really think it's possible, though? It seems like the Nazerazi Empire is too powerful for anyone to break free from. Nobody knows who they are or where they come from, and look how far they've spread their control."

"Anything is possible. Where there is life, there is

hope."

"I want to see Earth free again as well. It breaks my heart to see my people suffering. But even if that's not possible, I'm going to find my boy and escape to someplace peaceful, away from war, even if I have to travel to the far end of the galaxy to do it."

"You have a warrior's spirit," Boreas told her.

"What are you talking about?" Hero laughed. "I'm no fighter. I'd be the last person you'd want by your side in battle."

"Not all warriors enjoy fighting. Some of the greatest warriors are those willing to answer the call when it comes, only when it is absolutely necessary. Ready to defend those they love no matter the cost. You are one of those, I think. At any rate, eat your lunch. You need to keep up your strength."

"All right, Boreas. I'll do it for you. I'll eat the sand bitch."

"Thank you," he said, and headed back up the ladder.

Hero sat upon the cold steel floor and took a bite of the sandwich. It wasn't too bad. Lots of peanut butter and lots of concord grape jelly, just the way she liked it. Was Boreas right? Was she a warrior? A defender? A real warrior would find a way to fight back; find a way to thwart that teenybopper hologram and take back the ship. Yes, Hero thought as she forced another bite. She would find a way to do it; find another kill switch.

Shooting stars encompassed them, and Galin's hypnotic gaze was fixed in the center of the view-screen.

He felt surprisingly relaxed, considering the fact that his ship had just been commandeered. He hadn't had time to watch the stars and think much lately. 'Listening', Nicodemus had called it. But he was doing a bit of it now. Trying to anyway, on a ship full of distractions. Would it work with stars blasting past in every direction, or did the stars have to be stationary? At any rate, he knew he should feel a whole lot angrier than he did, but a calmness seemed to be sweeping over him despite himself, a feeling that they were on the right track. The right track for what, good or bad, he couldn't begin to guess. The situation had peaked his curiosity, that was for sure. The Katara had always been like a mysterious lover to Galin. She was his mistress, that's what Melissa used to say, and she was right, though he'd always denied it. Unlike a human relationship however, there were still many unanswered questions about this ship's past, and it wasn't like she could tell him. He knew the Katara inside and out, the placing of every nut and bolt. But in certain other ways he didn't know her at all. Perhaps now, all that could change. If he could figure out a way to sweet talk this TAII hologram, she could most likely tell him anything he wanted to know. The problem was, talking to her was a lot like talking to his own daughter, or one of her sassy little friends. He wasn't quite sure how to approach the girl without ticking her off, as he did on so many occasions with Sarah.

"So, why don't you tell me a little bit about yourself," Galin said, continuing to stare forward. There was no answer. "Come on, TAII. I know you can hear me. What is it that makes you tick?"

"What's that supposed to mean?" the girl asked, popping out of nothingness into the co-pilot's seat beside him.

"Well, you're not exactly like any other…what's the word I'm looking for- Artificial Intelligence that I've met on a military ship before. You've got a lot more personality, more emotional depth and spirit. Why is that?"

His soft tone and compliments seemed to please her. "Well, Captain, I was intentionally programmed like this. I was a birthday gift of sorts, to my father's biological daughter."

"It's Captain now, is it?" he said, giving her a smile. "So you believe I am who I say I am?"

"I've had time to download and review all the historical records. I've confirmed your story, but I'm sorry, Captain, until I get a few more missing pieces in this puzzle, security protocol dictates that I retain control of this ship. Too much is at stake."

"Of course it is," Galin sighed, but allowed her a grin. "All right, so tell me more about you being a birthday present. What's that all about?"

"Have you ever heard of a man named Shinmen Musashi?"

"Sure, he's the one who designed this ship. Supposedly some kind of genius."

"Yes," she agreed, "although the term genius might be an understatement. He designed me as well, and programmed me to have the appearance and personality of his seventeen year old daughter, Tae. It was a birthday present, to immortalize her in his work. She was a bit of a computer geek, but I guess I am too."

"Literally," Galin chuckled.

She looked at him as though trying to decide if it had been a compliment or an insult.

He quickly changed the subject. "So what can you tell me about this ship? I mean, I know all the unclassified historical details, but are there any juicy tidbits you'd consider sharing?"

"I'm sorry, Captain, but you don't have the proper clearance."

"I own the ship, don't I? Besides, I used to have a Top Secret security clearance when I held my commission with the UST Space Navy."

"You could be an Admiral serving in the fleet today and not have the proper clearance." She pursed her lips. "I kind of wish you did have clearance though, it's nice to have someone to talk to, and I could tell you some very wild stories, that's for sure." She laughed, but after a few moments it turned into a sob.

"What is it? Are you okay?"

TAII calmed herself. "It's just that, everyone I knew, the whole crew- they're gone. Captain Patel, Lieutenant Harrison, even Ensign McCoy. He was such a prick. But still…they're all gone now, all of them."

Galin found himself feeling genuinely sorry for her. It was a confusing sensation, having sympathy for a hologram. He nearly reached over to put a hand on her shoulder, but then thought better of it, knowing it would go right through. "I'm sorry. I know what it's like to lose people. Maybe you could look some of your friends up, though. A few might still be alive."

That only made her cry harder.

"I'm sorry," he said again.

"No. It's not a bad idea," she wept. "Maybe I'll do that when all this is over."

"Why don't you tell me about them."

"The old crew? You really want to know?"

"Sure. I'd love to know more about the people who took care of the old girl before I got ahold of her."

"All right," TAII said with a shrug. "Captain Patel was the greatest. He was the perfect leader, always level-headed and knew just what to do, even under the worst kind of pressure." She gazed out into the stars and then laughed. "He once took on fifteen Boreian Falcon class starfighters and slagged every one of them. You should have seen it."

Galin scrunched his nose at her. "You're making things up. Two or three of those ships would be more than the Katara could handle."

The girl smirked at him. "I'm sure you're aware that this ship was stripped of it's weapon systems when it was de-commissioned, but what you may not know is that it used to have ten times the fire power it does now."

"Bull crap."

"I'm incapable of lying, it's against my programming. The only exception is—"

"I know, I know. The only reason is to protect human life. But ten times the firepower? That's a little hard to believe. That kind of technology doesn't even exist yet."

TAII opened her mouth as if to say something, but then thought better of it. "I see what you're trying to do. You're just playing nice to try and get information."

"That's not entirely true," Galin protested.

"Whatever," the girl said. "Hey, that tickles."

TAII's form began to sparkle, and fade in and out. She put her hands on her hips and huffed in frustration before sizzling out into nothingness.

Galin scratched at his chin. Had Joseph figured out a way to turn the hologram off? He reached for the com, but before his fingers grazed the switch, the entire control panel flickered a few times and shut off. Then the rest of the lights on the bridge went out, except for the dim emergency strips along the floor.

"Oh, no. Don't do this to me. Not now."

"Warning," came the commanding female voice of the Katara's computer. "System wide failure. The reserve power core has been deactivated. Loss of reserve power and life support will occur in approximately twelve minutes."

"Frack me," Galin growled, jumping up and heading for the door. He had to push it aside manually.

By the time he got to the common room, Ulrick and Jace were already coming to meet him. "It was Hero," Ulrick told him. "She figured out a way to turn off the girl's program, but apparently everything else shut off too."

"Thank you, Doctor Obvious." Galin opened the engineering hatch. "You two wait up here, we don't need everyone getting in the way down below. Better yet, go monitor things from the bridge, just in case."

Jace nodded dutifully, but Ulrick growled in annoyance as they walked by. The big guy never had cared for any sort of problem he couldn't shoot at.

Galin scooted down the ladder to find Joseph, Boreas, and Hero scrambling around and attempting to restore power.

"Well, what the frack's going on?"

"Sorry, Captain." Hero cringed. "Looks like she had a backup plan. I figured out a way to divert power from the CPIC without her knowing. I created a power surge in the short range transmitter and yanked the thing out before she even knew what was happening."

"She must've known we might try something like this," Joseph said, fidgeting with one of the life support control panels. "Nothing appears to be damaged, but she's covered her tracks well. It's going to take a lot longer than we have to figure out what she's done and restore power."

Galin turned to Hero. "Plug the processor back in."

"But Captain—."

He placed his hand on her shoulder. "You did good, but the little girl was one step ahead of us this time. She knows this ship as well as any of us. Hell, she's a part of the thing. This isn't the way to beat her. Plug the unit back in."

Hero looked crestfallen, but she did as Galin said, and pushed the processor back into place. A moment later the lights came on, and the sound of circulating air hummed through the vents.

TAII reappeared with her hands on her hips and the same frustrated look she'd had when Galin last saw her. "You," she pointed and glared at Hero. "You're the one who did that, aren't you? I saw you fidgeting around with the communications equipment just before everything went black."

Hero didn't say anything. She just stood there, frowning defiantly.

"All right. I tried to be nice to you people. I gave you

a chance, but you wouldn't listen." She crossed her arms and sucked her teeth, as if thinking something over. "I want her off the ship."

"Off the ship?" Galin sneered. "What are you going to do, make us throw her out the air lock?"

"You think I'm joking? Well here's another one for you. This ship isn't going anywhere until she leaves. She can take that little shuttle in the docking bay."

"Are you serious?" Joseph huffed.

"I warned you. She can get on that shuttle and go anywhere she wants. Even follow us from a distance if she chooses. But the Katara doesn't move an inch until she leaves."

Galin gritted his teeth, and was just about to let the girl have it when Hero jumped in.

"It's okay. I'll go."

"Not a chance," Galin told her. "We don't leave our people behind."

"I can head back to Necron and wait for you there. Help out with the repairs on the other ship and try to get things back on schedule. I'm not doing any good here, not now anyway."

"She's right about the repairs, Captain," Boreas said. "I'll go along with her and assist."

"The Draconian stays here," TAII said.

"Hero is my friend. I'd be perfectly willing to —"

"No. You're staying on the ship," TAII insisted. "Someone else can go, but not you."

"Why?" Boreas asked.

"Because I said so."

"Frack it all," Galin said, turning to walk right through TAII so he could head back up the ladder.

She huffed at him angrily.

"Let's get this over with. Hero, get your stuff together. I'll go notify Jace."

"Notify Jace?" Hero asked.

"I'm sending him with you. He's a good pilot. Besides, I wouldn't be able to stop him from going. Omicron Five isn't far from here. The two of you can wait for us there, start shopping for parts." With that, he shot back up the ladder. Maybe it would be better to send them off to Omicron Five anyway. At least they'd be safe there. Anything could be awaiting them ahead.

"Man, I'd like to scramble her little circuits," Galin mumbled, heading for the bridge.

Jace handed his bag in to Hero before taking the seat next to her.

"Remember what I said," Galin told him. "Stay cloaked, and check in every four hours until you reach Omicron Five. You're only a little over a day away." He reached out to shake the young man's hand.

"Don't look so worried," Jace told him with a grin. "I'm not that bad of a pilot, and the Shiv seems to like me well enough." He patted his hand on the hull.

"You're not too bad at all, kid. You'll do fine. After all, you learned from two of the best." He formed a sad grin, and slapped Jace on the back.

The young man knew what he was thinking. Galin could see it spelled across his face.

"We'll be okay. I'll follow the plan. No monkey business."

Galin conceded a chuckle, and leaned in to give Hero a little squeeze. "You hear that? No monkey business. Captain's orders."

"We'll see you soon," Hero told him. Maybe even meet you in space before you make it back to the planet."

"No way. You two stay put at the trading post until we come and get you. Too many pirates in the area these days."

They promised they would, and Galin shut the door for them.

A few minutes later he watched from the bridge as the Shiv moved away and cloaked, leaving only a clear sea of stars behind her.

"I have a bad feeling about this," Ulrick said. He'd just come in from behind.

"I do, too. Then again, I can't remember the last time I had a good feeling about anything."

"True." Ulrick stroked his beard. "Things just aren't how they used to be. Things have changed. Everything just seems...."

"Just seems what?" Galin asked.

Ulrick shrugged. "Everything just seems wrong."

"Well, everything *is* wrong. Earth has been conquered. Peter's dead. My daughter and Starla are out there, who the hell knows where. My son's been acting like some kind of brain-damaged zombie. Can't get much more wrong than that."

"Yeah. That's not really what I mean, though."

"No? What do you mean then?"

Ulrick threw his hands up in frustration. I, I don't know. It's hard to explain. It's like we've been stuck in some kind of nightmare or something. I feel like I just need to wake up, and then everything would be okay again."

Galin didn't answer. He just gazed at the stars as they zipped by. Maybe they were in some kind of nightmare after all. Maybe he'd wake up one of these days and everything would be just like it used to be. If only it was that easy.

"Well, you two are quite the philosophers," came TAII's voice from behind them. "Who would have thunk it?"

"You again?" Galin said without turning. "Give it a rest. I'm not in the mood."

"Don't get pissy with me. I tried to warn you."

"Go away."

"You're just mad because your little plan fell through. I told you not to try and outsmart me."

The girl's voice was suddenly making him itch all

over, and he scratched at his scalp. It reminded him of the way Melissa used to get bent out of shape about something and then refuse to shut up. She'd make him itch, too.

"Fine. You win. Congratulations, you insufferable little twit."

There was nothing but silence for a few moments, and then he heard the quiet sounds of the girl's weeping.

Ulrick moaned. "Come on, cut the crap. You're a program. What kind of idiot programs a computer to cry like a baby every time it gets its feelings hurt!"

The crying grew louder before coming to an abrupt stop.

"Well, that seemed to shut her up," Ulrick said.

"Yeah." Galin closed his eyes. "I'm gonna get some shut eye. Wake me up if anything bad happens."

"Fat chance," Ulrick laughed. "I'll be sleeping too."

Galin watched his son in silence as the boy studied the chessboard. He'd gotten better since the last time they'd played. What had it been? Nine, ten months now? Back then, David had been a happy, energetic young man, prone to distraction by anything that seemed more exciting than a game of chess with his old man. Now, he seemed to be as calculating as he was emotionless.

My God, what's happened to him? Galin thought as he stared at his son. *Is there anyone out there that can help him come back from whatever this is?*

"Checkmate," David said, moving his queen into place.

"You got me. Wanna play something else now?"

"Yes."

"Okay. What do you wanna play?"

"I don't know."

Of course you don't, Galin thought. The kid didn't care about anything anymore.

"Captain, we're approaching the badlands," came Ulrick's gravelly voice from the com.

"All right. I'm on my way to the bridge. Come on, son. You're going to want to see this."

Galin led the way, and David shuffled along behind him. They entered the bridge to find Ulrick sitting in the Captain's chair, his mouth hanging open at the sight before them.

A massive asteroid field stretched out as far as the eye could see, and beyond that, the orange glow of a plasma storm shone back like some distant forest fire.

"Please don't tell me we're going to head into that," Ulrick groaned, looking sick.

"I'm not the one flying the ship, remember? TAII hasn't said a word for two days now, maybe you should apologize to her."

"Apologize to a hologram? Not. Slagging. Likely."

"Even if that hologram's about to fly you through one of the most dangerous sections of space in this quadrant?"

Ulrick gulped. He looked down at the poker-faced boy standing beside Galin. "So, watcha think, squirt? Pretty scary stuff, huh?" He looked back at the window, and a trickle of sweat escaped down his brow.

"He doesn't appear to be as scared as you do. You'd better go take a sedative or something."

Ulrick nodded and got up to leave. Then he turned back to them. "I hate space sometimes."

"We'll be all right. I'll wake you up when we get there."

Once he was gone, Galin took the Captain's chair and had David sit down beside him. "All right, TAII. I know you're listening. You gonna come out and talk or what?"

The girl appeared. "That depends. Do you think you can engage in a civil dialogue this time?"

"Most definitely."

"Good. Because you're going to have to fly us through this asteroid field to get back to Central Command."

"Me? You're actually going to let me fly my own ship? Well that's awfully kind of you."

"I heard you bragging to Jace about what a great pilot you are, now's the time to prove it. Kindness has nothing to do with it."

"You are a charmer," Galin told her. "That's one thing you've got going for you."

"Well?"

"Well what?"

She sighed in frustration. "Are you going to put your money where your mouth is, or not?"

He thought about it for a few moments. "If I refuse?"

"Then we'll stay right where we are until you change your mind."

"I thought you might say something like that." He reached out and unlocked the joystick, finding he'd regained full control. The center display popped on, outlining the course TAII wanted him to take.

"Okay, Captain, you're up. I'll man the phasers and do my best to keep any of them from getting too close."

"Piece of cake," Galin insisted as he guided the Katara into the field. He wasn't about to admit to being so nervous, and the funny thing was, he wasn't sure why. He'd flown through tighter spots than this before.

The outskirts of the area were calm enough, but the further in they went, the denser the asteroids became. Some of the rocks drifting past the ship were twice its size, and others off in the distance were much larger than that.

"Are you sure this is the best way in?" Galin asked as the number of asteroids continued to increase. "I know for a fact there are mining routes that run through this sector. Even with the sweeper ships they wouldn't dare bring their rigs through here."

"Hang in there, Captain. Just use your instincts. I'm

sure you can do this."

"I didn't say I couldn't."

"I know."

Explosions rocked the ship from every side as the guns seemed to turn and fire themselves. Galin had resorted to the auto-gunner program a time or two out of necessity over the years. It was a poor substitute for skilled humans behind the triggers, but TAII seemed to be much more skilled. She wasn't as good as some of the best gunners he'd seen, but she wasn't half bad, either.

Smaller chunks resulting from the explosions fizzled against the Katara's shields. Luckily, only a few of the big rocks made contact with the ship, and Galin managed to avoid all of the really large ones. After what seemed like an eternity, they cleared the other end of the field, and he sighed in relief.

The plasma storm that waited ahead looked even scarier than the asteroid field. Funnel clouds swirled through the thick orange glow, surrounded by bursts of lightning, explosions, and abrupt eruptions of fire. It was if they'd stopped to peer over the walls into hell.

"It's a good thing Ulrick's not up here to see this."

"Your engineer just finished modifying the shields to give us the best possible protection from the storm. Follow my coordinates without deviation, and you won't have anything to worry about."

"All right," Galin sighed. "Here we go again." He looked over at David to see that the boy was about as interested in what was happening as he would be by watching a round of golf on television. For the first time since they'd been reunited, Galin envied him. He moved the ship ahead, carefully following TAII's coordinates. Over the years, he'd flown through some pretty rough patches of space before, but had never entered a mess like this, even while being chased.

As the storm blazed on every side, Galin's eyes moved back and forth between his route and the shield monitor. To his amazement, the shields didn't seem to be having to work very hard.

"We're on some sort of pathway, aren't we?"

TAII nodded. "You can't see them, but there's a network of cloaked plasma dampeners that keep the tunnel open. I'm glad to see they're still functional."

"Me too," Galin happily agreed.

The trip took several hours, but when they emerged on the other side, a breathtaking nebula was spread across the view screen. It was if purple and blue lights had been painted across the sky on an ocean of translucent pink water.

That's when the vessels appeared on the scanners.

"Oh, come on. What's this?"

"Those would be the Sentinels," TAII told him. "There should be more of them, but it looks like two are functioning, anyway."

"So those things are friendlies?" Galin asked in relief, gazing out at one through the window. The thing was twice the size of the Katara, and reminded him of a mechanical shark with protruding arms. The thing was obviously designed to be intimidating, the only thing missing were the jaws painted on the front. From the look of those arms, and the clamps on the ends, the Sentinel was literally capable of reaching out to grab any ship it wished to capture.

"Friendlies?" TAII repeated. "That depends on who you ask. But to us, yes. At least, they should be, if they're still functioning properly."

Galin gulped as the other Sentinel caught up to them. They took position on either side of the Katara.

"Are those things vessels or robots?"

"A bit of both," TAII said. "But their programing is very basic. They exist to protect Mission Command and escort visitors." She watched them for a while. "They're not responding to my hails, but it's obvious that they recognize our ship. They'll guide us in. I'll take back control of the ship, Captain, if that's all right with you."

"All right. You're being awfully polite all of a sudden."

"Well, you're welcome to try to find the way to Command yourself, but those Sentinels aren't very forgiving when it comes to ships flying around off course."

Galin just grinned at her, and stood up out of the captain's chair. Then he waved his hand at it, as if to tell TAII to have a seat. Her eyes grew large.

"You mean...you'll let me sit in the Captain's Chair?"

Galin chuckled. "Sure. Why not? What's the problem? Are you telling me you've got no problem with stealing my ship, but you won't sit in the chair without my permission?"

"Captain Patel never let me do that! Besides, I haven't stolen anything. I'm just following—"

"I know, I know, you're following protocol. Have a seat."

He spun the thing around for her, and she looked downright giddy as she sat.

"Thanks. We're almost there, but you might want to find something to hold onto, because we're in for some chop."

"Oh, great. Seriously?"

"No. I've just always wanted to say that."

The thing that appeared in the distance looked like a hovering steel mountain, or perhaps a pyramid. It was certainly not what Galin had expected.

"Is that it?"

"That's where the Bleeding Star Initiative Command Center is located, yes."

"Bleeding Star Initiative? You mentioned that before. What is it?"

"Classified."

Galin growled at her, then got on the com. "All right,

everyone, we're there. You might want to come on up and take a look."

As they drew closer, he saw that a half dozen more Sentinels were moving about on patrol.

"That's odd," TAII said. "I've never seen them behave that way before."

"Great," Galin mumbled. "That's reassuring."

They were soon joined by the others.

"What the hell is that thing?" Joseph asked. "It looks massive."

"Classified," Galin told him, before TAII could answer.

"Central Command, this is the Tactical Artificial Intelligence Interface of the UST Katara, requesting permission to dock."

There were several moments of silence before the voice of a young man answered. "Well hello there, TAII. Permission granted. Release your controls and I'll bring you in with one of the docking bay tractor beams. Things are kind of a mess down here right now."

TAII made a strange face, as if the response had not quite been what she'd expected. "Controls released," she answered anyway. A few seconds later the Katara jerked as the gleaming blue beam encompassed her hull to draw them in.

The exterior of the station looked as smooth as polished stone, and the docking bay doors that were now sliding back seemed to be the only evidence that the thing was anything more than that.

"Well, I'll be slagged," Ulrick frowned. "I've never seen anything like this before. Kind of gives me the shivers."

"That voice sounded friendly enough," Joseph told him with a pat. "Don't worry. If things get out of hand, I'll protect you."

Ulrick sneered. "Thanks, that makes me feel better."

The ship came to a rest in a dimly lit docking bay. Not much could be seen until the beam released the ship and the lights came on. The place was littered with the wrecks of old ships, inactive Sentinels, and other mechanical junk that Galin could only guess the origins and purposes of.

A door slid open in the distance, and an excited young man came running out to greet them. He was rather short, and ran with all the gusto of an excited little cat. He was wearing blue jeans, a green t-shirt, and had on sneakers and a baseball cap, and appeared to be Japanese.

"He looks innocent enough," Ulrick said, stroking his blaster rifle as the man approached the ship.

Galin lowered the stairs and they all descended down to greet him. The young man standing before them looked like a child who'd just woken up to find a ton of presents beneath the Christmas tree.

"Hey, everyone. WOW, the Katara! All right! Last I heard she'd been captured by the Nazerazi. How'd you guys get away? How'd you find me? I mean, wow, my mind is kind of blown right now, man. Nice to meet you."

He thrust out his hand.

Galin took it. "Galin Winchester."

"Yeah, I think I knew that. I mean, I don't really know who you are. I just remember hearing a dude named Winchester ended up with the Katara. Great to meet you."

Galin suddenly realized that the man didn't seem at all surprised to see a Draconian standing among them. That was a bit odd. Whether people recognized the race or not, they were usually quite nervous, if not downright scared, to have one standing in front of them. "And you are?"

"Oh, sorry. I thought you already knew. Name's Kanbun Musashi." He scratched his head. "But, hold on. You didn't come out here looking for me? Then why are you here?"

"Kanbun Musashi?" Galin pointed at him. "You're the grandson of Shinmen Musashi, the man who designed my ship. I remember hearing you were out here in the badlands." He looked at the Katara and pointed back at her with his thumb. "It's great to meet you too, but no, we didn't come out here to find you. We're here because the Katara's old holographic interface—"

"TAII brought you here? Yeah, I guess that makes

sense. It's all falling into place now. What did you do, reinstall the ship's old CPIC without knowing what you were getting into?"

"Uh, yeah. The Chief here found it in a utility closet and—"

At this, Kanbun burst out laughing. "The utility closet? As if the thing had just been forgotten? That's fracking hilarious. I wonder who put it there, and when? I can't believe the thing survived. Do you have any idea what this means? You must have been meant to find it."

"Do you know why the Nazerazi might be after this ship?" Joseph broke in.

Kanbun crossed his arms. "Well, I think I can venture a pretty safe guess. How much do you guys know about the history of these ships? Hey, come here, I want to show you something."

As they walked, Galin recounted what he knew about the Katara's history. He felt oddly self-conscious while talking, as if someone had just asked when one of his children's birthdays was and he couldn't remember, but their host just listened enthusiastically and nodded his head as they walked.

Joseph looked like a kid in a candy store as they made their way through the docking bay. The place was like a poorly kept museum where all the exhibits were still under construction, and Galin could only imagine how much the chief would have loved to get his hands dirty on some of the things they walked by. When they got to their destination, Galin's jaw dropped in disbelief. It was yet another Dagger class starship, but this one looked like the Katara on steroids. A LOT of steroids.

Kanbun smiled at them proudly. "This is *my* ship, the Yoroi Toshi. As you can see, I've modified her quite a bit, just recently finished up. Not to brag, but she probably has about three times the shielding and five times the firepower compared to the Katara. She's also the only Dagger class I'd ever lain eyes on before you guys arrived. There were originally five ships, but two were destroyed. I haven't been able to determine the fate of the third."

"She's parked under a mountain on the planet Necron."

For the first time since they'd met him, the man appeared speechless. He eyed them over suspiciously, as if thinking it might be some sort of joke.

"That's kind of the reaction I had, but believe me, it's there."

"Wow. This is turning out to be a really strange day."

Just then, a beautiful brunette appeared out of nowhere. She had long, flowing hair and was wearing only a blue bikini bottom. "That girl keeps calling," she said with an irritated scowl. "She wants to come onboard."

"*WHAT* are you doing?" Kanbun demanded, his face turning red. He frowned over at his guests before turning back to the girl to snap his fingers. "You can't walk around like that when we have visitors. Put something on!"

The woman eyed them over quizzically. "Well, how would I know that? We've never had visitors before." As she was speaking, the top of the bikini appeared.

She was a hologram.

Kanbun turned to Galin and shrugged. What can I say? The perfect woman. Still looks as good as the day I made her and agrees with everything I say."

Ulrick let out a booming laugh that made them all jump.

"Come on." Kanbun sighed and waved them on toward the door. "We need to talk."

In a room at the end of a winding metal chamber, Galin found himself standing on a sandy beach, watching the sunset. A number of torches were burning on poles around them, and the sloshing of gentle waves came whispering up from the shore. Even the air smelled moist and salty.

"I've been on a few holochambers in my time," Joseph said, "but I've never experienced anything as realistic as this."

"It's pretty…ah, amazing," Ulrick agreed. His eyes followed a pair or bikini-clad girls as they ran down the beach. Until a few moments ago, they too had been topless. He leaned over to Joseph and whispered, "I guess being a brainy little nerd has its benefits, after all."

"Thanks," said Kanbun, coming up behind them. "I've added some improvements, but I can't take all the credit." He looked at Boreas. "The circuitry and programming is actually Draconian technology. There's quite a lot of it on the station. Apparently, your people played an important role on this base back in the day. Not entirely sure what that role was, though."

"Fascinating," Boreas said, running his clawed feet through the sand.

Kanbun plopped himself down in a lawn chair and tapped his fingers across a data pad. "Please, have a seat, you guys. Just tell one of the girls if you want anything to drink."

"Thanks," Galin told him. "But what I'd really like more than anything is answers. I reckon we've earned some."

"Sure. I'll tell you whatever you want to know. Or at least, everything I know, anyway." He continued to tap away. "I'm giving TAII permission to transfer her program over. I'm hoping she might be able to shed some light on some of this as well."

A moment later, TAII popped in out of thin air, her hands on her hips. "Well it's about time. Are you going to explain to me what exactly is going on around here?"

Kanbun chuckled. "So, this is what my Aunt Tae looked like when she was younger. Not too shabby. You should see the old bat now," he added in a whisper.

"Where's General Williams? I demand to spea—, ooh, that tickles. Hey, are you tinkering with my program? Why are you re-routing my rainwater thunder berries?"

"Huh? You want to run that past us again?" Galin said.

"It's just a side effect," Kanbun told him. "I'm reprogramming her command protocols and installing some updates. I assume she's been a bit uncooperative? She'll take her orders from *you* once I'm done."

The girl began to flash like a surging light bulb. "Not you command I or authority this station. Security sequence Alpha, Uniform, seven, one, one, three, Bravo." She flickered away for a moment before reappearing. "I'd appreciate a little warning before you do something like that again."

Galin looked over to see that Kanbun had finished typing. He flashed a confident grin.

"Like I said, she'll listen to you now."

"Let's try her out, then. Hey, TAII, go get me a Bahama Mama."

"Fine," she huffed, taking off for the bar.

"So," Galin said. "Let's get down to brass tacks. Maybe you can tell us what the hell's going on here."

"Well, I don't really know where to start. Let's see...."

"TAII said this place was the command center for something called the Bleeding Star Initiative. What's that?"

Kanbun snapped his fingers. "Well, I could try to tell you, but it'd be easier just to show you." He snagged one of the girls walking by. "Hey, Sarah, bring up a movie screen and show them that orientation video I unscrambled."

"Okay, sweetie," she said cheerfully, rubbing his shoulder seductively.

A large view screen appeared in the sky over the water. And the face of a grizzled, yet kind looking man clothed in military dress appeared.

"Hello, and welcome to the Bleeding Star Initiative Command Center. I'm General Williams. I'll be making your acquaintance personally sometime over the next few days, but I've created this briefing to explain some of the basic and most frequently asked questions about serving on this station, as well as the Initiative in general." He smiled. "First let me say, I'm glad you're here. Your appointment to this station means that you've already proven yourself to be one of the finest officers or enlisted persons in Earth's fleet. You've already been briefed about the importance of secrecy on this mission. With the exception of the people stationed at this center, few men and women even know this program exists. It is absolutely essential that you never speak with anyone about the things you witness here. As you've been told, there is no statute of limitations on this order. Anyone caught revealing information about the Bleeding Star

Initiative will be promptly executed. There are no exceptions to this rule."

Kanbun glanced over at his visitors and shrugged.

"Now, let's talk about the program. You may have already been briefed on some of this, but if so, we'll fill in the gaps," the general winked. His face disappeared, and an image of the station appeared. "Nearly twenty-five years ago, an exploration vessel from the United Earth Government happened upon this station. It appeared to have been abandoned long ago, by a race of aliens we have come to know as the Nexans. Through years of careful research, it was determined that this station served as a waypoint, a deep space outpost on a sort of...super-highway through the galaxy."

Galin finally took a seat. "How's that possible?"

As if in answer, the General continued. "A series of star-charts, found upon this station, was deciphered, revealing a network of traversable wormholes located throughout the Milky Way." An image of one of the star maps flashed across the screen, following a path through several sections of space, from one side of the galaxy to the other. "Although the charts were detailed and clear, our greatest minds could not discover how to open up the wormhole, presumably located just a few short miles from this station's location. Finally, one of Earth's top scientists, Shinmen Musashi from the United States of Texas, was recruited to work on the project. Musashi was known for his unconventional thinking in regard to space-time theory. Without getting into too much detail about things that neither you or I could hope to understand, I'll just tell you that Dr. Musashi was able to design a ship capable of opening up and traveling through the wormholes. Five of these ships have been built. I'm sure you've all heard of the Dagger class starship. The existence of these vessels was leaked a few years ago, with the belief that they were some sort of elite, diplomatic transports. Needless to say, their true purpose has never been made known to the public."

Galin looked over to see Kanbun grinning and nodding his head. "Keep listening."

"In addition, a select group of men and women was needed to pilot these ships. Musashi soon discovered that only a few, rare individuals had the necessary skills and ability to navigate the space-time fluctuations found to occur within the wormholes. An exhaustive screening and training process was developed to identify and prepare those who showed promise. Musashi began to call such men and women Clockwalkers." The General gave a broad smile. "You see, once we began to explore the system of wormholes, we determined that, not only did these tunnels lead us to different points in space, they also led us to different points in time. For some, this revelation was even more shocking than the original discovery. We now have a series of starcharts, which if carefully plotted and followed, can take us to anywhere, and any time we want to go, in the galaxy." Now the general's face became very stern, and his cheeks flushed red. "I assume you're beginning to realize the immense gravity that has been placed upon every person associated with this program, and why guarding its secrecy is essential. I cannot overstate the responsibility that has been thrust upon every individual who has access to this information, nor the terrifying possibilities of what could happen if such information was ever abused."

A number of thoughts were pulsing through Galin's brain. The general was right, the possibilities of what all this could bring about were quite terrifying, but at the same time, a renewed sense of excitement and hope surged through him.

The general continued. "Perhaps some of you watching this are candidates yourselves. If so, best of luck to you in the days to come. However, regardless of why you are here, thank you for volunteering for this mission. Things won't always be easy, but you truly are about to embark on the experience of a lifetime. Once again, welcome to the Bleeding Star Initiative, and good luck."

The general's image faded, and the screen quickly followed, leaving only a clear, darkening sky above the rippling waves. Galin turned to Kanbun, and recognized the same sense of hope and determination he felt within himself.

"If we can figure this out," the young man said, "we

can turn back the clock. We can save Earth from invasion."

Galin burst out in a grin from ear to ear. Kanbun was right. Maybe it was possible to stop the whole thing from happening. He could save Melissa, keep his children safe. And Peter, he would never have died in the first place if all this hadn't happened! He could even find a way to save his sister- stop Jamie from walking off alone on the night she was murdered. He could save them all.

Joseph didn't look so pleased. "What about the Nazerazi?"

"Frack the Nazerazi!" Galin yelled. "We can stop them!"

"Maybe it's not that simple," Joseph said. "They want our ship. They've always wanted it. It has to be because they know about this program. The star-charts, the Bleeding Star Initiative...maybe they know about everything."

"They don't appear to know about this station," Boreas said. "If they did, wouldn't they have come here and commandeered it by now?"

"But if the Nazerazi do know, if they were ever able to get their hands on any of this, they truly *would* be unstoppable. It could mean the end of the galaxy as we know it."

"They can all get slagged," Ulrick growled. "We're the ones with the ships. Now we just need to find us one of those Clockwalker characters."

TAII reappeared, handing over Galin's drink. "No, you don't. You've already got one."

"What do you mean I could be one of them?" Galin jumped to his feet, nearly dropping the glass TAII'd just given him. He set it down upon a nearby end table.

"It's the reason I had you navigate through the asteroid field," TAII said. "I needed to find out. You never could have made it through there if you weren't a candidate."

"You knew about this?" Galin asked, turning back to Kanbun.

He nodded. "I wouldn't have shared that video with you otherwise. Like the general said, it's pretty sensitive information."

"What about you? You're not one of these 'candidates?'"

"Me? Heck no. I couldn't pilot my way out of a wet paper sack. But it really isn't about piloting skills, at least that's not all it's about. Clockwalkers seem to have the ability to sense disturbances in the time-space continuum. Every Clockwalker is an excellent pilot, but not every great pilot is a Clockwalker. TAII must have noticed your abilities and decided to run you through the first test for new prospects."

"Spotting new prospects is part of my protocol," TAII

said defensively. "He wasn't the only candidate on his ship, either. I picked up signs from another member of his crew as well. A man named Jace Chang."

"I thought the General said such people were rare. What are the chances of two of us being on the same ship?"

"Pretty good, actually," Kanbun said. "These ships are special. Candidates seem to be drawn to them, somehow. Tell me, Captain, what exactly was it about the Katara that drew you to her? I mean, why'd you end up with her and not some other ship?"

Galin shrugged. "I don't know. She just seemed to be exactly what I was looking for. Besides, I kind of fell in love with the old girl the first time I laid eyes on her."

"It wasn't a coincidence. Your crewman might have been drawn to her the same way. You just knew there was something special about the Katara, didn't you? And you were right."

"Well, can't argue with you there."

"So tell me," Joseph cut in, "If Galin has these abilities, what does he have to do to work them all out? What about that training program the General mentioned?"

"That's something I'm still working on. When the Initiative was abandoned, all of the records were destroyed or taken off this station. I've only been able to piece a few things together, like that initiation video. I salvaged it off an old data pad I found lodged in a garbage compactor. I've found some other things too, and I've got some old computer systems I'm trying to bring back online, but it's going to take time. Even if we knew what the training process was, it would take months to complete, and that's assuming you'd be successful in finishing it."

Galin felt deflated. "Well, I guess it's back to plan A, at least for now. We need to get our tails back to Necron and help those people off the planet, then resume the search for Sarah and Starla, and Hero's kid." He turned to Kanbun. "You'll have to keep us informed about your findings. If I can go back and fix all this, I will. But we need to keep in mind that it might never be possible."

"Perhaps I could be of some assistance," Boreas said, tapping his long claws against his scaly face. I fear my presence upon the Katara is not as valuable as it once was, now that you have your engineer back. My time might be better spent upon this station, especially since Draconian technology was utilized here. I have also proven to be somewhat skilled in working with the systems of other species."

Galin crossed his arms. Boreas was right; he could probably do more good here than he could upon the Katara. Kanbun's work was important, and it might lead to saving them all. "You sure about this? I'd hate to see you go. But I think you might be right. You'd be an asset in helping Kanbun figure this out. But you'll always be welcome on the Katara, I want you to know that. You're part of the crew now, whether you like it or not." He turned his eyes to Kanbun. "Maybe we should ask the landlord. How about it, techie? You think an extra set of eyes might come in handy?"

"Sounds okay to me," the young man shrugged. "I've got my girls to keep me company, but living only with artificial intelligence makes you pretty lonely after a while. Besides, you seem like an okay guy for a Draconian."

"I'll take that as a compliment."

"All right, it's settled then," Galin said. "We'll come back as soon as we can, but we need to make tracks. Jace and Hero are waiting for us, and so are the people on Necron. We've lost too much time already."

Kanbun cringed. "Necron? So you really are serious about going back there? What's the big rush?"

Galin filled him in. By the look in his eyes, it was obvious that the gears were spinning as he tried to think of a way to help.

"Well, it's clear you need parts. You're welcome to anything you can find on the docking bay." He squeezed his chin thoughtfully. "I know you're in a hurry, but I'll tell you what, if you can give me two days, I'll bet we can have the Katara on par with the Yoroi Toshi. How would you like that?"

Ulrick raised his eyebrow. "Two days? That's impossible."

"Not if we all work together. I've got the parts, and

I've kept meticulous notes from working on my own ship. I've also got a team of crew-bots who've done the job before. Like I said, three times the shielding and five times the firepower."

Galin ran his hands through his hair and let out a quick breath. "It's tempting. Seems like we've been pretty good at getting our tail kicked lately. Just can't seem to keep from getting in over our heads."

"Those upgrades would definitely give us the upper hand," Joseph said.

"Yeah, but I think we're going to have to take a rain check. Hundreds of lives could depend on us getting back to Necron before the Claymore arrives."

Kanbun smiled thoughtfully, and then nodded, as if making up his mind about something. "All right, here's what I'll do to sweeten the deal. There's an engine I've been working on. I planned on installing it in the Yoroi Toshi next week." He clapped his hands together. "I'll give it to you guys instead. It's quite a design. My grandfather conceptualized it, by I'm the one who finally built it." He pushed his chest out proudly. "It allows warp to be used in hyperspace. Get you where you wanna go twice as fast as either technology alone."

"How's that possible?" Joseph muttered, as if trying to work the problem out in his head.

"If you really are interested, I'll try to explain it to you sometime. But right now, we've got a whole bunch of work to do."

—NAZERAZI BATTLESHIP CLAYMORE—

The steel tip of the blaster pistol felt cold against her head. Its pulsating hum always seemed to have a calming effect, despite what she was trying to do. Every day, for as long as she could remember, she would place a gun to her head and try to pull the trigger, but was never able to follow through with it. Why was that? She certainly wasn't scared. She had no one to care for, no real purpose to serve, not even another being she could so much as relate to. For years and years, she had tried to think of a reason not to pull the trigger, and she still hadn't thought of one. She simply had no reason whatsoever to live.

For a while, it had seemed likely that her father had done something to prevent her from taking her own life, had placed some psychological barrier inside her head to keep her from ending this walking nightmare of an existence, but she didn't believe that to be the case any more. Now she knew that to pull the trigger would somehow mean that she cared, that she felt something.

Not even her father's experiment with the boy had made her feel again. The short amount of time they spent together was enough to prove that it hadn't worked. She'd felt nothing. No love. No companionship. Not even any remorse. Anger would have been a welcome change when the admiral had torn the boy from her arms, but she'd not been granted even that.

And that was why she could never pull the trigger. It was clear as day now. She simply didn't even care enough not to care.

Why then, did she bother to do this any more? That was the mystery now- the thing she couldn't understand. To take out the gun, place it against her head, and hold it there with seemingly no chance of being able to pull the trigger

She didn't hear the admiral come in.

"JAMIE! Where the HELL did you get another gun?"

She turned it on him, and pulled the trigger, but his arm deflected hers and the charge struck the painting on the wall by the door, knocking the seascape onto the floor amidst shards of sizzling glass.

"Come with me, right now." Her father wrestled the pistol away and latched onto her arm, forcing her onto the couch in front of a short, wide window.

"I don't know why you continue to insist on this behavior." He sat down next to her and took a long, deep breath. "I've explained this to you a dozen times. I'm only doing what needs to be done. That planet needs to be cleansed. Inoculated, from those filthy things that we never should have allowed to exist there in the first place."

"But you're the one who let them live. You're the one who made a deal with my father—."

"Why do you INSIST on calling him that? He's not your father. He's never BEEN your father. I AM!"

"Yes," she said, looking into his eyes as if just remembering something. "You were. But that was before. Before I was…empty."

"No. I'm still your father, Jamie." He rose to his feet and clasped his hands behind his back. "I'm sorry you have such a hard time seeing that, but perhaps one day soon you will." He gazed out the window. "The Genesis Torpedo will be loaded onto this ship in two days. Once it arrives, we'll return to Necron and re-terraform the planet. Every living thing residing there, including Dr. Mengele, will be annihilated." He studied her for a moment. "How does that make you feel?"

She rose to stand beside him, and watched the stars blast by. "It doesn't make me feel anything."

"One day, Jamie, I'm going to find someone who can finally help you. Someone who can fix whatever it is that went wrong in your brain." He placed his arm around her. "I haven't given up yet, have I?"

"No."

"That's right. And I never will."

"I'm going to kill you."

He squeezed her lovingly. "So you keep saying, my darling. But you aren't the first who's tried, nor will you be the last." He turned to leave. "Is there anything I can get for you? Anything you need?"

"I want him back."

"The boy has been returned to his father," he said pointedly.

"He belongs to me now. You had no right to take him."

"You do go on about things, don't you?" He stopped at the door and turned his head to face her. "Perhaps I can arrange to have someone find you a cat, or some other little pet. You'd like that, wouldn't you?"

"If you don't bring me the boy, I'll go and find him myself. I'll kill anyone who tries to get in my way. Do you want your son to die like his friend did?"

He looked into her eyes for a few moments before walking out. The door slid shut behind him, and he turned to the heavy-set enlisted man standing guard.

"Sergeant, she somehow got ahold of another blaster pistol. I want her visits to the recreational area stopped until further notice. No one goes into this room but me. Understood?"

"Yes, Sir. Understood."

The sergeant breathed a sigh of relief as the admiral strode away and turned the corner at the end of the hall. Admiral Winchester always made him nervous. There was just something about the man's eyes, they were downright creepy, haunted even.

He'd be back at the same time tomorrow, unless some pressing business prevented it. The admiral came to visit his daughter like clockwork, every day at the same time. And every day he had to look at those damned, creepy eyes.

The sergeant startled a bit when Jamie's voice came over the intercom by her door.

"Sergeant Reynolds, is my father still there?"

"No Ma'am. He left about two minutes ago." Jamie Winchester was probably the only thing in the world that scared him more than her father. She was just as stoned faced and serious, but even creepier. In fact, she was freakishly creepy, but she was also one of the most beautiful things he'd ever seen, especially in comparison to Martha, his obese, sharp-tongued wife. Just thinking about Martha had been putting him in a foul mood lately.

"Are you alone?"

"Yes, Ma'am."

"I'm going to need another gun."

He grunted indecisively for a few moments. "I don't think that's such a good idea, Ma'am. He gave me strict orders, trying to make sure you don't get another. If he finds another pistol in there, he's gonna know where it came from."

A few moments of silence passed. "But, Sergeant, I thought we were friends. Haven't you been enjoying our time together?"

He felt his head begin to sweat. "Oh, yes, Ma'am. Never enjoyed anything so much in my life. Honestly."

"I'll make you a deal then. Three times."

"Th-three times? Three for one gun." For some reason, the fact that Jamie scared him made her that much more desirable. Desire wasn't quite the correct word anymore, however. This was fast becoming more of an obsession.

"Yes. And when I leave, I'll bring you along with me. You'd like that, wouldn't you? To come along with me?"

"Uh,uh-oh, yes Ma'am. I…I believe I would."

"Good. If you can, bring it with dinner tonight. Baked chicken and potatoes, please."

"Baked chicken and potatoes," he repeated stupidly. "And a gun."

"Yes, Sergeant. And a gun."

Book 8

Scar Tissue

"Stop that," Hero yawned, following Jace's example. "Don't you know those things are contagious?"

He laughed. "There's no reason for us both to be bored out of our wits. Why don't you try to get some shut eye."

Soon, he was gazing off blankly into space again, longing for sleep himself. Not only had the last few weeks been more than hectic, whatever TAII had drugged them with while taking over the Katara seemed to have lingering effects. As much as he wanted to sleep, he didn't fully trust the Shiv's autopilot in pirate infested space. There were too many traps scattered about. Galin and Peter had taught him how to keep his eyes out for them, but the task required vigilance.

"Hold on a minute," Hero said. "Are you saying I'm *boring*?"

"Huh? No. I didn't say anything like that."

"You just said you were bored out of your wits. My conversation isn't stimulating enough for you?"

Jace felt himself going red. "No. I...I just meant that, that we're both really tired, and...."

"Relax, Big Boy. I'm just yanking your chain." She leaned back her head, closed her eyes, and let out a tired sigh. "The truth is, a nap sounds pretty good."

Hero reached over and placed her hand on Jace's leg, just above the knee. He felt a surge of excitement run through his body that worked like a shot of caffeine. Looking over, he saw a troubled grin on the young woman's face. She was so beautiful. He suddenly wanted more than anything to see a look of peace on that face.

He'd never loved anyone the way he loved her, he suddenly realized. He'd had crushes, been in lust, even been in love a few times in his life, but he'd never experienced anything like what he was feeling now. There was a new kind of longing involved, a sensation not unlike pain, that was mixed with the excitement and joy and everything else that went along with loving someone.

"You should put on some music," Hero said, her eyes still closed. "It won't bother me, but it might help you stay awake."

"Maybe I will," he said with a shrug. "But I can wait until you've gone to sleep. Besides, I don't really know what I'm in the mood for."

They sat together in silence for a few minutes, and after a while Jace thought she'd gone to sleep. He gazed at her, wondering what it might be like to kiss her, and even felt the urge to lean over and plant one on her. Maybe she wouldn't notice. He grinned at his own stupid thoughts.

Maybe he should put some music on, or perhaps find something to watch on the view screen. Some action flick to keep him awake. Where were the headphones anyway?

But then Hero began to sing. Her voice was soft, but the ship was so quiet that it still startled him.

By the side of the pure crystal fountain
There is a lonely church yard nearby
There's a tombstone covered over with primroses
In the memory of a loved one passed away

Shall I ne'er see a more gentle mother
In the fields where the wild flowers grow
I am sorrowed for the loss I can't recover
Neath yon willow lies my gentle mother's love

Some children take a liking to their parents

While others fill their mothers' hearts with pain
But some day they will be sorry for their blindness
When the crying will not bring her back again

Shall I ne'er see a more gentle mother
In the fields where the wild flowers grow
I am sorrowed for the loss I can't recover
Neath yon willow lies my gentle mother's love
Neath yon willow lies my gentle mother's love

"You have a beautiful voice," Jace said, and he meant it. "What was that you were singing?"

"Something my grandmother used to sing to me when I was little." She opened her eyes and turned to him. "I used to sing it to Stephen."

"You will again," he said, catching up her hand in his." He expected to see tears, as he always did when she spoke of her son, but this time, the grin remained, and no tears came.

"I know." She squeezed his hand, and closed her eyes again.

Jace turned back to watch the stars as they blasted by. He always found doing so quite hypnotic, and knew he was going to have to come up with something to keep his mind active. Looking down at the control panel, he began to run a series of scans to look for traps. Everything looked clear enough. It was smooth sailing, at least for the time being.

"Did you mean it?" Hero asked a few moments later.

"Mean what?"

"Back on Necron. You told me you loved me. Did you mean it?"

"I did," he told her, staring into closed eyes. "More than I've ever meant anything."

For a few seconds she was silent, unmoving, but then her smile deepened and she turned her head to peek at him. "I love you, too."

Jace said nothing, though he felt like shouting for joy, like getting up and jumping right through the roof. She loved him, too. Euphoria seemed like too feeble of a word to describe what he was feeling.

A light began to flicker upon the com, and Jace looked down to see a distress signal coming through. It looked like a standard message, asking for assistance from any other ships in the area. Peter had warned him about distress signals in pirate-infested space. They were often used to lure in well-intentioned travelers, who suddenly found themselves in an ambush. Peter had told him of a time when the Katara received such a message from a supposedly stranded young mother with three young children on board. The woman had begged for someone to come and help before pirates showed up. *"Galin took us to the ship,"* Peter had told him, *"but he insisted we sit and watch for a while, keeping the ship cloaked, to make sure it wasn't a trap. We waited there for nine hours, and were finally about to move in when four Zandorian Strikers decloaked. The whole thing was a trap, and they would have turned us into mince meat for sure."*

Was this signal a ruse, too? Probably, but Jace scanned for the source anyway.

"That's weird," he mumbled under his breath.

"What's weird?" Hero asked, sitting up to take a look.

"It's a distress signal. Standard canned message, but the weird thing is, its source seems to be following us."

—GCW Navy Earth Star-Base
Three Years Before—

Hero awoke to the sound of classical music blaring from the alarm clock. She growled like a bear woken too early from hibernation and reached over to smack the thing off, knocking her book off the end table instead. Last night, she'd changed the dial from the hard rock station Will always turned to in search of something that would wake her with a less jarring blow. She didn't recognize the composer whose music was thundering out of the speakers, but her idea hadn't worked.

"HORNS," she moaned angrily. "SMASH THEM ALL!"

"Oh, come on," Will whined, covering his head with his pillow. "Don't tell me it's time to get up already."

"At least you get to sleep in," she growled. "Besides, whose idea was it to stay up half the night making love?"

He whipped the pillow off his face. "I'm married to the most beautiful girl in the world. You can't hold that against me. Besides, you didn't seem to be complaining at the time."

"No, I suppose I wasn't." She leaned over and kissed him on the forehead, and smacked away his roaming hands. "Go back to sleep, and enjoy your day off. I'll meet you tonight for dinner."

"I love you so much." He sat up and squeezed her tightly. "Have a great day, okay?"

"I love you, too. Get some rest." She closed the bathroom door behind her and a minute later was in the shower. It was a short one, and she kept it cold with hopes of waking herself up a bit. After that she slipped into her uniform and headed to the kitchen for a quick breakfast. Will was just plating up some eggs and bacon. He slid her food onto the counter as she climbed upon a barstool.

"I thought I told you to get some sleep," she reprimanded him with a smile.

"I might take a little nap later. I've got some things to catch up on first. It's been a while since I've had an entire day off at home."

"Did they ever find out who hacked into the central computer system?"

"If they did, nobody's bothered to tell me. Major Hanson said it looked like someone was fishing for weaknesses. The virus wasn't malicious."

"Maybe it was just some kind of joke. A prank?"

Will shrugged. "That would be a pretty dangerous prank. Tampering into a space station's security system is a capital offense. I don't know many people willing to pay with their life for a dumb joke."

Hero laughed. "It wasn't that dumb of a joke. It had you laughing."

"Well, I have to admit, watching a barrel-throwing gorilla pop up on every screen in the station was not something I ever expected to see."

"What was it called again? Donkey Kong? That's hilarious."

Will looked her over suspiciously. "You seem to be pretty impressed with the whole thing. Maybe it was you. *You're* the one who cracked the system."

That made her chuckle. She bit into a lightly charred bit of bacon. "Yup. You caught me. I'm the one who did it. Gonna have me arrested?"

"Maybe, and I might have to frisk you."

Hero shoveled in the final bits of breakfast and hopped to her feet. "Not right now, you won't, I've gotta get to work." She leaned over the counter to kiss him. "Thanks for seeing me off."

"Thanks for making me the luckiest man alive."

She blew him a kiss and headed out the door. It was going to be a long day. The Battleship Claymore had just arrived with a squadron of beaten up fighters. The truth was, she'd be lucky to get off in time to meet up with

Will for dinner, but she hadn't had the heart to tell him. As she walked toward the docking ring, an incoming call lit up her wrist com.

"Great," she mumbled, and clicked it on.

The stern face of a woman in her early fifties appeared. "Are you someplace where we can talk?"

"Hold on a minute." She went a bit further down the corridor, turned the corner and stepped into a utility room, pulling the door closed behind her. "I'm alone."

"How's the assignment going, Lieutenant? The life of an enlisted mechanic treating you well?" The older woman had a bit of a smirk. Hero hated that smirk.

"It's fine. Everything's going according to plan."

The woman waited for more, but Hero remained silent.

"And your…assignment? I assume he's treating you well?"

"His name is Will. Don't pretend like he's just some damned *thing*. He's a person, a real person with feelings and, and…."

"Get ahold of yourself right fracking now, Lieutenant. You're the one who convinced me you could handle this. You're the one who volunteered, remember?"

Hero nodded. "Yes, Commander."

"Then stop acting like a spoiled twelve year old, and send me the fracking report that was due two days ago. Understand?"

Again, Hero nodded, and wiped the tears from her

face.

The older woman stared her hard in the eyes, but then her expression eased. "We knew this was going to be a tough one. I tried to warn you."

Hero nodded. "I know."

"You aren't falling in love with him, are you?"

"Of course not. Don't be foolish."

The woman stared back, as if she wasn't quite convinced. "Guard your emotions. Your role is an important one." She paused. "If you want to be re-assigned, I need to know NOW. Before it's too late."

Hero shook her head, and forced a professional smile. "No. I'll be fine. This is just…harder than I thought it would be, that's all."

"All right. I expect that report by tonight. Any more excuses and it'll be your ass. You understand me?"

Hero nodded.

"And call me if you need to talk, I'm always here for you, okay?"

"Okay. Thanks, Mom."

The screen turned black, and Hero opened the door to peek out. No one was coming. She zipped back out and resumed her course toward the docking bay. "Keep it together," she warned herself. "It's just like she said, you knew this assignment was going to be difficult."

Two civilian contractors passed by with bemused grins on their faces.

Hero knew she needed to stop talking to herself out

loud. It was an old, nervous habit she just couldn't seem to get rid of. Her thoughts turned to Will. He was a good man, and he didn't deserve to be used as a pawn in some stupid political game like this. And truth be told, she *was* starting to have feelings for him, though she tried hard not to. He was kind, thoughtful, and attentive. The two of them didn't have much in common. He really liked sports, and although she'd been pretending to be a fan for the last ten months, none of them had really grown on her. She'd always had a love for all things mechanical, especially ships. He didn't seem to care much about those, but he did know a lot about classic hover-cars. In fact, the two of them had spent hours looking at magazines and talking about which ones they'd like to fix up together. The thought made her smile.

Maybe she *should* call her mother back and ask for re-assignment. It might be better to let Will believe she'd died in some obscure accident at work than to let their relationship continue to grow. He adored her, that much was clear, and the truth was there was no way out of this now that wouldn't cause him a great amount of pain. But Hero had been forged in a family that held the importance of duty above all else. It was in her blood. She would succeed, no matter how painful the cost, for her, or for those around her.

—NOW—

"Put that thing on silence, will ya?" Hero said, reaching up to rub her head. "God, that sound is irritating."

"Well, it's a distress signal, that's kind of the point." Jace reached over and switched off the speaker, though the accompanying light continued to flash. "So, what do you think we should do?" The ship had been trailing them for nearly an hour, continuing to transmit the same signal. "We could drop back and try to get a closer look."

"You think that's a good idea?" Hero sounded nervous, but curious.

"It's a weird situation. It's almost like…." He didn't want to say it.

"Like that ship knows we're out here? Like it's transmitting that distress signal for us?"

Jace cringed. "Yeah. It's just too coincidental, a ship showing up like this, headed in exactly the same direction we are."

"But there's no way anyone can see us. Not unless they have technology we don't know about that can see through our cloak. That's not very likely."

"They would've had to have seen us depart from the Katara, but we weren't picking up any ships nearby, and the Katara was cloaked at the time. It's impossible." Jace ran a series of scans. "I'm not able to get anything useful. Can't even tell for sure what kind of ship it is. I think they might be disrupting our scanners."

"Looks like it might be some kind of corvette class, judging by the size and energy signature. If it is a hostile, they'll have us way outgunned." Hero let out a long breath of air. "We could change course and see if they react."

"Yeah, that's not a bad idea. I'll decrease speed a bit as well."

Hero watched the scanners as he adjusted the coordinates. For the next few minutes, the ship continued along its path and maintained speed. The distress signal continued to come through on the com. "What do you think? Should we go in for a closer look?"

"I guess it couldn't hurt. I'll re-adjust our course and come in alongside her, its safer that way."

Minutes later, they were close enough to bring a visual image up on the display. The ship was long and sleek, and its hull was black. It was the kind of ship you could tell had a dangerous bite from looks alone- a beautiful thing, but deadly.

"That's a UEG ship, isn't it?" Jace asked.

Hero jumped to her feet. She gaped at the ship as if seeing a ghost, and Jace watched the blood drain from her face. "Yeah. Warbird class. Can you magnify that squadron insignia?"

He did as she asked. The image of a Red-Tailed Hawk appeared upon the view screen. Blue flames were shooting from the bird's beak, and its talons were snapping a pair of crossed bones. *Death's Echo* was written across the ship's nose, and below it, the painting of the grim reaper swinging his scythe. The burning blue skull beneath its hood was that of a hawk, grinning hungrily.

"You need to get us out of here," Hero whispered, as if afraid the ship would hear her. "Please. Do it now."

Jace leaned forward to reset the coordinates. "Hey, relax. Whoever's on that ship can't see us. We're cloaked, remember?"

Hero's breathing began to race. Her hands were shaking furiously. "Please. Please get us out of here. We need to leave."

"We're going." He drew her in close. "Look. We're already drawing away. I'm gonna put plenty of distance between us, okay?"

As they watched the other ship get further and further away on the scanners, Hero began to calm down a little, yet her eyes remained glued to the screen.

"You're shaking." Jace ran his fingers through her hair, trying to calm her down. "What is it? Who's on that ship you're so afraid of?"

"No...nobody. It's just, I used to work on ships like that."

Jace stared at her doubtfully.

"Just before the invasion. It was one of my last assignments before the invasion."

"Do you know the guy flying that ship?"

She shook her head frantically, eager to deny it, but then looked from the view screen into his eyes, and suddenly seemed to melt. "I think I do. Maybe…."

Finally, the ship disappeared from the short range scanners.

Jace helped her sit back down. "You want to talk about it?"

She shook her head. "No. Not now."

"Let me get you some water." He headed for one of the cargo bins toward the back of the shuttle, and a few moments later handed her a bottle. "Do you think that ship could be headed for Necron?"

"Its course certainly suggests it." Her voice trembled.

"Any idea why?"

She didn't answer, but finally shook her head, this time more slowly.

Jace took his seat. "Well, it's far ahead of us now. That distress signal's still active, though. It sure didn't appear to be in any kind of distress. Looked more like it was out for a Sunday drive."

"Today's Thursday."

Jace's laugh made Hero surrender a tiny grin.

For a while after that, they both remained quiet, holding hands and staring off into the stars. Jace wished that she'd talk to him, but wasn't about to push her. Whatever seeing that ship had triggered, she'd talk about it when she was good and ready.

He leaned over and kissed her on the forehead, gently squeezing the back of her neck. He wanted to say something to make her feel better, but wasn't sure what. He pulled back a little and gazed into her eyes. Before, those eyes had always seemed guarded, but now that was gone. Sadness and fear were in those eyes now, along with a love that made him feel sure that her words had been true. She really did love him, just as he loved her.

She drew him in for another kiss, a real one this time. It made him feel warm all over, and for the next few moments he almost forgot where he was. Their lips parted, and he caressed her face. Had she felt it, too?

"Hey," she said, looking over to the control panel, "it's stopped."

Jace had noticed as well. The light had stopped flickering. "Well, that's good, I suppose. I guess they solved whatever problem they were having."

"I guess," Hero agreed nervously. She stared at the scanners and began to breathe fast again.

Jace was about to place his arm around her when the ship reappeared on the screen.

Hero let out a gasp, and dug her nails into his hand. He winced.

"Listen, they don't know we're out here. There's just no way."

The com lit up, indicating an incoming transmission. Jace looked over at Hero hesitantly before clicking it on.

"He-ro," came a sing-songy female voice. *"Heeer-rooo.*

You're being rather rude. Aren't you happy to see me?"

—GCW Navy Earth Star-Base
Three Years Before—

"Mrs. Anderson, nice of you to come to work today." The bulky Deck Chief looked like a grimacing rhinoceros as he strode up toward her.

Hero finished lacing her boot, pushed her locker door shut, and checked her watch. "It's five minutes to eight."

He nodded his head mockingly, and Hero envisioned a large horn swaying up and down above the man's pocked, bulbous nose.

"Yeeeees. But like I've told you, if you're not fifteen minutes early, you're late. That's how it is on *my* deck, anyway."

"Well, you could always have me transferred," she mused.

"The men would riot. You're the only thing that pretties this place up. You're like a lily growing in the middle of a parking lot. Besides that, you're not the worst monkey I've ever seen wield a wrench."

Hero scoffed. "One of the *best* with a wrench, isn't that what you meant to say?"

The Chief laughed. It was booming and guttural, the kind of laugh that caused anyone nearby to smile in joy and cringe at the same time. "Don't get ahead of yourself, little lady. You've got a way with machines, that's for sure. But there're still plenty of tricks to learn with that pretty little head of yours."

Hero picked up her toolbox, which was about half her size, and followed the chief out onto the flight deck.

"You still want me to finish patching up that supply ship?" she asked. "I think I can get it done today if third shift followed through on installing those refurbished deflectors."

The chief turned his head and grinned. "No. I'll have Burke finish up on that. I think I've got something a bit more interesting for you to sink your teeth into, if you're feeling up to it?"

She looked at him quizzically, about to ask for an explanation when she saw them there lined up down the flight deck. "The Red Tailed Hawks? I've heard of them. They're probably the most feared and respected squadron of fighters in the fleet."

The chief nodded. "That may be the case, but they got themselves clobbered pretty good yesterday in a skirmish with the Nazerazi. You wanna help me and the boys patch 'em up?"

The boys was an unofficial term for the chief's inner circle of best mechanics. The man played favorites, sure enough, but it was obvious that a person's skills, attitude, and work ethics were the things he valued most. The Chief took his role very seriously, and that's why people had faith in him. It felt surprisingly good to be trusted by the man, but also made Hero feel uncomfortably guilty.

"I'd love to help," she said with a grin. "If you really think I'm ready. I don't have much experience with starfighters. Not yet."

"I know that, but there has to be a first time for everything. You can work with me. I'll keep my eye on you." He gave her shoulder a loving smack as they strode up to one of the ships.

"Death's Echo," she read while examining the nose art. "That's kind of cryptic. I wonder what kind of guy would give his ship a name like that?"

"This kind of guy," said a woman, stepping out from the front corner of the ship. She had long, auburn hair, a strikingly beautiful face, and wore the tight black uniform of a Red Tailed Hawks fighter pilot, minus the gloves and helmet.

Hero snapped to attention as the officer sized her up. She looked stern and judgmental, the way that her mother always had whenever she'd made a questionable decision growing up.

The pilot smirked, and turned her attention to the chief.

"Hello there, Chief Henner. What's it been, a year or so? Good to see you again."

"Nice to see you, too, Captain. I heard your team gave those Nazerazi scum a run for their money out near the demilitarized zone yesterday."

"You heard right. We lost three ships, and got nine more beat up pretty good, but we took out their entire squadron- fifteen ships in all. Their fighters were an even match for ours, but that doesn't matter when you've placed Bantheon pilots at the helm. Those furballs couldn't fly their way out of a beautiful sunset."

The chief chuckled and nodded his head, though Hero suspected he didn't have much of an idea of what the woman was talking about.

"So tell me, Cap, how many times have you gone up against the Nazerazi now?"

She looked over at her fighter, leaning against it with her right hand and stroking her hair with the left. "Oh, I don't know. About a baker's dozen, I guess."

"And have you ever seen one of them? Not one of the conquered races, but an honest to goodness Nazerazi?"

She shook her head. "Can't say that I have. I did meet a guy in a bar last year who claimed *he* did, though. He was a science officer stationed on the Battleship Warhammer. Said he encountered a group of 'em on an away-team mission."

"Oh, yeah? And what did he say they look like?"

"'Imagine a seven foot tall large mouthed Bass,' he said." She threw her voice mockingly. "'Only with a man's arms and legs. They smelled like fermenting garbage and were the bloodthirstiest race I'd ever come across.'"

The chief grinned from ear to ear. "And did you

believe him?"

The captain shrugged. "I don't know. He was pretty drunk at the time, and he was trying to get laid. Would you have believed him?"

"No," the chief laughed.

"So what's your story, sweetheart?" the Captain asked, turning to Hero. "I assume since you're still standing here, the chief's going to put you to work on my baby. You know your way around one of these things?"

"Never touched one," Hero answered, somewhat defiantly. "But there's a first time for everything."

The captain looked as if she were about ready to coil up and strike, but after a few moments she grinned. "I think this one might be a keeper, chief. I can tell she doesn't take much crap." She turned to leave. "Make sure she doesn't screw anything up. I'm heading for the chow hall. Killin' makes me hungry."

"You've got it," the chief answered. He watched her walk the entire strip, despite the obvious presence of Hero's glare.

"Really, Chief?" she whispered. "Are you trying to get brought up on harassment charges?"

The man guffawed. "You think she squeezes into that suit because she *doesn't* want to be looked at? Listen, kid, that woman is one of the top fighter pilots in the Space Navy, but the deadliest weapon she has is the one she carts around behind her, and she knows it."

"You're a pig," Hero told him, raising her eyebrows.

"Maybe. But I'm a pig who knows how to glue these things back together," he gave the hull of the ship a pat, "just as shiny and nice as the day they rolled off the assembly line. And she knows that, too."

Hero followed him to the other side of the plane, where a charred section of the hull awaited their loving care. She opened up her toolbox and retrieved a pneumatic wrench. "Well, she seems like a real character. I'll bet she drives all her male colleagues wild. There aren't that many women behind the sticks of these things. And that's the first one I've seen who looks like she missed her calling as an underwear model."

The chief grinned, knowingly. "Ah, huh. So that's what's got your feathers all ruffled, is it? You kind of like being the only drop-dead beauty in the room, don't ya? Another hen shows up in the rooster house and it's straight to hen-peckin'. I've seen it before."

Hero's face turned red. "What a load of bull. You don't know what you're talking about." She pulled on a face shield, and lit up her blowtorch.

"Yeah," he said, grinning smugly. "Sure, I don't. Don't worry, Anderson. Your husband is the envy of every man on this station. You'll always be our number one gal."

She fumed, but felt oddly comforted, though she wasn't about to give him any sign of it. She was silent for a few minutes as they worked, and then decided to change the subject. "So, this boat of hers, why'd she name it Death's Echo? Has she ever told you?"

The chief placed a cigar in his mouth, and borrowed Hero's blowtorch to ignite the end. He handed it back, and took a few puffs while directing the young woman in her work. "It didn't always have that name," he said. "It used to be called...ah hell, I can't remember. Her teammates renamed it for her. You see, our redheaded cutie has quite a reputation. Once she has a target in her sights, she always gets the kill."

"That's kind of the point of being a fighter pilot, isn't it?"

"Yeah," the chief chuckled, "but this one's different. She takes it to a whole 'nother level. Nobody's ever escaped her. *Nobody*. You could wiggle out of her grasp a dozen times, it wouldn't matter. She comes back. She stays on you until the job is finished. Seems to take the game *real* personal, see? She says an enemy's dead, they're dead, and you'd better stay out of her way until the job's finished."

Now it was Hero's time to laugh. "I think you're telling ghost stories, Chief. You almost sound afraid of her yourself."

"Me? Naw, I've always stayed on her good side. Takes a bit more than watching her butt wiggle to get the kiss of death from that one." He took a few more puffs of his cigar, looking like he was tempted to say more. Hero waited him out, knowing she might get more information if she didn't ask.

He continued. "You ever hear about the Greenleaf encounter?"

"I think so. It was a few years ago, right? When our ships engaged those Pleiadian strikers?"

"That's the one. But it was only one of our ships that engaged its target- this one." He gave the Death's Echo's hull a thump. "The whole thing was a misunderstanding, see? As you know, the Pleiadians have always been allies, but they can be an odd bunch. Very protective of their technology. Apparently, an Earth science vessel picked up one of their malfunctioning probes- the Greenleaf. They became quite perturbed, and were a little undiplomatic in the way they asked for the thing back. Fighters were scrambled, and things got a bit tense, as you can imagine. Our captain here flew a bit too close to one of their freighters, and a fighter took a few warning shots over her nose. That was a few more than she gave him. Everyone was ordered to stand down as soon as the first shot was fired, but she claimed she never received the order. Communications malfunction, she said, though it was never proved true." The chief tossed his cigar butt onto the floor and mashed it beneath his boot. "Anyway, that's one of the more light-hearted stories I could tell you about her. I've heard a few that made even my skin crawl."

"If she's that reckless, why hasn't she been grounded? Why hasn't she lost her commission?"

"*Well,*" the chief answered, pretending to think really

hard. "Fighter pilot's are supposed to kill things, and she's very talented at it. Besides, she *is* quite charming. Looks to die for. But most importantly, she's on *our* side."

—NOW—

Jace stared into Hero's eyes. Neither of them said a word, but the voice of the woman flying the ship kept coming, every few seconds, as her vessel drew closer and closer.

"Hero? How about it Hero? Care to join me for a drink? Catch up on current events?" Jace found the woman's voice quite sexy, but it seemed poisonously sweet. It reminded him of a girlfriend he'd once had. She'd turned out to be a humungous psychopath.

"Or maybe we could talk about...the future? Got any plans for the future, Hero? Of course you do. You've always been quite good at making plans, haven't you?"

"Can we outrun her?" Hero asked. "How fast is this little ship, anyway?"

Jace was sure she already knew the answer. "Not fast enough. Not if she knows where we are. I still can't figure out how she even knows we're out here."

"Well, try. Get, get us out of here some...somehow." She was on the verge of hyperventilating.

"Who is that woman? How do you know her?"

Hero shook her head. "She's…she's someone very dangerous. Wants me dead. She'll kill us both."

Jace took her in his arms and squeezed tightly. "Hey, I'm not going to let that happen, okay. You need to calm down. Try to steady your breath." He clicked off the com, and continued to hold her as she tried to calm down. "That's it. Whatever this is, we're going to get through it. Now tell me who she is. Is there any way we can reason with her?"

Hero gave him a panicked grin, and then shook her head. "No. No way. You don't know what she's like. I'd hoped she was dead. But she's never going to stop. She won't give up until she's finished me."

"She hasn't blown us out of the sky yet. There must be some reason for that."

"I don't know," Hero panted. "Maybe."

"Well, we can't outrun her. What do you want to do?"

Hero was silent for several minutes, but she'd managed to calm back down. They looked at the scanners. Death's Echo had fallen into position behind them, and matched their speed.

"I don't know what other choice we have," Hero told him. "I'll try to talk to her."

He looked deep into her eyes. "You sure?"

She nodded.

Jace clicked the com back on.

"I'm here," Hero said.

"Oh, I'm well aware of that. You know why I've returned, don't you?"

"Yes."

"Are you ready to get this over with?"

"There's an innocent man on this ship. He has nothing to do with this."

"Is that so? An innocent man? Really? And what gives you the ability to judge whether or not he's innocent? You, who are the farthest thing from it?"

Jace just sat there looking at her. He had no idea what this woman was talking about, and he didn't really care. There would be time enough to talk later, right now they needed to find some way out of this.

"So who is this innocent young man, Hero? Some unsuspecting patsy of yours? A new husband maybe? When do you plan on stabbing him in the back?"

"This is Jace Chang. Would you care to tell me who we're speaking with?"

"Hello there, Jace. My name is Captain Sonja Howard, of the United Earth Government Space Navy. Tell me something, Jace, are you a military man?"

"No. I tried to enlist in the Space Marines, but they wouldn't take me. High School football injury."

"Ooh, football hero, huh? I'll bet you're a real piece of eye candy. Why don't you put me on the view screen so we can talk face to face?"

"Not a chance," Hero told her.

"That's a shame. I'd love to meet your new boyfriend, Hero.

What do you say? I'll tell you what, the two of you can come aboard. We'll drink some tea, swap old war stories, what do you say?"

"Just leave us alone," Hero pleaded. "I'm not the person you think I am. You have me all wrong."

"I know exactly who you are," the woman said, her voice growing cold. *"I've seen who you really are. Better than anyone, even your football player boyfriend."*

"You want me dead? Why haven't you destroyed us yet?"

"I have my reasons."

Hero's face began to boil with anger. "I'm not going to play your games. Just get out of here and leave us alone."

"Oh, Hero. You poor, stupid girl. You sound like a broken record. Saying it enough won't make it so. I'm not going anywhere. We both know that there are several ways this encounter could end. Each of us going away quietly on our own is not one of them. So what do you say? Uncloak your ship, drop out of warp, and I'll bring you on board."

"And why exactly would we do that?" Jace asked.

"Because I have something that Hero wants."

"Is that so? What could you possibly have that she wants?"

"Oh, take a wild guess. Don't tell me you're as dense as she is. Tell him, sweetheart. What's the one thing in this universe that I could have that you might want?"

A look of terror spread across Hero's face, and she

lunged to flip on the view screen.

The woman staring back at them was downright gorgeous, though her eyes were like cold, angry sapphires. A young child lay sleeping in her arms.

"Stephen," Hero whispered as her entire body began to shake. "Please. Please don't hurt him. Don't hurt my baby."

"Me? Why would I do that? You're not going to give me any reason to do that, are you, Hero? Besides, I've been looking after this little animal for well over a month now. We're practically best pals." She looked down at him and smiled. "Hell, he probably thinks of *me* as his mother by now."

Hero was growing more frantic by the second. "Don't hurt him. Please! I'll do anything."

"Uncloak your ship and drop out of warp. Lower your shields."

Jace reached for the console.

"NO," Hero told him, blocking his hand. "How do I know you won't just kill us both?"

"Oh, I could have done that by now. Granted, I wouldn't be able to get a lock on your ship while it's cloaked, but I'd hit you eventually. No, sweetie. You and I are going to have a little talk before I punch your train ticket to hell. It's been a long time coming."

Hero just sat there, like a deer caught in the headlights, confused about which way to go.

"I can tell you need some convincing," Sonja said.

She lifted the boy up into the air so they could see him better, and smacked him hard across the face.

He jolted awake, screaming.

Hero looked furious, as if she might try to leap right through the view screen.

"What's wrong, sweetheart," Sonja asked the boy sweetly. "Did you have a bad dream?"

He hugged her tightly around the neck.

"Shush, everything's going to be fine now." Her fingers gently stroked his dirty blonde hair. "Your mommy's going to make the right choice, isn't she? That way, I won't have to break your little arms." She reached down and took hold of his hand, daring the boy's mother to challenge her.

Jace looked Hero in the eyes as he reached up to drop the ship out of warp. She made no move to stop him. Once they were at a stand still, he dropped the cloak, and then the shields.

"We're all dead," Hero whispered.

—GCW Navy Earth Star-Base
Two Years Before—

Hero rubbed her eyes before checking the time on her wrist com.

"You look really beat." The voice startled her. It was Petty Officer Iglesias, who reached out and snatched the remaining bolts from her hand. "Get the frack out of here, Hero. You look like you're about ready to fall over, and the sarge made it clear, you're not to work a minute over six hours. You've been here nearly seven."

"I'm almost finished. Fifteen more minutes, that's all I ne—."

"Am I going to have to call the old ball and chain to come get you again?"

She pursed her lips at him.

"Go on, beat it. I'll finish things up for you here. You're not the only one who knows your way around one of these cruisers." He hammered the ship with his fist to assure her.

"I know. But Captain Howard doesn't like anyone she doesn't know working on her ship."

"Well, she's gonna have to live with it. Don't worry about your tools, I'll clean all that crap up, too."

She hesitated. The truth was, she felt better when working. It took her mind off everything. Sure, she was tired, but fatigue was better than worry.

"Go rest. You look about ready to pop, and I'm a mechanic, not a fracking midwife."

"I think you missed your calling," she sneered. "You would have had such wonderful bedside manner."

He winked at her, and she shuffled back to the locker room, where she washed up and retrieved her things before heading off toward her quarters. About halfway there, she finally realized just how tired she actually was, and how much her feet hurt, and decided that making dinner was the last thing in the world she wanted to do.

Meet me at The Rib Shack when you get off work, she messaged to Will, and headed for the restaurant. His shift would be over in about an hour. Walking through the entertainment district, she waved to those people she knew, and even a few she didn't, as friends and strangers alike gave her warm, congratulatory smiles. Carrying a beach ball around beneath her shirt made everyone look at her in a whole new way, which was nice, although she could do without the uninvited hands that occasionally came reaching out to pat her.

What the hell were you thinking, came the voice of her mother, ringing through her head once again. *Getting pregnant? Are you out of your mind?*

I love him, Mom, she'd answered. *He is my husband, after all. Besides, you said he'd be protected.*

I said I would try. But I can't promise you anything. You know that. You're playing with fire, Hero.

She'd been running through that conversation in her head for months now. Maybe her mother was right. Maybe she was screwing this up just like she screwed up everything else. Maybe she didn't care. None of this made any sense to her anyway. It was about time she started living life for herself, and for her family.

Even before the doors of the restaurant slid open, Hero was met with the wafting aroma of flame-broiled meat. The place was well lit, and decorated like a wooden hut that one might find in the Louisiana bayou. Hero gazed up at the stuffed alligator hanging above the bar and wondered if it might be real, then her eyes sank down to examine the beers on tap. What she wouldn't give to have a nice cold glass of ale, but she'd waited eight months, she could wait one more.

"Grab a seat wherever you want, honey," a waitress told her as she hovered near the entrance.

Hero found a nice secluded corner bench, which was a bit more dimly lit than the others.

"Just you tonight, sweetie?" her waitress asked, sliding a menu onto the table.

"I'm waiting for my husband, but he'll be a while."

"Start you off with a drink then?"

"Water, with a slice of lemon."

"Any appetizers?"

"Bring me the sampler," Hero told her, not needing to check the menu. She had it pretty well memorized. It seemed like she'd eaten more in the last few months than she had in the last few years. That was going to need to change soon, too.

After a while, the waitress returned with her food and Hero dove right in.

Will turned up just in time to find her polishing off the last potato skin.

"Hey, I thought we were going to have dinner together? You already ate?"

She shook her head defensively. "Just had an

appetizer."

"An appetizer, or all the appetizers? You've still got a little bit, right there on your cheek," he said, pointing. "Here, let me get it for you."

"Sit down and shut up so we can order," Hero told him. "I'm hungry."

"Yeah, I'll bet you are." He slid into the seat beside her and placed a kiss upon her nose.

The waitress returned to take their order, but before they could finish giving it to her, a commotion broke out at the bar. Will leaned to look past the waitress's sizable rump to see what was happening.

"Uh, oh. Looks like your old pal Captain Howard is trying to make new friends again."

Hero leaned over on top of him to get a look. Sure enough, Sonja Howard was standing near the bar, and she had a fellow officer's head pinned against the counter. His arm was locked behind his back, and he shrieked with pain every time she gave it a twist.

"Maybe you should learn to keep your hands to yourself," Howard growled at the man.

"I'm sorry, okay. I'm…I'm sorry. It'll never happen again. I promise."

Howard's companions laughed every time her victim squealed.

"Say uncle," she told him, twisting again.

"Uncle, okay? UNCLE," he shrieked. "I'M SORRY!"

With a final motion, she broke his arm at the elbow, and the man fell to the floor in agony.

"MEDIC!" one of her friends called, and they all laughed again; everyone but Howard, who's face was stern and satisfied.

The bartender and a few waitresses rushed to the injured man's assistance.

"Wow. What a psychopath," Will whispered, shaking his head. "Doesn't that woman scare you?"

Hero shrugged. "Not really. I keep her boat patched up whenever she's in the neighborhood. Besides, she's loved me ever since I re-calibrated her phasers and fine-tuned her target locking system."

"Well, every time she comes in here," butted in the waitress, "she beats the crap out of someone, or worse. The woman is a menace. This is supposed to be a family friendly place, you know. Anyway, this guy got lucky, the last one was in a coma for over two months after she got through with him."

"Good Lord!" Will said, shaking his head in disbelief.

They finished placing their order, and after the broken-armed officer was escorted out, things calmed back down.

"Do you ever get sick of all this?" Hero asked Will as they waited.

"Sure. Crap like that shouldn't be tolerated from anyone. I don't care how many confirmed kills that woman has. She's a loose cannon."

"I know, but that's not really what I'm talking about. I mean, just all of this in general. The whole military type of life. Your enlistment is almost up. So's mine. We could leave all of this behind. Go someplace far away, start our lives over together."

"Wow, where's all this coming from? I've never heard you talk like this before. I thought you loved your job."

"I do. It's just...I want our baby to have the best life possible. I want to make sure we're doing what's right for our family. Our future. Wouldn't it be better to get out of here, especially with all this friction with the Nazerazi Empire. Things are only getting worse."

"Maybe you're right," he said, taking her hand. "But I don't think it's as bad as all that. Besides, we don't have to make this decision right away. We could still serve another term before moving on. You know, set ourselves up a little better financially."

Hero nodded. "You're probably right. Maybe I've just got the nesting bug, because of the pregnancy."

Will reached over and gently turned her head toward his. "You look so sad. Does this really mean that much to you?"

"I don't know." She stared into his eyes. "I love you so much, I just want us to be okay."

"Why wouldn't we be? I'll always take good care of you, and our baby, too." He smiled and pecked her on the lips. Then his smile broadened.

"What do you look so happy about?" she asked suspiciously. "Is there something you're not telling me?"

"Yeah, I didn't want to say anything until I was sure."

"What?"

"I've been put up for promotion. It would mean transferring over to the Axalon, but the C.O. personally assured me that you'd be transferred, too."

"That would be a great opportunity, for both of us."

He nodded. "You still look sad, though."

"No," she said, forcing a smile. "I'm happy for you. I'm just a little emotional right now."

"Well, I guess you're allowed to be." He placed his hand upon her stomach.

"I wish I could have a beer to celebrate."

"I'll have one for us both, if your nutty friend and her buddies up there left any for me."

"Thanks," Hero said, smirking.

Their order arrived and she dug into her brisket. It was settled then. There was no turning back now. All she could do was hope for the best.

—UEG Axalon
One Year Before—

Hero collapsed upon her mat to rest for a few moments. She steadied her breath, and then rose up to knock out the final set of sit-ups. After reaching the count of twenty-five, she dropped back to the mat with an anguished, yet satisfied growl.

"Come on, you can do more than that."

Hero looked over to see Captain Sonja Howard, dressed in a midnight-blue leotard. Her long, auburn hair was tied into a ponytail, and her body glistened with sweat. She'd obviously just finished a workout.

"What are you doing, stalking me?" Hero jested. "Anyway, that was my final set. I'm up to three hundred a day."

"Relax, grease-monkey. I'm just yanking your chain. You look a little thinner than the last time I saw you, that's for sure. What's it been, about a year?"

Hero nodded.

"Anyway, congratulations. Boy or girl?"

"Boy. We named him Stephen," Hero said, crossing her legs to stretch out. She looked at the captain's body with envy. "Now I'm just trying to get my form back. It's harder than I thought it would be."

Howard nodded. "You'll get there. You're pretty good at fixing things. That's why I requested we come aboard the Axalon for maintenance. The last jackass that touched my ship screwed up those improvements you made to my shield generators. You mind taking care of that for me?"

"Will do, Cap," Hero said with a smile.

Howard grinned. "I hope I'm not getting too personal, but was that a C-section scar I saw?"

Hero laid back and lifted her shirt. "Yeah. It's quite a story. You get wind of that accident we had on the docking bay about a year ago?"

"Sure. Some idiot drove a forklift into a loading rack of proton mines, right?"

Hero nodded. "One of the mines rolled into a pool of water and the containment shield collapsed. Then it kept rolling until it got sucked into the intake of a medical shuttle we were working on. Damned thing exploded, taking out half the docking bay with it. It was a freak accident, never seen anything like it before. Anyway, the little guy living in here," she pointed to her stomach, "I guess he decided he wanted to come out and see what was going on."

"So why'd you need a C-section? That's a bit archaic, isn't it?"

"Emergency shielding had gone up all around the bay, and emergency responders were fighting the fires all around us. I was lying on the floor, unable to move. My water had broken, but something was wrong. Luckily a couple of interns from that medical shuttle had been hanging out, watching their ship getting repaired. They spotted me through the smoke and came to help, but they didn't have any of their equipment. I still don't know what they used to cut me open, I'd passed out by then. I probably don't want to know."

"So what's up with that scar? The doctors should be able to erase that thing for you, good as new, just like it never happened."

"That's just the thing," Hero told her. "It did happen. There'll always be a scar there, whether I can see it or not. Some scars last forever. You can't ignore them."

Howard crossed her arms. "You're a gorgeous young woman, Hero. The first time I met you, I thought I had you pegged, but I was wrong. Hypocritical of me, I know. Women like us are both blessed and cursed by our looks."

Hero laughed.

"I don't mean to sound vain. You know what I'm talking about, don't you?"

"Sure. You judged me by my looks the first time you saw me. I guess I did the same to you. Kind of funny how we complain when men treat us the same way."

"True. But men have different intentions. That's what makes them so easy. They all think the same way, some have just been trained to hide it better than others."

"You ever think about settling down?" Hero asked with a grin. "Starting a family?"

"Me?" Howard laughed. It was the first time Hero had ever heard her really laugh with her guard down. "Frack no. The first time my husband and I had a bad argument, he'd end up with a broken bone. There aren't many guys who would put up with that kind of action."

"You just need to find one stronger and meaner than you are."

"Stronger? Easy enough. Never met one meaner

than me, not that I didn't end up killing."

Though she said it all with a grin, Hero could tell she meant every word. Good God, this woman was certifiably crazy.

"Anyway, I've got some old friends to catch up with." Howard turned to leave. "Thanks for taking care of my girl out there. I know I make it difficult sometimes."

"It's what I do," Hero said.

"And, uh…I really like that scar." She gave a little wink, and headed toward the showers.

—NOW—

Once the bay doors were down the tractor beam turned off, and the sound of restraining clamps rung out as the Shiv was locked down onto the deck.

Jace held Hero as they waited, he wasn't sure for what. "I'll go first. Just stay behind me."

She kissed him fiercely upon the lips. "Listen, if you're both able to get out of this, take care of Stephen for me."

"Hero, I…."

"Promise me." She stared him down with a pleading ache that nearly broke his heart.

"I promise. But don't talk like that. We're all going to make it out of this. You'll see."

She kissed him again. "Let's get this over with."

Holding hands, they opened the hatch, not knowing what to expect.

A crew-bot stood there waiting for them. The android's silver face took a bluish tint under the docking bay lights. It gazed up at them stoically. Jace wasn't sure what to think about a robot being sent to greet them; he was just relieved they hadn't been met with a blaster bolt to the face.

"Lieutenant Anderson," the android said, "Captain Howard is waiting inside to speak with you."

Jace turned to her in confusion. "Lieutenant? What's that supposed to mean? You get a field promotion I don't know about?"

"It doesn't mean anything," Hero told him.

"I'm afraid I must ask for your sidearms," the android said. "I'm sure you understand."

They had expected nothing less, and didn't have much of a choice in the matter. If they made too much of a fuss all Howard had to do was open up the bay doors. Blaster pistols wouldn't do much good in that situation. They held out their weapons, and the robot scanned them to make sure they didn't have any more. Then he passed them off to a smaller repair droid, who'd been waiting off to the side just out of view. The boxy little robot zipped out of sight like a dog that'd just been awarded a fresh bone.

Hero released Jace's hand, and stepped out onto the deck, stumbling down to her knees in front of the crew-bot.

"Hey, take it easy," Jace said, reaching down to help her. She'd already taken the android's hand, and as he pulled her to her feet, Jace observed her reach up to place something behind its neck. She locked eyes with him and shook her head discreetly.

"Thanks," she told the android. "Guess I've got a glitch in my programming. Need to reboot."

The android stopped in its tracks, and its eyes flashed brightly for a few seconds before it continued on as if nothing had happened. Jace wasn't sure what she'd done, but he hoped it was going to work.

The android escorted them out of the shuttle bay, through the short corridor, and into the small dining chamber. There, Captain Howard was sitting at the end of the table waiting for them, a raging fire burning behind her eyes.

"Hello, Lieutenant. I wish I could say I was happy to see you again." Her glance turned to Jace, and softened slightly. "Nice to meet you face to face, Jace Chang. You *are* a handsome young stud, aren't you? Certainly an upgrade from that boring John Doe you hooked up with last time, Hero."

"Where's my son?" Hero demanded.

"He's safe, for now. Can't promise that his future looks all that bright, though. If I decide to let him live, he'll likely spend the rest of his life in a cage."

Hero moved to lunge across the table, but Jace took

hold of her around the waist.

"Really?" Howard chuckled. "Honestly, girl. Nothing would make me happier." She turned to Jace. "You'd better help your girlfriend to her seat, before she gets hurt. Have some water," she gestured to the pitcher the crew-bot had just placed before them. "I'd offer you something stronger, but supplies are running a bit low. I'm sure you understand."

Jace forced her to sit down, and then took the chair beside her. "Look, I don't know what's going on here, but maybe we can talk all this out. The way things are right now, with the invasion and all...we need to stick together. Come together, no matter what's happened in the past."

"You poor little idiot." Howard gave him an exaggerated sigh. "You honestly don't know what you've gotten into, do you? You want to tell him, Hero? Want to show him all our old wounds? Explain how some scars never go away?"

Hero sat silently, chest heaving, her eyes boring into the woman across the table.

"Tell me, Jace...Can I call you that? Tell me, what is it that you look for in a woman?" She waited a few seconds. "It's not a trick question. Let me help you out. Beauty- this girl is obviously a knock out. I'm sure you're the envy of every man around. There's not a boy in this sector who wouldn't like to get himself a taste of that." She pointed to the fuming girl. "How about honesty? Loyalty? A partner you can depend on? All of those things are important, too. Right, Jace? You look like a man who can think with the head above your waist just as well as the one below."

Jace had no answer for her. "What exactly are you getting at?"

She looked at him dumbly. "I can't say I blame you. She had me fooled, too. In fact, that pretty little dumpling was one of the few women in my life that I might have considered a friend. See, I've always seemed to get along better with the boys than I have with the girls. Just always been a tomboy, I guess. But Hero was different. Here's a tough, no-nonsense gal who seems a bit timid at first, but once you get to know her, you realize she doesn't take crap from anybody. She's strong, in here, where it counts." She made a few thumps on her chest. "That's what I *used* to think anyway. But she had me suckered, the same way she's got you suckered. Go on, Hero. Tell him all about it."

Hero said nothing.

"Tell him how you betrayed all those people who loved you, *trusted* you. Tell him how you betrayed your own people! Tell him about how you murdered your husband, Hero. I'm sure he'll understand. He looks like the forgiving type. Me, on the other hand...."

Jace looked at her in shock. "What's she talking about?"

"It didn't happen like that. She doesn't know. SHE

WASN'T THERE."

"No?" Howard laughed. "What about Will? Does he know what I'm talking about? Too bad we can't ask him."

"SHUT YOUR FRACKING MOUTH," Hero screeched, picking up the pitcher of water and throwing it at her. "YOU DON'T KNOW. HOW COULD YOU?"

Howard sprang out of the way and drew her blaster pistol, pointing it at Hero's face. "How could I know? Are you serious, Hero? You *told* me, don't you remember?"

Just then, the crew-bot, who was standing behind her, struck the back of her head, and Captain Howard crumpled to the floor.

—UST Claymore
A Few Months Before—

Hero stormed into her mother's office, saluted, and stood at attention. "Lieutenant Hero Anderson, reporting as ordered."

The admiral rolled her eyes. "Stop being so dramatic and have a seat."

She sat.

"Honestly, honey. The attitude is getting a little old, its a bit immature, don't you think?"

"Why did you have me transferred?" she huffed, throwing her hands in the air. "I was happy on the Axalon. My family was happy. I had to leave Stephen with my Earth parents because Will's schedule is so hectic."

"He'll be fine with them for a while. They took good care of you, didn't they?"

"That's not the point. Look, just tell me what this is all about?" She already knew what it was about, she just didn't want to believe it.

"It's time. I've gotten word." She frowned sympathetically. "I *am* sorry, but you knew this day was coming. Are you prepared to carry out your orders?"

"Do I have any other choice?"

"Not if you want to live. You know the consequences of failure. And open defiance? I've seen what he's done in such situations, and it's not a fate I'd wish on my worst enemy."

Hero's head sank. Her eyes settled on her feet, but it was the face of her son and husband her mind settled upon.

"You've prepared the code? You're sure it will work?"

"Yes. It's gone through years of testing. Right under the UEG's nose."

"I knew we had the right person for the job. You've done well, sweetie. Just a few more days, and this will all be over. Then you can meet up with your family and relocate to wherever you wish to go. Even stay on Earth, if that's what you choose."

"I want to get as far away from all this as possible. Just because I'm cooperating doesn't mean I agree with what's happening."

"I can't say I blame you. Just remember, what we're doing...what *you're* doing, it's going to save a lot of lives."

"That's why I'm doing it. When does he want the virus activated?"

"Tomorrow afternoon. Fifteen hundred hours, sharp. A large portion of Earth's fleet will be convening to receive a virus prevention update. Kind of ironic, isn't it."

"The window of opportunity will only last about two hours. Do you really think the Draconians will be able to commandeer Earth's entire fleet by then?"

"That's what I've been told. But don't worry about any of that, it isn't our concern. Just focus on executing your portion of the plan, the rest will work itself out."

Hero looked down at her wrist com and scrunched her nose in frustration. "Will's not answering the message I sent him. I know he's busy, but I've told him how much I worry when he takes so long to get back to me.

Her mother suddenly looked suspiciously guilty.

"What is it, what did you do?"

She hesitated, taking in a deep breath. "The counsel wanted him taken into custody on some trumped up charges. Don't look at me that way. It's just a precautionary measure. He'll be released tomorrow evening."

Hero's blood began to boil. "Are you kidding me? After all I've done, this is the amount of trust I'm shown? They think they can just take my husband as some kind of...some kind of HOSTAGE?"

"It wasn't my idea. Damn it, get ahold of yourself. Now you can focus on what you need to do. Like I said, this will all be over soon."

Hero felt like screaming, but she choked the desire back. "May I please be dismissed?"

"Of course."

She rose and bee lined for the door.

"I'm here if you need —."

The door slid shut behind her before the woman could finish. She suddenly felt sick to her stomach, and wanted nothing more than to find a dark hole where she could crawl away and hide, but for now, her quarters would have to suffice.

When she got there, she threw herself onto the bunk and looked around. Everything seemed so empty. No pictures on the wall, none of Will's things scattered about, none of Stephen's toys to trip over. Sure, this place was only temporary, but it seemed so empty and lonely. It felt as if everything had been taken away, and despite what she'd been told, all the assurances she'd been given, she couldn't shake the feeling that her world was about to shatter.

"Pull yourself together, for God's sake," she whispered. "It's just like she said, this is almost over. Then we can start again, someplace far away from the Empire." Somehow, saying it out loud seemed to make it more likely.

But would he really let her go? She'd been told that the King was known for rewarding those who pleased him, but only when that person was of no more use to him. What would he think of someone whose idea of a reward was to get as far away from him as possible? Wouldn't he be insulted? Perhaps she was too insignificant for him to even bother with. That was her greatest hope.

Hero didn't get much sleep that night. Worry and anxiety about the following day kept her tossing and turning. She got up early and wandered the halls of the Claymore, exploring every section she could gain access to. It was truly an impressive ship. She would have liked the opportunity to serve aboard a vessel like this, and almost lamented the fact that her ruse was coming to an end.

The following day was one of the longest of her life, and as fifteen hundred hours approached, Hero got a knot in her stomach that nearly knocked her over. She dreaded having to return to her quarters, which now felt even lonelier than they had the night before.

Clicking on the wall monitor, she turned to the GCW

Navy Earth Star Base news channel. They were sure to start covering the story as soon as it happened. In fact, images of the fleet were already scrolling across the screen.

"Seldom do so many of Earth's vessels return to orbit all at once," the large chested brunette reported, popping on screen. "But due to increased friction with the Nazerazi Empire, Admiral of the Navy Justin Woods tells us that some essential security updates are long past due."

The image of the balding, squinty-eyed old Admiral appeared onscreen. The wavering flag of the United Earth Government floated in the air behind him. "Budgetary constraints have hindered us over the last few years, but I'm extremely happy that the President and Parliament have finally approved these upgrades. Our fighting men and women risk their lives to protect our own planet, as well as those in the United Confederation of Worlds. Giving them the latest technological safeguards is the least we can do."

The reporter re-appeared onscreen. "With the wide variety of military ships gathered together in orbit, a number of curious spectators have assembled to show their support." The camera panned over a number of civilian vessels passing through space nearby. "It's not often that one gets a chance to see such a wide variety of Navy starships. Of notable absence is the Red Tail Hawks squadron, led by Commander Timothy Gunn.

The squadron was scheduled to be here today, but was called away at the last minute to investigate the sighting of Nazerazi vessels inside UEG space. I spoke to one disappointed fan just a little while ago over in the entertainment district."

The screen switched to the brunette reporter holding her microphone in front of a little boy's face. A girl, presumably his sister, stood beside him, as well as his father, whose eyes were glued to the reporter's strategically displayed breasts.

"Tell me, young man, which ships are you most excited to get a look at today?"

"Well, my dad brought us up here to get a look at the Red Tailed Hawks." He held up his toy ship, a small replica of one of their cruisers. "But that man over there just told us they aren't gonna be here. What a load of Bull-sh-BEEEP."

The reporter looked up sheepishly as Hero clicked the mute button. She checked the time. Five minutes to go.

The transmitter was set up and ready, but she double checked the code and frequency one last time. With the push of a button, the virus would be transmitted from the Star-Base to every ship in the fleet, dropping the shields and disabling the targeting and navigational systems. Before they even knew what was happening, the Draconians would fly in and force their surrender.

"You're doing it to save lives," Hero reminded herself as the clock ticked down. "Fifteen hundred hours sharp," she breathed, and pressed the transmit button.

—NOW—

Jace scrambled to retrieve Howard's blaster pistol. "What did you do to this android?"

"I slipped a scrambling bolt onto its neck. Parts of its programming have been re-written. He'll take orders from us now."

Jace kneeled down to inspect Captain Howard. She had a nasty bump on the head, but didn't seem too badly harmed. "What are we going to do with her?"

"We need to find something to tie her up with." Hero disappeared through the entrance and returned a few moments later with some plastic zip ties. "These ought to work." She gave them a toss.

He reached down, taking hold of Howard's hands and pulling them in front of her.

She opened her eyes and gazed up at him as if she were drunk. "Don't…don't hurt me. Please."

"Oh, no," he said softly. "We aren't going to. I just need to tie you up."

CRACK

Before Jace had time to react, the woman had slammed her forehead into his jaw, and he went sprawling down onto his back. She punched him twice, hard across the face, swiped back her gun, and somersaulted away, turning back to fire a few bolts into the android, which crashed in a fiery heap in front of the sink. Jace turned his head to find Hero, and caught a glimpse as she dodged out the doorway. A blaster bolt struck the wall behind her.

"You're not getting away from me, Hero. You know that." Howard was back on her feet and after her.

"LEAVE HER ALONE," Jace yelled, grabbing the woman's ankle. She fell to the ground, cursed him, and tried to kick away.

"You still don't get it, do you?" She flipped onto her back, sat up, and pointed her pistol right between his eyes. "I don't want to kill you, but I will. She needs to pay for what she's done. You won't be able to stop it."

"You said she was your friend once. Maybe she had a good reason for doing whatever it is she did."

"You don't know what you're talking about." She kicked him in the face, and he felt his nose break. Then she got to her feet and bolted out the door. Jace struggled to pull himself up to the table. It took a moment for the room to stop spinning. A stream of blood gushed out to run down the front of his shirt.

By the time he got into the hallway, both women were gone. He tried to open the door to the cockpit, but it was locked. Just then, a heavy clank came echoing through the chamber, as if someone had just slammed a hatch. He made his way back toward the docking bay, from where he thought the sound might have come, and walked along lightly in order to listen, having to fight back the instinct to call Hero's name. Their psychotic hostess had shown him mercy once, but he might not be so lucky if he jumped her again.

Stopping to listen, the hum of the ship's air filtration system soon became the only sound he heard. Where would Hero have gone? She didn't know where Stephen was being held. She could be hiding anywhere.

The engine room, he suddenly realized. That's where she would hold up, maybe find a way for them to get out of this alive. But this wasn't the way to the engine room, was it? Maybe there was a service hatch in here, that led to the engine room, perhaps that was what he'd heard. The surrounding docking bay was a quarter of the size of the Katara's, and it didn't take long to examine the place, though the fear he felt for Hero made time crash to a halt. He had to find her, had to keep her safe. Where could she have gone? His heart was pounding.

No hatch was in sight, but a steel grating on the back wall covered a shaft just big enough for someone to crawl through.

"Hero, you in there?" Jace whispered, kneeling before it. No answer.

He walked back over to the Shiv, lifted the door and looked around inside. She wasn't in there. Going back to the grate, he gave it a yank, and the thing sprung open from the bottom, coming to rest on its hinges. He crawled into the shaft, reaching back to pull the grating closed behind him. It clunked down with a bang, creating the same sound he'd heard just a few minutes ago.

"Hero?" he whispered. "Hero? If you're in here, don't hit me in the face with anything." Before long, the shaft turned sharply to the left, and sure enough, came out in the confined engine room.

"What happened to your nose?" Hero asked, rushing to embrace him.

"I guess your old pal Captain Howard decided I needed a nose job."

"I'm sorry I took off like that. I didn't know what else to do." She pushed him aside before moving some crates into place to block off the grating. "There was nothing I could do in there. I had to get someplace where I could do *something*."

"It's okay. Just tell me you've got some kind of plan."

"Sure I do. It's not ideal, but we don't exactly have a lot of options, do we?"

"So, where is she? The cockpit?"

Hero nodded. "I think that's where Stephen is. I checked the door after I ran, but it was locked, that's why I headed down here."

"That's what I figured. So, what's the plan?"

"Little trick I picked up from TAII. I'm going to flood the air with engine coolant vapor. That'll put us all to sleep for a while, but you and I should wake up first if we open up the valve on that oxygen tank over there."

"Are you sure that's a good idea? I mean, how long will we be out?"

"About an hour or two. It's safe enough. We just have to cross our fingers that one of us wakes up before she does. Chances are one of us would anyway, since there are two of us."

"How long will it take for the gas to knock us out?"

"Only a matter of seconds once I vent it."

"You think Howard knows what you're doing?"

As if in answer, Sonja's face popped onto the small view screen by the door. "So, locked yourselves up in the engine room have you? Just what is it you're planning on doing, Hero?" Her voice was calm and patronizing.

"You'll find out soon enough."

"Have you forgotten that I've got your little snotling up here with me?"

"No," Hero said coldly. "I haven't forgotten."

"Good. I imagine you think you've got some brilliant scheme worked out in that pretty little head of yours. I've got a better idea. Come up here and say goodbye to your son. You've got about fifteen minutes."

"Oh yeah?" Hero asked, preparing to vent the gas. "What happens in fifteen minutes?"

"Well, that's when this little guy runs out of air." She held up Stephen, who had a space helmet secured onto his head. Such helmets were made to be put on during emergencies, and self-adjusted to the size of its user's neck. They had a limited supply of air. Stephen was obviously balling his head off, though the sound was being silenced.

"Yup," Sonja said, tapping a gauge on the side of the helmet. "Fifteen minutes and six seconds, to be exact. I even sealed it with a security code. But you can unlock it. I won't stop you. I used a code that only the two of us would know."

Hero looked over at Jace with a renewed sense of terror. She turned back to Sonja. "If I come up, will you let Jace and my baby go?"

Sonja stared back at her with eyes full of fire. "*You're* the one I want. Not them. I might be a killer, but I'm not like *you*. I'm not a murderer."

—UST Claymore
A Few Months Before—

Hero's palms began to sweat as she watched the Nazerazi vessels drop out of warp onscreen, and move in to engage Earth's fleet. She wiped her hands on her pants. Would they really be able to commandeer the UEG ships within the window of opportunity? Everything would have to be orchestrated perfectly. How many people did the Empire have planted on each ship? Whatever happened now, her part had been played. She just prayed there would be minimal bloodshed. Then it would all be worth it. Will would be released and they could start their lives anew.

But what would happen if he ever found out it had been her? That she'd played such an instrumental part in the Nazerazi takeover of Earth?

He could never be allowed to know.

Earth's ships hung in space like deer caught in the headlights of the prowling enemy vessels, which circled like hungry vultures, observing their prey to be sure of its demise.

Hero realized that the volume was still muted, and clicked the sound back on, catching the nearly hysterical voice of the brunette reporter mid-sentence.

"Ladies and Gentlemen, we still don't know what's going on, but our ships appear to have been disabled. None of them are maneuvering to engage the invading force. We can only—" And then all hell broke loose behind her.

Hero's breath was taken as she watched the Nazerazi ships open fire, sweeping through the fleet and picking off each of their targets one by one. Not even the mighty battle cruisers were spared.

And then the panning camera caught the remnants of the Axalon, flashing and erupting with fire. Hero dropped to the floor, and pain shot through her knees and up her legs, but she barely noticed. So many people, friends, were dying as she watched, and there was nothing she could do, and it was all her fault. She couldn't make a sound, couldn't even bring herself to scream at the horrors on the screen before her.

The picture cut back to the space station, where most of the people were shrieking and running about, but there were a few standing at the windows, watching quietly. The reporter turned back to the camera. Her face was wet with tears, and she struggled to regain composure. She opened her mouth to speak, just as the windows behind were struck with a plasma blast. The final images Hero saw were those of the reporter and civilians around her being sucked out into space. Then the screen went black and everything went silent.

This couldn't be real. It had to be some sort of nightmare. Hero's head was pounding. She continued to stare at the blank screen, half expecting the brunette reporter to come back on, and began to sob. She would have thrown up had there been anything in her stomach. It wasn't supposed to have been like this. What had just happened? What had gone wrong?

Will had been taken into custody, her mother had said, but that didn't mean he'd been taken off the Axalon. Was he dead? She loved him, despite their differences. Despite all the times she'd questioned herself. She knew it for sure now, and hated herself all the more for it.

Even if he was alive, what did it matter? She was still responsible for all this. She was the one who'd authored the virus, tested it, and uploaded it into the system. It had been her work that had made all this horror possible.

She'd never be able to look her husband in the eyes again.

But she'd done it to save lives; everyone told her it would save lives. Why would the Empire do something like this? The Krimson King's ruthlessness was known to all, but Hero had never imagined that even a man like him could be capable of ordering such a massacre.

She staggered to her feet, and made her way to the dresser by the window, where she stood for a few moments staring out into the stars. Had her mother known all this would happen? Had she intentionally lied to her? Without even consciously realizing what she was doing, Hero reached down to open the top dresser drawer. She pulled out her blaster pistol and rested the barrel against her forehead.

"I'm sorry," she whispered, thinking of Will, thinking of all the human beings who had just lost their lives because she had been so stupid and gullible. Her finger began to squeeze the trigger, but stopped when her thoughts turned to Stephen. What would become of him if she did this, if she took the coward's way out?

The gun dropped to the floor.

She threw herself onto the bed and curled into a ball, holding her stomach as if to contain the agony that threatened to set her off like a bomb. Her com rang, and she ignored it. Perhaps it was her mother. What was she calling for? To sympathize? To congratulate her on a job well done? Whatever the reason, she couldn't bear the thought of hearing the woman's voice.

But what if she had news of Will? Hero frantically moved to answer the call, and saw that it wasn't her mother after all. She clicked it on.

"Hero, it's Sonja. Listen, I need your help. I couldn't get ahold of anyone else."

How could Howard be calling her? Her communicator should be offline. Suddenly Hero remembered that the woman always carried an emergency hyperspace transceiver on her ship. She'd noticed it while conducting repairs on the Death's Echo. "I'm listening."

"Something really strange has happened. Our ships, the whole damned squadron, have just cut out on us. They're completely unresponsive. We were scheduled to receive some kind of security update, but it's almost like the thing contained some kind of virus, or…hell, I don't know. That should be impossible, right?"

Hero opened her mouth to speak, but no words came out. She wasn't sure what to say, what to do. She just stood there in silence.

"Hero? You there?"

"I'm here."

"Can you do anything? Find out what's going on and get back to me?"

"There's no time for that. Listen to me carefully. I want you to plug your computer's interface cable into the transceiver."

"Why?"

"Just do it. You need to trust me. You don't have much time."

A few moments of silence passed. "Okay, done."

Hero struggled to stay calm while bringing up the Death's Echo's security code on her computer. Once the code had been transmitted, she followed it with the deletion code for the virus, and waited nervously to see if it would work.

Moments later, Sonja responded. "I don't know what you did, but she's coming back online. You're really something, you know that, Hero?"

"Do the other ships have emergency transceivers, too?"

"Yeah."

"Listen, the Nazerazi could arrive at any moment. You need to retransmit everything I'm sending you to the other Red Tails. Tell them to do what you did."

"Okay. Hey, these are the security codes for every ship in our squadron."

"That's right. I'm sending you the deletion code for the virus. You need to hurry. It's your only chance."

"But how do you have these codes? Why would you have a deletion code? WHAT HAVE YOU DONE, HERO?"

—NOW—

"Hold on a minute. Maybe there's another way," Jace said, stopping Hero in front of the door.

"No. There is no other way. Not now. He's running out of time."

"You really think she'd just let him suffocate like that?"

Hero placed her hand upon his right shoulder and her head on his left. "In her mind, I'd be the one letting him die, not her. She doesn't think like other people. She's crazy."

"We'll go together, then. Armed. She won't be able to take us both." He wasn't all that sure of it, however. And he knew it came through in his voice.

"No. There's still a way that you and Stephen can get out of this." She pulled his head into hers, so that her tears ran down his neck. "I know you don't want me to die. And believe me, that's not what I want either, but we can't do anything to jeopardize the life of my son."

Jace's heart was pounding. He said nothing.

"Promise me." She pulled him in so tightly that it hurt. "Even if it means letting me go. Promise me that his life, and yours, come before mine."

Jace had never felt more helpless. He had to do something to save them all, but what? There must be something. "I promise you," he whispered. "That I'm going to save you both."

"NO!" She slapped him, hard. "If you love me, then

promise me that you'll take care of him for me. I can't lose him, too. You have to understand that. I do love you, Jace. But I can't lose him, too. Not after everything I've been through. Everything I've done."

She began to go limp. As if the last bit of energy was being used up within her. As if her will was water in a cup, being poured upon the sand. He squeezed her tightly, smelled her hair, and kissed her wet neck.

"All right. I promise."

She began to cry harder than ever, but a smile of relief spread across her face.

I will save you, he thought. *Somehow*.

"We need to go." She took his hand and opened up the door. The short walk to the cockpit seemed surreal, like something from a waking nightmare. Jace franticly ran through scenarios in his head. How could he save her? What could he do?

When they reached the door, it slid open. Sonja Howard was sitting there waiting for them, the screaming, but silent child upon her lap.

Hero leapt for him, but Sonja held up her gun. "Wait. Just one more thing, and then you can say your goodbyes. I want to know why you did it."

Hero froze. A terrified guilt appeared on her face, as if she were standing before God searching for an answer for all her sins.

"I…I already told you why. But I never meant for all those people to die. I didn't know. You have to…."

"I have to what? Believe you? I do. I believe you when you say you didn't know that Earth's fleet would be decimated. You didn't know, because you aren't capable of committing such acts. You aren't capable of doing what needs to be done. That's why your superiors were able to manipulate you, you poor, stupid girl. But does any of that make you less responsible for all those dead men and women?"

Hero stood in silence for a moment, locking eyes with the woman before her. "No," she answered. "They died because of me. All of them."

Jace couldn't believe what he was hearing. Could Hero be the one responsible for the fall of Earth's fleet? How could it even be possible? He gaped at her searchingly, not knowing what to feel. She looked so utterly broken. Whatever she'd done, she hadn't known what would come of it, that much was clear.

"Whatever she did," Jace said, turning to Sonja, "it's all over now. Killing her won't change anything."

"I know that," Howard snapped. "But she needs to pay for her crimes. Look at her. Even *she* knows that. You can see it in her eyes."

Jace looked back at her. Then he moved to stand in front of her. "All I see when I look at her is the woman I love."

"Then maybe you aren't looking hard enough," Sonja told him. "But, we digress, and this little guy is running out of air. So tell me, Hero, why did you do it? And I'm not talking about the virus. I get that. What I want to know is, why did you save *me*?"

Hero continued to stare into Sonja's eyes, but something in her face changed. A bit of the fear and guilt seemed to melt away, and something not unlike love appeared.

Sonja's face was getting redder by the second. "I watched my companions die! The Nazerazi fighters showed up before I could pass on the virus deletion code you sent me. I fought to hold them off, watching my fellow officers, MY FRIENDS, get picked off like they were nothing more than a bunch of damned space junk. But not me. I lived. I kept fighting. And when my ship was damaged to the point when I was no longer a threat, they left me there adrift. Maybe it was some kind of punishment. I had taken out three of them before they abandoned me there to die. So, I'm going to ask you one more time. WHY did you save me?"

"Because…" Hero stumbled, wiping the tears from her eyes. "Because you were the only one I *could* save. And because…because you were my friend."

Sonja glared back at her for a few moments, and Jace thought he caught the glimpse of an escaping tear before she turned her head away. "Come get your son."

Hero rushed to the boy, snatched him away as gently as she could, and sank to the floor a few feet away. She held him on her lap and entered the Death's Echo's security code into the helmet. It worked. The self-adjusting seal retracted and the thing fell to the floor with a clacking thud.

You can do it, Jace told himself, cautiously creeping toward Howard. *You can get that gun, just go slowly.* She wasn't even looking at him, but somehow knew what he was doing. "Don't." She waved the gun toward Hero. "Over there. Sit down next to your girlfriend."

He forced himself down onto the grating beside her.

Hero smiled at him before looking back at her son. "You're okay now, my love. You're going to be all right."

The boy stared up into her eyes as she rocked him. He calmed a bit, but continued to weep.

"Mama," he muttered, miserably, touching her cheek.

"That's right. I'm here now. You're going to be fine." She continued to shoosh him, holding him close and running her hand along his face. "I'm so sorry that I lost you, but I'm here now."

"Hero," Sonja said, nearly in a whisper, "do you know what this is?"

Hero looked up to see a small rectangular object in Sonja's hand, and shook her head.

"It's a device sometimes used by undercover operatives and their handlers. It's a tracking device. Nano-transmitters are injected into the agent's blood stream. They're virtually undetectable, unless you know what you're looking for, which is why you never even suspected they were inside you."

Hero turned back to her child and continued to gaze

into his beautiful blue eyes. He was looking more like Will, more like a little boy than a baby, but she could still see her own face there as well.

"I had a friend serving aboard the Claymore inject the transmitters into your bloodstream for me. You may remember him. Doctor Hanson? The man has been hitting on me every chance he gets for the last five years. Jumped at the opportunity to help me out."

"But the last time Hanson treated me was just a few days after the invasion. If you knew where I was all this time, why did you wait to come get me? Why didn't you just come for me then?"

Sonja looked down at Stephen, who was now smiling up at his mother's worried face. "Because you saved me, and I always pay my debts. And like you said, you were my friend." She turned to Jace. "But now we're even. Are you willing to be responsible for the brat after his mother goes?"

Jace gritted his teeth. He wanted nothing more than to jump on her, but the only thing that would earn him was a blast in the chest.

"We already talked about it," Hero answered for him. "He is."

"Good. I'll give you six hours. After that, I destroy the nano-transmitters."

"What happens then?" Jace demanded.

The look on Sonja's face would have been enough, but she answered anyway. "You know what happens then. Now get the hell off my ship."

Hero handed Jace the baby, and rose to her feet. Then she led them to the door. For an instant, she turned back, as if to say something, but instead she took Stephen and headed toward the Shiv.

"How can you do this?" Jace said, turning back to Sonja. "You know what kind of person she is. She may have been tricked into working for the Nazerazi, but you know as well as I do that she'd never intentionally hurt anyone."

Sonja leaned back in her chair, and looked him deep in the eyes. She looked angry at first, and then sad. And then tired. "You still don't get it, do you, kid? Hero *wasn't* working for the Nazerazi."

—USTS Claymore
A Few Months Before—

"Dammit, Hero, answer me! How could you possibly have security access codes to the ships in this squadron? You're the one responsible for this?"

There wasn't any reason to deny it now. "Yes."

"Oh…oh my God. These reports…. THE ENTIRE FLEET IS BEING DESTROYED. Oh, God. They're coming."

Hero just sat there, listening to Sonja's desperate shrieks as she frantically tried to pass on the instructions to the other ships. She listened helplessly as Sonja engaged the Nazerazi attackers. She heard the cursing and screams as, one by one, the Red Tailed Hawks were targeted and destroyed. She listened until the only sounds left were the angry, heavy breaths coming from the captain of the Death's Echo. How was she still alive? She couldn't possibly have defeated them all. Hero longed to say something, but was at a loss for words.

The two women were silent for some time, each painfully aware of the other's presence. It was Sonja who finally broke the silence.

"Why? Tell me why you'd do this, Hero? Why would you betray your own people?"

The sadness in Howard's voice was as piercing as an ice cold knife.

"Sonja, I.... It wasn't supposed to be like this."

She was silent for a moment.

"Oh, yeah? Then tell me, how was it *supposed* to be, you fracking traitor?"

"Nobody was supposed to die." She struggled to keep her composure. "It was supposed to be a peaceful transition. They promised me that what I was doing would protect innocent lives."

"What did they offer you?" Howard demanded with venom in her voice. "What did they give you to betray your own people, to lie to yourself about what you were doing? Was it worth becoming a traitor?"

"I'm no traitor."

Howard laughed disgustedly. "No? Tell me, Hero, what would you call a woman who betrays her own people to join an invading army? To work for the fracking NAZERAZI?"

Hero was silent for a few moments. She had nothing left to lose, she knew that now. "I haven't been working for the Nazerazi, Sonja. I *am* a Nazerazi."

Despite everything that had happened, she felt a small amount of relief in saying it. The lie, the masquerade she'd been living for so long was finally over. None of it mattered anymore. And perhaps this woman, this person who'd become at least in some small way a friend, would understand what she'd done; why she had done it, if only a little.

"Sonja? Are you there?"

The silence that followed seemed to bear the weight of an eternity.

"I'm coming for you," Sonja finally answered before clicking off her transceiver.

Hero sunk down to the floor. She had never felt more broken or alone.

—NOW—

The remaining hours of flight to Omicron Five were the most agonizing that Jace had ever experienced. The waiting, the despair, the tiny seedling of hope in his heart that Howard would change her mind and decide to show forgiveness. The helplessness of it all was the most maddening thing of all. Were these things, the helplessness and anxiety, the same emotions Hero had felt while fretting over the whereabouts of her missing son? They must have been, and he understood her, sympathized with her and loved her more that ever because of it.

Docking orders came in over the com, and Jace set the Shiv down upon the assigned landing pad and powered down the ship. He opened the hatch to find a waiting attendant.

"Welcome to Omicron Five," the chubby young woman said happily. "Can I be of any assistance?" She reached up to tickle Stephen's belly, which was sticking out beneath his shirt.

Jace nodded, grateful for the offer of help, even if it was the young woman's job. "I've got a…a body that I could use a hand with. Have you got a mortician or something around here?"

The girl's expression changed to one of genuine concern. "Oh. I'm sorry to hear that. Shepherd Moyer usually takes care of things like this, unless you have any objections. Would you like me to go and fetch him for you?"

"Please. Try to hurry, okay?"

"Absolutely," the girl said, rushing off.

Jace unstrapped Stephen, exited the ship, and took a

look around. Then he walked the short distance to a grassy area and knelt to set the boy down. Perhaps some fresh air and colorful reminders of life would do them both some good.

"I wouldn't do that if I were you," a woman told him as she walked by. She pointed to a sign with a variety of different creatures on it. One of the few that Jace recognized was a German Shepherd. "People walk their pets in there. Kinda nasty. There's a nice little playground over that hill right over there."

"Thanks," Jace told her, doing his best to force a grin. *How am I going to do this?* he thought. *I don't know the first thing about taking care of a kid.*

He walked back to the Shiv and sat down under the hatch, where it was rather hot, and the mechanical, oily smells of the landing pad wafted back over them. Stephen began to fuss.

"I know pal. It's been a hell of a day, hasn't it?"

Stephen waved his arms toward the inside of the shuttle. "Mama?" he whimpered. "Mama?"

Jace held onto the boy tightly, knowing that his mother was not going to come. The two of them struggled together uncomfortably until two men appeared, hurrying toward them. One of them was older, with salt and pepper hair and a kind face. He wore the brown and black robes of a Christian Shepherd. A younger man, perhaps an assistant, strode along beside him.

"I'm Shepherd Moyer. Peggy told me you required assistance."

Jace shook the man's hand and did his best to remain calm while explaining the situation, omitting the more sensitive details. Then he led the two men inside the shuttle where Hero's body rested upon the cot in back.

"She looks like an angel, resting there," the Shepherd told him. "I'm so sorry for your loss."

It was then that Jace began to weep. He'd told himself he wouldn't, not in front of strangers, but he couldn't hold it in. His mind kept turning to Hero's last few minutes of life. He'd sat there on the floor of the shuttle, holding onto her as if she were the most precious thing he'd ever laid hands upon. She nuzzled up into his arms, holding Stephen the same way that he was holding her.

"She told you, didn't she?" Hero asked, looking deep into his eyes. "Just before you walked away? She told you."

"Yeah."

"Do you hate me?"

Jace had never in his life been flooded with so many different feelings. Should he hate her for what she'd done? For who, or what she was? A Nazerazi, what had that even meant? She was human, wasn't she? She looked human, felt like and acted human. "Hate you? No, I don't think I do."

She was silent for a moment. "Do you still love me?"

Jace felt a tear escape to run down his cheek. "With all my heart."

"Good," she whispered, and her body seemed to relax in his arms.

"Don't let him forget me. Tell him how much I loved him. That I never stopped looking until we found each other again."

Jace nodded, and she smiled. He tried to smile back at her, and although he couldn't see whatever expression he'd managed to make, knew that he had failed.

She pulled him down for one last, gentle kiss, which seemed to express all the things that they wouldn't have time to say. Thank you for loving me, thank you for understanding, if only a little, and thank you for saving my son. The kiss said all those things, and as their lips parted, he knew it was saying goodbye, which was the most painful part of all.

Then, Hero turned her head back toward Stephen, and began to sing.

By the side of the pure crystal fountain
There is a lonely church yard nearby
There's a tombstone covered over with primroses
In the memory of a loved one passed away

Shall I ne'er see a more gentle mother
In the fields where the wild flowers grow
I am sorrowed for the loss I can't recover

Neath yon willow lies my gentle mother's love

The child was soon asleep, and Hero again cuddled her head upon Jace's breast as if to sleep herself. He'd never seen her look so calm, so at peace. It was if a great burden had finally been taken away from her.

Without warning, she dug her nails into his arm.

"Oh," she whimpered, as if something pained her. That was the last thing she ever said.

"My wife and daughter are on the way," the Shepherd said, reaching down to touch Hero's cheek. "You and I can take a walk while my wife prepares her for burial. And if you'd like, my daughter can watch your boy for a while. She's very good with children, and will keep a good eye on him."

Jace nodded. "I'd be grateful."

The woman and her daughter soon arrived, and the Shepherd spoke with them alone for a few moments while Jace waited outside. After that, the man led him out on a trail that winded behind the Safe Haven Trading Post to a clearing on the edge of the jungle, where a small, well-kept graveyard awaited them in the hollow.

"This is where we usually lay people to rest. It's a beautiful area, as you can see. But there's one other place I'd like to show you, and then you can decide where you'd rather place her."

Jace then followed him out past the side of the trading post to the cliffs overlooking the ocean.

"It's just up ahead," the Shepherd said, heading over the edge of the rock to a naturally formed path, which went along the side. The waves crashed threateningly against the crags far below, but there was plenty of room to walk along the trail where the holy man was leading him. "My daughter and I were out here exploring a few months ago when we found this place. Only a few of the locals know about it."

The path opened up onto a little flat area where a patch of grass and even a few flowers were growing. Jace couldn't remember seeing their variety before, but thought they looked something like Tiger-Lilies.

"Over here," the Shepherd said. He was standing near a small opening in the rock, holding a little flash light. He stooped down and disappeared inside, and once again, Jace followed. A dozen feet in, the passage opened up into a small cave, where veins of crystal glimmered through the surrounding rock.

"This is a special place. Your girl up there seems special, too. I thought you might want to place her at rest in here, but the choice is up to you."

"This is perfect. Thank you."

The Shepherd nodded. After that, they went back outside and discussed the remaining details.

Upon returning to the Shiv, Jace found Hero dressed in a modest but lovely blue dress. She was wearing more makeup than he'd ever seen on her before, but it wasn't too much. She was stunning, yet empty somehow. All traces of her tomboy persona were gone, and she now looked like she'd passed away while on her way to the ball.

The Shepherd smiled up at him kindly. "I've sent for some men to bring a casket. When they get here, we can proceed down to the cave. Would you like to go and change your clothes?"

He hadn't even thought of that. "Yes. I would. But I don't really have anything…." He thought he might panic. How could he attend Hero's burial looking like he'd just come from watching a baseball game? It would be disgraceful.

"The trading post should have something you might find more appropriate. Do you need any money?"

"Thank you, but no. I'll be back as soon as I can."

"Take your time, dear," the Shepherds wife told him. "She'll be in good hands until you return."

He rushed into the trading post and found a grey and black sports jacket and black pair of pants. It was the closest thing to a suit they had that fit him. He washed up, got dressed, and was about to head back to the ship when he suddenly thought of something.

Heading back to the jewelry counter, he picked out a wedding ring, which had two golden roses intertwined around a small diamond. It wasn't the most expensive piece by far, but Hero would have liked it. Then he picked out a gold chain, and put the ring on it.

Everyone was waiting for him when he got back to the ship, even the Shepherd's daughter had returned with Stephen, whom she had dressed in black pants, black socks, and a white button up shirt.

Curious bystanders stopped to watch as the small funeral procession moved toward the cliffs. The pallbearers proceeded cautiously over the edge and along the rock wall until reaching the grassy clearing, where the casket was set down, and the lid was opened. After that, the Shepherd said a few words, and his wife and daughter, along with another young man, sang an old hymn. Jace might have joined them, but he didn't know the words. He was then asked if he wanted to say anything.

"No. Not in front of everyone. But I do want to thank you all for being here. It means a lot."

"Please bow your heads with me," the Shepherd said, and closed with the Lord's Prayer.

They carefully carried the casket into the cave, and Jace asked for a few moments alone. When everyone was gone, he took the ring and chain out of his pocket, and gently lifted Hero's head to place it around her neck.

"I never got a chance to put this on your finger, but maybe you wouldn't mind wearing it like this. He kissed her cheek, which felt disturbingly cold, and gazed at her for a few long minutes.

A wave of guilt rushed over him, which was

accentuated by the distant sound of crashing waves, coming in through the cave opening. He was supposed to have saved her. What good was a man who couldn't even protect the woman he loved? "I'm sorry," he said. "But I won't forget my promise. I'll make sure that Stephen gets someplace safe, where I can keep an eye on him." He reached down to touch her hair one last time before lowering the lid. "Goodbye, Hero."

Once he was back outside, the other men helped him place large rocks in front of the entrance. Then the young man who'd helped sing the hymn handed Jace a paint pen.

He wrote-

HERE LIES HERO ANDERSON-CHANG
DIED FEBRUARY 2390
LOVING MOTHER
BEAUTIFUL HUMAN BEING

That night, Jace joined the Shepherd's family for dinner, though he couldn't bring himself to eat very much. He thanked them for their kindness and went out to the cliffs with Stephen, where he set up a tent, and lied down under the stars. It was a warm night, and a cool breeze was blowing in from the ocean. He listened as his own tent, and a few others that were scattered off in the distance, flapped beneath the breeze. It reminded him of the times his father took him camping as a child. The only thing missing was the sound of the wind blowing through the pine trees.

Stephen soon fell fast asleep, and as Jace lied there, gazing up at the stars, he felt strangely at peace. So much of the day's sorrow and grief seemed to be getting carried away by the breeze. It almost felt as if Hero was there with him. He arose, and made sure that Stephen was settled upon his blankets in the tent. Looking down on the child, who looked so much like his mother, Jace had a sudden surge of love and pity. What a horrible shame that he would never get a chance to know her, but at least he would know of the love she had for him. How she had been willing to give everything to make sure he was okay.

Lying down and settling himself in, Jace watched through the canvas wall of the tent as the final flames of his campfire flickered away into the night, leaving only burning embers to shine out in remembrance of the tiny blaze that had just passed away. They would linger for a while before turning gray, unless some wandering wind came to breathe new life into the flames, or carry a spark to resurrect the blaze in some unexpected, nearby place. Fire seemed to have an uncanny desire to carry on, and would do just that if you didn't watch it carefully.

Jace turned upon his back, his attention returning once again to the stars, which could be seen quite well through the thin, nearly transparent net of the tent.

They danced and sparkled before him, almost as if they were singing, and he found himself listening, hoping they might have something to say, hoping they might tell him that Hero was out there somewhere. That she was all right, that she was happy, and that her spirit had simply traveled on.

Again, he felt the sensation of her presence. It was as if she was there. He could feel her. He closed his eyes, and when he opened them again, he could see her, lying on her side next to him upon the blanket, smiling and gazing into his eyes longingly. But she looked somewhat different now. Her blonde hair, which had come to her shoulders, was now long, and intricately braided. She wore a long blue summer dress, not like the one she'd been buried in, this one was much simpler, and hugged her form with a modest elegance that he found intoxicating. Her gorgeous blue eyes sparkled with the orange flames of the fire that had reignited itself outside the tent, just as he thought it might. Those eyes looked like they hadn't shed a tear in years. *But why would they,* Jace thought, laughing to himself. The two of them had so much to be happy about.

"I love you," Hero said to him, snuggling down into his arms. "So very, very much."

"I love you, too," he told her, as the breeze bathed him with the smell of her hair.

She stretched up to place a gentle kiss upon the tip of his nose. "Promise me we'll always be together."

Jace released a satisfied sigh and squeezed her in close. "Always. No matter what."

Book 9

Spirited Away

—EARTH—

Nicodemus pushed himself from the ground to rise slowly upon his gnarled wooden cane. The utter darkness of the surrounding chamber was strangely peaceful and comforting after the plethora of images he'd just seen. The experience had been quite overwhelming, nearly too much for even his own, well-honed senses. He staggered toward the door, carefully taking one small step at a time. Some rest would be required before his journey began, that much was clear, but he could not put his departure off for long. He would need to act quickly before any more damage could be done.

Upon reaching the doorway, he placed his hand against the hard stone of the temple wall. It felt unusually cold, as it often did when he listened for so long. The phenomena did not mean that his surroundings were any colder than usual, but that he himself had a fever from the long hours spent in quiet meditation.

"Master," came a heavy voice, which echoed through the passageway toward him. "Let me assist you."

A few moments later a strong arm was secured around his waist, guiding him patiently along the path as his eyes adjusted to the firelight that flooded the halls.

"Thank you, my friend," Nicodemus said. "Help me to the well, won't you? I feel as dry as an old bone upon the desert sands."

As they approached their destination, the smell of moist air wafted past the reptilian's nostrils, giving him an even greater thirst. They entered the chamber to find two more Draconians waiting, who promptly rose to greet them. One handed Nicodemus a drinking bowl, which he gratefully accepted, and slowly drained, taking care not to spill even a drop.

"More?" the reptilian asked, whose name was Sobek.

"Please," Nicodemus said, as his head began to clear. He looked at the other Draconian standing before him, and smiled warmly. "Farwalker, my friend. And Sobek, is that you? Please forgive my being rude. It is good to see you both."

"We know how the visions cloud one's head," Farwalker told him, helping Nicodemus to sit upon a stone bench. "We have not mistaken your behavior for rudeness, have we Sobek? But tell me, why have you sent for us?"

Nicodemus received the bowl again and finished another refreshing draught. "There, that is much better. Thank you, old friend." He turned to Farwalker, frowning gravely. "My watch upon this world is coming to its end, I'm afraid. I find my age getting the best of me these days, but there are still a few things left to do." He arose again upon his staff, the cold drink of water having re-filled him with some vigor. "A temporal splintering event has occurred, and I must go and attempt to repair the effects."

Farwalker ran his large claws down the side of his scaly face. "A splintering? I too have sensed a disturbance while listening, but as of yet, I have failed to determine any cause for it. Do you believe this event is the causal occurrence? The origin?"

"I do not know," Nicodemus admitted. The fatigue in his raspy voice surprised even him. "I fear that the temporal waves surrounding this event have made listening very difficult. I have spent many long hours sifting through them. It has been like searching for one faint beacon on a vast, tempestuous ocean. However, I am confident that I am close to the source. This splintering must be corrected. If it does not clear the storm, then at least it will calm it a bit, and buy us time to continue our search." He placed his hand upon Farwalker's shoulder. "The time for my journey draws near. You must continue your training, and take up my office once I've departed."

Farwalker looked down toward the bubbling water of the well. "But master, I have not yet achieved the rank of Paladin. I cannot take your place here. I am not ready."

"You are ready when I say you are ready. And I say, you have been ready for several years. You still have much to learn, but your skills have come far enough for this. You are already more knowledgeable than I was when I stepped into this office. I will bestow the title of Paladin upon you tonight in the Garden of Departed Echoes."

They all sat in silence for a few moments, listening to the calming sounds of the bubbling water.

"Your words are kind, and I thank you for them, but please, listen to me now, and consider my words. If this disturbance that you speak of was not the causal event, then your skills will be required to continue the investigation. Tell me what needs to be done, and allow me to go on this journey in your stead."

Even as the younger reptilian was speaking, Nicodemus recognized the wisdom in his words. But the idea of sending Farwalker upon this journey greatly displeased him. Farwalker had a great future ahead of him as a Pneuma-Tal Paladin, and their people would need such leaders to guide them, especially in what could turn out to be such dark days ahead.

"No," he forced out. "I do not wish to send you upon this mission. This is not the reason I sent for you. I cannot ask this of you."

"You do not need to ask. This is what must be done. It is the wisest course of action; you know that as well as I. If this event is not the causal event, I do not have the necessary skills to look any further. I cannot replace you, Nicodemus, old master. I am many years away from doing that."

"Curse you to the desert, Farwalker. And curse my aged body, which is fading into the penalty of its years. My words about you are proven true. You are wise and brave. But perhaps you should give this some thought before you decide."

"The way forward is clear," Farwalker said. "No amount of thinking will change what must be done. We each know what role we must play, though neither of us likes it."

Nicodemus breathed out a low, mournful hiss. "Come then, there is no time to waste. I must show you what needs to be done."

"But shouldn't you rest a while first?"

"There will be time for that soon enough," the old reptilian assured him. "Come, we must listen together. Sobek, prepare Farwalker's things for his departure."

The reptilian bowed, and hurried away.

Farwalker accompanied Nicodemus back to the chamber upstairs, where he allowed the flood of starlight to fall upon them from the opening above.

Several hours later, once Nicodemus was convinced the younger Draconian's instructions were clearly understood, they left the temple and walked to the nearby Garden of Departed Echoes, a place where the community gathered for special occasions and ceremonies. Nicodemus smiled to see the vast crowd that had already gathered there, eager to witness a ceremony that most Draconians never had the opportunity to see.

He walked up the steps to a small platform in the center of the garden, and once the crowd had been hushed, began to recite the required verses from the Holy Collection of Scrolls.

Before he had finished speaking, Farwalker appeared on the platform before him, as if materializing out of thin air. Nicodemus was pleased. If his young friend had been seen by anyone before reaching his current position, he would have failed the test, and would have been required to wait another two Draconian years before attempting the walk again. But Nicodemus had reserved no doubts. He had been honest when speaking the young reptilian's praises, and knew he would perform well. Upon finishing his recital of the required verses, Nicodemus retrieved the object resting behind him. It was long, and wrapped in a red, velvety cloth.

The people stared in awe as the old master unwrapped the sword, which they all recognized instantly. It was a relic of legend, and until that moment, many of them hadn't believed the thing even truly existed. Its blade was white, fashioned from the tooth of the greatest specimen of one of Draconia's mightiest creatures, a Ghost Dragon from the icy mountains of the south continent. It was said that any Paladin ordained with that blade would forever carry a ghostly echo of it along with him. It would be a weapon that no one else could see, with the exception of another Pneuma-Tal Paladin, or anyone unlucky enough to find himself dying upon it.

Nicodemus raised the sword into the air, and carefully lowered it to each side of Farwalker's head. Then he rested its blade upon his forehead, and whispered a few more verses.

Farwalker rose, and Nicodemus handed him the sword. He swung it around through the air in a figure eight pattern until it was moving so fast that a white, shimmering blur was all that could be seen above him.

The surrounding Draconians began to thud their tales upon the ground, creating a thunderous series of booms that echoed mightily throughout the vast underground cavern.

Once they were finished, and the ceremony complete, the crowd broke out in cheers, and as Nicodemus led the newly ordained Paladin back to the temple, many excited bystanders rushed up to greet him. *If they knew he would be leaving us so soon,* Nicodemus thought to himself, *their hearts would be full of sorrow, just as my own is. But I do not have the heart to tell them. Not tonight.*

They entered the main chamber of the temple, where Sobek and a handful of attendants awaited.

"Are you ready to depart?" Nicodemus asked.

"Delaying my journey would do no good," Farwalker told him. "I will go now, while I still draw strength from the encouragement of our people. Their spirit flows through my heart like life-giving blood."

Nicodemus embraced him. "Journey well, my friend. And remember, keep straight to the path I have shown you, until your mission is complete. Do not become distracted by the things you will see. Do not wander, to the right or to the left."

"Listen for me," Farwalker said. "I will speak with you again before completing my walk." Then he dropped to his knees, picked up the long dagger that Sobek had placed there for him, and with one determined thrust, ran it through his heart.

Nicodemus reached down to help Sobek guide Farwalker's lifeless body to the floor. "Journey safely, my dear, beloved friend."

—BLEEDING STAR INITIATIVE COMMAND

CENTER—

"Boreas, you in here?" Galin asked, sticking his head into the dimly lit chamber.

"Yes, Captain, right over here. Watch your step. I have several large cables running along the floor. I should have had the patience to run them more safely."

Once the door slid shut behind him, it took several moments for Galin's eyes to adjust. "Thanks for the warning," he said, stepping carefully, though his attention was drawn to the middle of the room, which was lit up with an expansive star map. The image was flickering in and out of view.

"So, this is the celestial cartography chamber. What section of space are we looking at?"

"Your guess is as good as mine," Boreas said. "I don't read Nexan, and I have not yet interfaced this database with the central computer."

"You sound like a lizard who's been working too hard. Why don't you come take a walk with me, I've got something interesting to show you."

Boreas cocked his head in the way he always did when he couldn't tell if someone had just told a joke. He set down the circuitry he was working on, and walked to Galin. "How are the upgrades on the Katara coming along?"

"Just finished up with the engine this evening. Got a few diagnostics to run first thing in the morning, and if everything checks out, we'll be on our way."

"I'm glad to hear everything's gone to schedule," Boreas said, following him into the hallway.

"I just hope it was all worth it. If we don't get back to that planet on time, a lot of people are going to lose their lives. That Genesis Torpedo is going to wipe out every molecule of life on Necron."

"I am fascinated at how often the greatest instruments of science have been used as history's most lethal weapons. In fact, I find myself wondering if the beings that created this station fell into some such trap that led to their own demise."

"Well, I suppose anything's possible. Once one starts reflecting on all this space-time mumbo jumbo all kinds of theories crop up. Most of 'em are like something out of those old sci-fi novels Peter used to read. But, pretty much everyone agrees that messing with things such as time and space can get more than a little dangerous."

Boreas curled his lips in a grin, revealing long, sharp teeth that would have sent anyone who didn't know him running toward the hills. "Agreed. I'm going to miss my conversations with you, Captain. I must admit, in the beginning I wasn't entirely sure you had an advanced level of intelligence. You have a rather colloquial way of stating things. However, I am now convinced I was wrong. You can be quite eloquent and concise when you wish to be."

Galin scratched his head. "Uh, thanks? One thing's

for sure, Boreas, you are an unfailing charmer."

"Thank you."

Galin grinned. "I think you're going to have quite a time on this station, putting the puzzle-pieces of this mystery back together. Kanbun told me there are sections of this place he hasn't even been able to get into yet."

"Yes, he told me the same. He was hoping that I might be able to gain access to areas that appear to have been sealed off by Draconians. Two doors that he's shown me were sealed off by the Pneuma-Tal. I'm afraid I won't be much help gaining access to places such as those. As I explained in the tunnels back on Earth, if the Pneuma-Tal don't want any intruders, entry is virtually impossible."

"Heck, you almost make it sound like magic."

"Do I?"

"Well, I reckon you're the best lizard for the job, time being. One thing I've learned over the years is that every problem has a solution, you just need to hunker down and find it."

Boreas clicked his nails together. "Ah, yes. I see. I shall hunker down, then." His fangy grin was one of mischief. "If only my people had learned this trick several thousand years ago. The Pneuma-Tal would have been powerless to guard their secrets."

"And to think, here we are parting company just when I'm getting so good at reading Draconian facial expressions, and you're getting so good at sarcasm." Galin clapped him on the shoulder. "It's just down this passageway to the left."

He led his friend into a large chamber with murals painted across the walls. The murals ran from floor to ceiling, and down the entire length of the room. There had to have been thousands of species and races depicted, in scenes that streamed seamlessly into one other, linking worlds together as a children's book might link landscapes.

The center of the room was empty, which seemed wrong somehow. Perhaps it was because the place felt like a museum, but one where all the displays and artifacts had been taken away to be cleaned.

"Fascinating," Boreas said, examining the wall. His voice echoed through the chamber. "Could all of these beings and worlds be real? Or is some of this simply the imagination of the artist?"

"Or artists'," Galin corrected. "Who knows? I did find a section over there which I found particularly interesting." He pointed, and led the reptilian to one of the far walls in the room. "I recognize a lot of the peoples depicted here." He pointed up.

Boreas examined the mural. There were many alien races in the painting that he did not recognize, but just as many others that he did. "Yes, this appears to depict our section of the galaxy." He hissed excitedly. "There. Do you see? Draconians in the jungle of my home world.

These are gardening, and just there, a group of hatchlings preparing for their first hunt."

"I see them," Galin nodded with a grin. "You notice anything odd about this section of the painting? Look closely."

Boreas stared back at the image in front of him. Of course, why hadn't he seen it sooner? "The images, they appear to be moving. It's like watching the waves of an ocean from a great distance overhead."

Galin nodded. "I knew you'd see it quickly. Took me a while, but then, you're always bragging about how you lizards have better eyesight."

"Fascinating. And you're correct; the movement seems to be limited to this section around our home worlds. It grows more calm the further you look out, and then stops moving completely."

"That's not all." Galin reached up and lightly touched a section of the mural in front of him, a section that wasn't moving, and then showed the tips of his fingers to Boreas. Nothing was there. Boreas seemed to get the idea, and touched a section that appeared to be moving. Looking at his finger, he found paint.

"Paint's still wet," Galin said.

Boreas grimaced. "What does it mean?"

"Don't know. I guess that's for you to find out while I go play shuttle pilot. Looks like you've got one more mystery to solve."

The Draconian remained silent, and continued to gaze

ahead at the painting.

"I guess I over-estimated my ability to read Draconian facial expressions. Can't really tell what you're thinking."

Boreas turned to him. "I'm thinking…that this scares me."

—DEEP SPACE
EN ROUTE TO ZETA RETICULAN—

"I never knew space could be so boring," David said, gazing off into the emptiness before them. "My dad's stories were always exciting. This whole trip has been nothing but blackness and stars, blackness and stars. When's something exciting gonna happen?"

"I'm not bored," William Marshal answered. "In fact, I've found this entire experience quite fascinating. Sharing my thoughts with you, and hearing your own has been a very enlightening study on the way humans think. Though I still don't understand why you insist on the two of us speaking out loud. As I've stated, it serves no practical purpose and is a waste of energy."

"So what? You've got plenty of energy, it's not like you're going to run out. Thinking everything inside your head makes me feel weird. This seems more normal."

"Define the parameters of 'normal.'"

"You ask too many questions. It's like talking to a

fracking baby."

"I apologize. However, my last statement was technically a command, not a question, grammatically speaking."

"Can't you just be quiet for a while?"

"Affirmative."

David stared back out at the stars again. He felt so cold, so alone. Even as such sensations passed through his mind, he felt his emotionless comrade strive to analyze them. The whole experience was maddening. He'd never felt so intruded upon and yet so completely alone.

"William, I'm sorry," David said, instantly regretting his own thoughts. William was a good friend, and the last thing David wanted to do was upset him.

"Remember, David, I have no feelings. You have neither said, nor thought anything that could give me offense."

"Well, I'm sorry anyway, okay?" He wanted to change the subject. "Can you tell me another story?"

"Affirmative. Have you heard the one about the Princess and the Pea?"

"That's a kid story. I want something with murder, or sex. Or maybe both."

"The elements of such a story would not be considered appropriate for a human child of your age and cultural upbringing."

"Come on, please?"

"I shall see what I can do." The android searched his databases for something the boy might find acceptable. "Have you ever heard the story of Romeo and Juliet?"

"My sister had two hamsters that she named Romeo and Juliet, but then found out they were both boys, so she changed Juliet's name to Jabber, cause he had black over one eye and she thought he looked like a boxer."

"That is an interesting tale, although it wasn't the story of Romeo and Juliet I was referring to."

"I know that. I'm not stupid."

"I did not mean to imply that you were."

"Whatever, just tell me the story."

"Would you like to hear it in the form of a play, or a novel?"

"Novel, I guess."

"Would you like to hear it in modern English, or the original Elizabethan?"

"English. I don't know any Lizabethean."

"Would you like to hear it in my voice, or the voice of—. Well, this is interesting."

"I see it too." David could barely make out the twinkling form in the distance, which had just popped up on William Marshall's scanners. "Is it a ship?"

"Possibly, although we'd have to move in closer to be sure."

"Can we? Please? At least it'd give us something to do for a while."

"It isn't too far off our course. I suppose a small

detour wouldn't hurt. However, we are still approximately three weeks away from your sister's first possible location. We can not allow ourselves to become distracted."

"I know. I want to get to Sarah more than anything, but I kind of feel like I'm losing my mind. I can tell how curious you are about that ship. And it is a ship, I can see that now. It's not supposed to be out here, is it?"

"I could not hope to guess the intentions of the ship's crew," William said, "but some would consider its presence in this region of space rather perplexing. Especially since it is simply stopped in the middle of nowhere."

"Maybe it's somebody who needs our help," David said, hoping for an adventure, hungry for anything that might make him feel a little bit alive again.

"Perhaps it is," William agreed. "Or it could be a trap, someone lying in wait to attack any unsuspecting rescuers."

David could sense that William didn't really believe that. He was just attempting to play along, trying to encourage his excitement by increasing the sense of danger. David was grateful for the effort.

"I know you don't really believe that."

"Well, it is possible, though I would estimate the odds to be only about .0072 percent likely."

"Whatever. Even if it was a trap, you'd be more than a match for them. Let's just get over there and check it out, okay?"

"Agreed," the android said, boosting his speed.

Finally, David was going to see something more interesting than blackness and stars, at least he hoped so.

—OMICRON FIVE—

Jace approached the apartment door and held up his hand to knock. Changing his mind, he lowered it. Then he raised it again. Then he lowered it. Stephen giggled, apparently taking his guardian's indecisive actions as some kind of game. Then an even bigger smile spread across the boy's face, and Jace lifted his eyes to see Abigail, the shepherd's daughter, making faces through the window and scrunching up her hand in a wave. The girl then caught his gaze and pointed over to the door, letting him know she was going over to let them in. There was no turning back now.

The teenage girl pulled the door open and caught Stephen up in her arms; he instantly began to bounce up and down excitedly. "Come on in, Mr. Chang. My Ma and Pa are just gettin' cleaned up. They've been out working in the garden all afternoon."

"Thanks."

"Can I get you a glass of water or somthin'?"

"That'd be great."

The girl gave him a warm smile and headed off into

the kitchen, with Stephen as a happy stowaway.

What a sweet young girl, and so beautiful. She was going to make some lucky man very happy one day. It made Jace wonder if he'd ever find another girl as special as Hero, and immediately he regretted the thought. It felt too much like betrayal. Hell, her body wasn't even cold yet, it had only been four days. Thoughts such as these were the least of his worries, however. Even if such thoughts were a betrayal, at least they were rational. At least they were sane; grounded in reality.

Jace tried not to think at all as he sat on the living room couch and waited for his water. He was tired of thinking, of trying to rationalize and reason out all the things that were happening. He was just about to doze off when Abigail reappeared.

"My Ma just made a pitcher of fresh lemonade. I thought you might like that instead." She handed him a tall, icy glass.

"Even better. Thanks."

The girl nodded and smiled, and then sat on the floor with the baby, pulling out a little box of toys from beneath the nearest end table. Jace could see the joy in her face as she began to play with him.

"You really like kids, don't you?"

"Yeah, I love the little rug-rats. And this is my favorite age. They're old enough to play games and communicate some simple things, but still too little to give you any lip. And look how happy he is just to get a bit of attention. Hand over a few simple little trinkets and he thinks he's in heaven. This is the very best age of all."

"I'll have to take your word for it. I haven't been around too many kids."

"Oh, I have. I've worked with all kinds of little ones at my pa's congregation. Seen all kinds of parents, too. I can tell you're going to do just fine. You've got a lot of love to give."

"I hope you're right. You're going to be an awesome mother, that's for sure. You seem to have some crazy skills with kids."

Her face went red and she smiled at him shyly. "Thanks."

A few moments later, the shepherd and his wife came in. Jace stood to greet them. The shepherd offered his hand and Jace took it.

"So glad you could make it tonight, Jace. It's good to see you."

"You, too." He held out his hand to Ruth-Ann, the shepherd's wife.

"Don't be ridiculous." She hugged him fiercely and kissed him on the cheek. "I hope you came hungry, young man."

He hadn't had much of an appetite lately, but he didn't want to come off rude. "Always." He mustered the best grin he could manage.

She patted him on the shoulder, winked at her daughter, and headed for the kitchen.

Shepherd Moyer took him by the shoulder and led him out the back door, where the residents of the apartment building had created a community garden. A number of brightly colored flowers were scattered about, but most of the plants were tended to provide fresh fruits and vegetables.

"Is this where you and your wife were just working?"

The shepherd nodded. "Digging in the dirt can be surprisingly therapeutic. Have you ever tried your hand at it?"

"Not really. I grew up in the city, and there's not much opportunity on a spaceship."

The Shepherd laughed. "I suppose you have a point. So, you wanted to talk to me about something?"

Jace let out a long, measured sigh. This was the moment he'd been dreading. He wasn't very good at this sort of thing, talking about his feelings, but he feared he was literally going insane, and wasn't sure where else to turn. Heavy breathing betrayed his discomfort and nervousness, as did, or so he imagined, the look on his face.

"Take your time, son. I don't bite, you know."

Jace struggled to steady his breath. "I think I'm going crazy. I mean, honest to God, certifiably crazy."

The Shepherd nodded patiently, but didn't speak.

"The night Hero died, after her funeral, I set up a tent

out there on the cliffs. I don't really know why. I just...it just made me feel close to her somehow, like we were looking at the stars together or something. I know it sounds stupid."

"I don't think it sounds stupid in the least."

Jace cleared his throat. "Well, later that night, after Stephen had gone to sleep, she...she came to me."

"Hero? In a dream, you mean?"

He shook his head. "No. I mean, in the flesh. She came to me. I saw her, just like I'm seeing you. I touched her. We...we even made love."

The Shepherd raised his eyebrows, but not unkindly.

"Everything was different, though. We were married. We'd been married for quite some time, over a year I think. That's what I got from what she was saying. When I acted like I didn't know what she was talking about, which I didn't, she laughed it off like I was playing some kind of joke on her."

The Shepherd was silent for a few moments, obviously at a loss for words. "Well, this certainly is a new one for me. What did you do then?"

"We talked, I held her. We fell asleep together. Then in the morning she was gone." Jace's eyes began to swell with tears. It embarrassed him, and he wiped them away. "I'm telling you, it was real. I wasn't dreaming. It wasn't just some kind of vision. It actually happened."

"And was it just that first night, or...."

"No. I thought I'd just imagined the whole thing.

You know, grief or whatever. But it happened again last night. She showed up just after Stephen fell asleep. She even held him in her arms, and told me that the two of us had made the most beautiful baby boy in the world, and that next time maybe we'd have a girl, just as beautiful." He held his hands against the sides of his head, as if it might explode if he didn't hold it together.

"I need to know why this is happening. I need to know that I'm not losing my mind."

The shepherd nodded once again. Jace could tell by the look in his eyes that he was genuinely concerned, and it made him feel a little better. He'd half expected to be tossed out on his ear, or perhaps even have someone called to come and restrain him.

"I have a few ideas. First of all, why don't you stay here tonight? We have an extra room, set aside for guests. It might help you remove yourself from the situation, clear your head a bit?"

Jace shrugged. "Maybe. I don't want to impose, though. That's not why I came here."

"I know that. We'd be honored to have you as a guest. Besides, Abigail can play with the baby, and give you some alone time to think things through. Losing the one you love and inheriting a child all at once, I can only imagine how confusing and frightening it all must be."

Jace looked out across the garden and shook his head. "You can say that again. To be honest, confused and frightened don't even begin to cover it. Thanks for understanding."

"Of course. I have one other idea that might help. I'm quite friendly with Dr. Mason, the resident physician. He can run a paternity test for you. Show you physical proof that you're not the boy's father. It would just be one more thing to keep you grounded in reality, since your mind seems to be merciless in playing tricks on you. What are your thoughts on that?"

"Sure. I mean, it might help. Definitely couldn't hurt."

"I might be able to lure the old sawbones over here for dinner, or at least for desert. He loves Ruth-Ann's cooking."

"Okay, sounds great." Jace was already feeling somewhat better. It felt good to get everything off his chest. It didn't diminish the grief, but it did sate the despair, and the feeling of being alone. Even crazy people needed to have friends, he supposed.

"You don't know any psychiatrists do you?"

—DEEP SPACE—

William Marshall alighted gracefully upon the hull of the vessel. Its shields fizzled and cracked, making David laugh as a hot, tickling sensation ran over the robot's body. The android matched his shield's frequency to align with the ship's, and the blanket of tempestuous energy surrounding them merged with his own, settling back down with a pleasant hum.

William put his hands on his hips and gazed down for a closer look. This was a small rectangular ship, not much bigger than a shuttle, although it didn't match any shuttle he had in his databanks. For its size, the thing had impressive weapon and shielding systems, but the design had obviously not been developed with battle and maneuverability in mind, so it wasn't a fighter, not primarily. It was, in fact, not a match for any of the vessels he had on file.

"Maybe it's a secret model," David suggested. "It wouldn't be listed if it was. Nobody would even know about it."

"Its design and systems layout is consistent with many other human ships, although the technology appears to be more advanced than what is commonly found, even among higher grade military crafts. Although I must admit, I am a bit perplexed about what this ship was designed for." William adjusted the frequency modulation of his scanners to penetrate the hull. "The life support system still appears to be active, though I am only reading one faint life signature on board, a human female. It appears that your original theory may have been correct, this is most likely someone who needs our help."

"All right, a damsel in distress. How do we get in? You can't just tear through the hull. That would kill the woman inside, right?"

"Correct. That would be a highly inadvisable course of action." William's feet clanked heavily as he walked toward the back of the ship. "We may be able to access the engine compartment from the rear thruster maintenance panel, and then re-pressurize said compartment before entering through the service hatch inside the ship."

David knew the plan would work. He watched William's thought process as the entire strategy was outlined in his head, down to the removal and re-insertion of each screw.

"This ship's propulsion system is quite interesting," William said as he worked his way into the engine compartment. "I'd like to study it further to determine exactly how it works."

"Maybe later. We don't have time for that now."

"Agreed," the android said, opening up the control panel to pressurize the compartment. "Still, part of my protocol is to make note of those things that merit further investigation, once my primary mission has been accomplished."

"If you say so." David was amazed at the speed and precision with which William performed his task. He knew exactly what needed to be done and executed each action in sequence one after the other. It would have taken a human three times as long, even if he was trying to hurry. On top of that, David knew that this wasn't even close to being as fast as William could work. It was kind of like a walk in the park to him.

Once they were in, William pulled himself through the access panel and stood to look around. A few dim lights were flickering along the floor, and the place felt cold and unusually moist.

"The environmental controls appear to be malfunctioning. There were no signs of battle damage on the outer hull, perhaps an internal systems malfunction has occurred."

Even though David heard the voice in William's head as the android spoke, he wasn't really listening. All he cared about was finding the woman, which he did almost instantly. "Look, there she is!" David said, pointing up toward the cockpit.

Her body was sprawled on the floor near the pilot's chair.

"Let's go check on her," David urged, moving William's body forward.

The android nearly tripped over his own feet.

"Sorry about that, I forgot."

William had allowed the boy to take control of his functions on occasion, but whenever he tried to do it without asking for permission, or at least giving some kind of warning, the control systems became confused, trying to execute two sets of orders at the same time.

"Humans often do when they become emotional," William said, scanning the woman's body as they approached. "Human female, approximately thirty five years of age. Her body appears to be in shock, but I can detect no signs of physical trauma."

"Turn her over so we can have a better look."

William gently slid his hands beneath her and guided the woman over onto her back. When David saw her face, a surge of emotions shot through William's circuits like a dry, summer clap of lightning.

"MOM? The boy yelled. "IT'S MY MOM. BUT HOW DID SHE GET ALL THE WAY OUT HERE?"

William's body began to shake. He'd not yet experienced such strong emotions from the boy, and his systems had never reacted in such a fashion.

"David, try to calm down. My circuits weren't designed for this, and they may become damaged if exposure continues."

The confusion that set in next was nearly as strong as the excitement.

"I…I don't get it," David said. "This isn't my mom. But…she looks so much like her. Almost exactly like her. But, her nose isn't quite right, and…and her boobs are too big; way too big. Other than that, she looks just like her."

The woman opened her eyes to gaze up at them, groggily. For a few seconds, there was only confusion, but a moment later a smile dawned, and she reached up to touch the android's cold face. She looked so happy; so relieved.

"David, are you in there?" she said, though it took some effort.

As soon as she'd spoken, David knew who the woman was. But that was impossible.

William immediately scanned her to confirm the boy's thoughts. He was right. The woman was Sarah Winchester, his sister.

"David? You are in there, aren't you? I've…I've found you." She struggled to push herself up, and William reached down to help.

"Yeah, I'm in here. But how'd you know that? And why are you so old?"

She smiled, and perhaps would have chuckled if she'd had the energy. "Over there." She pointed. "Can you get me some water?"

William followed her eyes to the bottle, which rested on its side a few feet away. He retrieved it for her, and she took a long drink, spilling a good amount down the front of her shirt.

She slowly scooted back a few inches to lean against the rear side of the pilot's chair. "I know this is confusing, but I need you to do something for me, okay?"

William sat down in front of her.

"What is it?" David asked.

"I know you and William are looking for me, but I'm okay. I'm going to be okay. You need to turn around and go back to dad. He's going to need your help with something very soon. Something he can't do by himself."

"I don't want to go back to dad."

"Why not?"

"I don't know. I just...I guess I don't want him to see me like this. Mom either. I wanted to find *you* first. I wanted to rescue you, and I knew you'd help *me*, too. You always know what to do."

She smiled at him sadly. "Not always. I wish I did, that's for sure." She reached up as if to ruffle his hair, but then realized how foolish the gesture would be. She let out an exhausted sigh. "But, I do know what to do now. At least, I know what *you* need to do. You need to go find dad. He really needs your help. And it's something that only you and William can do."

"What?"

"Don't worry about that. You'll find out soon enough, and you're going to be fine, too. I promise. This is going to set things right for you. You're going to be scared, but it will all turn out okay. You trust me, don't you?"

She put her hand in his. It felt soft and warm, and rather small as it rested in William's large metallic paw.

"Yes, I trust you."

"Good. Then do what I'm asking. I need you to give dad a message for me, too. I need you to tell him not to come after me. He needs to go back to the Bleeding Star Initiative Command Center, and do everything he can to stop the invasion. Tell him I...." Her voice broke, and she put one hand to her head, and another to her heart, as if her own words pained her. Tears began to stream from her eyes, but she wiped them away, and forced a cheerful smile through her reddening face. "Tell him that I tried to stop it myself, but I failed. I made a horrible mistake."

"You failed? Failed what? I don't understand. Are you all right?"

She nodded, wiped her face again and rose slowly to her feet. "Just pass on the message, okay? Dad won't understand it all either, at least not right away. Just promise me you'll do what I'm asking."

He didn't want to promise her; didn't want to do what she was asking. The idea of going back to his father scared him. What if he was angry? What if he blamed him for what happened to Peter, or for ending up on Necron, or even for being taken out of his body and ending up in William's. Still, Sarah always knew what to do, even if she said she didn't. He did trust her, and had an overwhelming urge to please her, just as he always did.

"I promise. But then can I go find Mom?"

She looked stunned, as if she might start to cry again. *My God, he doesn't know yet,* she thought. *Nobody's had the chance to tell him how we lost her.*

Now wouldn't be the time, she realized. Not only would he have the journey back to agonize over her death, but he was currently inhabiting a walking, talking, nearly indestructible killing machine. There could be no worse time for a grief-ridden fit.

"Just…just do what I ask, and after it's over you can talk to Dad about Mom, okay?"

"All right."

She threw her arms around William's torso and squeezed. "You need to get going, and so do I."

"Going? Where are you going?"

"I'm going home. I need to report what's happened. See if…if anyone knows how to fix what I've done." She gazed at him longingly. "I'm sorry we don't have more time to talk. I know how lonely you are, sweetie. I'd give anything to stay here with you, if only for a little longer."

"You know I'm feeling lonely? How?"

She released a sad sigh, and tried out a smile that was a few sizes too small. "Because you told me. I'll see you soon, though you won't be seeing me for a while." Kissing William's knight-like face, she gave one last squeeze before pushing away. "I love you, David."

"I love you, too."

After a few moments of silence, William spoke. "My command was to find and protect you until help arrived, Sarah. I'm afraid I can't let you go anywhere."

"But that was me as a child, not an adult, isn't that right?"

David could tell that the question confused him. "She's right. Besides, we know she's telling the truth about being okay. Otherwise, how could she be talking to us now?"

"I suppose that is a logical line of reasoning." It didn't take him long to decide. "Very well, reporting our findings should be a sufficient fulfillment of my commands."

She led him back to the hatch where he'd entered. "I guess this way out's as good as any. Fly fast, and don't stop until you get back to Dad."

"I love you, Sarah," the boy said again, more emphatically.

She answered with her smile, the same smile she'd given him whenever he'd gotten a scraped knee or when someone had bullied him at school. The smile that told him she was looking out for him, and everything was going to be all right.

She pushed them away, and David felt his heart sink, though it wasn't even there, and then the hatch closed behind them, and she was gone.

Once they were outside and away from the ship, David turned back to take another look.

"Are you all right, David? You seem very sad."

"I'll be okay. I just miss her is all. I don't want her to go."

The lights along the vessel's hull lit back up, and the two of them watched as it changed course and shot off with a stream of light into the distance. David would have given anything to be going along with her.

—OMICRON FIVE—

Morning came much too soon. The alarm had managed to draw Jace back into the realm of the living, though he felt as if he was rising to the surface from the depths of a great pool of water, and the throbbing in his head was maddening. When had he finally gone to sleep? One, maybe two hours ago? It seemed like five seconds.

The doctor whom Shepherd Moyer had spoken of had not been able to come to dinner the night before. He'd been detained by an emergency, something about a young trading post worker who'd gotten his foot run over by a hover lift. Luckily, the doctor had agreed to an appointment in the morning if Jace could get in by eight.

Dragging himself out of bed, he pulled on his shirt and went to the mirror to run a comb through his hair. What had seemed like a reasonable idea the night before now seemed like a foolish waste of time. He wanted nothing more than to crawl back into bed, but given the fact that the shepherd had gone out of his way to call in the favor, he wasn't about to disrespect the man or thumb a nose at his family's hospitality.

"Did you sleep well?" Ruth Ann asked as he emerged into the kitchen.

There was no sense in lying about it, he'd seen what he looked like in the mirror.

"Not really. I just couldn't get my mind to calm down and stop thinking about things. Maybe I'll sleep better tonight."

She set a plate of fruit, bacon and eggs in front of him. "Why don't you ask the doctor to give you something to help you get some sleep at night? You're going to be working through a lot of anxiety and grief in the days to come. That's natural, but your body still needs rest."

He nodded. "You're probably right. By the way, thanks for everything you and your family have done for me. I wish there was some way I could repay you."

"It's our pleasure. You know where the clinic is?"

"The shepherd told me. Second floor, across from the saloon?"

She smiled at him playfully. "Convenient, don't you think? There's been more than a little business drummed up for the doc from that bar. Things have a tendency to get rather wild in there from time to time."

"I can imagine. Nothing aggravates inter-species relations faster than getting everyone liquored up."

She pointed at him, as if to say he was on to something. "My husband is becoming well acquainted with a number of different alien burial traditions, thanks to that bar. If you happen to go in there, be careful. They do have their own form of security, but we're a long way from any kind of law out here."

Jace toasted her with his coffee. "I've never been much of a drinker, black with no cream or sugar is about as wild as I tend to get."

She raised her own coffee to toast him back. "Let me go check on your boy for you. Abigail's gettin' him ready."

"Thank you, Ma'am."

When he was finished with breakfast, he gathered up Stephen and headed for the main building. They were still a few minutes early, and he decided to take a stroll past the gun counter. It hadn't been long since the last time he was here, when he'd bought his first blaster and shared his desire to procure a laser sword with the Boreian behind the counter. So much had happened; so much had changed since then.

He suddenly remembered what the Boreian had told him about the guns he'd been looking over, how every one of them had a story, and would tell it if you just took the time to listen. It had seemed a bit foolish at the time, but given recent circumstances, now it made more sense. Why had the salesman told him all that? Was it some kind of bizarre closing tactic, or had the man been able to sense something strange about him? He wished the guy were here now so he could ask him, but the only salesperson in sight was a giggly female from a race he didn't recognize. She was helping another customer, but would occasionally look over to grin and wink at him through double eyelids. She was an odd looking thing, whatever she was, and her appearance wasn't helped by the way her orange skin clashed with her bright blue dress.

Finally making his way up to the clinic on the second floor, Jace signed in and thumbed through some magazines on a rack, finding nothing of interest. He sat down and picked up a picture book on the ABCs to read to Stephen. As the child clapped and jumped up and down on his lap, Jace was overwhelmed with pride. He hadn't been prepared to love someone as much as he loved Stephen. Sure, he loved Hero with all his heart, but this was just…different somehow. This was a protective, self-conscious, hopeful sort of love; the type of love that only a father could know for a son. But Stephen wasn't his son, was he? Jace twitched as a few sharp pricks of pain ran through his head. How could he be? He tried to remember the details of the boy's birth, but his thoughts became so clouded that he struggled to hold on to his own name, or where he was. What was this place again?

"Mr. Chang? Excuse me? Mr. Chang!"

He lifted his eyes to see the irritated nurse tugging at his shoulder. By her expression, Jace couldn't tell if she was irritated or concerned.

"Are you all right?" she asked, the concern winning out.

Her voice seemed to help him snap out of it. "Yeah. Sorry about that. Guess I was daydreaming or something."

Her eyes didn't believe him. "Doctor Mason is ready

for you now."

"Okay, thanks." He followed her into an examination room behind the front office.

The doctor, who appeared a few minutes later, was a tall, bald man with a salt and pepper mustachio. He shook Jace's hand, and from his kind, yet whimsical grin, Jace guessed that the Shepherd had done a good job filling him in.

"Thanks for seeing me. I know this whole thing sounds crazy…."

The doctor had already started poking and prodding, intent on earning his money by performing a thorough physical exam.

"Not at all," he tickled Stephen's belly before placing a cold medical scanner against Jace's chest. "Losing a loved one can be a horribly traumatizing experience. You've nothing to be embarrassed about. Why don't you start from the beginning and tell me the whole story, keeping in mind that I have another appointment in about twenty minutes." He winked playfully.

Jace recounted briefly how Hero had died, and how she'd been appearing to him.

"And when she appears to you, she claims the boy is yours?"

Jace nodded.

"How many years did you know the girl, before her passing, I mean?"

"Only a few months. Look, I know this whole thing's

stupid. The Shepherd suggested, well I guess he just thought that a DNA test would be one more piece of evidence to help me get my head on straight."

The doctor shrugged. "Couldn't hurt, I suppose. There doesn't appear to be anything physically wrong with you, with the exception of that knee. Has it given you any trouble lately?"

"Not really. I'll have it taken care of properly some day. Just haven't had the money to do it yet. I've been getting headaches lately, though. My thinking gets really foggy, too. It just happened again a few minutes ago in the waiting room."

"Well," said the doctor, consulting his scanner, "I don't see anything unusual in your brain scans. It's probably just due to the trauma and stress you've undergone. I can prescribe some meds to help out with that, as well as something to help you get some sleep." He poked Stephen in the belly again, and handed over the medical scanner for the child to examine. "Let's get on with that DNA test, okay?"

"Will it take long?"

"Only a few seconds." He swabbed the inside of the boy's mouth, and drew a different scanner from his jacket pocket. Then he handed a swab to Jace, who ran it along the inside of his cheek and handed it back. Placing the samples beside one another on the scanner's screen, the doctor waited for a beep and then lowered his hand so that Jace could take a look. The screen was red, the results read negative. Of course they did. Jace didn't feel any different; he wasn't being shown anything he didn't already know.

"Well, that's that, then."

"That's that," the doctor agreed. He wrote a prescription and handed the paper over. "Take this downstairs to the grocer. She serves as the pharmacist 'round these parts." He gave the smiling boy one last jab in the tummy, and he in turn released a cackling giggle.

Jace gave his thanks, and then headed back to the trading-post downstairs. When he got to the grocery market, he noticed a trash bin in the produce section and tossed the prescription in. He suddenly had a great longing to see his friends; to speak with Captain Winchester and Chief Joe, and tell them about Hero. He wouldn't tell them about the hallucinations, not yet; just of her death. He felt like a child who'd spent one too many nights at a friend's house. He was scared and unsettled, and he wanted to go home.

—BLEEDING STAR INITIATIVE COMMAND CENTER—

The smell of burnt food greeted Galin as he walked through the door of the dining hall. What kind of food it was, he couldn't tell, just that it had spent more time than it deserved in the oven.

Kanbun Musashi had been excited for the opportunity to prepare dinner for all his guests that evening. He'd told Galin all about his passion for the culinary arts as they were bolting the engine down earlier that afternoon. Judging by the wafting aroma, it was a good thing the young man had decided to follow in his grandfather's footsteps.

"My apologies in advance, this probably won't be the greatest home-cooked meal you've ever had. I haven't been to the store in a while. None of the ingredients were fresh." Kanbun presented the meal before them and proceeded in dishing out generous proportions.

Galin looked down at the clump of pasta upon his plate. It looked quite overcooked, but didn't appear to be burnt. He wondered if they were supposed to have had bread with their spaghetti. He took a bite to find that his meal was just as tasteless as it was rubbery. Galin patted his stomach. "Not too bad, all things considered," he fibbed, and forced another bite past his lips. "Compliments to the Chef."

If either Starla or Melissa had been there, they would have scolded him for talking with food in his mouth. Irritation with his poor dining manners was one of the few things the two women had in common. Another was that they were both lousy cooks, but he would have traded this mess he was eating for anything either one of them had cooked on their worst day of the week. At that moment, he found himself missing them both, and his heart sank just a little.

Ulrick scowled and smelled the sticky ball of noodles at the end of his fork before biting into it cautiously like an untrusting puppy. The half scowl that followed had been seen on his face before, whenever trying to determine the level of drinkability on souring milk. Finally he shrugged, dumped on some salt, and dug in as if he'd never questioned it in the first place.

TAII had even shown up to join them. She sat in her chair quietly and stared at them all in turn while they ate. It seemed to be creeping everyone out for some reason, which Galin found quite amusing.

"So tell me, old woman," he said, waving his fork at her. "You said earlier that Jace might be another candidate for this here clockwalking gig of yours. When you threw Hero off the Katara, how come you let him go, and demanded Boreas stay put? Didn't you care to examine his moves, or some such business?"

TAII glanced at him doubtfully. "When the station was still active, there were standing orders that any Draconian found in this sector be detained for questioning."

"Why was that?"

She huffed, as if the effort bothered her. "It was believed that a reptilian insurgency group called the Sobek-Tal may have been sending spies into the area. The station's CO didn't want to take any chances. And I wasn't about to risk my skin on this big dummy."

Galin glanced at Boreas, who returned a light shake of his head. "I've never heard of the Sobek-Tal."

"Few people have," TAII answered, "even among the Draconians. They were a small group of renegade Pneuma-Tal warrior monks who dedicated themselves to interfering with the work being conducted on this station."

"Why?" Joseph asked.

"I don't know, but of the six known members of the group, five were captured, and or killed. The final member managed to evade that fate."

Galin pointed at Boreas and grinned. "You think that might be him?"

TAII looked Boreas over like he was a blind date who hadn't quite measured up to expectations. "No. I'd say the chances are pretty slim."

"Okay, so that answers that question. But how come you let Jace run off with Hero if you thought he might be a candidate?"

"I couldn't assess you both at the same time, and I had his information. My protocol required that I collect information on candidates, not that I had to kidnap them. Besides, I could tell that he and the girl care for each other and I felt, well…I felt a bit guilty about sending her off in the first place. But I did try to warn you all, right from the beginning," she added defensively.

Galin snapped his fingers. "I knew it. You do have a heart after all, you little sweaty-pie."

TAII rolled her eyes at him.

"So here's another question for you, and you, too," he pointed at Kanbun, continuing to speak through a mouthful of food. "Boreas and me looked at a big fancy mural in a room a few levels down. What can you tell me about that place?"

TAII shook her head.

Kanbun pushed his own half-eaten plate of food away. "That place is called the Record of Ages. I've found a few references to it in some of my research, but I never paid much attention. I think it's some kind of art gallery. They must have taken all the pieces with them when they abandoned the station, except of course for the murals on the walls."

"I'm not so sure about that," Galin said, and he and Boreas recounted what they'd seen.

"Weird," Kanbun said. "Really weird. I'll see what I can dig up on the place. Could be more important than I thought."

They all ate quietly for a while before Joseph broke in. "I've been thinking, once we return to Necron and get everyone off that planet, where are we going to go?"

Galin chuckled. "I guess you had your nose buried too deep in ship repairs to catch wind of all those conversations. No definite plans have been made. Several ideas have been tossed around, heading to this or that planet in the United Confederation of Worlds. Problem is, Earth isn't a member anymore. Humans are a conquered race, and becoming the vagabonds of the GCW isn't going to do us any good, especially since each of those worlds will most likely fall themselves now that Earth's fleet is out of the picture."

"So what's the solution, then?" Joseph put his elbows up on the table, one on each side of his untouched plate of spaghetti. "Head into uncharted space? Look for a new home on some as of yet undiscovered, hospitable world?"

"I reckon that's the idea for some. Though the ones who intend to stay and fight, which appear to be most, have the intention of following our lead, if I'm not mistaken."

"You could always bring them back here," Kanbun offered. He sounded willing, yet apprehensive, like a child who'd just been asked to share his toys.

"Didn't realize that was a possibility," Galin said. "I barely brought the Katara through those barriers in one piece. Can't imagine leading a caravan along the same path. And I'm for damned sure not about to play shuttle pilot, not through there. Is there a friendlier way in."

Kanbun grinned and nodded. "Uh, yeah. There are several."

"Hey, where are you off to?" Galin asked as Ulrick rose and left the table.

"Gotta go see a man about a horse. Why? You wanna watch?"

"Think I'll pass just this once." He looked back at

Kanbun. "What passes as interesting conversation to most folks is more often than not lost on that one."

Then he looked over at the boy sitting next to him. David was the only one who'd seemed to be able to finish his food.

—BLEEDING STAR INITIATIVE COMMAND CENTER—

Joseph handed the final crate up to Ulrick and wiped off his brow.

"You done good, Chief," Galin told him, smacking him on the back. "I'd venture to say that you've earned yourself a vacation, though I can't promise you'll be cashing it in anytime soon."

"What am I, chopped liver?" Ulrick asked.

"You? You've already had your vacation. Remember all those pirates you got to slag?"

Ulrick stopped in his tracks for a moment before conceding the point with a shrug and moving off to tie down the crate.

Galin leaned against the hull of the ship and crossed his arms. "You look a little nervous, Chief. That shiny new engine in there giving you concern?"

"Yeah," Joseph admitted. "I just don't understand how the damned thing works. I like to understand how the mechanics in my engine room work, call me crazy."

"Well, don't worry too much about it. The kid gave you the specs manual, didn't he? You can run diagnostics on it and fix it if it goes all funny?"

"Sure. But that's not the point."

"I know that, old friend. Just remember, we may not know how or why, but we're going to be going very, very FAST."

"That's supposed to make me feel better?"

Galin chuckled as he got up to greet Boreas, who was coming to say goodbye.

"I guess this is it, big guy, at least for a little while. Keep those gnarly clawed fingers of yours crossed for us, all right?"

He nodded. "I hope that all goes well, and that you make it back soon."

"Thanks, and I think you made the right decision. You two get everything worked out on this end, and maybe we can start hopping through the stars and all that, next time we meet."

"I shall do my best, Captain. Give my regards to Hero, and wish her luck for me. Tell her I'll be in contact as soon as we have the communications array back in order."

"I will. Take care of yourself 'till we get back."

The reptilian nodded, and turned to speak with Ulrick.

Kanbun Musashi was running some final sweeps of the Katara's systems as Galin strode over to place a hand on his shoulder. "You do good work, kid. I can't tell you how much I appreciate what you've done."

"Don't mention it. Honestly, I'm doing it for the good of us all."

"I know that, but still…you have my thanks. And just so we're sure, this snazzy engine of yours isn't going to malfunction and blow up the whole ship or anything is it?"

"Well, that *is* what test runs are for." He surrendered a little grin. "Just try to make it back safe. In the meantime, I'll keep you updated on any developments just as soon as I can."

"Sounds like a deal." Galin rubbed his hands together and gazed up at the Katara. The old girl never looked so good. She was like a brand new ship.

"And uh, Captain, try not to bang her up too bad."

"Who've you been talking to?" Galin said with a frown. "All right, everyone. Let's get going. We've got a whole mess of people depending on us to get back with these parts."

They boarded the ship, and Ulrick slid into the co-pilots seat next to Galin. TAII popped into view between them.

"Oh brother, is she coming with us?"

"You just try to stop me, you dumb, blonde ogre."

"Relax, sweetheart," Galin told her. "We're happy to have you on board. Especially since you're gonna do what you're told from now on, isn't that right?"

She glared at them begrudgingly.

"Now, go take a nap until we need you."

"Fine," the girl scowled before popping out of sight.

Galin lifted off and turned the ship toward the docking bay door. He guided the Katara out and fell in behind one of the sentinels, sent to escort him back to the plasma storm.

He looked over at Ulrick, nervously. "You think he's gonna show us to one of those kinder, friendlier routes Kanbun told us about?"

—OMICRON FIVE—

Jace had turned in early that evening at the request of the shepherd and his wife. He'd lain there for nearly three hours, just as awake as he'd been when he'd first lied down. Unable to stand it any longer, he got up, slipped on his shoes and shirt, and headed for the trading post.

The place seemed pretty lively tonight. There were quite a lot of customers perusing about, both inside and outside the building. Sauntering in, he saw that even more were going up and coming down the stairs from the saloon. He weighed the idea of going up, just to take a look around, and then decided against it. He'd never been much of a drinker, he hadn't been fibbing about that, but he did occasionally enjoy people-watching, when he was in the mood for it. The thought of doing it just now didn't hold much interest for him.

Jace knew why he'd wandered in, and it wasn't because he wanted the company of strangers. He decided to stop playing around with empty distractions and get right down to business. He headed for the gun counter to see if the Boreian clerk was in. At first he didn't see anyone apart from a few window shoppers, but then a door behind the counter opened and the fat Boreian attendant came shuffling in. He glanced up at Jace and wrinkled his big, flat nose, and slowly gave his beard a few thoughtful strokes.

"I remember you," he said toothily. "You're the lad that seemed intent on finding himself a laser sword, isn't that right?" he guffawed. "Ended up purchasing that Space Marine officer's service laser-pistol, if memory serves me right."

The Boreian glanced down to Jace's hip to confirm what he already knew, but the gun wasn't there.

"Don't tell me you lost the thing already."

"Actually, I did. It was taken from me a few days ago." He felt his chest tighten as an image of Sonja Howard flashed through his head. "But, I don't really want to talk about that right now."

The Boreian studied his face a moment, and then tapped his fingers lightly upon the glass counter. "Looking for a replacement, then?"

"To be honest, I hadn't really thought about it. But,

yeah. That would probably be a good idea. That's not the reason I'm here though. I…I wanted to talk to you about something. Ask you a question."

"Alright," the Boreian said, eyes twinkling with curiosity. He crossed his arms and cocked his head.

"Last time I was here, you…well, you told me that in some ways weapons are just like people, that each of these guns had a story to tell. Some good ones, and some bad. You said that if I listened close enough they'd tell them to me."

"Yeah. That sounds like something I'd say."

"Well, why'd you say it? Did you mean it, or were you just bull-crapping me?"

"Oh, I meant every word of it. I thought I proved my point the last time you were here." He bore into Jace's eyes. "I can tell something's really bothering you. What is it? What's got you all out of sorts?"

Jace still wasn't sure that he liked this guy. He just seemed like a smarmy used hover-car salesman. But perhaps that assessment wasn't fair. The Boreian hadn't done or said anything to cheat him, he just had that kind of look about him, the kind of look that could lose an otherwise worthy politician a race as soon as they put him on TV.

"I've been seeing people," Jace whispered to him, so the wandering passersby couldn't hear. "People that I shouldn't be seeing."

"Shouldn't be seeing?" The Boreian asked, confused.

"People that have died recently."

The Boreian squinted his eyes, which appeared to be more out of curiosity than to suspect that Jace might be crazy. That at least, was something.

"Seeing spirits? Their ghosts, you mean?"

Jace shook his head. "No, I've been seeing and talking to them just like we're talking to each other right now. I kind of, well I get confused about the things that have happened, start believing they're not really dead. My…the woman I loved, she was murdered just a few days ago. She's been coming to me at night. There's someone else as well, but I've only seen him during the day."

"Well that does sound rather strange, doesn't it?"

The Boreian scratched at his thick, black beard, and while looking into his crimson face, Jace felt as though he was at a confessional with the devil. From the alien's puzzled look, it was clear that he didn't know what Jace was talking about.

"So you came to me because you thought this might have something to do with what I said about listening to these weapons, is that it?"

"I don't know, yeah, I guess so. It's almost as if, and bear with me, this is all a little hard to explain, but it's almost as if I'm hearing these people. I mean, I can see them, feel them, it's all very real. But all of those sensations feel, at least in a way, more like I'm hearing them. It's like I'm listening to some distant voice that manifests into something solid, or having a vivid dream that doesn't fade away after it ends. But, how does any of that even make any sense?"

Jace waited for laughter to escape from his listener's lips. The things he was saying made him feel stupid and embarrassed, and he wouldn't blame this fellow for laughing, it wasn't often that one was approached with such absurdity, especially from a stranger.

But the Boreian didn't laugh. "Well, assuming you haven't lost your mind, perhaps you're on to something. Who's to say that you aren't hearing the voices of them that've moved on? Perhaps they have something they want you to hear. It's a very strange business, to be sure, but I've seen stranger." He picked up a bottle of cleaner, sprayed some on the counter, and started to wipe, looking around to see if anyone was listening in. "I'm afraid I don't really know how to help you." And then the look in his eyes changed, as if making an important decision. "But I know a man who might, that is, if he's still alive. I used to work for him. Name's Williams. General Tom Williams."

"And you worked for him? On what?"

"I can't talk about that, other than to say that the work we did, well it could be in some way related to the things you're experiencing now, and if that's the case, things might get worse for you before they get better. The General can help you. I shouldn't even be telling you his name, to be honest, but you seem like a good lad, and he'd want to hear your story, if I had to place a bet on it."

"Okay. Where can I find him."

"Last I knew, he was living on Malacandra Prime."

Jace's heart sank. Malacandra Prime was on the other side of the quadrant, if memory served. As far as he could guess, it would take a few months to get there.

The Boreian read his expression. "I wouldn't have mentioned him to you if I didn't think the trip would be worth it. And if there's any man alive who can give you guidance, it's him. But like I said, that's only if he's still alive. Last time I saw him was about five years ago, and he was older than dirt then, but fit as a fiddle and sharp as a tack as well."

Jace didn't know what he'd been expecting. Perhaps that the Boreien would have some magical answer- be able to tell him exactly what was wrong, and how to fix it. No, that wasn't what he'd been expecting, but it had been what he was hoping. But, why would this man have had such an answer? Just because he'd had some silly story about listening to guns didn't mean he was an expert on paranormal disturbances. Still, the answer he gave was better than no answer at all, or being laughed at.

"All right. As soon as I can, I'll go find him," Jace said, unsure if he'd get the chance anytime soon. He wasn't about to abandon his shipmates to start a wild goose chase because he'd been talking to ghosts.

Looking down at the guns, he noticed that the price had increased significantly on the remaining Space Marine service pistol.

"Won't be as many of those around in the days to come, will there?" the Boreian shrugged.

"I guess not," Jace said. He wouldn't have bought that particular gun anyway. It told bad stories, he remembered.

"I assume you neglected to take the sleeping pills I prescribed for you," came a voice from behind him.

Jace turned to see Doctor Mason standing there with a bemused grin on his face.

"You care to tell me what sort of a game you're playing at, Mr. Chang?"

Jace turned to face him. "Come again?"

The doctor rubbed his bald head and looked back and forth between Jace and the Boreian a few times before settling his eyes upon Jace.

"Come take a walk with me, if you wouldn't mind."

Jace followed the man back toward his office.

"I just came from the shepherd's house. I went there looking for you first. I've never seen such a thing before, Mr. Chang. In all my years of practice, I've never seen it happen." He unlocked the door to the clinic. The lights were already on. "The only thing I can figure is that you're some kind of aspiring magician, or perhaps a conman, trying to work a game on…who, the shepherd and his family?"

Jace was losing his patience. "Look, doc, I appreciate what you've done for me, but how about you cut the crap and tell me what's going on."

The doctor sneered at him, but was silent until they reached his office. He retrieved the medical scanner from his desk and held it out so Jace could take a look.

"Yeah, what about it? Am I missing something?"

The doctor looked down at it himself. His brow curled into a frown. "A few hours ago, the DNA results had changed to positive. Now, they're showing negative again. Are you telling me you've got nothing to do with this?"

"They changed to positive? Maybe there's something wrong with your scanner."

The doctor frowned at him. "Like I said, I've never seen anything like it before." He continued to stare with the contempt of a man who was the butt of some big joke, and saw not a lick of humor in it. "It's not a simple matter of a yes or no answer, the entire results of the test had changed. I had closely analyzed them all myself."

"Well, I didn't do anything," Jace said angrily, his fatigue and grief getting the better of him. He'd come to this man for help, not to be accused of whatever this was he was being accused of.

"Look," said the doctor flipping the scanner around. "Now it's a positive reading again."

"Let me see that," Jace said, whipping the device away from him. The screen was green, and the text indicated a positive paternal match. A series of throbbing pulses ran through his head, and he rose his hands to each side.

The doctor's expression softened a bit, but the doubt remained. Without saying another word, Jace stumbled toward the exit and left. If he was going crazy, it looked like he was going to take a few people with him.

The doctor popped his head out the clinic door. "I'm going to have to have a talk with the shepherd about this. I'm going to warn him about you."

"Yeah," Jace mumbled, going past the stairwell and toward the saloon. "You do that."

Jace awoke the next morning to a gentle hand upon his shoulder.

"I thought you told my wife you weren't a drinker," said the shepherd, sliding into the seat next to him.

He rubbed his eyes, and wiped the streak of drool from his cheek. An empty bottle of spiced rum rolled from the table and onto his lap. He looked around to see only a handful of patrons. A few, just like him, were left over from a bout of hard drinking the night before.

"I spoke to the doctor this morning. He told me you had quite a night."

"I didn't do anything to rig that test."

"I believe you," the shepherd motioned to a nearby waitress for some coffee. "Dr. Mason's a good man, but he's an unfailing skeptic. He's not the kind to easily open his mind to possibilities that can't be proven by some kind of calculation or theorem. We can't hold that against him."

Jace nodded. "Well, I'm sorry I didn't come back last night. It was late and I didn't want to disturb you. And then I had a few too many, and here I am"

"Looks like you needed a good stiff drink. Can't say I blame you, but you'd be wise to go back to coffee. Nobody's ever found happiness or answers at the bottom of one of these bottles." Just then, the waitress arrived. "Ah, here we are now. Thank you, my dear."

Jace took the bottle from his lap and set it upright on the table. "When I saw that medical scanner, I…well I guess I don't know what's worse. Before, I thought I might be losing my mind. According to that scanner, that isn't the case, and I think that scares me even more."

The shepherd nodded. "It certainly raises some interesting questions, doesn't it? In fact, I'm almost tempted to have a good, stiff drink myself." He smiled. "I do have some good news for you, however. The post's communications officer gave me a call this morning. They received an incoming transmission from your friend, Galin Winchester. The message was broken up a bit, must've come through some interference, but apparently they're on route to come and pick you up. ETA is sometime this evening. The captain said everyone is doing well, and that he has a lot to tell you."

Jace let out a long sigh of relief. Whatever his friends had been through, they were all coming back all right. Until this moment, he hadn't realized how worried he'd been about them. But now that they were coming for him, what was he going to do about Stephen? The Katara wasn't any place for a two year old, even under ideal conditions, especially one without his mother.

He'd been so preoccupied with questions of his own sanity, and with the strange events of the past few days, that he hadn't given enough thought to what he was going to do about Stephen. With what little thought he had given it, however, he realized that there were only a few real options. One was to keep the boy with him, which would expose him to danger and distract Jace from his duties, obviously not the best option. He could abandon his friends to settle down somewhere and take care of the child. But how we he support them? Even if he'd wanted to leave the Katara, which he didn't, at least not yet, the unstable political climate would make this difficult.

The third option was to leave the boy with someone he trusted. Someone who would love him as their own and enable him to keep an eye on him. For this option, he could think of only two possibilities, the shepherd's family, or his own parents.

Jace couldn't even conceive what it might be like trying to explain the situation to his mother and father. What would he tell them, that the boy was his? That he was sometimes his? Or perhaps that he was the mysterious DNA shifting baby of a Nazerazi infiltrator? Whatever he might tell them, New Lanzhou was a colony not far from the reach of the Nazerazi Empire, and if the people there had to flee, they would be driven out further toward the outskirts of known space- not exactly the best way to fulfill his promise to keep the boy safe.

"I've been speaking with Abigail and Ruth-Ann," the shepherd said, drawing him back. "Those two certainly have fallen in love with that little boy of yours."

Jace smiled apprehensively. It still felt strange to hear someone call Stephen his. It would take a little getting used to.

"Well, whether your DNA matches or not, he's your boy now, isn't he?"

Jace nodded. "Your wife and daughter have been such a help. And you…well, I don't know what I would have done if your family hadn't been here for me. I don't even know how to begin to thank you."

"No thanks is necessary. I and my house, we serve the Lord. And I learned a long time ago that the best sermons are lived, not preached."

The waitress arrived to freshen their coffee. She ruffled Jace's hair and gave them a wink before moving on.

The shepherd added some vanilla creamer and two packets of sugar. "Tell me if I'm speaking out of turn, but if you need a safe place to leave the lad for a while...."

What was this guy, a mind reader? Maybe he was just too easy to read. "I wouldn't want to impose." He ran his fingers through his hair and softly shook his head. "Besides, is it that obvious that I don't know what I'm doing?"

"I never said that," the shepherd frowned, "and neither did my wife or daughter. We all think you're a fine young man. But sometimes life throws us curve balls. Sometimes we're given burdens that we were never meant to bear alone." He gave Jace's shoulder a firm squeeze. "You *don't* have to do this alone. We're here for you in whatever capacity you need, but of course, the decision is yours."

Jace opened his mouth to speak, but what came out sounded something more like a whispered cough. Then he put his hands to his face, and began to cry. The tears poured out of him like they hadn't done in years. He didn't try to stop them, he simply let them flow. The grief, the confusion, the fear. He let them all drain out of him like dirty bathwater from a tub.

A few minutes later, when he had finally finished, he reached for his coffee. "I think it'd be the best thing for him, to stay with you guys, at least for a little while."

"He'll be in good hands until you return. And there'll always be a place for you, too. I want you to know that. You don't have to be a stranger. There are some good people around these parts, if you decide to plant roots someday."

"I know that, and I appreciate it." Omicron Five had never been a place where Jace would have considered settling down. It was a beautiful planet, but a bit too quiet and far from any kind of excitement. Sure, there were a lot of interesting visitors and plenty of bar-fights, but that kind of action wasn't really his idea of a good time.

Now that Hero was buried here, things were different. He was seeing the planet in a whole new light, and it seemed even more beautiful and full of life than it had before. The air was fresher, the flowers and grass more full of color, the birds more abundant with song. Jace was seeing this world through the love and sorrow he had for the woman who rested within its bones, and he now felt as though he were anchored somehow.

"Part of me wants to stay," he told the shepherd, "to sleep here every night out under those stars. To wait for Hero and live like it wasn't some kind of dream. But...."

"But?"

Jace swigged the rest of his lukewarm coffee. "Sometimes if you aren't careful, the best dreams can turn into the worst nightmares."

David sat next to his father in the Katara's copilot seat, as stone-faced and unenthused as ever, glancing out into the nothingness before them. The stars all around came to a halt as they dropped out of warp.

"We're coming up on Omicron Five," Galin told him. "This place is a hub for all kinds of alien species. You'll probably see more new peoples than you ever have before."

David glanced over at his father, but said nothing.

"I can tell how excited you are, just try to keep yourself under control down there, okay? We don't want to get thrown out of the place."

The boy nodded disinterestedly.

Galin would keep talking to him this way, he'd decided. He'd talk to the boy as if nothing at all was amiss. Perhaps in some small way it would help to heal him, help to snap him out of whatever darkness was holding him captive. Where there is life, there is hope.

Galin called for and received permission to set down the ship, so he headed for docking bay 7 and clicked on the com.

"All right, everyone, we're here. If there's anything on your shopping lists, pick it up quick. Once Jace and Hero are back on board we can finish up with business back on Necron. I don't know about all of you, but I'm ready to move on!"

When the Katara was set down, Galin and David descended the steps, the smell of moist ocean air filling up their lungs.

"I'll never get used to the way this feels." Galin

smiled down at his son. "I always know it's coming, that cool ocean breeze. But I'm still always surprised by the way it feels. Invigorating isn't quite a strong enough word. Can you feel it too?"

David didn't say anything, but looked as though he might be deliberating the idea silently in his head. At least that was something.

An outpost attendant in a khaki uniform had spotted them and begun his approach, but Galin waved the young man off and gave a friendly salute. "We all know where we're going from here, thanks anyway."

The attendant returned a thumbs up and moved on to the next ship in line.

"Last one off the boat, lock her up, will ya?" Galin said over his wrist com, and headed for the trading post. His eyes wandered to the left side of the building, where the cliff-side lounging area was located. An image of Starla, sitting there in one of those patio chairs popped into his head. It was almost as if she was there, looking beautiful as always, leaning back in her chair and gazing at him with that warm smile of hers. The ocean breeze lifted her hair from her shoulders, causing her to giggle.

But then some of the last words she'd spoken to him there came to mind.

"I'm glad you talked me into this, joining the crew I mean. At first I wasn't sure I could do it; live this kind of life. But it's been a wonderful ride."

"You talk about it like it's over. Are you still thinking about

staying on Earth once we make it back?" He had asked her.

"I haven't decided yet. It's possible. I'd miss the Katara, and the crew. I'd miss seeing new places like this, but I'm just not sure this is the life for me anymore."

Would she have really left the ship? Left him? Well, why the frack wouldn't she? God knows she should have, long before then, she should have. An ocean of sorrow began to sweep over him, ushered in by the crashing of waves from the waters below. He felt cold; his hands started to shake. What in the world was wrong with him, anyway? He knew what it was. It was the grief. The grief, and the regret for all the years he'd mistreated her.

He closed his eyes and took a deep breath. That conversation suddenly seemed like it belonged in another lifetime. But he wasn't the man now that he had been then. He'd changed. His eyes had been opened. Hadn't they? At any rate, one thing was certain; he was going to fix it all. One way or another, he was going to make things right. For Starla. For Jamie. For all of them. A rising sense of anger was beginning to drown out the sorrow, and he could feel his heart racing.

"Calm down," Galin whispered to himself. "Just calm right on down. What the hell's wrong with you, anyway?"

David looked up at him with a frown.

"I wasn't talking to you," Galin told him, forcing a smile. "What's the matter, never seen a grown man talking to himself before?"

"No," the boy answered stoically.

Galin just shook his head, and the two kept walking.

He scanned the patio for familiar faces. Jace and Hero should be on the lookout for them, and he half expected Hero to come rushing out to greet them at any second. She was an excitable little gal, that was for sure.

And then he saw someone stand, he was close to the building, somewhat concealed in the shadows. It was Jace. A smile spread across Galin's face as he headed to meet him; he'd been worried ever since they'd left the ship. What was that he was carrying? A little child? When he'd nearly reached him, their eyes met, and it was then that Galin knew something was wrong. Something was very wrong.

Where was Hero? She didn't appear to be with him.

A moment later they were standing face to face.

"She's dead," Jace said, his voice breaking.

A string of obscenities ran through Galin's head, though he only lowered his eyes and clenched his fists. "I'm sorry, kid. What the hell happened?"

Jace sat back down, placing the boy upon his lap.

"Is this her son?" Galin asked. He could see it in the boy's eyes. "Stephen?"

"Yeah, this is him."

Galin took a seat next to him and offered the boy his pinky finger, which he took and gave a squeeze.

And then Jace told him everything, how Sonja

Howard had stalked and killed Hero, and how she had died. He told him what Howard had said about her, that she was a Nazerazi, and about Hero's confirming words. Galin's eyes shot open as if he didn't know what to think about that, exactly, but he didn't say anything. Jace told him about the visions, and how Hero had come to him during the night, and what she'd said about Stephen being his son, and finally of the DNA tests that seemed to confirm it, at least part of the time. Up until that moment, Jace hadn't been sure how much he was going to say, but he found that once he'd started, he simply couldn't stop the words from coming. He was laying everything he had out onto the table.

Galin just sat and listened, occasionally nodding or shaking his head, trying to take it all in. He didn't know what to think, he didn't know what to feel. He, like his young friend, was simply lost and overwhelmed by what was happening.

When he was finished, Jace felt a little better, if only a little. He waited in silence for Galin to speak, not knowing what he was thinking.

"It's not your fault," he said quietly, "what happened to Hero. You did the best you could, kid. And you kept your promise to her. She'd be proud of you. Always remember that."

Jace nodded, though the words gave him little comfort.

"We're going to figure this out," Galin told him. "And

we're going to do it together. A lot of things are happening these days that don't make sense, but we might be on our way to getting some answers." Galin explained what had happened to them while they were away. He told Jace about the Bleeding Star Initiative, and what they'd seen at the Command Center.

"So that's who this General Williams guy is. The Boreian said he used to work with him, but he wouldn't say any more than that. Maybe he really can help us after all."

"Seems like things are lining up a bit, doesn't it?" Galin said. "Despite everything else that's happening, all the torture we've been going through, seems like things are starting to line up."

"Maybe," Jace said. "But lining up for what?"

"Redemption? A second chance? Least that's what I'm hoping."

They sat together in silence for a few moments, listening to the waves and watching the people.

"Want to see where she's buried?" Jace asked.

Galin nodded. He followed his young friend to the edge of the cliff, and then over the rocks and down along the path.

"So, Hero said she was a Nazerazi? What's that mean? Are they humans? Do they just look like humans?"

"Your guess is as good as mine. I mean, you know as much about it as I do at this point. She and Howard made it pretty clear, though. Hero wasn't just working for the Nazerazi, she was actually one of them."

"Maybe they're some kind of shape shifters. Maybe Stephen's shifting his DNA without even knowing it. You know, trying to be more like his new 'daddy' and all." He formed a sad little grin.

"I've thought a lot about it," Jace answered. "And the only thing I know for sure is, I have no fracking clue what's going on."

When they got to Hero's tomb, Jace sat on the grass and set Stephen down beside him. The boy immediately began to giggle and roll all around.

"Gass!" He observed excitedly, grasping a bunch in each hand. "Gass, gass!"

Galin stood looking at Jace's inscription, his arms crossed. "I'm glad she got her son back before she died," he said.

"Yeah. Me too." Jace looked off into the sky over the ocean. "Captain, are you…are you mad at her, at all?"

Galin thought about it for a moment. "No, I don't think I am. She didn't seem to mean us any harm. Helped us out on the ship quite a bit too, didn't she?" He scratched his head. "She didn't mention why her people wanted the Katara, did she?"

"No."

"She could have had the damned thing if she'd wanted it. She was smart enough to succeed in betraying us.

She could have taken our ship and the rest of us along with it right back to 'em, if that was what she'd wanted."

Jace nodded. "I know."

Galin took in another drought of the cool ocean air. "We didn't know what she was, but I'm pretty sure we knew who she was. I'm sorry we lost her…that you lost her, Jace."

"Yeah, I am too." He stood up, retrieved Stephen, and held him out to the captain. "What about this squirt, here? You think he looks like me?"

Galin held the boy out at arms length, examining him closely. He had Hero's eyes, that was for sure. "I hadn't noticed it before, but now that you mention it, I think that he might."

—DEEP SPACE
EN ROUTE TO NECRON—

David was not at all happy with the conclusion of William's story.

"That's stupid," he said angrily. "They were both a couple of idiots."

"Idiots? Why do you say that?"

"He killed himself, drank poison just because he thought his girlfriend was dead? Frack me, he could have found another woman easy enough. And Juliet's even worse. I can't imagine stabbing myself with a dagger like that, no way. What the hell's wrong with these people?"

"From the limited amount of research I've conducted on the subject, it appears that love, and the loss of love, can make human beings behave in very unpredictable ways."

"Yeah, you're telling me. That's why I'm never gonna get married. I'm gonna buy my women, just like my Uncle Jake does. He says that in the long run it's a lot cheaper anyway."

"If I'm interpreting your statement correctly, I believe that such behavior would be highly inadvisable. Intimate relationships can be unhealthy both physically and mentally when pursued with inappropriate types of people."

"Yeah, that's kind of like what my mom says when she cusses out Uncle Jake. Anyway, I was just pulling your leg."

The android paused. "Perhaps I can find a similar story with a happier ending."

"Ugh, I don't want anymore stories. I just want to get where we're going already. I'm so bored!"

"Yes, I know you are. But I'm going as fast as I can."

"I know that. I'm not blaming you. Hey, what's that?"

David saw that a massive ship had just come into view on the long range scanners.

"It appears to be an Earth vessel. A Battle Cruiser,

according to the energy signature. We'll have to get closer to determine its specific identity."

"Hey, my grandpa commands one of those ships. Where's it going?"

"It appears to be headed to Necron, just like we are."

"Try to catch up to it," David urged him.

"According to my calculations, we'll overtake the vessel in approximately twenty nine hours, just before reaching Necron, provided they retain current speed and do not deviate their course."

"When can we hail them? I want to know if my grandpa's on board. He's an Admiral. His name's Sebastian Winchester."

"We can send a sub-space transmission if you'd like."

"Yeah, let's do that."

William opened up the channel. "Attention, unidentified United Earth Government Ship. This is T3038 William Marshall. Please identify yourself. I am escorting someone who would like to speak with Admiral Sebastian Winchester, if he is on board and available."

A few seconds later, their hail was answered. "Greetings, William Marshall. This is the Nazerazi battleship Claymore." The voice was deep and grainy. "Admiral Winchester is currently indisposed. My name is General Soth. What is the nature of your business with Winchester and this vessel?"

"What do you mean 'Nazerazi battleship'?" David yelled, but his voice was that of the android's. "WHAT

DID YOU DO TO MY GRANDPA?"

There were a few more seconds of silence, and then Soth let out a series of hisses that could only be laughter. "What is this? Some kind of bizarre joke? With whom am I actually speaking?"

"David, calm down. Shouting won't get you any—"

"THIS GUY DID SOMETHING TO MY GRANDPA AND I WANT TO KNOW WHAT!" David continued.

Soth, presumably finished with hearing a confused android yelling and arguing with itself, ended the transmission.

"HEY, HE CAN'T DO THAT! REOPEN THE CHANNEL."

"I don't think that will do any good," William said. "But do try to calm yourself, and stop...stop...stop trying to take control...."

"NO!" David shouted, pushing William's voice away so that he could no longer hear it. He was sick of being told to calm down; sick of just being along for the ride. Diverting what little power he could from the android's shielding, he increased speed ever so slightly, rocketing toward the battlecruiser. He was going to find out what the Nazerazi had done to his grandfather, and make them pay for it.

— — —

Book 10

Dark Reunions

—OMICRON FIVE—

Galin stood behind Jace, massaging the young man's shoulders as a coach might rub down a recently injured player, about to get back in the game. The young man had looked a bit too nervous, sitting in the captain's chair as if he didn't quite trust himself in it any longer. Galin knew that it was like getting back in the saddle after being thrown by a horse. How many times had he seen this before, heck, even been there himself? A person gets traumatized out there in the stars, and it's not always easy for them to head back out again. He understood that space suddenly felt a lot more claustrophobic for the young man sitting before him, an ironic truth everyone who'd lived their kind of life eventually came to understand.

Jace took a long breath, and then lifted off and guided the Katara away from the planet's surface. The trading post would be shrinking into the distance behind them, Galin knew, and wondered if any of the crew was bothering to catch the view. Jace hadn't bothered to put the image on the view screen, and there was really no reason to remind him. The kid had asked to pilot the ship away from the planet, and it seemed of real importance to him. That was understandable. Jace had been forced to suffer through more than his fair share of loss, and if a little thing like this could help him get past it, that was all the better.

"How ya doin', champ?" Galin asked, when they'd put a few minutes behind them.

"Champ?" He looked up with a sad smile. "Nobody's called me that since my football days. I'm doing as well as could be expected, I guess."

Galin gave him a few final pats on the shoulder. He didn't like to see a friend suffering like this. He and Peter had come to think of Jace as something of a little brother since he'd joined the crew, and as such were accustomed to trying to look out for him whenever they could, make things better. But the hard truth was, there would be no making this better. Time alone would heal some of the pain of Hero's loss, but even then, there would always be scars. The pain would never truly go away, Jamie's death had taught him that long ago.

And now, they'd lost Hero. The girl's death had affected Galin much more than he'd expected. In the time they'd spent together, he'd grown very fond of her, and where he saw Jace as a brother, perhaps she was something like a little sister, part of which came simply from her being a member of his crew, but there was more than that. She was a special girl, every one of them had thought so. She could talk to Joseph all day long about ship mechanics, even to the point of driving Galin a little crazy, and he'd even heard Ulrick open up to her a few times, enlightening the delighted girl about the latest and greatest upgrades the brute had made to his favorite guns.

As delightful as she was to have around, there was always that unmitigated pain, brewing just below the surface. She and Galin had empathized with each other over the loss of their children. It was a communion of agony that neither had needed to share with words. It could be, and often was, expressed by something as simple as an exchanged glance, a momentary, hopeless flicker in the eye, like a slowly dying flame, that they could only hope to recognize in each other. No one else understood. The small comfort he'd found in their mutual sorrow and hopelessness was lost to him forever now, and perhaps the weight of that loss was the straw to tip the scales of his sorrow. It was just one more thing he couldn't find the energy to grieve.

"I'm going to miss that little guy," Jace said, drawing Galin back from his thoughts. "Despite all my confusion and…hallucinations, or whatever they are, he's a part of Hero, and that's a hard thing to leave behind."

Galin sighed. "I know what you mean." He sat down in the copilot's chair and folded his hands behind his head. "Over the years, I had to leave my kids behind more times than I could count, and each and every time, it felt like abandonment." He looked out into the stars. "I wanted to bring them along, but their mother wouldn't have it, even when they got old enough to want to come." He grinned. "Listen, if it makes you feel any better, I think you did the right thing. As hard as it is, you did the kid right. He deserves a woman's touch, and to have the beauty of that planet beneath his feet. He'll know how much you love him, and that you'll always be there for him. The shepherd's family will see to that."

Jace turned to him, his eyes wide and urgent. "Do you really think there's something to all that Bleeding Star Initiative stuff? You really think we can set all this right, somehow? Get them back?"

"Damned if I know, kid, but one thing's for sure, we're going to find out, and we're going to do it together."

Jace nodded, his lips contorting into a frown that would have scared off the most hardened of playground bullies.

"All right," the chief's voice came in over the com, *"all*

systems are set to go. You ready for round two?"

"Roger that, Chief. You heard him everybody, hold onto your butts." Galin turned to Jace. "I think you're gonna like this, kid, but you'd better switch me seats."

Jace got up and Galin took the captain's chair. "You thought the new armored hull and firepower were impressive? Check this out."

Galin made the jump to hyperspace, sending trails of starlight shooting past them like hundreds of burning meteorites. A mischievous smile formed, and he then initiated the warp drive. The world around them exploded into ribbons of rainbow colored light. It was hypnotizing and not a little disorienting.

"Don't worry," Galin said. "It's not so bad once your eyes get used to it. Best part is, we'll be at Necron in no time."

"Never thought I'd hear anyone say *that*," Jace mumbled.

Galin chuckled. "Yeah, never thought I'd be saying it. Hey, TAII, you ready to come back out and say hello yet?" The holographic girl hadn't made an appearance since Jace had returned to the ship, and Galin was sure he knew why. "She doesn't want to face you," he told Jace. "I think she feels pretty guilty about what happened to Hero."

Jace looked angry for a moment, but then his face softened. "It's not her fault."

They sat in silence for a few seconds, and then the girl

popped into the air beside them. Her eyes were red and puffy, and holographic tears were streaming down her cheeks. "You really mean that?" she whimpered.

Jace glared at her for a while, and then turned back to the colorful display streaming by outside. "To be honest, I can't help but be angry about what happened, but even if things hadn't gone down like they did, Howard would have gotten her eventually. It was just a matter of time. If she hadn't gotten us alone on the Shiv, more of the crew might have died, or Stephen could have been hurt. Who knows how things might have turned out."

The girl continued to look at him like she'd just run over his dog. "Well, for what it's worth. I'm really sorry."

Jace nodded, looking back at her. "Thanks, I know you are. But it wasn't your fault."

"I, I really wish I could hug you right now," TAII sobbed. She stood there hesitantly, as if there was something she was afraid to say. "I made you something. A gift, if you want it."

He shrugged. "Okay, why not."

All of a sudden, a holographic image of Hero appeared next to her, smiling down at them.

Jace jumped to his feet, barely aware of what he was doing, and stared into the hologram's eyes. It stared right back, smiling.

"She doesn't talk, I thought that might be creepy, but

she'll follow your gaze, kind of like a picture that's capable of looking back."

Jace didn't say anything, but Galin could tell he was touched. "She's lovely," he told TAII. "Looks just like her, far as I can see."

Jace nodded. "Yeah, it does. Thanks." He turned to the girl and gave her a little grin. After looking at his gift for a few moments longer, he sat back down. "Can you put her in my room for me.

TAII nodded. "You can call the image up any time you want to."

"Thanks. She really is lovely."

Both women disappeared, and Galin turned to see that Jace looked worried.

"You okay?"

He nodded. "Seeing her image like that, it just made me wonder, are the visions over, now that we've left the planet, or is she going to come again?"

Galin had been wondering the same thing himself. "I wish I knew. Do you want her to?"

"In a lot of ways, yes. But…in other ways, no. It's hard to explain, but I guess it's like having something really nice that you can't enjoy because you stole it. You know it's not really yours, that you shouldn't have it. Does that make sense?"

Galin nodded. "Sure, I suppose so."

"And then, there's the confusion that sets in. I swear the whole thing's maddening, not being able to recognize what's real and what's not. Not knowing if she's alive or dead, if we're married…I just want to figure out what all this means and get it fixed."

"Hang in there. We're headed in that direction, I can feel it."

"I wish I could feel it, too."

Galin smiled at him with as much encouragement as he could muster. He got on the com. "Hey Ulrick, how about fixing us up with some of that supercharged coffee you're so proud of, you know, the kind that looks like motor oil?" He turned back to Jace. "I have a feeling neither one of us is gonna get any sleep tonight, even if we tried."

—MERLOS III
FIVE YEARS BEFORE—

Galin pulled himself to the top of the utmost boulder, and let out a satisfied grunt. He pointed down into the valley, and whipped off his night vision goggles, careful not to disturb any black face paint. "There it is," he whispered to Peter. "The entrance to the Temple of the Ever-Hungry Thunder Gods." He turned to Starla. "That's what you said it was called, right, little girl?"

"More or less. A bit gets lost in translation. You're sure you want to go through with this, huh?"

Galin whispered an indignant laugh. "What could

possibly go wrong?"

Starla's nose twitched with irritation, just as he knew it would. "Sometimes I wonder if you even bother reading my assessment reports. You really think the amount of money we're going to get for that thing merits this level of risk? We're not even one hundred percent sure it's still down there, or what condition it's in."

He pursed his lips at her. "Don't give me any more of that bologna, you know good as I do that it's down there. Anyway, I read every report you give me. Well, most of them anyway, I mean, I skim through them. And yes, I think it's a reasonable level of risk."

She gave him that look again. The one that said he was utterly full of crap, and both of them knew it.

"All we have to do is creep in there nice and easy while all of those frogs are sleepin', and then tiptoe back out with the carcass in tow. I've done harder jobs before shaving my face in the morning."

She looked like she had at least a few witty remarks to that, but didn't care to waste them on him. "And what are you going to do if anyone sees you? Murder a whole village full of Merlocks because they're trying to protect their temple?"

He shot her an exasperated frown. "Yeah, that's exactly what I'm gonna do, because I'm Galin Winchester, notorious frog murderer. I left Ulrick back there to guard the ship, didn't I?"

She continued to stare at him doubtfully, hands on

her hips.

"All righty then. We need to get going." He turned to Peter, who was dressed all in black just as he was. "You ready to become the ninja?"

"Ninja!" Peter whispered to Starla while performing a few blocks and punches. He pecked her on the cheek, and then descended off the opposite side of the rocks.

"*Please* be careful," Starla told Galin as he followed.

"We will. Just stay on those binoculars and give me a buzz if you see anything funny."

She sighed in protest, as women often do. "Fine."

He flashed his most charming grin, and her eyes eased just a bit. It wasn't much, but he'd take it. And with that, he was over the edge.

The two men crept down the rock face into the swampy jungle below, which was lit up by their night vision goggles. There wasn't much to see, apart from the occasional small, scurrying creature, until they reached the bottom.

"So, what *are* we going to do if these frogs wake up?" Peter asked when his friend caught up.

"Have you ever seen a Merlock run?"

"I've never seen a Merlock, period."

Galin sniggered. "Well, let's just say that I'm fairly certain we can outrun them."

"They jump though, don't they? Starla said they can jump really long distances, and really high."

Galin shook his head. "Not at night."

"Why not?"

Galin's finger went to his lips, then pointed up ahead. He slid off his goggles, and Peter did the same. A set of Merlocks was walking toward them on a path that wound up to where they'd seen the temple entrance from off in the distance. They were tall, thin creatures. Standing at about seven feet each, they *did* look a bit like frogs, stretched out and walking on two legs. Their heads and faces were the only thing about them that were un-froglike. The faces and ears were more feline than anything else, but instead of whiskers they had short, mossy beards. Their skin was rubbery, and had a greenish-blue tint under the light from a lantern that one was carrying from the end of a long, wooden pole. The lantern bore no flame, but rather, some sort of lightning bugs that were flittering around inside the glass, sending out an impressive amount of light, which was occasionally interrupted by a sizzling flash, which shot an even greater wave of illumination, momentarily lighting up the immediately surrounding jungle.

Peter found himself grinning from ear to ear, suppressing a little laugh as he watched the Merlocks walk. They truly were ridiculous looking creatures, a fact that was emphasized even further by their bow-legged stride.

Galin pulled his friend down, and the two of them hid quietly until the creatures had passed.

"We should be able to walk along the path safely

enough," Galin said. "There's just enough moonlight to see where we're going. Our eyesight is better than theirs, but there's nothing wrong with their ears, so let's try and keep it down.

As they walked, the sound of drums began to emanate from the depths of the jungle, followed by an ethereal chorus of clicks and howls.

"Get a recording of this," Peter whispered. "It's pretty catchy. We could listen to it on the way back to Earth."

"Not fracking likely," Galin smiled.

As they continued, several more groups of Merlocks passed by, heading off toward the source of the music. The two men slipped into the shadows each time, letting the natives go by, and making their way toward the temple a little bit further whenever they had the chance. Before long, it loomed up before them in the distance, and Galin could make out the front entrance.

"Doesn't appear to be guarded," Peter whispered.

"Doesn't appear to be," Galin agreed, examining the area thoroughly through his goggles. "Now's our chance, let's go. Remember to stay low."

Peter rolled his eyes. "How long we been doing this?"

The two jogged toward the temple entrance, stepping out of the shadows just in time to sprint for the door. They scrambled inside and hid themselves once again, taking a moment to wait and listen. All appeared to be quiet, though the orange glow and shifting shadows down the passageway suggested a sizable fire.

"That blaze isn't tending itself," Peter whispered.

Galin nodded, and drew his phaser. "Let's try not to stun any of 'em, if we can help it. This is a temple, after all. These Merlocks probably wouldn't take too kindly to us shootin' up their holy men."

"I am ninja!" Peter assured him.

Galin moved quietly along, sidestepping with his back to the wall, phaser pistol held up and ready if one of the natives happened to see them. But that wasn't really what he was worried about. Starla had warned them that the Merlocks were known for building traps in and around their buildings. Such traps were not constructed for intruders, as they didn't get too many of those, but for some of the predatory animals that would approach when they got hungry enough to risk tangling with civilization. Their little ones were taught from a very young age how to avoid such traps, Starla had said, but they were still advised to be vigilant. They would have been anyway, even if she hadn't warned them. This wasn't Galin's first trip to the rodeo, he'd been in places like this before, and there were always traps. Constructing them seemed to be a favorite pastime of primitive goons like these. Still, he did get a certain kick out of worrying her.

When they arrived at the end of the hall, Galin peered cautiously around the corner. "You gotta take a look at this," he whispered, easing out to get a better look.

Peter followed his example, grinning whimsically at the scene before them.

In the center of the room was a large, elevated pit, where the fire was blazing, and around that was a ring-shaped pool, where at least a dozen of the natives were lying, bodies partially immersed in the water. They appeared to be passed out drunk, or stoned from some ceremonial drug they'd been taking. The bottles and bowls that littered the floor were proof enough to support the theory.

One of the Merlocks opened his eyes and looked them over for a moment before returning to his slumber, clearly uninterested in the alien life before him.

"Stay off drugs, kids," Peter said with a grin.

Galin just shook his head. "We need to keep moving."

And so they did. Another passageway awaited them on the opposite side of the room, but unlike the first they'd come through, this one sported no warm, flickering light. The pitch-black opening gave Galin the shivers as they passed through, and as soon as they were beyond the firelight he re-positioned his goggles.

They crept along silently, Galin keeping one hand against the cool stone wall for support; it seemed that whatever had been burning in the previous chamber had begun to disorient him. The effect wasn't bad, but he was eager to leave the tainted atmosphere behind.

The air was becoming clearer the further they walked, and if the map of the temple that Starla provided in her report was accurate, then they should soon be coming into another large chamber, though he had no idea what might be in it.

Galin was pondering what might be found there when he heard a heavy click. He turned to see Peter gazing down toward his feet before looking back up with a guilty smirk.

A low, grinding sound began to echo through the corridor.

"RUN!" Galin yelled, turning back to rush for the chamber ahead. A few seconds later they were treading water. Ten seconds later it was up to their knees. Thirty seconds later, they had reached the end of the tunnel to find a stone door blocking their escape. The water was up to their chests, and still rising.

"Why can't anything ever be easy?" Galin moaned.

—NECRON
NOW—

The night was cold. Unusually cold. Too damned cold to be running around like some kind of thrown away pet, left alone in the woods because the family had too many mouths to feed.

Hopeless. Dejected. Betrayed. What had he possibly done to deserve this kind of luck. His own family, sons and daughters alike, had not only abandoned him, (as if that wasn't bad enough,) but now many of them were trying to kill him. Hadn't he always been there for them? Hadn't he always taken care of them, understood them when no one else would?

"Sons and daughters of bitches," he mumbled, and spat upon the vine-covered ground. "I curse every last one of them, especially…." His eyes welled up as he remembered. He'd been seeing it play over and over in his head, the day she'd left him. She'd snatched away the boy and then abandoned him. It was if she'd known that the Claymore was coming. Had she known? The ingratitude of it all was disgusting. Perhaps she couldn't help her lack of compassion for him, her inability to love, but it didn't matter. He couldn't help but hate her for leaving him there, for stranding him to watch the destruction of his own home. The dying screams of his reapers, his loyal and loving children, still rung cruelly in his ears.

And now…. Now all he was left with was *them,* and they wanted to eat him. *Him,* for God's sake, their own father. He repented of the fact that he'd ever made them, ever protected them. He should have let them all die long ago. He should have let Winchester destroy them.

So why hadn't he, then?

The moist ground saturated his pants as he sat; he cursed, and crossed his arms to draw in his coat a little tighter. A few matches remained in the book inside his pocket, which he caressed with his fingers and thought how nice it would be to strike a fire. Even if the forest weren't so wet, he wouldn't dare create such a beacon, lest it draw his lost children in closer. They were somewhat afraid of fire, but the light would still bring them, and then they would linger, patiently waiting for the flames to go out, and then it would be time to feed.

"To hell with them all," Mengele whispered, unaware that he'd spoken out loud. If they killed him, they killed him. What did he have to live for these days, now that his home and his most beloved children were gone. He had no one left to love, and even worse, no one left to love him.

Finding the driest spot he could, which was under the trunk of a thick, fallen tree, he scanned for unwanted critters, assembled the best bed he could out of leaves, and lied down in an attempt to get some sleep. How long would he have to live like some mangy, unwanted dog?

Just as he was nodding off to sleep, the sounds of distant screaming rang through the air. Such laments had resounded through the night several times since his displacement, but had seemed to lessen over the last few weeks. If fact, he'd been beginning to wonder if he was the only normal (if that word could be used to describe him) person left.

Without giving it much thought, he rose to his feet, picked up his pack, and headed off toward the screams. Perhaps it was simple curiosity, he pondered, or boredom with the ridiculous turn his life had taken. Or, perhaps he'd finally given in to despair. He didn't *want* to die, necessarily; he just wouldn't care much if he did. At least death would be something, an end to this pointless wandering. And if nothing else, he could provide one last meal, a final sacrifice for his ungrateful, starving children.

The twin moons were gracious enough to escort him along, gliding overhead like cautiously empathetic prison guards, popping in and out of view from beyond the trees. Their lights shown down upon his path, the beams of two flashlights, tracing the steps of his last walk.

Yes, it was time to pay the piper for all the great things he'd done. Perhaps some of his accomplishments were questionable, at least to common minds, but his intentions had always been pure. Couldn't God, or the gods, or karma, or whatever force was playing chess with the universe see that he'd always meant well? The old saying was true, he decided with a nod. No good deed goes unpunished.

The worst of the screaming faded away into the night as he walked, but one voice carried on, that of a woman.

A survivor? Perhaps he wasn't walking to his death after all. The resolution was somewhat disappointing. He turned to head back from the direction he'd come, and then realized just how foolish the idea was. There was nothing for him back there, just as there was nothing for him ahead, so what did it matter?

He stopped in his tracks to listen. The woman was

calling for help. No surprise there. Her voice was weak, and wracked with pain, but she *was* persistent, you had to give her that. But why was she carrying on so frantically? Had she been driven crazy? Her screaming was bound to attract more of his children.

No. He had to stop thinking of them like that, they weren't his children, not anymore. He realized that his feet were moving once again, heading through the jungle toward the miserable woman's voice, curious to see what she was carrying on about.

It only took a few minutes to reach her position. Peeking cautiously through the trees, he saw that she was sitting alone in the middle of a small clearing, surrounded by a sea of gore.

The men and women she'd been with had fought their attackers to the bitter end, until this blood covered woman on the ground was the lone survivor, and she didn't look like she had long.

"Is somebody there?" she sobbed, staring toward him.

Mengele spun, looking all around and behind him to make sure no one had snuck up. He cursed himself, imagining he'd been much quieter.

"I, I can see you moving out there. I can see your eyes sparkling in the moonlight. You're not one of them. Come…come help me, PLEASE!"

She seemed to be guarding something, there on the ground in front of her, but it was too dark to tell what. Curiosity once again got the best of him, and pulling his hood up to cover his scarred head, Mengele crept out to meet her. The ground was slick with gore, and he had to move carefully as not to trip over the bodies.

"I'm injured," she sobbed. "Very badly, I think. I've already lost so much blood. I, I don't think I'm going to make it." She gazed at him pleadingly.

Whatever was lying on the ground in front of her began to writhe. Was it a dying comrade, a loved one? No, he saw as his eyes adjusted to the light. It was two loved ones. Two babies. They looked to be no more than eight or nine months old. They, like everyone and everything else in sight, were covered with blood, though they appeared to be uninjured, and quite content.

"Are they twins?" the doctor asked in fascination.

The woman nodded. "My beautiful, twin boys," she laughed through tears. "Clark and Clint."

"And they were born here? On Necron?"

Again, she nodded. "My friends and I…," she glanced around in horror at the surrounding bodies, "we were dumped here a little over a year ago. That one there's the father," she said, pointing. By the way she said it, Mengele wasn't entirely sure the relationship had been altogether consensual.

"I've heard all the stories," she went on. "Even seen another baby born on this planet with the disease. I don't know why mine were born healthy, do you?" She looked up at him. "Though, I thank the good Lord they were."

Mengele kneeled, and shook his head. "No, I'm afraid I don't know, not yet."

She stared at him pleadingly. "I'm dying. I can feel it. Those things managed to take too many bites out of me. But my boys…you'll take them won't you? Try to keep them safe?"

Mengele looked at the babies with a hungry sense of wonder. Perhaps he'd been destined to come this way after all. Yes, he was meant to find these boys, meant to have them for himself. "Yes," he told the woman eagerly. "Yes, I'll take good care of them. I'll do all that I can to keep them safe." And he meant it. In fact, he hadn't been so sure about anything in a long, long time.

"Don't let them die," their mother said, kissing each in turn, and looking deep into their eyes. Tears washed the blood from her cheeks as she handed them over. "Promise me, that you won't let them die." Her voice was fading as fast as her body.

"Don't let them die?" he repeated. No, he wouldn't. He would never let them die, not if he could help it. But this time wouldn't be like the last, not like it had been with Jamie or the boy. He wouldn't make the same mistakes again. Never again. Not for anyone. "I'll make sure they're loved," he promised. "And I pray that one day, they'll come to love me."

"Tell them that I loved them more than anything. Will you?"

He supposed that would be all right. It wouldn't

change the way they'd feel about him, someday. In fact, telling them about their mother might even endear them more closely to him. "Yes. I can do that. Tell me, what's your name?"

"Mara. Mara Krimson."

"I'll tell them about how much you loved them," he told her, "and about what you did to save them. I give you my word."

The woman smiled at him, and eased her broken body to the ground. "Good," she whimpered. "That's good." And then, wearing that smile, her eyes closed for the last time.

A rustling sound arose somewhere in the distance. Mengele looked all around, and saw something curious toward the eastern edge of the jungle. Could it be…smoke? Smoke from a campfire? But who would dare light a campfire in a place such as this? Someone who wasn't afraid of his wandering children.

"Someone who can help us, perhaps?" he said to the babies, who were now nestled safely in his arms. "Let's go and have a look, shall we?"

General Soth stood fixed before the view screen, arms crossed, glaring at the T3038 that was getting closer and closer. There was a reserved kind of excitement in his eyes, the kind you might see in those of a tiger getting ready to pounce.

The surrounding crew waited at their posts for his command, a blanket of nervous tension having settled down to thicken the air. Except for the whirs, hums, and occasional beeps that emanated from the ship's control systems, the bridge was silent; the General's presence always seemed to have that effect on people.

Security officer, Lieutenant Lihnda Moore watched the android as well, gaping from her post on the rear, port side of the bridge. She hadn't been in attendance when the Claymore had first answered the robot's hail, but had been briefed upon resuming her duties. Hardly able to believe what the thing had said, she reviewed the record herself to confirm it. This bot had claimed to be carrying David Winchester, but one could plainly see from the image on the screen that he wasn't carrying anything. He'd even spoken as if he *was* the boy, demanding to know what had come of his grandfather, Admiral Winchester.

It wasn't all that long ago when Lihnda herself had escorted David Winchester down to the surface of Necron, to personally hand him over to his father. The Admiral had said something then, just before they left, that she hadn't really understood. *'Those monsters did something to him, but they won't get away with it. I'm going to find them. I'm going to make them pay.'*

She knew he'd been speaking of Dr. Carl Mengele, the man he blamed for the condition of his daughter, Jamie, and Lihnda had spent just enough time with the boy to recognize similarities between him and his aunt. Whatever Mengele did or didn't do to the pair of them, Lihnda had reached the conclusion that the whole damned family had something wrong with them. Then again, the Admiral's son Galin had seemed normal enough, though she'd only been in his presence for a few, brief moments.

Over time, she'd learned to take the Admiral's grumblings with a thick grain of salt. His mind had been slipping for a long time, everyone serving beneath him knew that very well. But the way the boy was acting, and now this business with the android- it was all too much to digest. Something very peculiar was going on here, that much was clear. But, what? Curiosity had gotten the better of her; perhaps her fascination with mystery novels while growing up was to blame for it.

If only she could speak with the android, question him about what he'd said, but Soth had refused to answer any more of the thing's communications, and she wasn't about to question the General's orders; no one on the bridge ever did if they valued their life. Soth hadn't actually harmed anyone, but there was something about the Draconian that erased every doubt that he could, and would blow out your candle if you crossed him the wrong way. He reminded Lihnda of a tigress she'd seen on a third grade trip to the Houston Zoo. The she-cat had locked eyes with her from behind the bars, and hissed with a hatred in its eyes that she had never, and would never see from another living creature- until she met Soth. The only thing that had stopped that tigress from eating her were those bars. She didn't know what it was that kept Soth from sinking his fangs into her and the rest of the crew, she was just glad those invisible bars were there, and wasn't about to reach through to give him a poke.

"Commander Maeng, run a full sweep of that android's systems," Soth hissed.

The man sitting at the science station quickly did as he was told, and a full analysis appeared on the view screen.

Soth studied the results intently for a few moments, and then began to laugh, a sound that clearly chilled the bones of everyone around him. Lihnda cringed.

"The fool has diverted every bit of available energy to its propulsion systems. In an attempt to reach this ship, it's left itself vulnerable. Prepare an anti-matter net."

"Aye, sir," Maeng told him. He sank his head into his console, and reappeared a few moments later. "Awaiting your command."

"Deploy."

Maeng took aim and released the net. They watched as the android flew directly into the trap, and began flailing around as it became more entangled before dropping out of view behind them.

"If that doesn't destroy him, it will keep him busy for a good long while." Soth returned to the captain's chair to have a seat, where he wrapped his thick tail around his legs like a vine. He might have looked comical there, being much too big for the chair, if he wasn't so downright terrifying. Soth could be dressed as a ballerina and wearing a jester's hat, it still wouldn't bring a grin to Lihnda's face.

"General Soth, we're receiving an incoming subspace transmission. It's from the Journey's End."

"Put it on screen."

The image that appeared made Lihnda take a quick step back, where she bumped into the wall as if she'd been pushed. Still, her eyes remained glued to the screen. A man sat before them on some kind of throne, though she couldn't make out any fine details because the place was so dark. Two large creatures stood on either side of him, their yellow teeth and eyes glimmering in the light.

Werewolves, was the first thought that came to her head. *They look like noble, self composed werewolves*. As amazing and frightening as those beings were, however, her eyes quickly returned to the man sitting on the throne. *My God. Is that him? Could this actually be the Nazerazi leader*? But the thing was- he appeared to be human.

"General Soth," the dark man said, "I expected a status report hours ago. Is everything proceeding on schedule?" His voice was heavy, and measured.

"Yes," the General hissed. "We have encountered a

few minor delays, but nothing completely unexpected."

The man frowned down at them, and Soth turned to gaze at the surrounding crewmen. He laughed. "If you fools were wise, you would bow in the presence of your king."

But Soth himself did not bow, Lihnda observed. In fact, nobody did, except for Fanmarr, a science officer and the one other Draconian on deck. Everyone else continued to sit or stand at their station, as if the command was some foreign custom they didn't quite understand.

The King rose from his throne, and strode from the shadows toward the view screen. His bright blue eyes gleamed with the contempt of a mad dog, barely able to restrain its bite. It was only now that Lihnda saw how unfailingly handsome this man was, even through his steely expression. He looked downright barbaric, wearing high boots and a long, furry loincloth. The muscles of his bare, tanned chest gleamed as if he'd just been oiled. Lihnda imagined this was the type of man who could be joyously lobbing off heads one moment, and then getting rubbed down the next by exotic slave girls for his troubles. His jet-black hair was slightly curled, and hung just above his shoulders. He wore no crown or jewels, but held a long, golden scepter with a wolf head on the end, and a crimson-colored fur cloak, which was draped from his shoulders, swept the floor as he walked.

The King glared at the unmoving men and women before him, drinking them in as if to memorize their faces, and when his eyes met hers, Lihnda felt a wave of panic wash over, as if in imminent danger.

"Bow, you fools," Soth warned. "Otherwise, he will kill every one of you."

They must have believed him, because the decision to heed Soth's advice seemed unanimous. Within ten seconds, every person on the bridge had taken a knee, including Lihnda, though she was one of the last.

The King's eyes eased a bit, and then returned to Soth. "Has the Katara returned to Necron?"

"I don't believe so, but they may be waiting in orbit under cloak."

"Just remember," the King said. "Galin Winchester must not be interfered with until the operation is complete."

Soth nodded. "Put your concerns to rest. I have not forgotten the terms of our arrangement, and do not need to be reminded. Nor will I betray them."

"Very well." The King returned to his throne, crossing one leg over the other. "Have you selected a volunteer for the journey?"

Soth's eyes fell upon Lihnda, and something not unlike a smile spread over his lips. Her heart skipped a beat.

"Yes. I have the perfect woman. She should suit your needs nicely."

"Excellent."

"Would you care to say hello?"

"As we both know, that would not be wise," he sneered. "Please keep me informed of your progress."

Soth gave a nod, and the view screen returned to the image of stars zipping past. He turned, and headed toward the door to leave. Lihnda watched him nervously, and shuttered to see his eyes fall upon her once again before stepping through the door.

Was she this "volunteer" they'd just spoken of? She hadn't volunteered for anything. With people such as these, however, one probably didn't have to.

She reached down and touched her stomach, just realizing how much it had begun to hurt. It seemed that every time she assumed things couldn't get worse, they did.

And now he was drifting.

The more frantically David struggled, the more the anti-matter net tightened around William's frame. He couldn't remember ever having been so terrified.

"William," he pleaded. "WILLIAM! I'm sorry. I'm so sorry, please answer me. *Please.*"

But William wasn't there. He hadn't said a word since David pushed his voice away, hours ago. He still didn't know what he'd done or how he'd done it, but he'd done it well.

Loneliness was something he'd struggled with even while William was with him, but now he would give anything to hear his friend's voice again. A vast sea of blackness spread out around him, only a handful of stars shining through the emptiness, and David felt as though he were drowning, that the nothingness was some great monster's belly intent on slowly digesting him.

As time ticked away, it was becoming harder and harder to think, more difficult to focus on finding a solution for survival. If only he had a clue for what that solution might be.

Diverting all energy sources back to the shields, he ceased struggling, and waited to see what would happen. The net continued to tighten; not nearly as fast as when he was fighting, which was good, but it was still tightening, nonetheless.

What would William do if he were here? What would he do to get this thing off? David didn't know, nor did he have any way of finding out. All of the robot's thought processes seemed so clear and easy to understand when the android was thinking through them in his head. David could see what was happening, as if it was all being written out like a mathematical equation in his own brain. But now that William was gone, he had access to none of those sources. He could still control the body, that much had been left to him, but now it was more like operating an advanced remote control car than moving his own body, having to think about each movement and push all the correct buttons to make it respond. Not that it mattered now; because of the net, having any amount of control would do him no good.

"William, I don't know how to bring you back, how to turn you on again. I don't want to die like this. Please!"

But he *was* going to die here, wasn't he? Die for a second time. And what would happen then? Would his soul drift among the stars like some kind of cosmic space junk, until he really and truly *had* gone mad from being alone? Or would he simply be free? Unhindered? Able to go wherever he wanted to go without restraint? That wouldn't be so bad, not for him. But then what would happen to William?

Minutes turned into hours, and hours into a disorienting blur as David tried to think of a way out of the trap, but he continually came to the same conclusion- it was no use. He was at a loss for answers.

So now what? Should he pray? That's what his grandmother would have told him to do.

Please, God! If you're out there, if you can hear me, please help me. I don't know what to do.

But if God was even out there, was he listening? He didn't seem to have cared enough to intervene when Earth was invaded.

He gazed out at the stars, keenly aware that there was nothing else to stare at, and they shone back uncaringly, unable to offer any comfort, even if they had wanted to. But then another light appeared, coming at him like a ship in warp, though it didn't appear on the scanners. It seemed to be moving quite slowly, but there was no way that was possible. Whereas a ship would be rocketing toward him, whatever this was came gliding, like a fishing lure being drawn back over the water. David's mind made all these observations at once, though he had no time to process them.

They're coming back for me, he thought, remembering the forms he'd seen after being torn from his body. But he wasn't scared, for some reason, he was actually relieved. He wouldn't be left alone, after all.

And then, sorrow came over him yet again. What about William? Would he be abandoned to drift lifelessly through space until the end of time? If so, David realized, he had as good as killed him. He was the one responsible. Some friend.

Struggling to focus on the thing coming toward him, he decided that it could only be some sort of angelic being. Perhaps God really had heard his prayers. Maybe Grandma had been right all along. As the thing drew closer, he struggled to bring it in focus, but could not. Not with William's eyes, at any rate. It suddenly struck him that he was seeing this being not through the android's sensors, but rather with his own soul, as he had seen things during that short time while being absent from a body.

Suddenly, panic swept over him as he saw what the thing really was. It wasn't an angel; it wasn't anything like that. It was an enemy, one of the creatures who'd tunneled into his school and taken him away, along with all his friends. It was a Draconian. No, even worse than that, it was a Draconian's ghost.

The shimmering reptilian came to a halt before him, hovering there to examine him quizzically. "David Winchester?"

His voice was surprisingly gentle. He didn't sound like an evil, cold-blooded ghost. His face looked kind enough as well.

"Yes," David said softly, surprised to find that the voice was his own.

"A most fascinating state you've gotten yourself into," the reptilian said, glancing over William's body and the anti-matter net that was tangled around it. "My name is Farwalker. I have come to take you back to your body."

"You have? But…why? Why would you?"

"Because, you were never have supposed to have left it. I have seen you from afar, and have come to help. I can explain more as we go, but we mustn't delay. Come with me." He held out his arm, as if waiting for the boy to reach out and take it.

"I can't. I'm stuck."

"Nonsense," Farwalker said. "This robotic body is trapped, but you are not. Come out."

"NO. I'm not going to leave William trapped like this. You have to help me get him out."

The reptilian hesitated for a moment, as if about to

argue, but quickly softened his gaze.

"Very well." He caught the netting up in his clawed hands, and then proceeded to tear it apart as though it were tissue paper. It fizzled and cracked as he worked, though the effect didn't seem to harm him. After many long minutes, he was finished. "Come out of him now. We must be on our way."

David fired up William's rockets, and ran a systems check. Everything appeared to be working properly.

"No. We're taking him with us. I'm not going to abandon him here. Besides, my sister came from the future and told me we both had to go back to my dad."

Farwalker said nothing at this, though his face tightened, and he seemed troubled. He gazed away into the stars for a few moments as if he was looking beyond them, seeing things that the boy couldn't before finally turning back.

"It will be as you say, but you must tell me more of this visit from your sister, for there are very strange things afoot. Come, we must hurry."

Farwalker turned, leaving a glimmering streak in his wake that fell immediately away like stardust, and David followed, realizing he wasn't afraid anymore. Maybe he should be, but he wasn't. More than anything, he was relieved to no longer be alone.

The purple glow of Necron's twin moons was swiftly

being consumed by the yellow rays of morning, and Dr. Carl Mengele was still walking. Dense tropical jungle was giving way to a sparse scattering of trees, and the scattered rocks and occasional boulder that ushered in the awaiting cliffs beyond. It has been quite a long time since Mengele had seen a sunrise such as this, unhindered by buildings or forest.

He looked down at the twins, almost as if to ask if they might be thinking the same thing. Both were fast asleep.

The stream of smoke he'd seen earlier that night had dwindled to almost nothing, but the remnants appeared to be coming from somewhere in the rocky terrain beyond, over the edge of the cliffs. There was nothing to be done but keep moving toward it, and hope that whoever had built the blaze wasn't going to shoot them dead or eat them, or both.

It didn't take long for the morning to grow hot, and by the time he'd reached the cliffs, both boys were awake and fussing. They were hungry, he knew, thirsty for their mother's milk, and it was only then that he realized how thirsty he was, as well. He had no provisions for any of them, however, and raised his eyes longingly to gaze into the great distance ahead. It had been a number of years since he'd travelled out this way, or to the lands beyond. Exactly how many years he couldn't remember, but it had to have been at least twenty if it was a day- not since he'd led a band of his reapers to drive off those troublesome ranchers at that old homestead. A river flowed through that place, he remembered, but how long would it take him to get there? Five, six hours? Probably more since he had two squirming snotlings in tow.

His decision was made. He would continue toward the smoke, and if he couldn't find anyone there, since survivors on this planet quickly became very good at hiding, then he would continue on to the river, however long it took, and hope for the best.

Carefully maneuvering along the edge of the cliff, he found what looked like an old goat trail, and headed over the rocks to try his chances. The way was going to be a bit difficult in places, he saw, but as they proceeded, his patience was usually rewarded with a somewhat easy way down, even if he did occasionally have to sit and slide along on his rear.

Only once, as he'd set off sliding, had he gained an uncomfortable amount of speed, and been unable to slow down in time enough to stop where he'd intended. His feet had brought them to a hard stop against an awaiting boulder, and he promptly found himself lying on his stomach atop of it, a screeching baby having been cast to the ground on either side of him. He slid off the rock, amazed to find his injuries limited to a scraped belly and two sore ankles. The babies too, it seemed upon examination, were more insulted than injured, one being virtually unmolested, while the other had suffered a small bit of road-rash on his forehead and nose. They both screamed for a long while after that, until Mengele was tempted to bash them both upon the rocks as payment for their unceasing racket. But no, he had promised to guard them, and guard them he would, though if he'd had his surgical equipment he'd be half tempted to detach their vocal cords, he pondered indignantly.

Suddenly, he forgot his anger, and a surge of excitement ran through him when he looked down to see the green grass, blowing upon the plain. They were almost there now, he could nearly reach out and touch it, and he had to force himself to slow down, lest there be a repeat of the prior incident. They might not be so lucky if they crashed like that again.

Eventually, they reached the grass, and Mengele laid each baby down, a bit more roughly than he'd intended, letting himself fall down beside them. The grass felt cool compared to the oven-like air upon the rocks, and he thought that the only thing that might feel better at that moment was sinking into the awaiting river. The promise of the cool waters ahead didn't allow him to linger long, though the prospect of sleep was tempting.

Sitting up, he opened his eyes to something entirely unexpected. A ship, swooping in from the jungle not far from where he'd come, passed overhead, and set down near the edge of the cliffs about a mile or so away. It was an odd looking vessel, reminding him more of an ancient sailboat than any type of spacecraft he could recognize.

He realized at once that it was the area where the smoke had come from, where he'd intended to go before the path in the rocks had led him astray.

"Pirates," his dry voice whispered. "Stinking filth."

But he'd never known pirates to set up camp on the surface before. They'd always just set down long enough to round up a number of his children, which he imagined would be used for whatever dark purposes the buccaneers had on their agenda, before taking off and disappearing into the heavens once again. His reapers had taken care of many such men, but the majority had been able to escape without too much trouble, they simply had never had the resources to put a stop to it.

Mengele found he was grinding his teeth while thinking about it. He didn't want anything to do with pirates, but was that what these men truly were? And if they were, what kind of bargain might he have to make with them to get safe passage off the planet? Perhaps he could offer his services. They wouldn't deal with him fairly, that much was certain, but he was vastly more intelligent than any such curs, and could turn the tables around on them quickly enough if it came to a game of wits.

Sebastian Winchester was coming back, bringing certain death along with him; it was just a matter of time. He couldn't know when, and no one had told him as much, but he was as certain of that as he was of anything. Winchester was going to come back and finish the job he'd started, and when he did, Mengele wanted to be as far away from this doomed experiment of a world as he could possibly be. Necron was his own creation, truth be told. It had been he, and his colleagues, who'd invented the virus, and Bios had become as much a victim to it as any of the human beings who'd lost their minds and humanity to its imperfections.

So, if taking up with pirates was a necessary step in getting himself, and his new children to safety, then he would just have to hold his nose and do it. He knelt down, took one baby in each arm (they felt three times as heavy now as they had before), and headed off toward the ship.

Mengele clung to the rocks, trying to remain hidden while moving as swiftly as he could. The dryness in his throat had passed through to every other part of his body, and his legs felt heavy and wooden. One of the babies had drifted back to sleep, and the other looked lethargic, staring off into the sky with arid, unseeing eyes. Mengele realized that he had no knowledge about the time they'd last eaten. How long had their mother been stranded there with them amidst that carnage? How long had the whole skirmish taken? He had no idea. It was possible that the lads hadn't been nourished in the last twenty-four hours or so, and he needed to get them something quickly. Under the full heat of the morning sun, they would soon dry out like raisins.

Abandoning all pretense of stealth, Mengele returned

to the edge of the grass and beelined for the ship, stumbling along clumsily until he could make out human forms in the distance. The closer he got, the more people he saw. There were dozens of figures up ahead, perhaps a hundred, perhaps more, and with great relief he saw that they didn't look anything like pirates. This was an odd sight, indeed. What could these people possibly be going on about?

"Hello, down there," came a voice from the rocks above.

Mengele scanned the area for a moment before finding the two men climbing down to meet him. Lookouts; they probably had him spotted long minutes ago. He jerked down his hood to make sure his scars were adequately covered. His condition had been better than normal, as of late, but still might be a point of concern for some.

"Wow, what have you got there, mister? Babies?" said the first man. He was approaching cautiously, but trying his best to seem casual.

"Yes," Mengele rasped. "But please.... Water? Do you have any?"

The second man was already unstrapping his canteen.

"My name's Andrew. This is Will."

"Carl. Carl Me...." No, what was he thinking? He couldn't give them that name. Carl Mengele had to remain on Necron, had to die here with the rest of the disease. He coughed. "Sorry, my throat's so very dry.

Name's Carl Krimson."

He allowed them to each take a baby while he partook of a good, long drink.

"Were these little ones born here on the planet?" Will asked.

Mengele nodded, and carefully tipped the canteen to the first child's lips, allowing a few drops to trickle in. "Yes. Yet they were born uninfected. It was quite a surprise to their mother and me. This one's called Clark, and that one there's Clint. They're my two miracle boys."

Will nodded. "Never heard of one being born here and making it before. Good for them, I'm glad to see they're all right."

"Is anyone else traveling with you who might need our help?" Andrew asked.

The doctor shook his head. "Their mother, and all the others, were overrun and killed. We're the only survivors. Haven't seen anyone else."

"Well, you don't look so good," Andrew said, motioning him to come along. "Come with me up to the camp and we'll get you taken care of."

"I'd be very grateful." He was already feeling a bit better. "Tell me, what's going on here? Who are all these people?"

"Looks like you wandered in at just the right time," Will answered. "We've been rounding up survivors wherever we could find them. Gonna evacuate this place; apparently the planet's been scheduled for re-terraforming. Ain't that the craziest thing you ever heard? I guess the powers that be decided to get rid of the remnants of the zombie virus once and for all."

"And us along with it," agreed Andrew. "If we don't get our tails out of here quick enough."

"And…pirates are assisting you in this?"

"Heavens, no," Will laughed. "Some friends of ours commandeered that ship up there. It's been renamed the One-Eyed Maiden, formerly known as the infamous One-Eyed Whore. We've got that and another ship, though we're waiting for a few parts to be delivered for it, and the ship that's bringing them for us, the Katara.

"The Katara? Galin Winchester's ship?" Mengele didn't like the sound of that.

Will nodded. "That's right. You know him?"

"Heard of him," Mengele said, holding back his disdain. He didn't think he wanted anything to do with any more Winchesters.

"Well, you'll get to meet him, soon enough. And then we're all getting out of this hellhole together, how's that sound?" Andrew grinned at him giddily.

"Sounds good to me," Mengele said. "Seems like I've been here way too long." He shuffled the babies to get more comfortable. "Seems like years upon years."

The ship was approaching Necron when Galin finally

snapped out of his daydreams. "All right, kid, we're nearly there," he said, failing to hold back a yawn. "We'll drop out of warp and run scans before approaching the planet."

Jace nodded. He wondered where the captain's mind had been over the last few hours, as it had definitely been somewhere else. Maybe he'd been thinking about Starla, just like he had been thinking about Hero. Was Starla dead too? He hadn't believed it, not before they'd lost Hero, but now he wasn't so sure. Optimism was in short supply these days.

"Think there'll be pirates?" Jace said haphazardly.

"God, I hope not. We could use a little reprieve, couldn't we?"

The answer went without saying.

The Katara dropped out of warp, and Jace began the sweeps. It only took an instant to find what he'd hoped he wouldn't. A large vessel appeared on the scanners on the other side of one of the planet's moons.

"Frack me," Galin said, peering over his shoulder. "It's the Claymore."

"The Claymore? I didn't think they'd return so soon."

"Neither did I. Please tell me they haven't released that torpedo yet."

Jace scanned the planet. "No. Necron is still Necron, at least for now."

Just then, a hail came in from the Claymore. Galin flicked the switch, and winced to see that it was General

Soth, not his father, looking back at him.

"Greetings, Captain Winchester. I knew our paths would cross again."

"General. The pleasure's all mine."

"Yessss," he hissed with a laugh, detecting sarcasm. "I'm sure it is."

"I don't see my father with you, is he well?" The Admiral's absence was concerning.

"He is currently unavailabe. But, we have our own to discuss. I am aware of your intended rescue efforts down on the surface. Please do not let my presence stop you. Feel free to proceed."

Galin stared him in the eye, looking for any sign of the reptilian's real intentions. Soth seemed like a being capable of a good, many things, but being charitable and empathetic to the needs of others wouldn't be placed high on the list.

"You don't look like you trust me, Captain. Is it your intention to insult my honor?"

"No. Just, uh…trying to understand your reasoning. Why would you let us help the people stranded down there?"

"Because I made a deal with someone, someone who cares very much about the fate of your beloved castaways. We will hold our position in orbit while you carry out your work. I will even send a team to assist, if you so desire. And once you've completed your heroic quest, you will come on board this ship, so that we can have one last meeting, face to face." His eyes seemed to burn with hunger as he spoke the words.

"Is that a condition of you letting us go about our work, that I come aboard the Claymore when it's finished?"

"A condition? Not at all. I would call it more of a prediction. I have something to show you, Captain, that you would chase me to the ends of the galaxy to get a better look at." His guttural laughter made Galin's skin crawl. "But we shall save that discussion for later. For now, you and your associates will not be hindered until your efforts are complete. You have my word." His glare was harsh, and deadly. "Is it enough?"

Galin stared at him speechlessly for as long as he dared. "It's enough."

Soth made a slight bow of his head, and then the screen flashed off.

"Do you believe him?" Jace asked nervously.

Galin turned the Katara toward the planet, and increased speed. "Yes. He's too arrogant to lie to us. For whatever reason, I think he's gonna let us do what we need to get done."

"What about your father? Do you think Soth hurt him?"

"No, I don't. I don't know what's going on with him, and to be honest it's got me a little worried, but I don't think Soth did anything to him, or else he would have said so. People like him don't beat around the bush, and he wouldn't give a damn about sparing me my feelings."

"I don't know," Jace said. "Seems too easy. I have a bad feeling about this."

The kid was right. Soth was up to something, and before long, they were going to find out what. Thing was, there was no way out of it now, not without abandoning the people down below, and that wasn't an option.

"I've been in tighter spots before," Galin said, though he knew it wasn't always easy to escape without scars.

—MERLOS III
FIVE YEARS BEFORE—

Galin was starting to feel like a slime covered raisin. Thanks to Peter, they had been fully submerged in water for nearly an hour now, and still had no idea as to how to get out. Lucky for them, Joseph had suggested they bring oxygen extractors along in case they needed to breathe underwater. It seemed a bit ridiculous at the time, but now.... Galin made a readjustment. The devices became somewhat uncomfortable to hold in one's mouth for long periods of time (he suspected they'd been invented by a dentist), but having them was a whole lot better than trying to figure out how to breathe like the fishies do.

He swam down to the base of the stone wall to take

yet another look. There had to be a switch somewhere, a release for those frogs unlucky enough to stumble down the wrong passage and step on that switch after a hard night of worshiping whatever the hell it was these things worshiped. He swam the entire length of one wall before Peter came up from behind and tapped him on the shoulder. He pointed over and up before swimming away, and Galin followed.

They came to what looked like a solid section of the ceiling, and Galin was pleasantly shocked to see Peter put his hand right through it. Examining it more closely, he saw it was simply a well designed illusion. The rocks had been placed in such a way as to make the ceiling look solid, but the concealed hole was just big enough for each of them to slip through comfortably, which they did.

Emerging in the small crawlspace above, they were able to remove the oxygen extractors and enjoy some long, relieved breaths.

Looking at Peter, Galin grinned weakly while shaking his head.

"Hey, I got us out, didn't I?" Peter retorted.

Galin pursed his lips.

"What, you've never set off a trap before? I happen to recall a little incident in the mines of Cerberos a few months back."

Galin raised his hand. "I don't want to talk about that."

"No," Peter said. "I didn't expect you would."

They followed the crawlspace through to an outlet in the wall of the next large chamber. Sliding over onto his belly, and then easing out to hang from the ledge, Galin saw that there was still an eight foot drop to the floor. This was going to sting a bit. He dropped, and sure enough, pain shot through both of his legs as he rolled onto the hard stone and crashed to his side. He moaned, "Oh, frack me like a son of a—"

"Hey, you all right down there?"

"Never been better." Galin staggered to his feet, pleased to find that nothing appeared broken. "Hey, hold on just a minute."

Resting against the wall a few feet from the hole was a wooden ladder. That would have been nice to have a moment ago, but he never would have been able to reach it, even if he'd known it was there. He stretched himself out a bit, and then picked up the base of the ladder and scooted it over to Peter.

"Don't ever say I never gave you anything."

"Thanks," Peter said, looking pleased. He climbed down. "You sure you're okay?"

"Just bruised up a bit. I'll probably feel it tomorrow more than I do right now."

The surrounding chamber echoed with their whispers. It was empty except for a stone well in the middle of the room, which had twice the width and half the height of a typical water well. A thin stone cover rested across the top.

"That's where they place their dead," Galin said. "Starla told me they hold their funerals in here, and then lower the bodies down into that pit."

"I thought this place smelled funny. Yuck!" He scrunched up his nose. "Kind of a creepy way of handling the dead, isn't it?"

Galin shrugged. "I suppose, but I can't think of a way of handling the dead that isn't. Burial, burning…taxidermy," he added with a chuckle. "Death is death. Ain't nothin' pretty about it."

"I suppose that's true. Still, if I don't make it out of this, don't throw me in that pit, okay?"

"Nor you, me."

Peter crossed his arms. "No, I think I'm gonna have you stuffed. Put you right back there in the captain's chair to resume your duties. Ship won't be flown any worse, and I'll win all the arguments."

"Well, just be sure to dust me off now and then," Galin said, scanning the opposite wall for an egress. "I have my reputation as Mr. Alpha Quadrant to uphold."

"There it is." Peter pointed to a small passageway, only a few feet high, near the far end of the room. "I assume we're going to head into that place through the backdoor?"

"Yeah. There are easier ways to get in, but Starla outlined this route as the least likely to draw attention. The sanctuary isn't far now."

"Guess she wants to keep us around for a while after

all."

When they reached the passage Galin stooped to go through, then turned to face him. "Hold on a minute, didn't you read her report?"

"I skimmed it," Peter said, holding his hands up.

They shimmied along, walking like ducks for a few dozen feet until the passage opened up on the other side. Firelight could be seen once again, and Galin peeked out to see a large courtyard, opened up to the sky above, a garden spread across the entire length. The sounds of a strange conversation could be heard in the distance. Galin turned and raised a finger to his lips.

"There's somebody out there, talking," he whispered. "Can't tell what they're saying." He reached into his ear and gave the universal translator a few sharp taps. "Damned things are supposed to be waterproof."

Peter shook his head. "Water resistant, there's a difference. Can you tell how far away they are?" he asked.

"Not far," Galin told him before leaning out to take another look. "Three of 'em, over there on a bench a few dozen yards away. We'll have to try and sneak around."

Peter leaned over him to take a look for himself. "This'll be a perfect place to make the extraction if we can get rid of those frogs."

Galin nodded. He waited several moments, and then set off in a roll, tumbling to a crouch behind some flowering bushes where the Merlocks couldn't see him.

As soon as Peter got the chance, he followed.

"I think we can stay out of sight by going around those trees," Galin indicated with a tip of his head.

"That's going to take us right up behind 'em. We'll have to be careful."

"I don't see any other way around, do you?"

Peter scanned the area again. "Nope. I think it's our only option."

Galin gave him a nod, and crept along silently on his hands and knees until reaching the tree line. The Merlocks were completely out of sight at the moment, though their voices were louder than ever. He waited for Peter to catch up, and together they made their way to the other edge of the tree line. Once there, they paused, waiting for another opportunity to go, and Galin was just about to bolt when a sudden movement at the base of the next tree froze him in place.

Focusing through the shadows, he saw a small, collared creature not unlike a toad, or perhaps a bulldog, staring back at him. Its eyes were bugged out in fright, and it barked a series of clicking croaks, jumping up and down threateningly before finally making a lunge. Instinctively, Galin punched the thing squarely in its toady little face, and it promptly sped off, releasing a series of offended, whimpering moans.

Galin raised his eyes to see the three Merlocks standing before them, utter shock and bewilderment written upon their faces. Unlike their previous counterparts, these were completely awake and aware of what was happening.

They've never seen alien life before, Galin realized, feeling a bit sorry for them yet groping for his blaster nonetheless.

A shot flew past his head, and one of the Merlocks dropped. Peter had been able to draw while he'd been fending off the mutt.

The remaining Merlocks, though in shock, were quick to remember their duty, and one was already in the midst of throwing his spear when Galin lunged for them. He caught each one by the waist, taking them down with surprising ease, and realizing as they dog-piled to the ground that these beings were much lighter than they looked.

Peter's cry of pain had just registered in his mind as he got ahold of his own blaster and gave one of the struggling frogs a shot to the upper leg. The Merlock quit struggling, but his companion began to fight all the more, slamming a rubbery fist into Galin's jaw, causing his teeth to rattle and resulting in a nasty bite on the tongue. Then the creature swung up upon his back as if he were a rodeo bull, forced his chest into the ground, and delivered a quick series of jabs to the back of his head before the sound of another blaster shot rang out into the air. The Merlock fell off.

Galin flipped over to find Peter standing over him, the Merlock's spear buried into the upper right side of his chest. He jumped to his feet.

"God, Peter. You okay?" It was a stupid thing to say, he realized immediately. Of course he wasn't okay, the man had a fracking spear stuck through his chest, the point of which was protruding about six inches from his back.

"Yeah," Peter answered. "I will be, I think. He didn't get me in any of the vitals."

They looked at each other, both wondering the same thing, but neither saying it. Had the spear been poisoned? Starla hadn't mentioned anything about that.

"You'll be okay," Galin finally agreed. "But we need to get you out of here. I can use one of the beacons to extract you right now—"

"No." Peter shook his head forcefully. "We're nearly there. I'll wait in the passage and keep watch."

Galin stared him down for a moment. He knew that his friend wasn't going to budge.

"The package is too important. Just, just hurry, okay?

"All right, then. Wait there in the entrance while I hide these bodies. They should all be out for a while, and nobody'll be able to see them in those shrubs over there."

It was quick work, as the bodies were so light. Normally, Galin would have felt sorry for the headaches they would all be feeling upon waking up, but then he figured they'd gotten more than their fair share of licks in, and Peter had definitely gotten the crappy end of the stick.

Galin looked over to see that the little toady mutt was still hiding, peering out nervously from beneath a statue by the fountain. They shouldn't have to worry about him for a while either.

"Okay," Galin said, meeting Peter in the passage. "Let's finish this up and get the hell out of Dodge."

"Let's," Peter grunted, keeping a firm grip on the spear to prevent it from moving.

Together, they headed toward the final chamber.

—NOW—

The mob that had gathered upon the grassy plain below was considerably larger than the previous group they'd encountered while setting down on Necron. That had been a beautiful, clear day, Galin remembered, nothing like the torrent they were in right now, but it didn't appear that the people gathered to celebrate their return were going to let a downpour stop them.

Galin looked over at Jace with a big grin on his face, and the kid returned it, though it was a weak attempt. How could they not smile, seeing all those people clapping, cheering, and shouting for them? Their enthusiasm was contagious.

They landed, and upon descending the steps, Galin found James Locke and Angelica Garcia Ramirez waiting to greet him. Angelica threw her arms around him, and kissed him fiercely upon the cheek.

"I'm so happy you made it back okay."

"We all are," James agreed. "It was quite a shock to see the Katara just take off like that. We weren't sure *what* was going on. Thanks for sending word back when you did."

Galin smiled and waved to the dispersing crowd. "Yeah, sorry to scare you like that, but we didn't have much choice in the matter. I see you've been herding the strays; got a pretty sizable group now."

James nodded. "If they're not here, then they didn't want to be found. Daniel Butcher and Matt Anderson have been leading the rescue efforts in the One-Eyed Maiden. They've swept the entire planet, several times over. As soon as that other Dagger class ship is finished, we can be on our way. Were you able to obtain the necessary parts?"

"Oh, yeah. We've got parts, all right, and that's not all. We also have a new home, a safe place where everyone can put some stakes down and plan the next move." Then his thoughts turned to Soth. "Although, we're going to have some complications to deal with first. The Claymore's already here, in orbit, and General Soth knows all about us and what we're doing."

Angelica looked like she'd been slapped. "Soth? But if the Nazerazi are here, why haven't they attacked by now? We need to get out of here as fast as we can."

"I don't understand all his motives, but I believe we're safe for now. He said he made a deal with someone who wants to see everyone safely escorted off this planet. He won't make a move until we've evacuated."

"And you believe him?" James asked.

Galin nodded. "I do."

Angelica's eyes went wide. She didn't look so sure. "Well, I suppose it doesn't matter much. If they launch that torpedo, we won't even know what hit us. Either way, this nightmare will be over." She immediately looked sorry for saying it. "Sorry." Her shoulders slumped. "I've got to get back to the repairs."

Galin's eyes followed her as she headed back for the caves.

"She's been working around the clock on those repairs. A lot of us have. Really takes a toll on your spirit after a while."

"I can appreciate that," Galin said. "She'll feel better once she's lain her eyes on all the spare parts we've gotten ahold of. If you can collect a few of your men to help haul 'em in, we can get right to work."

"Absolutely," James said, and called one of his men over to explain the situation. Then he turned back to Galin. "And now, Captain, if you'd come with me, I have something very interesting to show you."

Galin followed him to the entrance of the caves, where someone handed him a towel so he could wipe the rainwater from his face.

James led him through the passages that led to the large cavern where the UST Rondel was docked. "We've found the control room that opens the bay door on the side of the mountain. I was getting a little worried that we'd have to blast our way out."

The ship had come a long way since the last time Galin had seen it. "Wow, you people really *have* been busy. Good work! These old girls clean up pretty nicely, don't they?"

"You said it. My mechanics tell me we should be up and running within a few days with those parts you brought. Does that sound about right to you?"

Galin nodded. "As long as we don't run into anything unexpected, I'd say two days at the most."

James looked pleased, yet irritated, like a boy who'd just been told it wasn't quite time for Santa to come. "I shall keep my fingers crossed, then."

Once they'd spent a few moments looking over the ship, James led him to the wall opposite the entrance. "A woman bringing in supplies just happened to lean against this wall for a little rest." He pushed the camouflaged rock, and it slid back. "Imagine how surprised she was to find herself lying on the floor in this hidden cave a few seconds later."

The room was small, containing a control panel, one chair, and a waist high bookshelf, which James walked over to and put his hand on.

"There's all kinds of information here. Electronics,

ship mechanics, a small library of wealth for anyone with the desire to perform their own work on a ship like the Rondel."

Galin looked them over with a smile. "Interesting. It's funny to think that this ship must have been somebody's weekend project. She must have been left here by whoever abandoned that old homestead."

James chuckled. "Reminds me of my father's obsession with fixing up this old Tesla Windchaser he kept in the garage. My mother hated that hovercar, hounded the poor man until he got rid of it, but not before he'd sunk a small fortune into the repairs. My father was a lot of things, but a mechanic wasn't one of them."

Galin smiled and looked back down to the books. "I wonder why whoever put these here wanted paper copies?"

"Some people just like the feel of antiquated books," James said.

"Yeah. Peter was like that. He loved to read, and preferred paper editions. I always teased him about it."

"Really? Why?"

"I don't know." Galin gave him a sad grin. "It was just one more thing to rib him about, I guess. You know how it is."

James fell into the chair and placed his feet up in front of the control board. "I get it. Male camaraderie. Iron sharpening iron and all that. Men share a form of friendship that's hard for most women to understand."

"That's true. Still, they're twice as hard to figure out as we are."

"Yes," James chuckled. "As far as we've come as a race, it's funny how the opposite sex sometimes seems more alien than aliens do."

Galin nodded, and stooped down to take a closer look at one of the books. "Hey, what's this?" He leaned over to retrieve a leather journal, which rested on the bottom shelf in a spot by itself. "*The Bleeding Star Chronicles*," he read. The title was located beneath a line of words that were written in a language Galin couldn't read, but vaguely recognized.

"The whole thing's written in that language on the cover," James said. "You know what it is?"

"I'm not positive, but it looks like Greek," Galin said.

"Yes, that's what I thought as well."

"We can scan it into the Katara's computer to try and get it translated." He flipped through the pages, continuing to stare at the words as if they might suddenly start making sense.

"You think that thing holds some significance?" James asked, seeing his interest.

"Let's just say the title kind of grabbed me."

James stared at him expectantly until Galin filled him in on the details of where they'd been, and everything they'd learned about the Bleeding Star Initiative. James listened intently, looking as if he didn't quite know how to wrap his mind around it.

"We can talk more about this later," Galin said. "It's not gonna make much sense until we have a long time to talk through it all, and there's a lot I still don't understand myself. Right now, we've got bigger fish to fry. So tell me, have you tested out these docking controls yet?"

"We've run diagnostics on everything, and the system appears to be functional, but we didn't want to open the doors just yet. We thought it best to avoid drawing attention from pirates or the Nazerazi."

"I don't believe that's a concern anymore. Is it okay with you if I hang onto this?" Galin gave the journal a few pats, and James grinned back and nodded, so he slipped the book in his pocket and leaned over to examine the control panel.

"General Soth seemed pretty invested in making sure we all get off this planet alive, though I'm not sure why. I reckon he'll blast any pirates that are stupid enough to approach while the Claymore's in orbit."

"Well," James said, running his fingers through his beard. "I guess now's as good a time as any. Hows about we open up the doors and let some of that cool air in?"

"It's your show," Galin told him.

James reached up, flipped a few switches, and hit the big green button.

"You're not even going to warn anyone?" Galin

chuckled.

"Naw, I like to keep 'em on their toes."

There was a loud, metallic thunk, followed by a steady grind as the horizontal doors began to rise. The light that beamed through was surprisingly bright, given the cloud-covered skies overhead. Dirt and rocks tumbled away until the doors came to a rest, letting in the smell of heavy rain. The people working in the bay clapped and a few looked over toward the hidden control room to give them waves.

"Guess they were getting sick of this stuffy, cave air," James said. "That, and it's just one small step closer to getting off the planet."

They left the control room to find Chief Joe heading up the steps of the Rondel.

"I'll talk to you later," Galin told James, shaking his hand. "I want to catch up with the chief on a few things.

He sidestepped some men carrying a crate and darted up the stairs, nearly running right through TAII, who was standing there glaring with her hands on her hips.

"Excuse you," she griped.

"Hey, aren't you on the wrong ship; what are you doing over here? It's not like you could walk over."

"Joseph brought me over to assist with the repairs. Integrating the Katara's old CPIC with this ship's systems will move along more smoothly if I keep an eye on things from the inside."

"Makes sense to me. I'm glad to see you helping out.

I'm sure your expertise on these ships will come in quite handy."

She beamed at him. "Thanks. I'll do what I can."

Galin winked at her before heading for the engine room. As he walked through the ship, he saw things both familiar and unfamiliar. It was like coming back to visit an old home you'd moved out of long ago, after someone else had moved in. He smiled, taking it all in. Not long ago, he'd thought the Katara was the only one of these girls still around; he was glad that wasn't the case. There was something about these ships that drew him in, Kanbun had been right about that. Having two more of them in the family made him feel happy, and these days he could use every little bit of happiness he could get.

Galin grinned expectantly into the clear, blue sky. The day was warm and bright, without a cloud anywhere in sight; it was almost as if Necron's sun itself was turning a curious eye to the festivities. The crowd waited impatiently upon the grass, knowing that at any moment, the starship Rondel would emerge from the side of the mountain for her first flight in decades.

Potential crewmembers for the Rondel had been nominated in a meeting two nights before. Only the most experienced and trusted candidates were selected. Galin and the crew of the Katara had then screened them, in order to confirm their capabilities, and from those found worthy, the crew had been selected by a simple majority vote.

Angelica Garcia Ramirez would serve as captain. Her co-pilot would be a man by the name of Ezra Steward. Jason Hawthorne would serve as gunner and weapons specialist, and Andrew Black was appointed engineer. Two interns had also been selected, to serve in whatever capacity was needed, and learn from the more experienced crew. Their names were Elizabeth Story and Zach Hayes.

An additional crew member had also joined the roster the day before, though his addition was neither planned nor expected. While searching through some encrypted data files, TAII discovered a backup copy of the Rondel's own Tactical Artificial Intelligence Interface unit, which was called Squire. This hologram took the form of a pre-teen boy, and seemed to Galin to be much more amiable than TAII. In the one afternoon he had spent with the lad, he'd been quiet, helpful, and compliant with everything that had been asked of him. Galin imagined that this sort of personality must have been the standard type used on all the other ships. Only he would be lucky enough to get the one designed to emulate a real-life, bratty teen-aged girl.

Even as Galin's mind was pondering the previous few days' events, the Rondel breached the side of the mountain. The people erupted in cheers as the ship twirled a few circles overhead, and then shot off for the stars. It had been agreed upon that a short test run was in order before loading the ship up with passengers, and if everything went well, they'd be leaving within the hour.

"Looks like she's a fair enough pilot," Galin told Jace. "Definitely doesn't seem to be shy of the gas peddle."

"No, she doesn't," Jace agreed somberly.

The kid didn't have much to say these days. The old Jace would have eaten up a celebration like this, shared in everyone's happiness and even have been the life of the party; these days he just didn't have it in him.

Galin put his arm over the young man's shoulder and gazed into the horizon where the Rondel had vanished just moments before. "We'll be up there soon ourselves, and then we can get back to putting all these pieces together."

"Yeah. And then this place will be re-terraformed. It'll be wiped away, just like it never existed."

"At least it'll be the end of that virus. There are still hundreds, maybe thousands of those infected zombies out there."

"I know." Jace looked around, back toward the cave entrance and off in the direction of the apple orchard and old homestead. "Most of the memories these people have made on this planet will haunt them for the rest of their lives, but most of mine are good ones. Hero and I had some great times here together, in the short time we had.

It makes me kind of sad to see the place destroyed."

"I can understand that; after all, it really is a beautiful planet. Bios was a good name for it back then, a place so full of life, a fresh start for so many people. And it still is beautiful, even with the remnants of that plague running across its surface." Galin sighed. "And it will be again, much like it was before, everything's just going to look a little different."

"It's a planet," Jace frowned, "not an Etch A Sketch."

That made Galin chuckle. "Never thought of it quite like that. I'm going to head over to Peter's grave one last time before we go, you want to tag along?"

"Sure," Jace said, rising up from the grass. They walked in silence for a while before he spoke again. "I don't get it, if the zombies don't breed, won't the planet be hospitable again after they all die off? It's not like the UEG is around to dump any more prisoners here."

Galin shook his head. "Some of the animals on this planet act as carriers, and there's always a risk that the virus could mutate and cause another outbreak. Some alien species could be susceptible as well. That'd be a real nasty planet-warming gift to leave for any would-be visitors."

Arriving at the gravesite, the day seemed even more beautiful than it had before. The sunlight sparkled upon the trickling stream, a light wind blew through the trees, and a small family of rabbits was just disappearing into the brush on the other side of the bank. Everything in sight seemed to be singing a tribute to life, except for that one section of disturbed earth beneath the shady tree.

Jace looked down to see that grass had begun to grow up over the ground that marked their friend's final resting place. As he was looking on, a bolt of pain shot through his head like lightning, forcing him to his knees. For a few disorienting moments, everything went black.

"Hey, kid, be careful. You gotta watch your step around here." A strong hand reached down and pulled him back up to his feet. He recognized the voice before his vision cleared. It was Peter.

"Yeah, I know. I, I'm just…not sure what happened. Got a horrible headache all of a sudden."

"Maybe that new wife of yours has been working you too hard. I know how it can be for young, married couples." Peter gave him a few slaps on the back and looked hard into his eyes, as if to determine if he might take another stumble. Apparently satisfied with what he saw, he made a sad grin, and looked down toward the grave. "I hate to leave him on Necron like this. The chief was one of the greatest men I've ever met."

The chief, had he said? What had happened to the chief? Jace couldn't seem to remember.

"We've got to help Galin go back, put everything right, if we can. You understand me, kid? We're running out of tries." He looked at Jace pleadingly for a moment, and then a realization dawned across his face. "Hold on. You don't know what I'm talking about, do you? You look confused."

"I am. My head's really clouded. I mean, I thought...I thought...."

"You thought *I* was dead? Frack me, I guess to you, I am. I can tell I'm already losing you," he grabbed Jace by the neck, drawing him in close. "I need you to remember something, okay? Focus, kid. Look me in the eyes, damn it! I'm from the thirty-eighth journey, you understand? Tell Galin, the thirty-eighth journey, you got that?"

Peter was shaking him back and forth, telling him to focus, but his head hurt. It hurt bad, and he couldn't.

"Okay? Hey, Jace, you okay?"

Peter was gone, and the shadowy figure, shaking him lightly by the shoulders, slowly turned into Galin.

"You okay, Kid? Hey, look at me."

"I'm fine," Jace said. "Come on, let go." He pushed Galin away, done with being shaken about like a child's rag-doll. "I've got a splitting headache."

"Sorry," Galin said, sitting down next to him on the grass. "I didn't mean to hurt you. You looked like you were about to pass out." He reached up to feel the young man's forehead. "Who were you talking to just then? Hero?"

"No," Jace said, rubbing his head. "It was Peter. He wanted me to tell you something. Said he was from the thirty-eighth...something or other. That mean anything to you?"

Galin thought for a moment. "No. Doesn't mean anything to me. How about you?"

Jace shook his head. "I know how weird it sounds." He rubbed his temples. "Seemed pretty important to Peter, though." He stared at Galin, almost guiltily. "He was standing right here, I swear it. You didn't see any trace of him?"

"I wish I had, kid. I'd give anything to talk to him again."

Jace shook his head doubtfully, as if to say that Galin's opinion might be different if he actually had gotten the chance.

They sat for a few moments in silence before Galin stood up. "You feelin' well enough to walk back, or you wanna' go piggy-back."

Jace sneered, surrendering a half-hearted grin. "I think I'm okay now, but going piggy-back might be a nice change; give me a chance to really take in all the sights."

"Maybe another time," Galin chuckled, retracting his offer. He looked back down at Peter's grave.

Jace saw a great sadness in his eyes, and the horrific uncertainty of someone forced to peer down at his own grave. But then dawned the steely resolve of a man making some great and unspeakable promise.

Galin piloted the Katara through Necron's exosphere

into the awaiting vastness of space. The ship felt a little heavier somehow, as it always did when human passengers were traveling onboard. Following the Katara was the One Eyed Maiden, bearing the greatest bulk of castaways due to her size and resources, with the Rondel finishing the caravan in the rear. The ships had no more than broken orbit when the gleam of the Genesis Torpedo's thruster appeared out in the distance, rocketing toward the planet like a fast-pitch thrown by God. It made a slight hook before disappearing from view. Jace switched on the view screen just in time to see the torpedo collide with the planet's surface, sending out a purple shockwave that encompassed all of Necron in a glittering cloud of plasma.

"I wonder what the Nazerazi have planned for this place," Jace said.

"Who knows," Galin answered, switching the screen back off. "At the very least, it's one more world on the star charts they can blot with a checkmark." He clicked on the com. "Daniel, Angelica, we're gonna take this nice and easy. I expect the Claymore to fall into pursuit. If it comes down to it, I'll try to lead them off. Don't worry about us, we can easily outrun them. Just stick to the plan, whatever happens. If we get separated, Squire knows the way home."

"Roger that," said Daniel. *"And Galin, if you do end up going aboard that ship, be careful."*

"Not to worry, brother. Careful's my middle name.

How you guys doin', Angelica?"

"The old girl's still doing fine," she said. *"Listen, thanks again for everything. We couldn't have done it without you. And Daniel's right, be careful. I have a bad feeling about all this."*

"You're welcome, and I will. Happy flying, everyone. I'll check in with you in an hour or so." He clicked the com off, and gave Jace a grimace. "Well, here we go."

"Maybe we shouldn't wait," Jace said. "Maybe we should just try to lead the Claymore off now. Wouldn't the others have a better chance of escape?"

"I wish I knew. For now, I think we just need to play this straight and see what Soth is going to do. He wouldn't have let everyone off the planet without a reason."

Sure enough, the Claymore fell in line behind them just a few moments later, though it kept a comfortable distance. This went on until they'd cleared the solar system, where Galin took the convoy to warp. Again, the Claymore followed.

"I expected them to hail us by now," Galin said. "What if Soth's just toying with us after all. He strikes me as the kind of guy who might like to play with his food before he eats it."

"Want me to change course?"

"Not yet. I'm gonna try to hail them." He opened a channel. "Claymore, this is Captain Winchester of the Katara. Is Admiral Winchester available?"

Nothing but silence.

"I'll take that as a no," Galin said. He turned to Jace, who's face was turning white.

"I think we might be in trouble." He nodded to the radar.

An entire squadron of Nazerazi fighters had just dropped out of warp in the distance ahead.

"They're not coming toward us," Jace said, "just waiting there, directly in our path."

Galin's heart began to beat faster, whether from fear or anger, he couldn't tell. He got on the com. "Daniel, Angelica, I'm assuming you guys see this. Lets bring the ships out of warp."

And so they did. The Claymore dropped out of warp as well, only to hang in the distance like a curious bystander.

Galin watched the screen. Neither the Claymore, nor the squadron made any move to intercept them. *Calm down*, he told himself. *Keep a cool head*. There were too many people depending on him, and this was no time to lose it.

"*What do we do now*?" Daniel finally asked.

The Claymore hailed them. Galin clicked on the screen to see Soth's smug face glaring back at him. "You can't go that way, Captain, and neither can your two other ships. My men won't allow it. So, where will you go now?" Without another word, the screen went black.

"Maybe you were right," Jace said. "He *is* just toying with us."

Galin was silent for a few moments. What happened now? What was he supposed to do? He looked out at the stars, and then glanced down to the radar screen, which was lit with dozens of Nazerazi fighters, then looked back out at the stars again. Where could he possibly go to keep these people safe? If Soth knew about the Bleeding Star Initiative Command Center, and was barring their way, did he have some other place he wanted them to go? If that was the case, why didn't he just say so, tell them where? He gazed out into the vastness of space. For minutes, he stared, as Jace spoke with the other pilots and crewmen about their situation, barely taking note of them. The stars shining in the distance had a calming effect on him, and he needed to clear his head; needed to figure all this out. He needed to listen. His eyes drifted across the expanse, coming to settle on those stars off the port bow. They seemed to be different somehow. In fact, the longer he looked, the more they seemed to be calling to him. Telling him to come on over and join the party. Hell, why not?

Galin leaned forward and put in the coordinates. "Follow me," he instructed the other pilots.

"Where are we going?" Jace asked.

"That way," Galin said, pointing, and Jace rolled his eyes.

The One-Eyed Maiden and Rondel fell in behind them, and just as Galin expected, the Claymore as well.

"Oh, God," Jace moaned. "That group of fighters is

coming after us, too. What's going on?"

Galin clapped him on the back. "I don't know, kid. But if they wanted us dead, we'd be dead, right?"

"Sure, I suppose."

Almost instinctively, Galin put in a set of coordinates and took the Katara to warp.

Jace entered the coordinates on his data pad. "The Zemeckis Nebula? What's in the Zemeckis Nebula?"

"I guess we'll find out when we get there."

Jace put his hand to his head. "Frack me. You're losing it, aren't you? We can't both be going crazy, I don't think I could take it."

"You're *not* going crazy, remember?" Galin continued to stare up at the stars ahead. Yes, they were calling to him somehow, he was sure of it. "And I don't think I am, either."

Upon reaching their destination, Galin ordered the convoy to drop out of warp. The streaking stars came to a stop and the radiant colors of the Zemeckis Nebula spread out before them.

"This must be where rainbows come from," he said with a smile.

Jace scowled at him. "Yeah, it's beautiful, but all those pretty colors aren't going to protect us from the Nazerazi. What are we doing here? What happens now?"

"Follow me, everyone," Galin said over the com.

"Where are we going?" Jace glanced at the radar to see that the Nazerazi ships had held position just behind them.

"Don't know," Galin told him. "This way just feels right somehow. You trust me, don't you, kid?"

"Sure I do. I guess I'd just like things to make sense for a change."

"You and me both," Galin said.

They flew on for what seemed like hours, though Galin never bothered to check the time. He guided them through the Nebula like he'd been there before. He hadn't; but it sure felt like he had.

Eventually, he brought the Katara to a halt. "This is it."

Jace joined him in looking out at nothing.

Galin stood up and crossed his arms over his chest. "This is where we're supposed to be."

"If you say so."

An incoming hail popped up from the Claymore, and Galin put it onscreen.

"Captain Winchester," Soth grinned. "I assume these are the coordinates? Why don't you open it now so we can move all this along, hmm?"

"Open what?" Galin asked.

Soth glared at him. "You annoy me, Captain. You humans have always annoyed me, it's the way you wallow in your inability to notice those things so plainly dangling right before your eyes."

It sounded like something Nicodemus would say, but devoid of tact. However, perhaps Soth had a point. Hadn't it been the stars calling to him that had brought them here in the first place? He closed his eyes, determined to relax, and tried to listen. This went on for several long minutes.

"You're trying too hard, Captain." The reptilian's voice startled him. "That is why you fail. Stop trying, and simply DO."

Galin let out a long breath, glared at Soth, and sank down into his chair. He let every thought, every care, drift from his mind like feathers on the wind. A moment later it felt like he was floating as well; resting on a cloud, sinking into a sky without a bottom. It felt like he was drifting peacefully in space at the end of a lifeline, just as he'd done so many times in the past, before this long nightmare had begun.

And then he saw it, clear as day, hanging there in space before him. He reached out and opened it, as easy as turning the handle of a door.

"Well, I'll be SLAGGED!" said Ulrick.

Galin turned to look up at him, a bit confused, as he hadn't heard the big man come in. Ulrick's jaw was dropped in amazement, as was Joseph's, who was standing right next to him. Galin then turned back to see what he already knew was there, the twirling wormhole, which glimmered and spun, be it ever so slightly, like a whirlpool in space.

All of a sudden, the Katara rocked gently as if she'd been struck.

"They've hit us with a tractor beam," Jace said, stating what the rest of them already knew.

"Command your comrades on the other ships to go through," Soth said. "And then disengage your engine so we can bring your vessel onboard."

Galin stared into his eyes, attempting to search his intentions. "And why would I do that?"

"That squadron," Jace said, nervously. "They've taken up a battle formation. They've got us surrounded."

Soth grinned, smugly. "I'm well aware of your ship's upgrades. You could easily outrun us if we hadn't locked onto you with a tractor beam, but even with your advanced firepower, you're still no match for a battle cruiser. Command your companions to go through. You and I both know that it's what they're meant to do."

"He can't be serious," Joseph said. "We don't know what's on the other side of that thing, or even if there *is* another side."

Galin stood, and stared into Joseph's eyes intently. "He's right. They'll be safe on the other side. It's what they're supposed to do." He opened a channel to the Rondel and One-Eyed Maiden. "Daniel, Angelica, I can't order you two to do anything, but I'm advising you both to go through that wormhole. I don't know where it'll lead you, but I know you'll be safe on the other side."

"What about you?" Angelica asked. *"Are they going to let you go through as well?"*

"No," Galin said. "But don't worry about us. You've got the people on your own ships to protect. They're your first priority." He turned back to Soth on the viewscreen. "And what happens to the passengers on this ship? And my crew?"

"I will provide a transport for your remaining passengers, so that they too may enter the wormhole. Your crew will surrender to me; if they are compliant, they will not be harmed, and your ship will once again become the property of the Nazerazi Empire."

"And if we refuse to go?" Daniel asked. *"We aren't leaving the Katara behind. We're all in this together."*

"Then you will all die together," Soth said. "My patience has its limits, I promise you. Winchester, what will it be?"

"He won't do it," Jace said. "He won't kill everybody. He kept us all alive for a reason, right?"

"He'll do it," Ulrick said. "I can see it in his eyes. I've looked into the eyes of a lot of killers. If we drive him to it, he'll kill us all."

"Listen to your friend," Soth said. "He may be ugly, but he is quite perceptive. I have held up my end of the bargain so far, but will do what must be done, if needs be."

"Bargain? Bargain with who?" Galin demanded.

Soth glared at him impatiently. "Send those ships

through, then come aboard, and I will answer your questions."

Galin looked around at each of his friend's faces. If he gave in, would they truly remain unharmed? And for how long? Surrendering to Soth wasn't an option he cared to consider, but he needed to get the other ships to safety before deciding.

"Angelica, Daniel, take your ships through the wormhole. He'll destroy you if you don't. You need to do it now."

A few silent moments passed, nobody moving.

"Do it," Galin demanded, sounding almost angry. "You accepted responsibility for everyone on those ships when you took command. You have to protect them."

"But what about all of you?" Angelica pleaded, sounding on the verge of tears.

"Don't worry about us. We'll be okay. Go, while you still can."

"He's right," Daniel said. *"Our lives aren't the only ones we're responsible for, Angelica. Not anymore. We need to go."*

"All right," she finally conceded, trying to hold it together. *"Then let's get it over with."*

Galin sighed in relief, and Joseph gave him an encouraging clap on the arm. The crew of the Katara exchanged goodbyes with those of the two other ships, and then watched as they reluctantly approached the wormhole. The Rondel went first, stopping just short before entering.

"Goodbye, and good luck," Angelica said. *"Thank you all again for risking your lives for us. God bless you all."*

The outside lights of the Rondel flashed on and off, and then the thrusters lit up, and she was gone.

The One-Eyed Maiden flashed her lights as well. *"We can never thank you enough. Take care of each other."*

"We will, Daniel. When this is over, we'll come find you, if we can."

They watched as the former pirate ship passed through to whatever fate awaited her people on the other side.

"Now, you will surrender your ship," Soth said. "I give you my word, your people will come to no harm unless they bring it upon themselves."

"What about Galin?" Joseph demanded. "You haven't said what you've got planned for him."

Soth laughed with a screech that made Galin's blood run cold. "Haven't I? No, I suppose not. The Captain and I are going to have a bit of friendly conversation, and then I will take the utmost pleasure in ripping him apart with my bare hands."

Joseph leaned to Galin's ear. "With that new engine, we have an excellent chance of being able to rip free of this tractor beam. Our shields are at full strength. If we do it now, I'm sure we can make it."

"Now, why would you want to do that?" Soth said, then turned to grin at Joseph. "We reptilians have much better hearing than humans give us credit for. He looked back to Galin. "Don't you remember? I said I had something to show you? A surprise. You humans like surprises, don't you? I'll even throw a party and wrap it up for you if you'd prefer."

Galin was starting to see red. "You've done something to my father, haven't you? Cut the crap, General. If you've got something to show me, then be quick about it."

Soth smirked menacingly. "Bring her out," he commanded.

Two security officers walked off screen, and a few moments later reappeared with the last person Galin had ever expected to see.

"JAMIE?"

Knees going weak, Galin sank to his seat. A tremble took hold of him, and he struggled to grasp the arms of the chair, squeezing as if the whole ship might fall out from under him.

"Jamie? Is it…really you? I don't understand."

"It's some kind of demented trick," Ulrick growled, veins bulging. "You cloned her somehow, didn't you? You cold-blooded bastard!"

Soth said nothing, but gently pulled away the gag in the woman's mouth.

"Jamie?" Galin repeated. It was almost a whisper.

"It's been a long time," she said, rubbing her jaw, and without a hint of care.

Tears had begun to escape down Galin's cheeks. He

wiped his eyes in order to see her better. "But, how? How are you…?"

"Where's David?" she demanded. "He's mine now. I want him back."

A storm of confusion swept through Galin's head. None of this was making any sense. What was she saying? How was *she* even possible? A woman who'd been dead for nearly fifteen years was now standing right there before him. The last time he'd seen her, she'd been a lifeless corpse in the morgue, and now here she was with her eyes wide open, staring back at him with nothing more than a bit of annoyed indifference.

"Do what Soth says. Surrender your ship, and come aboard so we can talk. Bring my… your son along with you."

"Take her back to her quarters," Soth interrupted, pushing her roughly back toward the guards.

Galin jumped to his feet, gritting his teeth as he stared at the grinning monster before him.

"This is no trick, Captain," Soth hissed. "Allow us to bring you in with the tractor beam. Do not resist, and I'll allow you to speak with her before you die. Everyone will live. Everyone, except for you." He pointed at Galin with a long, sharp claw.

Jace turned to look at him, a barely restrained panic on his face. Ulrick and Joseph were staring him down as well. Galin could feel the eyes of all the passengers from Necron, as if they were boring holes right through the walls to see what he was going to do. They were all depending on him, counting on him to save them. He was the one who'd brought them here. He was the one who'd asked them to trust him, if by doing nothing more than taking them aboard as passengers. But what of his father? What of the woman, long thought dead who awaited him upon the Claymore, what of Jamie?

His decision was made. He glared back up at Soth. "I'm shutting down the engine. Bring us in."

Galin stood silently with his crew and passengers, helpless within the walls of the Claymore's holding dock. He'd been a captive on this battleship before, not too long ago, awaiting his doom in the brig, but he'd managed to escape in the end. He would do so again, he promised himself.

Galin still couldn't believe what he'd seen just moments before; Jamie, his departed baby sister. Could he dare to hope that it had been something more than a cruel trick, orchestrated to make him surrender without a struggle. But if that were the case, why would Soth go to such lengths to bring him aboard? Did the Katara mean that much to him, and if so, why would it? He'd said he was aware of the ship's upgrades, but that didn't mean he knew about the engine, which was the only truly unique piece of technology. Whatever the truth might be, he was going to find out soon enough.

The door slid open, releasing a cool gust of wind that smelled like the guts of a UST Battlecruiser. It was a clean, crisp metallic scent weighed down with a strong dose of duty, but it was also marred with something else, a smell that took Galin only a moment to identify, because he had come to grow so familiar with it.

"Draconians," he mumbled.

The officer standing before him deepened her frown. "Yes," she said, having taken his meaning, though the thought hadn't been intended for her. "And I'm here to take you to one. The biggest, smelliest one of them all. But, you already knew that, didn't you? I'm Lieutenant Moore. Come with me. Just you for now," she said, holding up her hand when they all began to follow.

Galin recognized her immediately. This woman had been with his father when he'd brought David back to him on Necron. Her face was pretty, but stern, and he wondered if it had been so before the invasion. The two space marines she wore like accessories didn't look any friendlier.

"Galin Winchester," he introduced himself while handing over his blaster. "But *you* already knew *that*."

She nodded, curtly.

"Was that really my sister?" He blurted, abandoning pretense.

The question seemed to make her uncomfortable. A few moments passed, and he didn't think she was going to answer. Finally, she let out a short breath, and her expression softened. "Yes, I believe it is," she said. "At least, what's left of her."

"What do you mean by that?"

"I wish I could tell you more, but your father has always been very secretive...I probably don't know much more about her than you do at this point."

"Where is he? My father, I mean. Does Soth have him held up somewhere?"

"Don't know. The last anyone saw of him was about three days ago. We haven't made any stops since then, but I suppose he could have left on a shuttle. I'm sure the General will fill you in."

Damn, this woman was cold. "You don't like me very much, do you? Was it something my father said?"

She let out an agitated sigh. "I don't have anything against you. And to be honest, the Admiral has never talked about you much, not around me." She stopped in her tracks, turned to face him, and thrust a finger into his face. "It's always something with your family, though, isn't it? Some big fracking drama? It's like the whole universe revolves around you people and your stupid problems. While the entire human race crumbles around us, it's all about finding your kid, chasing down your sister, tracking down *your* sorry butt and escorting you to Soth. I'm getting just a little bit sick of you…you *Winchesters*!"

Her eyes were watery, her face red, and she spat out his family's name as if it were some filthy word she'd promised herself she wouldn't say anymore.

Galin just gaped at her in silence for a moment. "Well, I was going to ask you to dinner tonight, but if that's your attitude, you can forget it."

She only looked back at him with something akin to a hurt confusion, and then turned to resume her journey down the corridor. Galin followed, as did the Space Marines.

"I used to really love my job, you know that? Then I got transferred to your father's command. I mean, he was crazy enough *before* the invasion, but he's really gone downhill since then. Just when we didn't think it could get any worse, he brought Jamie and your son on board. He's kept her locked up in her quarters ever since. Let me tell you something, the phrase 'nuttier than squirrel crap' doesn't even begin to cover it for the both of them. And now, he's off and disappeared, leaving the rest of us to deal with Soth. Do you know what that's like? Do you have any idea? The guy is downright terrifying!" Her face was angry and pleading.

"I've met him. So, I actually *do* know what you mean."

She crossed her arms and shook her head angrily. "I swear to God, I think I'm going to have a nervous breakdown."

Galin wasn't convinced that it hadn't already happened. He didn't know why she'd decided to open up to him like this: perhaps it was just the way she was, but he didn't think so. She seemed like the type of woman who was a good officer; an officer that cared about her responsibilities and the lives of those around her, and he was pretty good at discerning that kind of thing. It was something one learned to pick up on after being in the service for a while, and he'd been exposed to the military all his life.

"Everyone has their breaking point," he told her. "Just try to hang in there. Things are bound to get better."

Her expression was one that dared not hope. "Why do you say that?"

He offered a little grin. "Well, things can't get any worse."

"Thanks. That's encouraging."

"Sorry. It's all I've got at the moment. Anyway, you think you've had it rough serving under the Admiral, you didn't have to grow up with the man. Just thank your lucky stars for that."

"Yeah, I suppose," she said, leading him into a turbo-lift.

She sure was a tough egg to crack.

"I think I can handle him from here, gentlemen."

The Space Marines saluted her, and she returned the gesture before the door slid shut.

"So, you have any idea what he wants with you? I mean, not to sound rude, but why are *you* so special?"

"Center of the universe, just like you said." He gave

her a wry smile; her pissy attitude was starting to get the best of him.

She remained silent until the lift came to a stop. The door opened and he followed her out.

"The General's quarters are right up here."

"His quarters? He wants to meet me there?"

"Those were my orders." She looked him over. "Nervous?"

"Among other things."

She came to a stop in front of Soth's door.

"Look, I'm sorry for being such a bitch, I don't really mean to be. You seem like an okay guy. Good luck in there, okay?"

"Thanks. You could come in with me. Moral support and all that." He smiled.

"Afraid you're on your own this time. Soth doesn't take too kindly to uninvited guests. I'll be waiting out here."

She rang the buzzer, and a few moments later the door slid open. The room was dark, and Galin couldn't see anyone or anything inside.

"Ah, Captain Winchester," Soth hissed. "Please, come in."

"Good luck," Moore whispered, looking scared for him.

He gave her a subtle nod, and stepped inside.

The room was as muggy as it was dark, and smelled like a pet shop. Galin stood in silence until his eyes, as well as his nose, adjusted.

The only traces of furniture were a large block of wood, which could have served as a bed, and a birdcage that extended across the entire far wall. Soth sat on the floor, studying him silently as a predator tracking its prey.

"Where's my sister? My father?"

"Why, Captain, you wound me. I thought we might enjoy a few minutes together by ourselves first." His words were saturated with a dark, cold anger.

"You want to talk?" Galin said. "Let's talk. Why do you want my ship?"

Soth smiled. "I don't want your precious ship, Winchester." He flashed his fangs. "But, an associate of mine does. I agreed to turn it over to him, and he agreed to help me get my hands on you. That's why I pretended your father was a traitor, an ally to the Nazerazi. I knew he'd play along in order to protect his people, thinking that someone, but not knowing who, had betrayed him. It would have driven him mad, if he wasn't already there. And it was all for you! Imagine how hard it was for me to let you go the first time I had you, to allow your escape, to stand by and do nothing while you flew that pathetic tin can of yours away as if it was *your* idea. But no, it was all part of the deal." He clicked his razor-like claws together. "But I have you now, and there will be no escape for you this time."

"You want little, old me? Why? What have I ever done to draw the affections of a big, lovable lizard like yourself?"

"What have you done? You ignorant, close minded little fool, it's not what you've done, but what you are doing. What you are doing right now, and what you are going to do. You are reckless and stupid, too concerned with your own suffering to recognize the consequences your actions might have upon others. But why do I waste my time and words on you? Perhaps I hope to see a hint of something that would lead me to believe you are capable of taking a different path. But no, thirty eight times I have tried to stop you, and each of those times you have slipped from my grasp. But I didn't know then what I know now, how to break you, or more accurately, how to allow you to break yourself."

"You're quite the jabber-jaw, Soth. Too bad I have no idea what your big scaly yapper's flappin' on about."

"Even now, you crack jokes. You refuse to listen, to recognize the things going on all around you. But I have seen inside you, Winchester. I have seen your heart. Your humor is only a thin veneer to the grief that drives your every turn, and that will be your undoing."

"You're mad," Galin spat at him.

"And you're boring. Boring, predictable, and one-dimensional. Yet, you have continued to evade me. You wonder why I want you? Why I hate you? This is the reason. You have evaded me. At every turn, you have evaded me, and until now I didn't know how, or why. But the thirty ninth time is a charm, I have already succeeded, you just don't know it yet."

"I didn't come here to listen to the ramblings of a insane reptilian. How about you shut your filthy canary muncher and take me to my sister."

Soth's smile was as refined as an old wine. "As you wish, but do hurry things along, I'm looking forward to killing you." He stood, and walked to the door. "Come, follow me. I shall serve as an escort for the dead calling upon the dead."

Soth said nothing until they reached the door to Jamie's quarters, and then he turned to look down, staring into Galin's eyes.

"Although I detest you, Captain, you have my respect as a fellow warrior."

"Well, goodness me, I'm honored."

The General flashed his fangs. "It is because of warriors' honor that I warn you, do not eat anything this woman gives you."

"Why not, are you afraid she'll poison me? Rob you of your chance to tear me apart with your bare hands, and all that?"

Soth pressed his finger against the access panel and opened the door. "Enjoy your visit. You have one hour;

after that, you belong to me."

Galin took a deep breath, trying to lighten the feeling in the pit of his stomach, and stepped into the room. The door slid shut behind him.

Jaime was standing by the window, most likely having just been interrupted from gazing at the stars, one of the things they'd always enjoyed doing together when they were young.

She started toward him, and as she came, he recognized the fact that she appeared just as lovely and young as the last time he'd seen her alive. She looked almost exactly the same, but for the emotionless, empty expression on her face. It was the same look he'd become accustomed to seeing on his own son, as of late. The look hadn't been as evident when he'd seen her on the view screen, but now that they were face to face, her utter lack of emotion sent ice through his veins.

Something else seemed strange about her as well; it was the way she was dressed. She was wearing an elegant gown, emerald green with golden laces, which exposed too much cleavage; her hair was braided into an elaborate bun, and her face had been made up. Her arms, neck and face were flawless, though pale, and no trace of a smile or frown appeared as she gazed back at him.

Galin had seen his sister in such garb only a few times since their mother had died, while going to the prom or some other pompous affair. She'd always been satisfied to dress herself more carelessly, sporting a natural beauty without augmentation. But why should her outfit bother him? Here was his sister, standing before him in flesh and blood. He knew not how, but here she was. Galin rushed forward to seize her, drawing Jamie's body into an embrace so fierce that had it been any stronger, he might have snapped her. Taking her by the shoulders, he stared into her eyes, his little sister's eyes, expecting to see the same joy and elation that he was feeling. But, it did not come. The young woman before him looked like his sister, but as he continued to search her, he slowly realized, with great agony and horror, that she was not there.

They stood together in silence, Galin continuing to search her eyes for something, anything, that would help him recognize the Jamie he used to know. When he could no longer stand it, he released her, stumbling back and beginning to hyperventilate. The pieces were beginning to fall into place.

"You've been alive this whole time, haven't you? On Necron? You're the woman who kidnapped David. But…why? Why'd you do that? And if you were alive, why didn't you ever come to find me?"

Her vacant stare told him that she was just as confused as he was. He remembered the old proverb, something about the eyes being the gateway to the soul. What were Jamie's eyes telling him? They didn't appear to be telling him anything at all.

His stomach sank even deeper, if that was possible. "Jamie, are you the one who killed Peter?"

She continued to stare back at him, her expression unchanging. Why wouldn't she say anything? Galin had to close his eyes and take some long, deep breaths to calm himself down.

"Let's just start at the beginning, okay? What happened to you? How did you end up on Necron?"

She cocked her head, her eyes narrowed. "Come," she said, turning to walk away. "I've prepared supper. We can talk at the table, as we once did, long ago."

He followed her into the dining room, where the smell of roasting meat greeted them. Despite the state of his stomach, Galin's mouth began to water. He sat down at the table across from his sister, where a place had been set for each of them. As she opened a bottle of wine, Galin looked over the table to see grapes and mixed berries, a loaf of fresh bread, and a large roast prepared with onions and red potatoes.

This is the food of the dead, he thought, though he had no idea why. He remembered the tale of the Greek goddess Persephone, who was tricked by Hades into eating a handful of pomegranate seeds, food from the underworld, thus consigning her to spend part of each year in his hellish abode.

Galin sat quietly as Jamie drew a carving knife, and began to slice the meat. He had to stop himself from pressing her to talk; perhaps she'd be more willing if he gave her a little time.

Once she'd placed a few slices of meat upon her plate, she rose and walked around the table, stopping behind him. Her hair brushed across his shoulder, and shivers ran through his body as she leaned over, drove the knife back into the roast, and cut him a generous portion. Casting the blade haphazardly onto the table, she retrieved the wine and filled his glass, then returned to her chair.

Knife and fork began to scrape across her plate as she cut her meat, and glanced back up at him.

"After I died, our father brought my body to Dr. Mengele, and he…."

"He brought you back to life?"

The question seemed to trouble her. "No, not really. He didn't bring me back, he woke me."

"He *woke* you?"

She nodded. "But it doesn't feel like being awake. It feels like being in a dream, a nightmare that can't be escaped. It always has."

Her words pierced him. What few remnants of joy at seeing his sister alive were being burned away as he watched her, and listened to her words. Was this body before him even his sister at all, or just some shell, which hadn't been allowed to rot after the young woman's departure? Galin felt sick, confused and angry. And what of David? Is this what his son was as well? He could not bring himself to speak, and hopelessness began to gnaw him like some insatiable predator.

"I can't feel anything. Not love, nor hate, nor desire. I haven't felt anything since the day my new father woke me." She took a bite of roast, chewed slowly, and swallowed it. "Why aren't you eating? Do you not hunger?"

"Why did you kill Peter? And what…what did you do to David?" He should have been angry, but his rage had given way to despair.

"I killed Peter because I wanted the boy." She talked through a mouthful of food, as if the concept of manners had escaped her. "I knew he wouldn't give him to me, and I needed him. I wanted my father, Mengele, I mean, to make him like me. I thought that perhaps if I had a son of my own, I might feel something again. Love. Concern. Annoyance. Anything. But, I never got much of a chance to find out. Your father returned to take him away from me. I didn't even know he was your son at first. It's a small galaxy, isn't it?"

Tears were now streaming down Galin's face, he no longer had the will to try to stop them. "You…you say that you made David like you?" He feared her answer, more than he'd ever feared anything. "How? How did you and Mengele do it?"

"We released his soul," she said, shoveling in an onion and slice of potato. "Killed him, I suppose you might say." She eyed him over searchingly. "You wouldn't have given him to me either, would you?"

"My God," he shook his head. "Where does this end?" His entire body was shaking; he was drained, weighed down, as if the very air he was drawing into his lungs was trying to crush him. She was lost, then, she and David both.

But not if he could go back; not if he could somehow fix this. And he must try, whatever the cost.

Galin wiped his eyes and gazed over at the creature that had once housed his sister. Damn their father for doing this! How could he have taken part in turning his own little girl into something like this?

The grief taking hold of him now was much worse than what he'd felt all those years before. Everything he'd experienced the day of Jamie's death, and the days that followed- the hopelessness, confusion, the anger, were nothing compared to this. His father's words, the sickness he'd felt, his own guilt and shame, and the unjustifiable way he'd taken it out on Starla. And now there was this. It appeared that some nightmares never came to an end.

A renewed sense of fury toward his father came welling up inside of him, but it was drowned almost immediately by pity. Would he himself have ever been tempted to do something similar if he'd known it was an option, if he'd known his sister could be brought back? *NO*, a part of him demanded. But he wasn't entirely sure.

Their father couldn't have known it would be like

this, couldn't have guessed that the daughter he'd loved so much would lose all traces of her humanity, or that the thing Mengele would reawaken would be an entirely different creature. He couldn't have known, could he? And this woman, if it was right to call her that, was another creature, some kind of monster, a fact that grew clearer every second. This thing was no more his sister than a coffin full of dry bones would have been, if her corpse had been allowed to rot.

"Why didn't you bring the boy, like I asked?" Jamie said.

"He's with my crew, they're looking after him for me."

"If you promise to give him to me," Jamie said, "I'll allow you and your crew to go on your way."

"You're mad. I'd never do that. NEVER. Besides, you think you're the one in charge here? Looks like Soth's got you under lock and key."

"I've made powerful allies since coming aboard this ship. The Claymore is mine."

"What about the Admiral? Don't you think he'll have something to say about that? Where is he anyway? Has Soth got him locked up too?"

She only looked down at her plate.

"Jamie, where the hell's our father?"

"I thought you'd want to see him one last time, so I saved some for you, but you're not even eating."

He looked at the roast, and then back to his sister's wooden face.

"You cooked him?" Galin managed to breathe, the horror of it taking hold.

She nudged his plate toward him. "You really should have some. You're going to need his strength when we retake the ship."

"Ah, Lieutenant Moore," Soth hissed as she entered his briefing room. "The time for your departure approaches. Thank you for volunteering."

She hadn't volunteered for a damned thing, but she wasn't about to protest.

The reptilian rose and walked over to tower above her, sending chills down her spine.

He held out a package. "Here, open this."

She did, and nervously began to thumb through the contents.

"These are your final orders. You will pilot the shuttle with the remaining survivors from Necron, who came aboard from the Katara, and rendezvous with the ships on the other side of the wormhole. Now listen to me carefully, once the ships have reached their destination, you will meet an old man who is caring for two babies- twin boys. You will protect them and their guardian, ensuring that no harm befalls them. Do you understand?"

"Yes, sir. Um, who's this woman?" she asked nervously, dropping a picture and then retrieving it to show him.

He didn't even bother to look at it. "That is a young woman who will one day prove to be just as reckless as the rest of her family. Her name is Sarah Winchester. All of her information is here, in this file. Remember her well, and teach your people's children to remember her. A day may come when she arrives upon the planet that will become your new home. When, and if she does, she must be eliminated immediately."

Moore gazed up at him, eyes flickering, trying to take it all in.

"In the days ahead, you must study that file. If I fail in my mission, then perhaps your efforts will prevail."

"Mission? What…what mission?" Although she was terrified of the General, he seemed to be in a pleasant enough mood, and the more information she could get out of him, the better. She was flying off into the unknown, after all, and on his orders.

"What little you need to know, you will find in this file. It will all become clear in time." He crossed his arms. "I know that you have little trust for me, and there is no reason you should. After you fly through that wormhole, you will be beyond my grasp forever, but remember my words, I am confident that you will do only what you believe to be right, and that will be enough."

His words shocked her. This did not seem like the same person she and every other member of the crew had come to fear.

Soth turned, and walked to the display screen on the wall. "I know you are already aware, and have spoken to others about your concerns for the Winchester family. Do not be surprised, I see and know much."

"They're, ah…yes," she mumbled, "they're a bit of a strange bunch."

"You don't know the half of it," Soth laughed, meanly. He turned on the screen, and footage of Jamie Winchester's quarters appeared. The young woman was speaking with her father.

"Everyone on this ship has been speculating about the whereabouts of their beloved Admiral. Why, some have even accused me of executing some dark plot against him."

Lihnda gasped to see Jamie pull a blaster pistol from her dress, and shoot her father from point blank range in the chest with it.

"Patricide," Soth said. "A horrific crime on your world *and* mine. But what comes next, I have to admit, caught even me off guard, and I have seen all kinds of sordid deeds, on all sorts of savage worlds."

He moved the footage forward, to show the admiral being butchered like a slab of beef, and after that, images even more unthinkable.

Having no control over it, Lihnda fell to her knees, and released what little dinner she'd eaten up onto the floor.

Soth knelt, and placed his arm around her. "Do not think me cruel for showing you that woman's crimes, distressing you was not my intent." He helped her stand. "And what do you suppose is transpiring in that ghoulish woman's quarters even now?"

He switched the view screen to the camera in Jamie's room, and the two of them watched together, Lihnda's body quivering beneath the would-be comfort of Soth's arm, as the Winchester children conversed, and began to feast upon what the Lieutenant could only guess was the unholy meal she'd just seen prepared. As Lihnda looked on, she noted that Galin did not eat, and soon became quite agitated. Although the sound was not on, she could see Galin yelling. Finally, he rose from the table, taking up the carving knife his sister had used on the roast. He walked slowly, clearly distraught and with measured steps to the other side of the table, where he plunged the knife up to the hilt into his sister's heart. The woman had seen it coming, yet made no attempt to stop him. Her body slid to the floor, and Galin fell down beside her.

Lihnda was still gaping on in horror when the reptilian gently turned her head to face him.

"And now, you have seen," he told her. "You have seen what these people are?"

"Y,yes," she stuttered. "I've seen."

The General reached down and retrieved the packet, which had fallen beside her to the floor. Reorganizing its contents, he handed it back. "Remember my words. Remember Sarah Winchester."

He gently pushed her toward the exit. "It is time. The shuttle awaits its captain."

She walked toward the door, recomposing herself, and as it opened, she turned.

"Why me?" she asked.

"Because," Soth answered, "you have proven yourself a loyal and competent officer. Besides, you look like a woman who's ready for a fresh start. Farewell, Lieutenant Moore, and good luck."

"Thank you," she said, and walked through the door. Lihnda felt sick, sicker than she'd ever felt, but as the door slid shut, she found that a smile had crept onto her face, a feeling that had become quite foreign to her lately. She knew why it was there; it was there because of hope.

Ulrick's face had grown red and puffy, he looked like an over-ripened tomato with wavy blonde hair, pacing back and forth between the walls of the holding cell like a lion.

"You need to sit down and relax," Joseph told him, "you're driving me crazy."

Ulrick stopped and turned to glare at him with a mad-dog stare.

"Don't look at me in that tone of voice, patience is a virtue, remember? Haven't you ever heard the story of the Crow and the pitcher?"

Ulrick continued to stare, eyes bulging.

"He doesn't look like he has," Jace said.

"Well then, I suppose I'm going to have to tell him. Once, there was a crow, who was so thirsty you would have thought he was half dead if you'd seen him. He came upon a pitcher of water, but the day was so hot, most of the water had already evaporated. He put his beak in, and found that it wasn't long enough to reach down to get a drink. Well, what do you think he did then? What would you have done? He took a pebble and dropped it into the pitcher. Then he took another pebble and dropped it into the pitcher. Then he took another pebble and dropped that into the pitcher. Then he took another pebble and dropped that into the pitcher. Then he took another pebble and dropped that into the pitcher. Then he took another pebble and dropped that into the pitcher. Finally, at long last, he saw that the water was almost within reach, and after casting a few more pebbles in, he was able to quench his thirst."

Ulrick looked at him dumbly for a few moments, like a big, bloated baby who'd had all his toys taken away. He shook his fists in the air. "I WANT MY GUNS! FRACK THAT CROW AND HIS PATIENCE, I NEED TO SLAG SOMEBODY!"

"Hey, shut up in there," one of the guards grumbled. "You're giving me a headache."

"GET SLAGGED!"

Jace lifted his head from his hands. "I don't think he wants to be patient."

Joseph leaned over to whisper. "No, but at least with him throwing a fit, the guards won't think we're up to something."

Jace rubbed his temples. Ulrick's rants were starting to get to him, too. "You really think Galin's plan is going to work?"

"It should, but we're going to have to move quickly once these force fields go down. We—"

"Wait, hold on a second," Jace put his finger to his lips. "You hear that?"

A few seconds passed, then Joseph nodded. "Blaster fire?"

The guards had noticed it too, and were disappearing through the door to go check it out.

"Well, this is interesting," Joseph said. "Sounds like somebody else has some kind of plan, too."

Even Ulrick had stopped pacing in order to listen. The shots continued for some time. In fact, it sounded like an all out war had broken loose, and the three men stared at one another, listening in amazement until the sound of gunfire dwindled, and eventually stopped altogether.

"A mutiny?" Ulrick asked.

"Could be," Joseph shrugged.

Ulrick's face grew red again. "And we missed it?"

The force field of their holding cell flickered, and then

collapsed altogether.

"Well it's about time." Ulrick bee-lined for the guard's desk to look for weapons just as TAII appeared before them.

"Good job, young lady," Joseph told her. "We were beginning to think you wouldn't show up."

"I almost didn't. This ship has some very impressive anti-virus programs. I had to convince the Claymore's main computer that I was an upgrade."

"Good thing you're such a flirt," Jace said.

"Well, it wasn't easy. We're lucky that group of insurrectionists showed up and installed their own virus when they did."

"So there was a mutiny?" Joseph raised his hand toward the door. "What exactly is going on out there?"

"Captain Winchester's sister had organized a sizable group of followers, and they just attempted to commandeer the ship. Soth's loyalists put them down, but I'd say at least half of the Claymore's crew is dead, though final numbers haven't come in."

"Well, that should make our escape a little easier," Jace said.

Joseph shook his head. "Not really. We've lost the element of surprise. There aren't as many men around to contend with, but those who are will be on a heightened state of alert."

"Looks like we'll have to shoot our way out then," Ulrick said, beaming.

"With what," Jace sneered, "our good looks?"

"Maybe," Ulrick said.

Joseph rubbed his chin. "No, things have definitely gone in the crapper. Looks like we're going to have to initiate Plan B."

Ulrick smiled from ear to ear.

"Whoa, whoa, hold on just a minute. There's no turning back from that, right? That's what Galin said. Once the command is entered, there's no turning back."

"That's right," TAII said. "You all need to be sure."

Jace retrieved his baseball cap from the guard's desk and slapped it back on his head. "But, what about Galin? Where's he?"

TAII closed her eyes, as if thinking. "He's in his sister's quarters, speaking with General Soth. It looks like things are getting out of hand. We need to do something to get him out of there."

"If that alarm goes off, Soth will kill him for sure, right?" Jace said.

"Not if it distracts him," Ulrick said. "How long will it take us to get down there?"

TAII shook her head. "Too long. If you tried to help him, you'd never be able to make it back to the Katara in time, even if you weren't required to fight your way through."

Joseph hit his hand with his fist. "We can't stand here and talk about this all day, we need to move quickly. The best thing we can do to help Galin is grab

David and head for the ship. TAII, initiate Plan B, and then see if you can distract Soth and help Galin escape before transferring your program back to the Katara."

"Roger that," TAII said. "Computer, initiate self-destruct sequence, beginning the countdown at fifteen minutes."

"Acknowledged," the computer answered. *"However, a T-minus fifteen minute countdown would begin at the point of no return. There will be no way to cancel this command. Please confirm."*

"Command confirmed," TAII said. "Authorization code Tango, Alpha, India, India, One- override sequence Sierra, Oscar, Lima."

"Accepted," the computer said. An ear piercing alarm began to blare, accompanied by swirling red lights. *"ATTENTION, THIS VESSEL WILL SELF DESTRUCT IN T-MINUS FIFTEEN MINUTES. ALL HANDS ABANDON SHIP."*

TAII grinned at them nervously. "Good luck, and remember to move quickly, I'll head up to help the Cap...." A curious, amazed expression dawned across her face. "Well, this is an interesting development," she said, and disappeared.

—MERLOS III
FIVE YEARS BEFORE—

The final chamber was just up ahead, and Galin knew that if he could pull this off quick enough, they might escape the Merlock temple without another incident. The task would be more difficult without Peter's help, but there was no way around it now, he had to man up and recover the package alone.

"You sure you're okay to hold up here for another few minutes?"

"I'll be fine," Peter told him. "But I'd appreciate your expediency, if it's not too much to ask."

"I suppose an encouraging hug would be out of the question?"

Peter glared at him. "I'll have to give you a rain check on that. Now move your butt. I'd kind of like to get to a med kit before this wound takes a turn for the worse."

Galin squeezed his arm encouragingly and headed for the chamber.

A warm breeze met him as he entered. The place was well lit with torches, and smelled of smoke. Galin stowed his night vision goggles and crept toward the center of the room, where a number of statues representing the Merlock gods were positioned in line one after the other. Each was about twenty feet high, some male and some female, but all were impressive, if not bizarre. One held a large war hammer, made from rope and stone; he was donned in leather armor and the snarl on his battle-hungry face made him look like a Merlock version of Ulrick. The thought made Galin smile. Another statue had a bow and full quiver of arrows, and another wielded a long, stone knife. Others had no weapon at all, but bore some other distinctive set of characteristics. Galin passed by one who was clearly a farmer, and a female with humungous breasts, certainly a fertility goddess. But the one at the end of the row looked quite different from the rest. This was unmistakably the one he was looking for.

He went to the statue and stood before it, hands on his hips. Whatever frog had done the carving hadn't done too badly, though some of the statue's proportions looked more like those of a Merlock than those of a human. Its face was the round, featureless dome of a space helmet, gazing up toward the roof of the chamber as if it could see right through the stone and into the stars, where it was pointing with two fingers on its right hand.

Just as Starla had promised, a primitive rock mausoleum had been constructed behind the statue. Galin entered, and there, resting on a long stone slab, was the thing he'd come to get.

The body of the United States of America astronaut had been laid there like an esteemed treasure, a museum piece for all reverent Merlocks to come and examine. Galin wondered if there was much more than dust inside the space suit now, though the suit itself had held up surprisingly well. It had obviously been cared for, considering the means that these people had to care for it. It was more to them than a curious oddity from the past, these Merlocks had come to worship it; this body was the body of a god, a deity who'd come to visit them from the stars, long ago.

Captain Jeremiah Winters had been one of Earth's first deep space explorers, and he had also been one of the first never to return home. Galin knew the man's story well, as this sort of history had always fascinated him. He never would have imagined that he would be in charge of the efforts to recover the Captain's body, but now here it was, resting before him like a mummified rag doll with its arms crossed over the top.

For nearly two hundred years, Captain Winters' fate had remained a mystery, but when word came to the man's descendants that his remains had been located in a temple on the obscure planet of Merlos III, and that they were on display and being worshiped, the idea of it all had not rested with them well. A mutual friend told the family about Galin's crew and the work they did, and a meeting was set up. The family took up a collection to cover the expedition fee, and Galin was asked to bring the remains home. As a last resort, if the body could not be recovered, it was to be destroyed, and proof brought back with his report. For that reason, Galin had decided to record the expedition. He took a moment to double check the camera, and ensure it was still working properly. It was.

There was no time to waste, Galin realized, rubbing

his hands together. Getting into this place had been surprisingly easy, even considering their run-in with the three Merlocks and Peter's wound. He needed to get moving before their luck ran out; they were still in danger of being discovered at any moment.

Galin took the force field generator from his belt and placed it upon the astronaut's foot. He turned it on and a blue wave swept over the body; he then modified the field to the desired parameters, until an oblong bubble had spread out to cover its entire length. Pulling a bottle of liquid from his pouch, he adjusted the generator to a position on the top of the bubble, and poured the liquid in through the hole in the middle. When that bottle was empty, he retrieved its mate and poured that one in as well. The two compounds mixed together, and began to bubble up, expanding until the inside of the field was filled to the brim with helium infused foam. Galin sealed the hole, entered the command to solidify, and collapsed the field. The protective coating around the Captain's body looked a bit like a flat, tan boulder, which would help serve as camouflage when trying to make their escape.

Galin grabbed ahold of the body, which had already begun to float a few inches above the slab, and led it carefully through the door of the mausoleum. Taking a quick look around, he rushed off toward Peter. With any luck, they could get away without raising alarm, and the Merlocks could believe this god of theirs had jumped off his uncomfortable bed of stone to return to the stars. And in a way, they'd be right.

He soon reached Peter, who looked very glad to see him.

"Any complications?"

Galin shook his head. "I talked him into coming along easy enough."

Together, they crept back to the courtyard garden. All appeared quiet. Galin saw that the little bulldogish creature had left its hiding place to return to the side of its unconscious master. It glared at them warily, but looked like it had been given its fair share of trouble for the evening, and wanted only to be left alone.

"Can you hold on to this?" Galin asked.

Peter nodded and took hold of the package with both hands, grimacing slightly for his effort.

Galin pulled three retrieval beacons from his pack. He fastened one to the back of Peter's belt, one to his own, and clipped one to the top of the foamed up Captain Winters, then he lanyarded all three together.

"You ready for this?" Galin asked.

Peter looked miserable at the prospect. "Just get it over with," he winced.

Galin hit the controls, and all three beacons immediately inflated, dragging them swiftly into the night sky. Peter suddenly had the image of a little pink piglet with party balloons being taken away by a great, blustery wind. He would have laughed had it not been for the agonizing pain.

They had no sooner risen above the roof of the temple when an enormous, mosquito like creature, about the size of a small hover-car, came buzzing toward them, swift as lightning. Its long claws were posed to skewer them. Galin's blaster had already been drawn, and he shot the hungering insect square in the face before it could reach them. The thing plummeted down toward the temple and bounced off the roof with a heavy thud.

"GOOD LORD!" Peter squealed. "You didn't tell me about those."

"Well, you wanted to know why the Merlocks don't go jumping around at night? There's your answer."

A hysterical eruption of babel filled the night sky, and Galin looked down to see two Merlocks, standing guard in a high tower of the temple, gazing up at them and shaking their spears. One of them looked quite conflicted; his face being filled with wonder at what he was seeing, and at the same time trying to determine if his duty demanded that he try to bring them down. Finally, he decided, and threw the spear with all his might. The choice had come a few seconds too late, however; and his missile fell short of Galin's leg by a few mere inches before sailing down toward the jungle floor.

They watched as a half dozen more frogs came to join their companions on the tower. The first two pointed up frantically, trying to get the others to see, though the darkness was swiftly consuming them.

"Might as well prove those guards right," Galin said, turning on the beacons' flashing red lights. "Now the others won't think they're crazy. It's the least we can do."

Peter let out a pained mumble that might have been agreement.

The flashing beacon lights seemed to draw more of the curious mosquitos, though they approached more warily than the first had. When one got too close, Galin blasted it, and the others withdrew for a while. These seemed smarter than the average insect, and Galin wasn't sure if that made him feel better, or worse about their presence.

By the time the Shiv arrived to collect them, the temple had faded in the distance. Ulrick opened the hatch and reached down to pull them in. He quickly stowed the encased body, and then helped Galin. Together, they carefully guided Peter through the door.

Ulrick examined his injured friend warily. "I thought you said you were a ninja."

"Well, now he's a ninja-kabob," Galin grinned as Peter scowled at him. "Just get us back to the slaggin' ship."

—NOW—

Galin Winchester lied crumpled upon the floor in a

pool of his dead sister's blood.

Soth burst in through the door, and he startled. The reptilian scanned the carnage before him in disgust, his eyes coming to rest upon Galin's.

"I can't leave you Winchesters alone with each other for five minutes," Soth sneered. "Count me out of the next family reunion."

Galin's eyes fell. He had nothing left with which to defend himself, neither in word, nor in action. His sister's body lie draining upon his lap, but he was the one who felt dead, felt like some empty, used up thing. No blood. No spirit, or soul. No love. He had nothing left to fight with, or for.

"My son," he sobbed. "My boy, David. They did this to him, too. He's, he's just like she was." He looked up at Soth, desperate to receive something from the only other being in the room. Was it sympathy? Understanding?

"Release," Soth told him, as if reading his thoughts. "That's what you want from me, Winchester. That's what you NEED!" He pulled a curved, ivory weapon from beneath his cloak, about the length of a saber, and swung it through the air with a speed that numbed the mind. "This is the jawbone of an Fire-Eyed Iguana," he said. "One of the most prized species of game upon my world. Ninety-four percent of the hunters who draw a license to kill this creature end their adventures in death. I hunted this specimen with my bare hands, and before it died, I pulled this choice bone from its mouth, to drive through it's heart. In a way, it died as a victim of its own miscreant nature, just like you will." He sank down to a knee, and looked Galin deep in the eyes. "A second warrior's courtesy I grant to you, Captain. Do you wish to be torn to pieces upon this rack of fangs, or shall I rip you apart with my own bare hands?"

"You choose," Galin said, not bothering to lift his head, looking instead at his slain sister's face. "Just shut up and do it already."

This is how it would end, then. Fighting would do no good, even if he'd had the desire to put one up. But as he gazed into Jamie's blank, yet peaceful face, his thoughts turned to Sarah, and to Starla, and he could feel a spark of something reignite within him. Whether of hatred or of love, he could not be sure, but he suddenly wanted to live. Perhaps if he could delay Soth just a little bit longer, it would buy his crew some time.

"So, this was your price? Killing me? Was my death worth your becoming a Nazerazi slave?"

"Slave?" Soth laughed. "I am no slave, you heckling corpse. I fulfilled my part of the bargain, and he fulfilled his. Now your life belongs to me."

"Who? The Nazerazi ruler? Your master? Someone who defeated you in battle, most likely, bent you to his will, manipulated your simple lizard mind to make it seem like you were getting what you wanted? You're just a pawn, Soth. A big dumb, Draconian bitch who was too weak to save his own people."

The General's eyes burned with fury, and Galin could see a war going on within them, one side hungering to slash him to pieces, and the other insisting he defend his honor.

"Who are you Soth? Who are you really? Tell me I'm not about to die by the hand of some common, Draconian slave?"

The flames within the reptilian's eyes died down, though the embers continued to glow. It appeared his honor had won the battle, delaying death a little longer.

"I tracked him down, tried to kill him," Soth confessed. He looked down at Galin and sneered. "I shall grant you this short reprieve from death, as you so transparently request with your vile insults, to recount the tale." Standing, and lowering the jawbone to his side, he continued, "We battled, the two of us, for many long hours. I had never before come across anyone, or anything, with such powers." He looked down to read Galin's face. "After hours of battle, we finally arrived at the same conclusion, he was unable to match my speed, and I was unable to harm him." He hissed. "You have been wise, Captain, to battle me with your words instead of your fists."

For all the creature's arrogance, Galin knew he was right. Reptilians were much quicker than humans, generally speaking, and this reptilian, whoever he might be, was something entirely different. In fact, he would bet that Soth was at least as fast as Nicodemus.

"What are you?" Galin demanded. "A Pneuma-Tal?"

For the first time, he saw surprise on the reptilian's face, but it quickly faded.

"I was, once, many years ago. But then my path took a different turn."

Suddenly, it struck him, and Galin remembered the words TAII had spoken back at the Command Center, she'd told them about a group of six reptilian insurgents, former Pneuma-Tal monks who'd dedicated themselves to interfering with the Bleeding Star Initiative. Only one member out of six had managed to remain at large.

"I know what you are," Galin grinned. "You're a member of the Sobek-Tal."

The General's eyes narrowed, and his lip curled in disbelief. "Very perceptive, but how is it that a cur like you knows of the Sobek-Tal?"

"Tell me what you know about the Bleeding Star Initiative," Galin retorted.

Soth studied him for a moment. "The Command Center still exists, does it? You've been there, haven't you? But how—?" A look not unlike panic dawned over him. "It appears I have some unfinished work to tend to. But, first things first. Are you prepared to die?" He stepped closer, raising his weapon.

Suddenly, an ear piercing alarm started to blare, red, swirling lights began to flash, and the ship computer's voice came over the com. "ATTENTION, THIS

VESSEL WILL SELF DESTRUCT IN T-MINUS FIFTEEN MINUTES. ALL HANDS ABANDON SHIP."

Soth hissed in annoyance. "You *do* have a way of complicating things, don't you, Captain? Very well, it appears I have an escape pod to get to." He gave his jawbone a few swipes through the air, preparing to strike, but then turned his head. "What's this?"

Galin looked up to see TAII standing before them, a blaster rifle pointed directly at Soth's chest.

"Zero in on my coordinates, quickly!" she said.

Hatred flashed in Soth's eyes as he shot to the girl and swept his weapon through the air; it passed through her as a hot knife through butter, yet she remained unharmed. The blaster rifle abruptly changed into a bouquet of red roses, which TAII offered to the General along with a coy grin. Even as Soth had begun to move, a loud series of booms, progressively getting louder, and which shook the floor beneath Galin's numbed body, came echoing through the ship. The General, distracted by the sound, turned his head to listen, and a look not unlike fear spread over his face. He glared at Galin, the prospect of losing his kill yet again driving him into a panic.

"NO," he screamed, lunging toward Galin and raising his jawbone as he went.

A final devastating boom pierced the room, sending debris in every direction, and Galin turned to see a tall, humanoid figure moving toward him faster than he'd ever seen anything move before, save perhaps a ship going to warp. The T3038 android, which he quickly recognized as William Marshall, came skidding to a halt in front of him, where Soth's weapon came cracking down upon his back to shatter into a thousand pieces. William swiftly picked him up, along with his sister's body, and darted toward the same hole he had just blasted through.

Looking back, Galin met eyes with Soth, and the General screamed in rage and disbelief, and then in pain. Galin could barely make out a ghostly, reptilian figure moving in behind Soth, and a long, spectral blade of light bursting through the center of his chest.

"No, you fool," Soth sputtered while dying. "You've killed the wrong—" A stream of blood shot from his mouth, and he fell.

Galin thought that he must be dying as well. He closed his eyes, and slipped into darkness.

"Release the docking clamps," Jace yelled into the com.

"Just hold on one fracking minute," Ulrick answered.

Jace could see him looking over the control panel through the window. "My God," he mumbled, "he has absolutely no clue what he's doing up there."

"I heard that, pup."

"Good!" Jace yelled back.

"Any sign of TAII yet?" Ulrick asked, finding the controls. The docking clamps squealed as they set the ship free.

"She's not answering," Jace said. "Look, you'd better hurry up and get down here. We've got three minutes tops if we want to clear the explosion."

"Keep your pants on. Remember the Crow and Pitcher of Beer story."

"It was water," Jace insisted.

"Not in my version. All right, the force field is set to auto, it'll collapse upon approach."

"I know what the frack it does, would you just get down here already. TAII, are you there?"

She didn't answer.

"How's everything checking out with the engine, Chief?"

"The old girl's purring like a kitten. Any sign of Galin yet?"

"Not yet."

"If he doesn't show, you pilot this ship out of here, got it? He might have already gotten to an escape pod."

"Understood." As much as he hated the thought of abandoning his captain, the chief was right. They could wait around for Galin to show, sacrificing themselves while he was jettisoned safely away in an escape pod, wondering when they were going to come pick them up.

He looked at the clock, one minute-forty five seconds to go.

Ulrick came striding quickly along the flight deck, disappearing from Jace's sight under the ship. He'd wait until the last possible moment, Jace knew, before boarding and pulling the stairs up behind him.

Seconds continued to tick, and Jace let out a long, frustrated breath. "TAII? Come in, are you there?"

Nothing.

The clock showed one minute. Fifty-nine seconds. Fifty-eight. Fifty-seven.

"HEY, LOOK AT THIS," came Ulrick's voice, nearly driving Jace from his chair.

The android running toward the ship was clanking heavily upon the grating with each falling step, carrying a body under each arm as if they were footballs, and he, headed for the End Zone. It was William Marshall, and one of the bodies was Galin.

"Is he friendly?" Jace pleaded, remembering their last encounter.

"Yeah, I guess so," Ulrick said. *"He ran right past me into the loading bay. I'm retracting the stairs. Get us out of here, shorty."*

"Gladly," Jace said, lifting off. "Everyone, hold onto your butts!" He guided the Katara out, much more swiftly than he was comfortable with, and his innards jumped as they rocketed through the threshold, force field collapsing just as he knew it would, though the prospect of failure still scared him.

And then, they were out. The Katara streamed away

like a missile, dodging this way and that to avoid the scattered escape pods. Jace glanced over just in time to see the wormhole collapse, and wondered what would happen to the friends he'd seen pass to the other side. He also realized that the people in the pods were a bit out of luck, the things weren't capable of long distance travel, and they sure were a long way from anywhere. He gasped, and veered starboard as another of the pods came blasting across his path.

"FRACK, YEAH," he yelled, just realizing how much fun he was having. He'd never piloted the ship before during any action like this, and as Peter had always told him, *'Calm seas don't make good sailors.'*

And then he saw Peter, sitting right there in the co-pilots chair with a big, dumb grin on his face. "You're doing all right, kid. Just watch that one on our six."

Sure enough, another pod was coming up fast right behind them. Jace veered to let it pass, and then looked over to see that Peter was no longer there.

"Thanks," he said anyway, not knowing if his friend could hear.

By the looks of the radar, they were finally in the clear. He turned the Katara just in time to see the Claymore, last behemoth of the United States of Texas, erupt into a hellish blaze of fire.

—MERLOS STAR SYSTEM, EN ROUTE TO

EARTH

FIVE YEARS BEFORE—

Galin was roused from his nap by a loud series of raps on the door.

"Just five more minutes, Mom," he called, knowing by the knock that it was Starla.

She burst in.

"*You* lied to me."

"How's Peter?" Galin asked.

"He's fine. He'll be good as new in a few days, but you knew that already. You *LIED* to me, Galin. Tell me why!"

Galin sat up and looked at her, a bit surprised by the fact that she was genuinely upset.

Starla waved a data pad in front of his face. "This contract. The one you signed with that astronaut's family- I found it in the cockpit. We're not getting paid half of what you said we were."

Galin lied back down, and turned his eyes to gaze at the starscape outside. "We should be out of the solar system by now. Why hasn't Peter gone to warp?"

She huffed at him. "Would you just answer me, damn it."

"You're all getting paid full shares. I didn't lie to you about anything."

"If we're getting our standard shares, then what's that leave you? You won't even make enough to cover expenses."

"No, I won't, but it'll come close."

She shook her head at him. "But...why? Why would you possibly take a job like this at a loss? I mean, your best friend got skewered like a pig, for God's sake!" She narrowed her eyes in suspicion. "What else is in it for you?"

He snorted and grinned at her. "What's the matter? Can't believe that I'd still chalk one up to charity now and again?"

She frowned. "That's not what I said. I just...I just really don't get it. Why on a job like this?"

Galin stared back at her for a few seconds, looking deep into those beautiful, brown eyes. "Because, it was all they could come up with."

"And?"

"And?" He smiled at her sadly. "And...everyone deserves to bury their dead."

He could almost see the thoughts of Jamie go rushing through her head. The memories, both good and bad, had come rising to the surface, as they tended to do now and then, when the two of them were alone. He wouldn't have to give her any further explanation. She understood, all too well. It didn't matter that Captain Winters' descendants had never even known him; to them, he was family, and separated by generations or not, they deserved the chance to see him properly lain to rest.

Starla gazed down at him, her face melting into an admiration that he'd almost come to forget. It was the same look she'd given him so often when they were young. A look that said that she loved him more than anything or anyone else in the world, in all of creation, she loved him, best of all.

She lifted her hand to his face, and caressed his cheek so lightly that it tickled, running her fingers across his ear and back down to a rest upon his chin, just as she used to. As she leaned over to place a kiss upon his forehead, he became lost in the scent of her hair, and her lips fell upon him as softly as they might have touched a newborn.

Galin, eyes closed, reached for her, eager to retain the warmth of that touch, but she had already retreated to a safe distance near the cabin door.

"Don't be late for dinner," she said softly, her glance falling upon a picture of Melissa and the kids that he kept on the nightstand. "Joseph's making fried chicken again, and if Ulrick gets to it before you do, well…." She patted her stomach, and smiled.

"No guarantees," Galin said.

She shook her head. "No guarantees." Her smile faded as she slipped away, and he thought he'd seen a tear in her eye as well.

The door slid shut behind her.

"I love you, too," Galin said, though she could not hear him. "And always will."

—NOW—

Galin sat up in bed, startled from the grasp of some insidious nightmare. A cold sweat covered his brow, and he shook uncontrollably. As the blurred worlds of dream and reality grappled for his attention, he began to remember. Everything slipped slowly into focus, those things that had been the spectral haunts of his nightmare, and those horrors that had not. He looked out the window, gazed into the stars, and began to sob. The nightmare had been better.

His room was empty, and he was alone, thank God. He couldn't bear the thought of anyone seeing him like this.

"But, are they still alive," he said to himself. "Did everyone make it?" He needed to get himself under control, set aside the horrors of what he'd gone through so he could emerge and account for his crew.

No, not his crew, they were more than that. He loved every one of them like family, and the reality of that fact seemed so important now; more important than anything. Still, he couldn't go out there. Not yet.

"TAII?"

The holographic girl appeared beside the foot of his bed, almost as if she were waiting to be asked. "Yes, Captain?"

"Did…did everyone make it back to the Katara? Is everyone okay?"

She smiled. "Everyone. Even the big, dumb oaf."

"Thank God," he breathed, feeling a little better. But the grief returned just as fast, and he knew why. The truth was, everyone hadn't made it back. Not David. Galin knew the truth now, knew that his son's condition wasn't going to just go away. It couldn't be fixed, or healed. David was dead.

Many parents had suffered the agony of outliving children, Galin knew; he wasn't alone in that. He'd had friends that had lost little children, and shared in their grief. He'd spoken to the parents of officers and enlisted men under his command, who'd been taken too soon, the casualties of accidents or battle. He'd seen and experienced every kind of grief imaginable. At least that's what he'd thought before today.

Not only had his boy been lost, but he was going to have to do to him what no father should ever be asked to do. He'd have to do the same thing he'd done to his sister.

But that wasn't her, he reminded himself, *it was just a corpse. I didn't do it to her, I did it for her.* Jamie had died a long time ago, and he was simply taking care of the body.

As gruesome and horrific as it was, he was going to have to take care of one more. But how could he? Was he even capable of such a macabre task? The thought of doing it made him ill, made him hate himself.

"The crew's waiting to see you," TAII urged. "They've all been very worried. You've been unconscious for over twelve hours now."

"Tell everyone I'm okay, I just need to get cleaned up, then I'll be out." He looked back out at the stars for a moment. "Where are we anyway? Heading back to the Command Center?"

"No. The Claymore was destroyed, and the wormhole collapsed. We're towing the escape pods in tandem behind us with a repeating tractor beam, and are headed for Merlos III. It's the nearest hospitable planet."

He moved to the aft window and looked out. Sure enough, there they were, what looked like close to a hundred of them.

"I've been to Merlos III. I'm not sure hospitable is quite the right word for it."

"Joseph said that one of the northern continents is free of intelligent life. He plans on dropping the survivors off there, unless you have other orders."

"No," Galin said. "It's a good plan. Tell everyone I'll be right out."

"Roger that." She hesitated, then grinned from ear to ear. "And Captain, I'm glad you made it back okay."

He surrendered a grin. "I did, thanks to you."

She beamed at him with reddened cheeks before vanishing.

He got undressed and stepped into the shower, and

found that the hot water streaming over his body provided little comfort. Images of Jamie, and what he had done, and what he still needed to do were burned into his head, and he once again found himself longing for the nightmare, though he couldn't remember what it had been about.

Maybe he didn't need to do it, didn't need to destroy David's body as he had Jamie's. The boy had done no harm.

Not yet. But he would.

What kind of horrors would he be capable of if he were allowed to live? No, live wasn't the right word for it. Linger fit better.

Galin would have to end it. If he loved his son, honored the boy's memory, he would have to put an end to it, and he'd have to do it himself.

But this time, it couldn't be violent, not like Jamie. This needed to be more dignified, more peaceful, more like a proper funeral. They'd have to come up with a shot or something that would just make the boy go to sleep, a final sleep, just as God and nature intended.

The water flowed over Galin's face, washing away his tears. He was going to have to get the deed over with, do it immediately, and then he could turn his attention back to the path ahead.

With that thought, a small bit of hope returned.

"You are a Clockwalker," he said, as if to fend off his specters. "You will learn how to put things right, all of it." He stepped out of the shower, continuing to grasp that little seed of hope. "God, if you really are out there, I could use a little help right now. Send me something. I know I don't talk to you much, but it seems like you've been out on the fracking golf-course a lot yourself, here lately."

He would get dressed, go meet his crew, debrief them, and then do what needed to be done. He would get through this. It would be agonizing, it *was* agonizing, but he would get through it. He always did.

Finally, when he was dressed, and as close to ready as he could be, he left his quarters and headed toward the cockpit, drawing in short breathes and trying to stay on his feet. The door to the commons area slid open, and he passed through.

"DAD!" David shouted, running to embrace him. He squeezed his father around the waist so hard that it took the wind out of him. Joseph and Ulrick looked on from the table with elated smiles.

Galin looked down at his son's face, more surprised by the expression there than he'd ever been by anything. Tears were streaming down David's cheeks, great tears of happiness and love.

But how was this possible?

Galin dropped to his knees, hugging the boy back.

"I don't understand," was all he could get out. "Where…where were you?"

"It was Farwalker," David said. "He brought me

back. I was with William, we were going to go find Sarah, and we did. She gave me a message for you."

Galin could only laugh.

"I have a lot to tell you," David said.

"Okay, but first just let me look at you." He held the boy's head in his hands, gazed deep into his eyes, and for the first time since their reunion on Necron, he could see his son.

—Bleeding Star Initiative Command Center—

Boreas hissed in frustration, scanning the mess of cables and circuit cards littering the floor around him, and deciding he'd had just about enough for the night. Perhaps knocking off early and spending a bit of time on Kanbun's holodeck would do him good. The man had created a new program just for him, allowing visits to the steamy forests of Draconia, and had even taken the liberty of copying over some of his favorite female holograms, which took the form of Draconian females. Although they looked the part, their human personalities were a complete mismatch, which Boreas found both humorous and discomforting. So much so, in fact, that the few times he'd visited the program, he'd turned the women off, and focused on enjoying the sights and sounds of nature, a fact which he didn't have the heart to tell the exuberant and well-intentioned Kanbun.

Abandoning the mess behind him, Boreas left the room and headed toward the lift, but soon found himself taking a turn toward the chamber of murals, *The Record of Ages* as Kanbun had called it. He found himself drawn there often, almost every day, as a matter of fact. There was just something about the place; he found it quite calming to stand back and gaze at the scenes depicted upon the walls. Besides, Boreas seemed to have a need to ensure from time to time that everything was still in order; the section of wet paint Galin had shown him troubled him greatly, for reasons he did not fully understand.

Just as he was crossing the threshold of the chamber, Kanbun's voice came over the com, *"Hey Lizard Lips, how about we both knock off early and catch a few drinks in the fire caves of Vermooth. I just finished up with the program. The women there are all really hot; pun intended."*

Boreas wasn't sure how the man ever got any real work done, he was so busy creating new holodeck programs, yet he did. Kanbun was as hard working as he was talented, a fact quite obvious from weeks of observation. His grandfather must have been the same way.

"I had similar thoughts myself," Boreas responded. "I'm just finishing up with something, but will be joining you promptly."

"I'll save some girls for you, just hurry up."

Boreas rolled his eyes, an expression he'd learned

from Hero, and then proceeded into the room. Walking unhurriedly, he studied the depictions of a thousand worlds, some in war, some enjoying peace, looking at the faces of species he would most likely never meet in person. He had come to realize after the first few visits that some of the scenes would change from day to day, and that just when he'd come to recognize a portion of the mural, a picture he thought he knew well had morphed into something different. Sometimes the changes were small, such as a group of aliens carrying guns instead of swords, or farming equipment instead of weapons, and sometimes a scene would change into something else entirely. The section just before him had people that looked a bit like the elephants of earth, though they were bipedal, and bright blue in color. A few played instruments, and others were practicing some kind of sport- a race in which they rode each other's backs. Boreas would have sworn that this world hadn't been depicted the day before, at least not in this way, so far as he could remember.

The room had proven to be as unsettlingly strange as it was fascinating, and because of this, when a change appeared to have happened, Boreas always checked the paint, which so far had remained dry. That at least, was comforting, the paint being dry, except of course for that one section depicting his own part of the galaxy. There, the paint was always wet, just as it was when Galin had shown him. Wherever else he looked during one of these tours of his, Boreas always finished by visiting that section, for it continued to trouble him the most.

"*Hey, are you coming up here or what*?" Kanbun called. "*Come on man, I mean, lizard-man. It's not a party until all the A-listers have arrived.*"

"My apologies. I'm on my way." Boreas could tell quite clearly from the slur in his friend's voice that the party had started without him.

He nearly left then, without going to check that final, familiar section. But almost against his will, he found himself turning toward it.

As he got closer, his heart began to pound, and then to race; something was not as it should be. Yes, he was sure of it, the paint was wet, much farther out than it had been the day before. He walked on, becoming more anxious with each step, seeing that the paint was getting wetter, and wetter, and beginning to blur.

Coming to the section where Earth and his own world should have been, Boreas found a vast, swirling ocean of multi-colored paint.

What did this mean? Whatever it was couldn't be good.

After a few long moments he turned to leave, more than ready for a drink.

—MERLOS III
NOW—

Jace watched as the last of the escape pods touched down on the planet's surface. The survivors gazed up at them, both human and reptilian, and while some looked thankful, others sported angry glares. You couldn't blame them, he supposed; they'd all been through a lot.

Galin flashed the lights and turned back toward orbit. "They should be safe enough until someone comes to retrieve them," he said, as if he felt guilty for leaving them, nonetheless. "I wonder who they'll decide to call."

"Well, it's like you said, we don't even have enough room for half of them, and if we did, there's no telling who the Nazerazi loyalists are. If Hero had us fooled, there must be others, not to mention the Draconians. Who knows what some of them might try to pull. A few might want revenge for General Soth."

"Could be," Galin shrugged. "I just don't like leaving anybody behind, I know there's some good people down there." He sighed. "At any rate, they've got more than enough food and supplies, they'll be fine. Set course for the Bleeding Star Command Center."

Jace put in the coordinates, and as soon as they cleared the solar system, he took the ship to warp.

"So, do you believe his story?" Jace asked. "I mean, I'm not saying that he's lying or anything, but this changes a lot of things."

Galin thought hard for a few moments. "I believe him, and the android backs it up. He even showed me the memory files, that woman David spoke to was my daughter. I'm sure of it."

"And she said not to come looking for them? That she and Starla were both all right?"

Galin nodded. "That's what she said. She said we shouldn't come after them, but head for the Command Center instead."

"And you're okay with that? You're sure?"

"Kid, I haven't been *completely* sure about anything for a long while now. These are strange days."

Jace snickered. "You can say that again."

"All I know is this, if I can use this clockwalking thing to go back and do things over, I'm going to do it. Starla and Sarah are both safe, wherever they are, and if this Bleeding Star thing doesn't pan out soon enough, we can head back after them. But, if we're able to figure it out, we can prevent them from ever being taken in the first place. We can save my sister, and Hero, just think about it, we can fix everything that's gone wrong."

"Okay," Jace said. "If you think it's legit, then I'm with you. Besides, it'll be nice to get to the bottom of these…these damned visions, or whatever they are. I still feel like I'm going crazy, whatever anyone says."

"How often are they happening?" Galin asked.

"Just depends, they seem to come in waves. Some days I don't have any, and some days it happens two or three times."

Galin pursed his lips and nodded. "We'll get it all

sorted out. Try not to worry too much."

"That's easy for you to say."

"I know, but I'm starting to feel a bit more optimistic. For the first time in a long time, I just have a sense that things are going to start going our way."

"I really hope you're right," Jace said, rubbing his eyes.

"Listen, I'll watch over the old girl for a while, why don't you go and get some shut eye."

Jace sighed. "Well, if you're going to twist my arm about it. It's been a very long day." He got up to leave. "Just one more thing, how did you manage to open up that wormhole?"

Galin smiled at him. "That *was* something, wasn't it? To tell you the truth, I have absolutely no idea how I did it. I just wanted it to happen, and it did. It was as simple as turning a doorknob." He smiled. "Could I do it again, right now if I wanted? I have no clue."

"Well, it was really something. Do you think all those people who passed through are all right?"

Galin nodded. "That's one thing I'm sure of. I don't know why, but I am. They're going to be okay. In fact, if things were different, I might have liked to go along with them."

"Really? Why?"

"A trip into the great unknown? Uncharted waters? What could possibly be any more exciting than that?"

Jace thought about it a moment, and grinned back.

"Now go get some rest, that's an order."

Jace made a few knocks on the door as he left, as if to say he would.

He stopped in the kitchen to get a drink of water, and then headed for his quarters. He went to the bathroom, brushed his teeth, and undressed. The room seemed a bit cold, so he told the computer to turn the temperature up, and pulled back the covers on his bed. Hero was already there waiting for him. Her long blonde hair was tied back in a ponytail, and a blue, silk nightgown hugged her hips and breasts. She looked like a princess lying there, head resting on her interlocked hands, smiling as if he was the most wonderful thing she'd ever seen.

Jace felt his heart skip a beat. Good Lord, this was the most breathtaking creature he'd ever lain eyes on, and she was all his.

She smirked at him, flirting. "You look tired."

He sat down beside her. "You don't know the half of it."

Sitting up, she began to rub his back. "Not too tired for me, I hope."

He laughed. "Are you joking? I'll never be *that* tired."

She kneaded his shoulders, and kissed his neck. "Listen, there's something we really need to talk about, but I'm not sure you're going to like it."

Jace closed his eyes, drinking in her touch like heat from a radiant fire. "What? What is it?"

"Well, remember the other night, when we were discussing what to do about Galin?"

He had to think for a moment, because everything seemed really cloudy. As she continued to rub, however, it all started coming back again. "Oh boy. You're not going to start that again, are you? You're right, I *don't* want to talk about it."

"But we need to. It's important. We have to decide what we're going to do. It might be time for something drastic."

Jace turned to look at her. "What's *that* supposed to mean?"

She frowned, looked at him sternly, and stopped rubbing. "Honey, we've talked about this, you know what it means. Soth failed. It's up to *you* to stop him now, no matter what." She kissed him fiercely on the lips, and climbed upon his lap, placing her forehead against his. "Even if it means killing him."

— — —

—Afterword—

The conclusion of this book brings to an end what I've come to think of as "The Necron Saga," a.k.a. the first third of The Bleeding Star Chronicles, for which I have thirty chapters planned in all. I am committed to tell this story in those thirty chapters, even if that means that some of the books, like this one, are a bit longer than the rest. Who knows, Issue #30 might be a tome, though I seriously doubt it. At any rate, I hope you've enjoyed the story so far, and if you have, then I would bet that you're going to love where it's going. Some aspects of this tale have been rather dark, and there are dark times still ahead, but lighter times as well, before we come to the end.

People sometimes ask me what The Bleeding Star Chronicles are about. This has always been a hard question for me to answer. Why? Because to answer that question honestly and thoroughly, I would have to give things away- things I'm not ready to give away just yet. The Chronicles is a space opera, a tale about a space ship and her crew, it's a story about an alien invasion, a futuristic dystopian adventure about survival and the agony of loss. I don't think any of these answers alone make these books sound very enticing, because none of them can fully explain what the BSCs are about.

That being said, I know exactly what this saga is

about, and perhaps you do too, or are at least beginning to pick up on it. For now, I'll say this- simply put, The Bleeding Star Chronicles is about human struggle, Galin Winchester's struggle, to be more precise, and by what regards this is true will become more obvious and fulfilling in the days ahead.

Issue #11, The Sounds of Wind and Water, will take us away from Galin and the Katara for a while, at least in their present condition, to focus on some other familiar faces, and fill in more of this story. I'm excited about the journey ahead, and I hope you're excited to read it. Thanks for giving me the opportunity to share these tales with you, and don't forget, if you enjoy reading these books, please tell a friend. Godspeed!

Ethan Russell Erway

ABOUT THE AUTHOR

Ethan Russell Erway, author of THE BLEEDING STAR CHRONICLES and the ADVENTURES OF MICHAEL BELMONT, has been a life long fan of the fantasy and science fiction genres. His third book, MICHAEL BELMONT AND THE CURSE OF THE THUNDERBIRD, is due for release in late 2014. Ethan has a Bachelor of Sacred Literature degree from Summit Theological Seminary, and is the Minister at Agua Fria Christian Church in Humboldt, AZ where he lives with his wife and children.

Connect with Me Online:

http://www.EthanRussellErway.com

http://twitter.com/@ethanerway

http://www.Facebook.com/EthanRussellErway

Made in the USA
San Bernardino, CA
26 November 2014